CINDERELLA'S NEW YORK CHRISTMAS

SCARLET WILSON

UNMASKING THE MAVERICK

TERESA SOUTHWICK

1018

MIX
Paper from
responsible sources
FSC C007454

This book is produced from independently certified FSC™
paper to ensure responsible forest management.

For more information visit: www.harpercollins.co.uk/green

Printed and bound in Spain
by CPI, Barcelona

MILLS & BOON

First Published in Great Britain 2018
by Mills & Boon, an imprint of HarperCollinsPublishers,
1 London Bridge Street, London, SE1 9GF

Cinderella's New York Christmas © 2018 Harlequin Books S.A.
Unmasking the Maverick © 2018 Harlequin Books S.A.

Special thanks and acknowledgement are given to Scarlet Wilson for her contribution to the The Cattaneos' Christmas Miracles series.

Special thanks and acknowledgement to Teresa Southwick for her contribution to the Montana Mavericks: The Lonelyhearts Ranch continuity.

ISBN: 978-0-263-26532-3

Sca_____Love and Medical Romance. She lives on the west coast of Scotland with her fiancé and their two sons. She loves to hear from readers and can be reached via her website: scarlet-wilson.com.

Teresa Southwick lives with her husband in Las Vegas, the city that reinvents itself every day. An avid fan of romance novels, she is delighted to be living out her dream of writing for Mills & Boon.

CINDERELLA'S NEW YORK CHRISTMAS

SCARLET WILSON

To my fab NHS work colleagues
Kathleen Winter and Janice Traynor.

I value the fact I work with such kind,
supportive friends.

PROLOGUE

Our dearest Leo,

You have no idea how much joy it gives us to write this letter. We have hoped and prayed for this moment for so long. We hope you are well, we hope you are healthy, and we want you to know that we've spent every day thinking about you, and the last thirty-five years looking for you. You have always been in our hearts, Leo, always. Please believe that.

Thirty-eight years ago we were young, foolish teenagers who fell in love. Our parents disapproved and when we fell pregnant with you we were forced to give you up for adoption.

We want you to know that it was never what we wanted. From the very first moment we knew you existed we wanted to keep you. But times were different then. Our parents bullied us, refused to support our relationship, and were ashamed of their illegitimate grandchild.

It broke our hearts, but we were penniless and had to agree to give you up for adoption, or we would have both been flung out of our homes.

Every day we talked about you and imagined

where you were. We prayed you had parents who loved you as much as we did, and who nurtured and supported you.

Despite what our families thought, we stayed together and eventually married. As soon as we had some money we started our search for you. But the world was full of paper records then—people who kept secrets and those who told lies. It took years for us to learn you'd gone to the US, and then the trail went dead.

It broke our hearts all over again.

You have a brother, Sebastian, and a sister, Noemi. We always found it difficult to talk about your adoption to your siblings, but now that we've found you we would love it if our family could be reunited.

It has always been our dream that one day we could have all our children sitting around our table for Christmas dinner, like the true family we always wanted to be. We would love it if this could come true this year and wish that you could join us at Mont Coeur, Switzerland—the place where we have always loved to spend Christmas.

We've missed you every day, Leo.

Knowing that you are alive and well has brought us so much joy. We know you may be settled in your life. We know that you may well think of your adoptive parents as your only parents, and we will always respect your decisions and your wishes, but, please, please consider our request to meet.

There is nothing we want more than to throw

our arms around our firstborn son and tell you
how much we love you.
With our hearts,
Mamma e Papà
Salvo and Nicole Cattaneo.

CHAPTER ONE

HE SHOULD NEVER have opened that letter.

His insides curled uncomfortably as he took the final few steps up to the veranda around the luxury chalet. Even though it was the beginning of November it seemed the Mont Coeur ski resort in Switzerland had moved into full Christmas mode. Maybe it was the cold weather and snow that made the whole population think it was normal to have Christmas trees up at the beginning of November. But as his car had woven its way through the resort it had seemed that every business and shop in Mont Coeur was fully on board for the festive season.

Everywhere he looked there were garlands, twinkling lights and piped music.

On any other day he'd think the whole place was picture perfect—like a scene on one of those Christmas cards. But today wasn't like any other day.

His parents' luxury chalet seemed to be a leader in the festive decorations. Through the glass-panelled doors he could see the Christmas tree decorated in reds and gold as a focal point in the spacious living area; boughs of holly had been wound around the banisters and across the mantelpiece, where a fire was roaring beneath. And above him, against night sky, gold twinkling fairy lights adorned the outside of the chalet. The quintessential idyllic Christmas scene.

This should be different. This should be so different.

He should be coming here today to meet the parents who had given him up for adoption thirty-eight years ago. He should be coming here to learn more about the people who'd said they'd thought about him every day since. Instead, he was here at the insistence of a family lawyer he didn't know and a sister, Noemi, whom he'd never met, for the reading of his parents' will.

The warmth and the family feel of the chalet felt totally alien to him. He'd never experienced this lifestyle. He'd never experienced the true joy of a happy, family Christmas. And he couldn't shake the guilty feeling that if he hadn't been found, hadn't answered their letter, then his parents would never have died in a helicopter crash on their way to meet him.

Now he was here at their request for the will reading—and to meet his two siblings.

Everything about this felt awkward and wrong.

His stomach churned again as he knocked on the glass door. Maybe no one was home? Maybe his siblings had changed their minds? It would be so much easier to turn on his heel, go back and find the alternative luxury chalet his PA had booked for him.

There was a flicker behind the glass. A woman rushed towards him. She was tall and slim with a short brown angled bob. Behind her, walking much more warily, was a tall, muscular man. Even from here Leo could see the creases along his brow.

The woman flung the door open. 'Leo?'

Her brown eyes were hopeful. He could see her hands twitching at her sides. She was barely able to contain herself.

'Yes,' he replied hoarsely. It was all it took.

She let out a squeal and flung her arms around his neck. 'Oh, Leo, I'm so glad to finally meet you.'

He stood frozen to the spot, not sure of whether he should lift his arms to hug this woman back. After what seemed like the longest time she finally pulled back, wiping a tear from her eye. 'I'm Noemi. You know that, don't you?' She wiped away another tear and gestured to the man behind her. 'And this is Sebastian, your brother.'

It had to be the most awkward meeting in history. Animosity was rolling off Sebastian in waves. He didn't even step forward, just gave the barest nod of his head.

Leo steadied himself for a second. This was his brother and sister. When he'd been growing up he'd always wished he was part of a large family. He would have loved to have had a brother and sister. But his adoptive parents had already decided one child was too much. He was never quite sure why they'd adopted him as they'd shown so little interest in him.

All he wanted to do right now was turn and walk out the door. It made him feel pathetic. He was a business-man, a CEO. He spent his life in difficult business deal-ings. This should be nothing to him. But everything about this was unravelling a whole pile of emotions that he'd never acknowledged.

It was obvious that everyone in Mont Coeur was rich, even by his standards, his brother and sister included. Maybe they were worried he was here for money? Money that he didn't need or want.

Noemi grabbed his hand. 'Come in, Leo, come in. I want to hear all about you. I want to know how you are.' She bit her bottom lip as a few more tears escaped. Was his sister always this tearful? He wasn't big on emotion at the best of times and he was already feeling the overload.

Her hands were warm against his chilly skin and she pulled him inside. She drew him straight into the heart of the house, between the Christmas tree and the fireplace. 'Give me your jacket,' she said enthusiastically, tugging his dark wool coat from his shoulders.

Sebastian had barely moved. The muscles around the bottom of his neck were tense. He glanced at Leo as he shrugged his way out of his coat. His words were stiff. 'My wife, Maria, and son, Frankie, hoped to be here but…' his voice tailed as if he were trying to decide what to say '…they've been unavoidably delayed.'

Something in his gut told Leo that Sebastian hadn't been exactly truthful when he'd spoken. He looked like a coil about to burst from into a spring. Either his wife and son didn't want to meet the 'new' brother, or Sebastian was hiding something else completely. Leo had done enough business dealings to know when someone was being economical with the truth.

Noemi patted the sofa next to her. 'Please, sit. Giovanni will be here soon, but I want a chance to chat first.'

Giovanni. The family lawyer who'd persuaded him to attend the reading of the will. Giovanni, who right now he wanted to email and tell him that he'd changed his mind.

He sat down on the sofa and was almost swallowed up by it. Leo wanted to laugh out loud, because that's how he was feeling in general about the visit here.

His eyes caught sight of family pictures on the wall. There was a whole array, obviously taken over years, starting with a young smiling couple with a baby and toddler, going up to four adults all standing with their arms around each other. Love was plainly visible in every picture.

Something gripped in his chest. The family that he should have had. The family he should have been part of.

It was like a million little caterpillars creeping up his spine. He actually thought he might be sick.

He wanted to go over and grab the photos, hold them up to his nose and study his parents. He wanted to see the last thirty-eight years. What they'd been like, how they'd grown, how they'd aged. All things he'd been cheated out of.

He pushed himself up from the impossible sofa. 'This was a mistake…'

'What? No.' Noemi looked instantly stricken.

Something twisted in his chest. He really couldn't handle this. He wasn't equipped to deal with this. He'd spent a lifetime devoid of any love. Forming relationships wasn't his forte. The last woman he'd dated had described him as 'cold' and 'hard'—two things he couldn't really deny.

Getting that initial letter from his parents had been like a bolt out of the blue. It had taken him two weeks to reply. When he had, he'd been hit by the overload that was his mother, who'd emailed every day, making plans to visit.

Getting the call from Noemi—the sister he'd never met—to tell him that their parents had been killed in a helicopter crash while on their way to visit him in New York had almost taken the air from his lungs.

He *so* wasn't ready for any of the emotions attached to having a family. Guilt. Expectation. Judgement.

He'd wanted to see them. Curiosity had made him fly to Switzerland to stand in the same room as his brother and sister and talk to them in the flesh. But now he'd done it.

He had to get out of here. He had to get some air.

A hand came down firmly on his arm. 'Don't go.'

Sebastian. His brother.

He could see Sebastian was struggling with this too. 'Not yet.' It was almost like he couldn't quite get the words out.

Sebastian shook his head. 'You just got here.' He wasn't really meeting Leo's gaze. 'Take a breath. Take a moment.'

Leo looked to his left. Noemi's chin was trembling. He couldn't watch her cry again.

Leo couldn't work out if Sebastian was doing this for him or for his sister. Their sister. Noemi was *their* sister. Not just Sebastian's.

Brain overload. This wasn't him. Nothing about this was him. All of his life he'd been cool, calm and collected. Those three words were synonymous with how most of his work colleagues described him.

He pulled his arm away from Sebastian's. He turned to face him. 'I know I was asked to listen to the reading of the will. But now I'm here, I can see this isn't appropriate. I don't want anything from you both. I don't need anything. I'm not here to take what you think is actually yours.'

A flicker of anger flashed across Sebastian's eyes. But before he had a chance to respond there was another voice.

'Ah, Leo, I see you made it. Perfect timing.'

Leo turned to face the figure standing at the now open door. 'Giovanni Paliotta,' said the grey-haired, designer-suited man as he closed the door behind him and walked over with his hand outstretched. He tilted his head to the side as he got closer. 'It's a pleasure to meet you. You're so like your father.'

It was like a kick in the guts.

Giovanni didn't seem to notice, and waved his hand

towards a large table in the corner of the room. 'Shall we sit?'

Noemi looked at the table, then glanced around the rest of the room, as if she were trying to find another place to sit, but Sebastian moved behind her, putting his arm at her waist and leading her over.

Leo's gaze flickered. Twelve chairs. Enough for a large family gathering. Was this the table that his mother and father had traditionally sat around at Christmastime? Was this the table that his mother and father had intended for him to sit around with his brother and sister?

Leo had never wanted to bolt from a place so much in his life. He steadied his breathing.

Giovanni settled in one of the chairs and spread his papers in front of him.

Sebastian and Noemi sat down with only a glance at each other. Leo took a few seconds then dragged out one of the heavy chairs too.

Giovanni waited until everyone was settled then gave them all a nod.

'We all know why we are here.' He nodded again in particular to Leo. 'I was your parents' lawyer for the last thirty years, and I loved them, and miss them, and everything I do today is in accordance with their wishes.'

There was an edge of anxiety in Giovanni's voice that Leo picked up on. He cast his eyes over his brother and sister again as he shifted in his seat.

Giovanni started reading from the paper in front of him. 'This is the last will and testament of Salvo and Nicole Cattaneo. Salvo and Nicole were the sole owners of Cattaneo Jewels, currently valued at around seventy billion euros.'

Leo blinked. He knew the jewellery line was famous

and international, but he hadn't realised his parents' fortune rivalled even his own.

Giovanni kept talking, 'It was the wish of Salvo and Nicole that in the event of their death, the business should remain with the family.' Giovanni pressed his lips together for a second, looking decidedly nervous. 'As such, the controlling stake in Cattaneo Jewels will pass to Leo Baxter, their eldest biological child.'

'What?' Sebastian's chair landed on the floor as he stood up and thumped his hands on the table.

Noemi's mouth opened, then closed again.

Giovanni cleared his throat, refusing to fix on Sebastian's red face.

'No,' said Leo, shaking his head. 'I have no interest in the family business. I don't even know anything about jewels.' He stood up too. All he wanted was to get out of there.

'I've trained for this my whole life,' raged Sebastian. 'Who is he to inherit the business over me?'

'Your brother,' snapped Giovanni. For the briefest second Leo realised why Salvo and Nicole had worked with this lawyer for thirty years.

Giovanni held up his hands. 'Sit down, both of you.'

Leo met his brother's angry gaze. He got it. He did. And he had absolutely no interest in this business, but his brother's reaction annoyed him. It didn't matter that he partially understood it. He couldn't hide his flare of anger. Sebastian had got to spend a lifetime with his parents—Leo hadn't even got to meet them.

Giovanni gave a shake of his head and Leo settled back into his chair, staring pointedly at Sebastian until he did the same.

Giovanni continued slowly. 'There are conditions attached.'

'What conditions?' Leo couldn't help it. He'd been in business too long to get caught out.

'Leo must hold the controlling stake in the business for a minimum of six months. The shares can't be sold, or transferred, to any alternative controlling company or family member.'

'What happens if he does?' Noemi's voice was shaky.

Giovanni looked at all three of them. 'Any attempt to violate the terms of the will mean that the company shall cease trading and will be liquidated with its assets distributed amongst the other existing four hundred shareholders.'

'What?' Sebastian's voice sounded wheezy. His eyes were wide.

Leo sat frozen in his chair. He was a businessman. He had a head for business. He knew exactly what this was.

'This is blackmail,' he said coldly.

'No,' said Noemi quietly.

'Manipulation, then.'

She turned to face him and gave a slow nod. 'You could be right.'

'But why?' Leo leaned across the table towards Giovanni. 'Why on earth would—' he couldn't even bring himself to say the words 'parents'—'Salvo and Nicole do this?'

Giovanni sighed and leaned back in his chair.

'Did this just happen?' interjected Sebastian angrily. 'Did they just do this because they found Leo?'

Leo drummed his fingers on the table. He couldn't get his head around this at all. 'Were they sick?'

Giovanni started.

Leo's brain was struggling to make any sense of this at all. He asked again, 'Were they sick?' He shook his head. 'This doesn't make any sense. I don't imagine for a second that they could have predicted the accident they were in, so the only other thing I can think of was that they were sick. They were trying to find a way that we...' he paused for a second at that word '...would all have to work together. Nothing else makes sense.'

Sebastian looked pale. His eyes found Noemi. 'We would have known. They would have told us.'

She gave a bewildered shrug. 'They didn't tell us about Leo until a month ago. And only then because I found his letter.'

Giovanni cleared his throat. 'Their will has always said this.'

'What?' This time it was three voices in unison.

Giovanni gave a slow shake of his head. 'They always believed they would find Leo. Initially, the will just named him as "the eldest biological child". They never stopped searching. Even if they died before they found him, they still wanted him to know he was always part of the family, and to give him the opportunity to know the family business.' Giovanni took a deep breath. 'They believed in family. You know that.' He shook his head. 'They changed the will to include his name as soon as they found him. But the truth is he was always included. In their eyes, he was always part of the family—whether they knew his new name or not.'

Noemi blinked and looked between Leo and Sebastian. 'This isn't about the business,' she said quietly.

Leo could tell Sebastian was still angry. There was a tiny tic in his jaw. But he met his sister's gaze and gave her the slightest nod. 'I know that.' It was the most conciliatory thing he'd said since Leo had got there.

Leo felt blindsided and he hated that. Every business meeting, every potential deal, he always went in prepared. He would know the background, the finances, the personalities and their quirks before he even set foot in the room.

But here? For the first time since he'd been a child he felt totally out of his depth.

It felt as if the room was closing in around him, suffocating him with the heat from the fire, the love from the pictures on the wall, and that horrible feeling of emptiness inside.

Sebastian's voice was tight. 'Mamma and Papà spent their lives growing this family business. It's gone from a few tiny shops in Italy to a billion-euro company with worldwide acclaim. You might know business, Leo, but you don't know *this* business. And I'm damned if I'm going to let their pride and joy fall apart around you for the next six months because you don't know what you're doing.'

He'd had enough. Leo had reached breaking point. He pulled back every emotion that he'd been struggling to keep in check. Business. Sebastian was talking business to him and no one was better at business than him.

'I might not know anything about the jewellery business, Sebastian, but one business is the same as another. Don't make any mistake, I don't want to do this, and I'm not interested in doing this. I don't need your *mamma* and *papà*'s business, and I certainly don't need their money. I could walk away right now quite happily, but where would that leave you?'

He let the words hang in the air. Noemi's face was pale as she stood up and reached out and took Leo's hand, stumbling. Leo caught her elbow but Sebastian was at her side in an instant. 'Are you okay?' He slid his arm around her waist, helping to prop her up. It was like she was caught between two brothers.

She gave a shake of her head as she steadied herself

for a few seconds, one hand still holding Leo's. 'Just a bit dizzy.' She pressed her other hand against her stomach as she took some slow breaths and the colour in her cheeks started to return.

When she lifted her chin, her eyes were filled with tears. 'Don't do this. Don't be like this.' Her head went from one brother to the other. 'I hate this too. But Mamma and Papà want us to work together. They want us to be a family.' She turned to face Giovanni. 'You've read the will, but I think we should have a little time to consider what it all means.' She let go of Leo's hand and reached for his shoulders, turning him to face her. 'Leo, I want to know you. I want to know my brother. I've already missed out on so much of your life, I don't want to miss out on any more. I'm not asking you to be my best friend. But family is important to me—now, more than ever.' She squeezed his shoulders. 'Why don't you both take a bit of time? This is a lot, I know that—for all of us. We all need to think—to process—and…' she glanced at Sebastian again '…probably to cool off. How about we agree to meet again later?'

Her eyes were pleading as she looked between the two men. Giovanni nodded. 'Sounds reasonable. Nothing will happen quickly in terms of the will. It will take around six to eight weeks for things to be legally tied up back in Italy, and I can string things out as long as you all need.'

'Fine.' Sebastian's answer was short.

'We can meet again around Christmastime?' Noemi said, her voice breaking with distress. 'Back here?' She pressed her lips together. 'It's what Mamma and Papà always wanted.'

There was an edge to her words. A hint of desperation. It brought it home to him again. She'd just lost her parents. They all had.

He moved from her grasp and collected his coat. The swell of emotion in the room too much for him. He gave the briefest of nods. 'I'll get back to you both,' he said as he walked swiftly towards the glass doors and out into the dark night.

He hadn't even bothered to fasten his coat again and the Swiss Alpine air bit around him. He could barely register the cold, his body was so flushed with heat.

New York. That's where Leo wanted to be right now. That was where he called home. He'd left Indiana and his adoptive parents behind a long time ago.

As he tramped along the snow-covered path he quickly realised he had no idea where he was going. The car from the airport had dropped his luggage at the luxury chalet booked by his PA. Trouble was, he didn't know where that was. He pulled out his phone to search on a map. Around him people were crowding out of bars and hotels. It only took a few glances to realise that the Mont Coeur ski resort was filled with the rich, the very rich and the very, very rich.

He knew how ironic that thought was. He was in that category—as was his newfound family. But Leo didn't usually willingly mix in these circles. He'd always been picky about who he surrounded himself with, preferring people with their feet firmly on the ground to those who worried about climbing the social ladder.

He could go into a bar—find somewhere to have a drink. But he wasn't really in the mood for a drink. Distraction maybe—but not a drink.

He checked out the map on his phone and headed down another street, this one a little quieter and leading away from the main thoroughfare.

He probably should have hired a car or tried to find

a taxi, as he realised the road towards his luxury chalet was mainly uphill. But the truth was he didn't really mind. It gave him a little time to think about what had just happened.

Several things burned in his mind. Giovanni had said the will had always included him. That made him feel… odd. His adoptive parents had always maintained that his real parents couldn't wait to be rid of him. The harsh words had felt as if they'd burned their way into his soul, wounding him in a way he'd never spoken about. He'd spent years resenting both his real and his adoptive parents, feeling as if he wasn't really wanted anywhere. Finding out now that was all untrue was more unsettling than he could have ever imagined.

He let out a long, slow breath, sending warm air out into the icy night, clouding around him.

Leo reached the end of the street and looked up from the map on his phone. His chalet should be off to the right, but to his left he saw Mont Coeur's practice slopes. Even though it was nine o'clock at night, there were still a few people getting in that last run.

They were illuminated with bright white lights, reflecting off the glossy snow, smoothed down hard by the constant traffic on the slopes. In most other ski resorts, the slopes were high above the actual towns. Mont Coeur was different. It was built halfway up the mountain, almost right in the middle of the slopes, which made them much more accessible.

He stopped for a minute, leaning on a fence as he watched a single figure head down towards him. Dressed completely in black, the figure zig-zagged down the practically empty slope at an alarming rate of speed. Skiing was something he'd loved to do over the years and he could appreciate the skill and expertise. He frowned. Wasn't the figure coming down just a little too fast?

There was a loud bang to his right. His head flicked to the side, just in time to see a car with a black cloud of smoke coming from under its bonnet.

He flicked back to the skier. *Oh, no.*

They'd turned to check out the noise too, and now it was too late. In the blink of an eye he realised they hadn't slowed their descent enough. That split-second distraction had been too much.

They desperately tried to slow, but it was too little, too late and they hurtled into the tyres at the bottom of the practice slope with a sickening crash.

Leo didn't think twice. He leapt over the fence and scrambled over the thick tyres. There was hardly anyone around, and it was clear he was the closest.

The figure was lying crumpled on the ground, skis askew and one of their legs in an awkward position. Leo slipped and slid on the snow. 'Are you okay? Can I do something to help you?'

He knelt down next to the figure in black. Now he was closer he could see it was a woman. The black salopettes and padded ski jacket couldn't hide the slim curves underneath. She still hadn't responded. He touched her arm, 'Hi, I'm Leo. Can I help you?'

There was a groan underneath him. The twisted leg moved and she gave a yelp. *'Foitrottl!'*

He smiled. He may not have understood the language—was it Swiss? German?—but he understood the sentiment. Not quite as ladylike as he might have imagined. 'Well, at least I know you're conscious,' he said.

Her arms shot upwards and she snapped the fastener on her ski helmet and pushed her ski goggles upwards, revealing a mass of ice blonde hair.

'What on earth was that noise?' she said, switching to English. She was mad. She was more than mad.

Leo couldn't help but smile again. As well as the avalanche of blonde hair, this lady had the clearest blue eyes he'd ever seen. She pretty much looked like some kind of ice princess but he could already guess how she would take that kind of comparison.

'It sounded like a combination of a car backfiring and an engine blowing up. Either way, it was loud.'

She was digging her elbows into the snow and struggling to push herself up.

'Can I give you hand?' He stood up and reached out towards her.

For a second he thought she might refuse, but after the briefest pause she pulled one hand from her glove and grasped his fingers tightly.

He tugged—maybe a little more firmly than he needed to—and pulled her straight up into him. His other arm caught around her waist just as her weight hit her feet and she yelped again as her leg buckled beneath her.

He tightened his grip and pulled her against his hip. 'Do you think something's broken? Do you want me to call an ambulance for you?'

She was breathing hard and fast but her skin was pale. 'Just give me a second,' she gasped.

So he did. And even though it was freezing after a few seconds he was struck by the heat emanating from her slight frame. She was taller than most women he met, but still at least six inches shorter than him. He stood silently, watching a little colour appear in her pale cheeks and her breathing eventually starting to slow. She was holding her left foot off the ground and tentatively put it back down, wincing almost immediately.

'Want me to carry you?'

Her frown was fierce but she didn't bite his head off. Instead she leaned a little into him. 'Nope, definitely not. Sorry to be a pest, but I've got a bit of an old injury. Would you mind just helping me limp back to the ski hut? There's a buggy I can use there to get back to my chalet.'

'Can you stand for a second?' She nodded and he bent to retrieve her skis and poles before sliding his arm back around her waist and taking some of her weight. 'Okay, then. What were you doing, practising so late? Most people are in the town by now.'

She gripped onto his arm with her other hand as she limped alongside him, being careful not to put too much weight on her foot.

Leo couldn't help but ask again. 'You're sure that's not broken?'

She shook her head. 'I'm sure. Believe me. I've broken a few bones in my time.'

It was just the way she said it. He couldn't help himself. 'What—yours or other people's?'

She threw back her head and laughed, then obviously put too much weight on her bad foot. 'Ouch.'

Leo actions were instinctual. He dropped the skis, bent down and swept her up into his arms.

'What are you doing?' Her eyes were wide. She glanced around but it was late, the slopes were quiet, and there wasn't really anyone else watching.

'I'm carrying you,' he said simply. He strode towards the large ski hut. 'No point hurting yourself when you don't need to. I'll come back for those in a second,' he said, noticing as she craned over his shoulder to look for her abandoned equipment. He looked down at her curiously. He could tell she was just about to object again. 'So, have you broken a lot of bones? What are you—a ski instructor?'

There was a flash of something on her face as they approached the ski hut. She sighed. 'Yes, I guess I am.'

He moved around the side of the building. Just like she'd said, there was a large SUV with snow tyres. 'Want me to drive?' he asked as he set her gently down next to the passenger door.

'Will you carry me round to the other side if I say no?' she quipped.

Leo smiled. Whatever else had happened today, things were definitely looking up. He winked at her. 'Your wish is my command, Ice Princess.'

Ice Princess? Had he actually just called her Ice Princess?

If she had been feeling herself she'd toss her head and stomp off. Trouble was, she wasn't feeling herself. She actually felt as if she might be sick all over her ski boots.

As her rescuer disappeared to retrieve her skis and poles, she wondered if maybe it was the shock of the noise of the backfiring car. Maybe it was her current feeling of stupidity for allowing herself to be distracted when she really should know better. Or maybe it was that whole host of memories that had come flooding back as she'd tumbled down the slope, too quickly and completely out of control.

She dug into her ski jacket and pulled out her key. As he returned, leaning her equipment against the SUV, she steeled herself to say words she'd never thought she would. 'Actually, would you mind? I promise I only live a five-minute drive from here.'

The guy—Leo he'd said he was called—gave a quick nod as she pressed the button to open the doors. 'Not at all,' he said graciously.

He was being a gentleman. There was obviously a cheeky demeanour hiding under there, but for now she'd take the gentleman. Anything to get home as soon as possible.

She slid into her seat, suddenly aware she'd been a little rude. 'And it's Anissa—not Ice Princess.'

He smiled as he slid into the driver's seat and pressed the button to start the engine. 'Anissa.' He gave a nod of approval. 'Sounds like a kind of ice princess name to me.'

'Do you know *many* ice princesses, Leo?'

He laughed and held out his hand. 'Leo Baxter. From New York. Just here for a few days on…' his face gave a little twist '…family business.'

She shook his hand. 'Anissa Lang. And this Ice Princess has the illustrious other titles of part-time ski instructor, part-time chalet maid.' He smiled. He had a nice smile, dark, curly hair a little longer than average and bright blue eyes that could stop a girl in her tracks. Just as well she was sitting down. She held his gaze just a few seconds longer than she meant to.

He didn't look away. His grin just got wider and she felt colour rush into her cheeks. What on earth was she doing? She took a deep breath and focused on the view through the windscreen instead. It was safer.

He pulled the car out of the parking lot and stopped at the road junction.

'Right.' She pointed.

'Were you doing a lesson?' he queried. 'I didn't notice any students on the slopes with you.'

She shook her head. 'Too late for lessons. And students wouldn't be allowed on that slope. Too dangerous.'

He gave a nod of his head as he continued down the dark road. 'You don't say.'

A wave of nausea rushed over her and she put a hand to her mouth. 'You okay?' he asked quickly, his cheeky quips instantly replaced by concern.

She swallowed and pointed a little further down the road. 'Take the next left, please. I'm just at the end of that road.'

She leaned back against the seat and gave a sigh. 'Maybe I hit my head. I'm feeling a bit queasy.'

His eyes were laced with concern, but he didn't say anything else until he pulled up outside her staff chalet. A few seconds later he'd stopped the car, jumped out, rounded the car and opened her door. 'Let's get you inside. Maybe if you sit down for a few minutes and get some water, you'll feel a little better. If you don't, I'm sure I can find a doctor in the resort to check you over.'

She really wanted to argue with him, but getting inside her chalet seemed like the priority right now, so she let him help her out and up the steps to the chalet, not even objecting when he took the key from her slightly shaking hand and opened the door for her. He flicked on her lights and slid his arm around her waist, helping her inside.

She sagged down onto her sofa in relief, unzipping her ski jacket and taking a few deep breaths. When she opened her eyes a few seconds later, Leo had already started the fire.

'Well, if I'm Ice Princess, you must be Prince Charming.' She smiled.

It was odd. She didn't feel threatened by the complete stranger who was currently inside her temporary home and finding his way around. She was actually feeling relieved there was someone else with her right now.

'Oh,' she said in surprise as he sat down on the coffee table opposite her and lifted up her ski boot.

Those blue eyes twinkled. 'Prince Charming? Isn't that the guy obsessed with shoes? Let's get these ski boots off and you can see if you've done any damage.' He really was too handsome for his own good.

He undid the clips, loosened the boot then gave it a gentle tug, pulling it off. She clenched her jaw, waiting for wave of pain she'd normally feel if she'd done some damage. There were a few twinges but nothing severe.

He pulled off the other boot, holding her foot for a little longer than necessary. 'Okay?' His question seemed sincere, so she nodded as he moved so her feet could rest on the table in front of her. 'You still look really pale.' He glanced around the room. 'How about something medicinal? I think you're in a bit of shock. Do you have any brandy?'

Her brain really couldn't think straight. Brandy. Yes. She had some of that. She waved her hand. 'Cabinet behind you.'

Two minutes later she heard the clink of glasses. She leaned forward and peeled down her socks. No obvious swelling. Thank goodness. She gave both of her feet a cautious circle. Whilst one was definitely sore, it wasn't as bad as she'd initially feared.

A glass was pressed into her hand and Leo lowered himself into the seat next to her.

She took a sip of the brandy and pulled a face. 'I'm not sure if giving someone alcohol for shock is really the official treatment.' She gave her head a shake. 'You know, St Bernards don't really have brandy around their necks.'

He smiled and raised his glass. 'What can I say? I've always been one for old wives' tales.'

She looked at him curiously. His face was a tiny bit flushed in her rapidly warming chalet, but there was no question that this was one of the most handsome guys she'd seen in a while. Mont Coeur was no stranger to numerous jet-set playboy millionaires, but he didn't seem quite the type. She took another sip of her brandy, which warmed on the way down.

'I'm not sure I believe you—you don't look like an old-wives'-tales kind of guy.' She sighed. 'But then again, I'm not the type of girl to let a stranger drive her car—or come into her chalet—so I guess it's just a night of firsts.'

There was a definite twinkle in his eye. She nudged him.

At any other time alarm bells would be going off in her head. But the one thing she instantly felt around this guy was safe. That was it. He had a safe kind of smile. She liked that—that and those bright blue eyes. 'Want to take that wool coat off before you die from heat exhaustion?'

Her heart skipped a few beats. Had she really just said that? More or less invited him to stay a bit longer?

Deep down something was flickering inside her—and it was nothing to do with the fire. Everything about this was so out of character for her. Under normal circumstances she would probably have tried to hound her rescuer back outside the door. But Leo just seemed... different.

There was something in his eyes that she couldn't quite figure. He had the tiniest air of mystery around him—that and a whole load of sex appeal. A lethal combination.

He laughed, unfastened the coat and shrugged it off. 'A night of firsts,' he repeated. There was a strange kind of look on his face. 'I guess it's certainly been one of those.'

There it was—the air of mystery that just seemed to reel her in. She turned a little towards him. 'What do you mean?'

He shook his head. 'Let's just say I'm glad of the distraction.'

Now she was definitely curious. 'Well, from my experience, most people come to Mont Coeur to either ski or...' she raised her eyebrows '...to show off how rich they are. Which category are you in?'

For a second he was silent, then he took a long, slow swig from the brandy glass. 'I can just about hold my own on a ski slope. But I've never skied at Mont Coeur before. I came here at kind of short notice. I didn't bring any equipment with me.'

'So you didn't come here for the skiing?'

He shook his head. He really wasn't giving much away. But the way that he looked at her through those heavy-lidded eyes, it was making her stomach do a whole lot of flip-flops. Never mind skiing. Right now her stomach thought she was a gymnast.

'But you were watching tonight?'

He nodded. 'I've only been here a few hours. I haven't even reached my...' he put his fingers in the air '..."luxury cabin" yet.'

Anissa's stomach gave a little twist. *Please don't let him be staying in one of the cabins I'm cleaning.*

'So, is it business or pleasure?' She licked her lips, a little nervous at asking the question. For all she knew, he could actually be here with a wife or fiancée, and really only was being gentlemanly by helping her home. She unintentionally held her breath as she waited for the answer.

'I imagine some people would expect me to say a bit of both.' He gave another sigh. 'But the honest answer is neither. In a lot of ways, I wish I'd never come. There's nothing I'd like more than to jump back on the soonest flight to New York.'

Her stomach gave a little pang. The first interesting guy she'd met in a long time couldn't wait to get out of Dodge. Typical.

But it was the way he'd said the words that mattered.

As if they made him sad. 'Then why don't you?' she asked quietly.

He met her gaze with his blue eyes. 'Because I'm a bit in limbo. What I do next could affect other people—whether I like it or not.'

Empathy swelled within her. Connection. Because those words were so familiar to her. What she did wouldn't affect anyone other than herself. But being in limbo? She raised her glass to him. 'Limbo. I see your few days' worth of limbo and raise you a whole year's worth.'

He turned closer towards her, leaning in and letting her see the shadow on his jawline and the tiny lines around his eyes. That tiny movement made her catch her breath at what might lie ahead. The woody scent of his aftershave filled her senses. She liked it. It had a hint of spice mixed with earthy tones.

He leaned his head on one hand and gave her a sexy kind of smile. 'How did a gorgeous girl like you end up in limbo in Mont Coeur? Have you always lived here?'

Gorgeous. He'd just called her gorgeous. She could almost hear the echoing voices of approval of her fellow chalet maids at her rapidly rising heart rate. For months they'd been telling her to pay more attention to the guys around her. For months she'd told them she had other priorities and that no one had captured her attention. And they hadn't. Until now.

She shook her head and tried her best to play it cool. 'I'm Austrian. But I've spent most of my life on skis, no matter where I've lived.' She lifted one hand. 'This last year? Let's just say it hasn't been my best—hasn't been my favourite. Limbo is exactly the right word to describe the last twelve months of my life.'

It hurt. Every memory about it still hurt. From the physical pain of crashing down a mountainside. To the psychological pain of realising her hopes of winning an international skiing championship gold medal had just been ripped from her grasp. Then there was the emotional trauma of her fiancé *and* coach, Alain, dumping her.

Leo reached out and grabbed her hand, the touch of his warm skin shooting an instant tingle up her arm. His voice was deep. His other hand reached over and tucked a wayward strand of hair behind her ear. It was a personal touch, an intimate touch, and the skin on her face was on fire with it. 'How about, for one night only, we try and forget about the stuff that's dragging us down?'

She blinked. Had he actually just said that?

The fire was flickering behind him, sending a warm glow around the room. Her heart missed a few beats.

No way. She wouldn't. Not ever. She wasn't that kind of girl.

But...

Somehow, tonight, she wanted to be.

She really, really wanted to be.

She prayed her voice wouldn't shake as she uttered the words. 'I could live with forgetting about everything dragging me down.'

He moved closer, his mouth only a few inches from hers, and she licked her lips in anticipation.

She paused for the briefest second. 'Promise me you have no wife, no fiancée, no girlfriend.'

He gave a flicker of smile. 'Promise. What about you?'

She smiled too as she leaned in. 'Oh, I don't have a wife, a fiancée or a girlfriend.' This was reaching the teasing stage. Her favourite part.

He smiled back as he reached up and slid his fingers through her hair, anchoring his hand at the back of her head. 'No significant other?'

She shook her head. 'No significant other.'

His lips brushed against her ear. 'Then how about we get ourselves distracted?'

She must be crazy. She must be losing her mind. But for the first time in a year all she could think about was how good it felt to be in the arms of this man she found wildly attractive and how in control she felt. She was making this decision. No one was doing it for her. Leo Baxter was hot.

And he was all hers.

This was one night. Everything else she could worry about tomorrow.

She smiled as she brushed her lips against his. 'So… distract me.'

CHAPTER TWO

LEO BLINKED AS he heard the faint noise of someone shuffling around. There was only a tiny glimmer of light outside. The bed was uncomfortable and his mind took a few seconds to orientate itself.

Mont Coeur. The will. Sebastian. Noemi.

And then there was last night. Anissa.

He rolled over and leaned on one arm. Sure enough, Anissa was padding around the room, pulling on some kind of uniform.

She looked up. 'Sorry, didn't mean to wake you. I have an early shift.'

He wasn't one for overnight stays and awkward next mornings. Seemed like he'd had more firsts than he'd expected to. The jet lag and emotional trauma of last night had obviously just wiped him out.

He watched as she pulled her hair up into a ponytail. He'd thought she'd looked good last night, but even early in the morning she looked good. Something twinged inside him and his gaze connected with hers.

This was where things got uncomfortable. This was where he had to make a hasty exit and try and find the luxury chalet he'd never made it to last night.

He glanced around the room, trying to find his clothes. Anissa pulled on her jacket and Leo instantly swung his legs from the bed. She had to leave. And she wouldn't want to leave a stranger in her house.

'Give me a second to grab my things and I'll get out of your hair.'

Images of last night flashed through his brain as he pulled on his shirt and trousers. Good images. Great images. And a connection he'd never thought he'd feel.

Anissa was standing at the bedroom door, watching him a little awkwardly. She sucked in a breath. 'Thanks for helping me last night.'

He pushed his feet into his shoes and moved closer. 'You're welcome. How's your foot this morning?'

She gave it a little stamp. 'A bit sore, but that's it.'

Maybe she hadn't realised it but she was blocking his exit to the door. He stopped in front of her. 'Last night was...' He let his voice tail off, unsure how exactly to end the sentence.

'The best sex I've had in years.'

He blinked, then laughed. It seemed that Anissa had no problem finishing the sentence for him. 'Okay, then...' he gave his head a shake at her quick words '... I guess I'd have to agree with that.'

Her blue eyes were fixed on his. His stomach gave a twist. Please don't let this be something it isn't.

His brain was all over the place right now, as were his emotions. In the space of a few months he'd found his parents, lost his parents, met a brother and sister he'd never known and been blackmailed into taking an interest in the family business. He didn't have room for anything else right now.

'I'm not looking for romance.' Anissa spoke quickly.

'Neither am I.' The answer came out automatically, with a sense of relief.

'And I never usually do anything like this,' she added.

'So please don't think this is normal for me. Last night was just…' This time it was her that couldn't find the words to complete the sentence.

'A one-off,' he finished for her.

She nodded in agreement. 'A one-off.'

They were still close. Close enough that he could smell the fruity shampoo from her hair that she'd pulled into a ponytail high on her head.

It would be so easy to lean forward and kiss her. To capture those lips in his again and pull her back down onto the unmade bed.

The truth was Anissa hadn't been wrong. Last night had unexpectedly been the best night of his life. But in reality he hardly knew her. And his timing was terrible.

She stood back against the door to let him pass. The early morning light was filtering through the windows of the small staff chalet. It was small, neat and functional, with only a few hints of the woman who actually stayed here. A framed photo of her standing in her skis, the two brandy glasses from last night, the ski boots still lying on the living-room floor. He was struck with how much it didn't really look like a home. The similarities between this place and his own penthouse apartment in New York sent a wash of recognition over him. How long had she said she'd been here? A year?

He picked up his coat and fastened it. Anissa moved in front of him and held out her hand towards him. 'It was nice to meet you, Leo Baxter.'

Her body was rigid, and she was being formal, but he could still sense the hint of humour in her eyes.

He slipped his warm hand into hers. 'It was nice to meet you too, Anissa Lang.' Her handshake was firm and he found himself in no hurry to let go. Her pale blue eyes were fixed on his.

His heart twisted at the first flicker of a connection he'd felt in, oh, so long. He tilted his head a little to the side. He wasn't sentimental. Never had been. Never would be—especially after recent events. But there was something about this girl beyond the obvious beauty and the passion she'd sparked in him last night. He gave a wry smile. 'Bad timing, but in another world, another place I would have very much liked to know you better.' He pulled her towards him and dropped a kiss on her cheek.

And before she had a chance to reply he turned on his heel and left quickly, walking out into the fresh snow and the rapidly wakening resort.

He had so much to think about. So much to consider.

And he didn't have a single clue what he really wanted to do.

Anissa held up the rota again. 'Oh, come on, someone swap with me. *Please.*'

Lucy leaned over Anissa's shoulder and looked at the list of occupiers in the most luxurious chalets in the whole resort. 'What's wrong with Leo Baxter, then? Bad breath? Wandering hands? Suggestive comments?'

Heat rushed into Anissa's cheeks.

Chloe laughed as she straightened her uniform next to them. 'Oh, no, none of that.' Then she glanced sideways at Anissa and shrugged. 'Or maybe two out of the three.' She laughed. 'But, hey, who doesn't want to go to the chalet of the gorgeous billionaire Anissa snagged a few nights ago?'

Lucy's eyes widened. '*That* was the guy?' She laughed too and shook her head. 'Oh, no way. I'm not swapping.' She pointed at Anissa. 'You've gotta go clean the hottie's chalet.' She swept up her equipment. 'And who knows what might happen—again!' she added with a wicked wink.

Anissa's stomach turned over as her colleagues left. Darn it. She'd managed to get out of cleaning Leo's chalet the last few days as she'd been working with other girls. But she'd made the mistake of telling Chloe all about her mystery encounter and great night before she'd realised Leo was actually staying in one of the chalets she was supposed to service.

She checked her watch. She had another chalet to clean too. Maybe she could time things just right and manage to avoid Leo. He was here for…business, wasn't he? Chances were he would be out at some point during the day.

She gathered her equipment and headed out towards the chalets. There was a large red SUV outside the one that a family was staying in, and nothing outside Leo's.

She licked her dry lips and headed towards his, turning the key carefully in the lock as her stomach did somersaults. 'Housekeeping,' she called. 'Anyone home?'

Her voice echoed around her. She stayed frozen for a few seconds, wondering if there'd be any delayed response, but after a minute she breathed a sigh of relief and closed the door behind her, looking around carefully.

Chalet was a bit of a misnomer. It might suit the place in which she lived, but it didn't suit these massive luxury houses halfway up the slopes. She grabbed some of her cleaning equipment. The people who stayed here were millionaires at a minimum. They expected impeccable service. And as the chalet had seventeen rooms, this wasn't somewhere you could whip round with a brush and duster in half an hour.

Her heart started to race in her chest. She really needed to use this window of opportunity wisely. She had to get in, and out, as soon as possible. Her brain tried to think logically. There was no way Leo was using all these rooms. Chances were she would have the main room, a bedroom, bathroom and kitchen to clean. She could do that before he got back. At least she hoped she could.

She automatically plugged in a fresh scented atomiser. It was changed every day—probably just to let the guests know that the chalet had been serviced. She grabbed her mop and bucket and dashed up the stairs to do a quick check around. None of the rooms on the top floor looked as if they'd been touched—everything was still pristine.

She ran down to the next floor. Leo was using the master suite. No surprise there. But it felt a little strange, walking into a room and seeing his belongings scattered around. The white bed was rumpled and unmade. She walked over and touched it, then pulled her hand back. It was weird. She was used to making strangers' beds, picking up their clothes and folding them, restocking their bathrooms and kitchens. But this wasn't a stranger. This was Leo. The guy who'd made her forget a year of feeling unloved and unwanted. A guy who'd actually made her feel attractive and sexy again.

She could smell him in this room. That woody aftershave he'd been wearing when he'd been with her, the way his stubble had scraped along her jaw...

She took a breath and sat down for a second on the bed. She'd been here a year and she'd never behaved like this. What on earth was wrong with her? What had changed the other night?

Even this, sitting on one of guest's beds, was something she would never do. She glanced around, almost expecting there to be hidden cameras taping this terrible misdemeanour. She ran her hand over the bed sheet. Leo had slept here last night. Had he thought about her? Had she even crossed his mind?

What if someone else had shared the bed with him? She jumped back up, annoyed that her thoughts had even gone there. It was enough to bring her back to her senses.

She started stripping off the sheets, remaking the bed with clean sheets in record time. She wiped around the room with a damp duster, picking up a discarded shirt and pair of trousers and hanging them up. The bathroom was messier. He'd managed to get toothpaste and shaving foam all over the sink. And all four towels were lying on the bathroom floor, indicating they should be replaced.

What was it with guys and towels?

Anissa worked as quickly as she could. Normally she would take longer, ensuring the glass shower door was smear free and the mirror completely spotless. But that would all take time she wasn't sure she had. A quick wipe would have to do.

She hurried down to the kitchen and started to clean there, scrubbing a little harder than necessary in some places. Her eyes kept glancing at the door. She really wasn't doing the job she normally did but she was willing to risk a complaint if it meant she could avoid coming face to face with Leo again.

Darn it. She picked up the discarded coffee pods. She'd forgotten the hamper to restock the kitchen.

There was noise outside and she turned in time to see a large black SUV pull up directly outside. *Oh, no.*

She gathered the towels and bed sheets in her arms, looking first one way then the other. Normally she would just put these in a black laundry bag and phone for them to be collected. But all of a sudden she thought about darting out the back door and taking them back to the service office herself. She looked at the back door again.

But it was too late. Her jumbled brain had waited too long.

Leo was at the door.

He'd met with Giovanni again. He'd called his own lawyers in New York, desperately trying to find any possible way to get out of looking after the family business for the next six months. But things were not looking good—and unless he wanted to ruin the Cattaneo family business, staying was beginning to look like a distinct possibility.

As Leo opened the door of the chalet he was struck by the fresh scent of pines and cinnamon. A hint of Christmas. A clear sign that the chalet service had visited.

Then he stopped. And blinked.

'Anissa?'

She was standing near the kitchen, a white pile of something in her arms. Her cheeks flushed pink instantly. Something she'd said the night they'd met pricked in his brain.

'You work here?'

'I... I... I...'

She was clearly flustered.

'I know you said you were a chalet maid, but I didn't realise you worked in these chalets.' He was surprised to see her. And even more surprised by the fact his heart was missing a few rapid beats.

He saw her swallow nervously. 'You didn't say where you were staying—'

'I didn't know,' he cut in. He gave a laugh. 'I hadn't made it to my chalet before we met.'

A frown creased her brow and she stared at him for

a few seconds with her pale blue eyes. 'Of course,' she said softly.

He moved towards her. 'Hey, why don't you dump that stuff and have a coffee with me?'

Something flitted across her eyes. 'I can't. I have another chalet to clean. And I haven't really finished in here.' She pulled a face as she glanced back at the kitchen. 'You might not even have coffee. I haven't replenished your supplies in the kitchen.'

He stepped even closer. As he breathed he felt a wave of familiarity. A scent. Her scent. The fruity one he'd smelt a few days ago. Orange blossom. The sensations from the other night flooded back. Her warmth. Her passion. The spark in her eye.

For the past few days he'd been buried beneath a mountain of legal stuff. Now, seeing Anissa again, it just made him regret the choice he'd made. He'd liked the way she'd distracted him. He'd more than liked it. And he kind of wished he could capture it all again.

He gave a smile. 'Hey, what happened to my brilliant chalet maid, then? The one who stocks up the coffee varieties every day, along with all the fresh bread and chocolate-chip cookies.'

Anissa let out a little laugh. She shook her head. 'Yeah. You've had Rena the last few days, but she's off now.' She shrugged. 'And you got me. The poor excuse of chalet maid. Sorry.'

She moved to the side. 'Give me a sec.' She walked over and dumped the laundry in a black fabric sack and sat it outside the front door. She dialled a number on the phone and spoke for a few seconds before replacing the handset and turning back around to face him.

'Okay, the restock hamper will be here in a few minutes. Don't worry, you'll have coffee.'

He gave a nod as his heart gave a little trip. 'And will you join me?'

She glanced at her watch then gave a small smile. 'Okay, a quick one. I do have a day job—no matter how much I don't want one.'

He raised his eyebrows in interest. Perfect. Anissa Lang was going to distract him. Again.

Her stomach was in knots. For the first few seconds she'd just wanted to run. Talk about embarrassing. The guy she'd spent a red-hot night with had just found her changing his towels. Hardly a great moment.

But it was odd. Leo had made her feel instantly at ease. And there was definitely still…something. It didn't matter that it had been a few days and she'd been deliberately avoiding him. It only took being in his presence again for a few seconds to feel that buzz, feel that attraction. And she wasn't imagining the sparkle in his eyes. For some crazy reason she liked being around this guy. And—no matter what some people might think—it was nothing to do with his billionaire status.

A few minutes later the supplies arrived in a wicker hamper. She unpacked the coffee, the bread, the milk and the cookies. Leo was at her elbow the whole time, starting the coffee machine, putting in the pods and lifting out the cookies.

The clients who stayed in these chalets were well taken care of. They could pre-order fresh deliveries for every day. Anissa was kind of surprised at Leo's response to everything in the hamper. 'Didn't you order all this stuff?'

He shook his head. 'No. Why? Can you do that?'

Anissa shook her head. 'Sure you can. Didn't you book this place?'

Leo pulled a face. 'Ah…maybe not.'

'So, who booked it for you? Your family?'

He shook his head. 'No. My PA.'

'Oh, of course.' Anissa smiled and rolled her eyes. 'The PA. Well, here's hoping she ordered what you like, and not what she likes.'

'I'm easy to please,' he said quickly.

'That's what they all say,' she joked.

Something flickered across his eyes and her heart sank. She touched his arm. 'No.' She shook her head and pulled a face. 'Absolutely, no. That's not what I meant.' Her heart was beating wildly in her chest. She breathed slowly and met his gaze. 'I told you. I never did that before.'

His bright blue eyes were fixed on hers. This guy could complain about her. This guy could cost her the job that she didn't even really love.

He blinked. 'I believe you. Now, what do you take in your coffee?'

A wave of relief swept over her. Thank goodness. She'd hate it if he thought she just jumped into bed with every guy she met. Some chalet maids had that kind of reputation and Anissa didn't want him to think of her like that.

She picked up the milk from the counter. 'Just this.' His fingers brushed against hers as he took the carton from her hand and splashed the milk into the cups. 'Want a cookie too?' He lifted the pack as he headed towards the table.

She shook her head. 'You missed out. The oatmeal and raisin are the superior cookie here, but everyone seems to order the chocolate chip.'

He raised his eyebrows as he sat down. 'Ah...insider secrets. Thanks. I'll order oatmeal and raisin tomorrow.'

She pulled out the chair opposite and sat down. This

was a little weird. A little formal. Last time they'd been in each other's company he'd been pulling off her boots and sitting next to her on the sofa.

'How's your leg?'

She shrugged. 'Okay. I strapped it up the last few days when I was doing lessons.'

He leaned his head on one hand, his fingers threading through his dark tousled hair as he sipped his coffee. 'How long have you skied for?'

'Practically since I could breathe. I'm Austrian. It's in my genes. The other day on the slopes? That was stupid of me. I lost my concentration. I never do that. Never.'

The last time she'd lost her concentration it had cost her a chance at the gold medal. She'd been stupid. The effects had meant her whole world had come crashing down around her. And she'd spent the last year trying desperately to reach the same level she'd been at before. But it didn't seem to matter how hard she practised, it was still out of her reach. The accident the other night had shaken her more than she could admit. If Leo hadn't been there to help her, then distract her…

He gave a slow, thoughtful nod. 'Maybe you had other things on your mind?'

'Like you have?'

She couldn't pretend not to notice that far-off look he got in his eyes.

He met her gaze and smiled. 'Am I that obvious?'

She sipped her coffee. 'Just a little.'

He nodded again. 'I thought I would have been back in New York by now.'

Her stomach gave a little flip. If Leo had gone back to New York she wouldn't have seen him again. It surprised her how much she didn't like that idea.

'Why aren't you?'

He bit his bottom lip. It was clear he was trying to find the right words. 'Family…issues. The matter I came to deal with should only have taken a day. But there's been…complications. And it seems I can't get away when I thought I could.'

He ran his fingers through his rumpled hair. She could tell just by looking how tense he was. The muscles around his neck and shoulders looked tight. His forehead marred by a deep furrow. And he looked tired. Like he hadn't really slept properly.

She could tell something was wrong. For the first time he seemed a little awkward. It was obvious the family stuff was getting to him.

Her heart gave a little tug. She remembered feeling as if things were pressing down around about her—in fact, it sort of resembled the whole last year for her. But a few days ago she'd met a gorgeous mystery man who'd pulled her out of her slump. Leo.

'It's a good time of year to be in Mont Coeur,' she said.

He looked up and gave an amused smile. 'It seems like it's Christmas already here.'

She shrugged. 'From what I hear, New York is pretty much the same.'

'Okay, I'll give you that.'

She waved her hand. 'Anyway, I was talking about the slopes, not the Christmas decorations.' She put her hands around her coffee cup and looked up at him. 'You should try them. Skiing at night—it's peaceful. It's calming.' She gave a smile, 'And the slopes are much quieter. Maybe it will help clear your head a little?'

He was watching her with those bright blue eyes. 'Are you asking me on a date?'

She laughed out loud as she felt heat rush into her cheeks. 'Nope. I was making a suggestion. You said you didn't have equipment, but I can tell you where to hire some. And it's good stuff.'

'Could be dangerous up on the slopes alone at night.' His eyes were twinkling.

'What are you suggesting?'

He gave a careless shrug. 'Well, you know. I was thinking that someone could come with me. It would be much safer. After all, I've seen you on the slopes. You might need rescuing again.'

'Ha!' She sucked in a breath in mock horror. 'Mr Baxter, that almost seems like an insult.'

He raised his eyebrows. 'How about, Ms Lang, you take it as a challenge?'

He let the words hang in the air between them. She liked this. She liked his humour. She pushed herself up from the chair. If she didn't get to the next chalet soon she would end up in trouble.

'Okay then. As a resident here, why don't I show you why the world loves Mont Coeur so much? Do you have any other plans for tonight?'

He shook his head. 'None. I'm all yours.'

'Then how about we meet later—around nine o'clock?' She grabbed a notepad sitting next to the phone. 'Here's the name and number of the place to hire gear. Okay?'

His hand touched hers as she slid the piece of paper across the table towards him. He smiled again. 'This sounds like a date,' he said, his tone teasing.

She shook her head. 'It's no date.' She wagged her finger at him as she headed to the door. 'Don't you be getting any ideas, Leo Baxter.' She gave him a cheeky wink and then hurried out the door before her rapidly beating heart exploded in her chest.

The hand he'd just touched was pressed up against her chest wall, still tingling. She looked down and smiled. What on earth had she just done?

CHAPTER THREE

LEO BAXTER WAS used to being in control. Anything else was alien to him. Which meant the last few months had thrown him off his game.

The letter he'd received from his birth parents was still in his briefcase. It had been there since it had landed in his penthouse mailbox in August. It had taken him weeks to reply, and then, when he had, his mother and father had sounded overjoyed and couldn't wait to come to New York to meet him.

He'd been struggling with the realisation that what he'd believed for most of his life had been wrong when they'd died in a helicopter crash on way to New York. He'd never even got to see them in the flesh. He'd never got to hug them. He'd never got a kiss from them. It was almost as if, since he'd received that letter, all elements of his normally micromanaged existence had spiralled out of his control.

The will was just another element. He hated being manipulated. He hated the thought that someone might be trying to take charge of his life.

His parents had had no idea where he was, or how life had turned out for him, when they'd included him in the will. Maybe they'd hoped it would give him the financial security that most people craved. But Leo had no need of financial security from his parents. He'd carved out his own successful business through dedication, hard work and a tiny edge of ruthlessness.

If they'd had a chance to meet they would have realised that Leo didn't need money. He had no need to be part of the family business—or any interest in it. But that chance had been stolen from them all, and right now the will was creating havoc with his own business interests.

He needed to be in New York. He had several large deals coming off and for Leo the devil was in the detail. The thing he prided himself on. Being in Mont Coeur, surrounded by family pressure, was messing with his head.

Anissa's idea to come up the mountain to clear his head had come at the perfect time.

There was a nudge at his back. 'Come on, then, Leo. Show me your moves.'

She'd arrived behind him right on time at the ski lift. Her eyes swept up and down his body. 'Did you get that gear from the hire shop?'

'Maybe,' he answered, noncommittal. He didn't want to let her know that he'd just gone to the most exclusive shop and bought a whole host of new gear and equipment.

She gave a nod. 'They've obviously improved their range. Cool.'

She gestured towards the ski lift. 'Ready, then?'

'Sure I am. You show me your moves, and I'll show you mine.'

She grinned and glided ahead of him on her skis, lining up with the swiftly approaching chair lift. He slotted in behind her in the queue and tried not to think about how neat her backside had looked as she'd been swept up by the seat. She was wearing the same black ski gear she'd been wearing the first time he'd seen her. And, boy, did it fit well.

They reached the top of the slope around ten minutes later. It wasn't for the faint-hearted, and just being here gave Leo a hint of mischief.

The whole of Mont Coeur lay beneath them, twinkling with lights, surrounded by a dark sky and white snow.

'I love it up here,' Anissa said quietly, her warm breath clouding the air in front of them.

'Impressive,' he said as he looked around. There were only a few other serious skiers. He watched them dart down the slopes in front of them, zig-zagging with ease.

Anissa was moving from foot to foot—obviously anxious to get started. He turned to face her with a wide grin on his face. 'Okay, so you might need to give me a few pointers.'

'What?' Her face fell.

He held up his ski poles. 'You know—the kind of stuff that you teach.'

Her mouth opened. 'But you said you could ski. That you could hold your own.'

He shrugged. 'I might have been a bit economical with the truth.'

Concern laced her brow. 'Please tell me you're joking. I would never have brought you up to this slope if you weren't experienced.'

'I am. I'm maybe just...' he grinned and shrugged again '...a little out of practice.' He loved teasing her. It was clear she was taking it all in and contemplating how to tell him he was about to kill himself skiing down this run.

She sucked in a deep breath and obviously tried to still the panic she was feeling. She shuffled over next to him. 'Okay, let's practise the basics. Positioning. Moving. Slowing and stopping.'

She seemed to go into automatic pilot, demonstrating each position and talking him through it. Leo took great pleasure in getting most things wrong, particularly when she came over and tried to move his body into the position it was supposed to be in.

'When was the last time you skied?' she asked.

'College,' he quipped.

'College?' It came out more like a squeak.

He could see her professional face slip into place. 'Leo, maybe this isn't such a good idea.'

'How long have you been doing this?' he asked. He was curious. Was her dual role between ski instructor and chalet maid her ambition or a convenience?

She bit her bottom lip. It made her look the tiniest bit vulnerable.

'Only for the past year. It's kind of a needs–must situation.'

Now he really was curious. 'Why? What were you doing before?'

She looked distinctly uncomfortable, shifting from ski to ski. 'I had other career plans. But they got…side-lined.'

He couldn't help himself. 'Why, what did you do before?'

She glanced over her shoulder, almost as if she were checking to see if anyone was listening. But the few other skiers up on the slopes were all occupied. She took a deep breath. 'I was a professional. Have been the last few years. I was training for the International Skiing Championship. I was hoping to get gold.'

For the first time since he'd met her, he was struck dumb. 'What?'

She looked a little hurt. 'Is it really so unbelievable?'

'What?' he repeated. 'No, of course not. But...' he paused for a second '...what happened?'

Her face was serious and her body posture tense. 'I had an accident. One that my surgeon termed "catastrophic". I broke my leg in three places. He said it would never be strong enough for me to ski professionally again.'

Leo reached out and touched her arm. 'Oh, Anissa, I'm so sorry.'

She tossed her hair over her shoulder. 'Don't be. I get better every day. I can feel the strength returning. I just need to keep practising, keep conditioning myself to gain momentum again.'

He heard the words she was saying but wasn't quite sure he believed them. He'd seen how much she'd been in shock the other night after her minor accident. And if her doctor had told her that being competitive wasn't possible again, could Anissa be deluding herself?

'What happened to the team you had around you? Didn't you have a sponsor?'

She pressed her lips together and looked off into the distance for a second. 'Yeah. They weren't interested in hanging around. They're in it for the here and now. They don't want to wait for someone to get back to fitness.'

He moved in front of her. It was awkward when they both had skis. Right now he wanted to touch her cheek, give her a hug, let her know that he empathised with her. Because he did.

Anissa sounded as if she'd been the next big thing—only to have it all ripped away from her. In a resort like this, she had a daily reminder of what she'd lost.

He knew how hard that was. He'd spent the last few days purposely avoiding Sebastian and Noemi—even though Noemi had called four times. He was trying so hard to think about the family stuff. He didn't even want to acknowledge how much his life had been turned upside down.

He reached out and took his Anissa's hand. 'I get it,' he said quietly.

Her pale blue eyes met his. 'Get what?' He could see a whole host of mixed emotions there.

'I get what it feels to have your life change completely.'

She narrowed her gaze, a little wrinkle appearing in her brow. 'You do?'

He nodded. He didn't want to say too much. 'Let's just say the reason I came to Mount Coeur is turning out to be tougher than I originally thought.'

Anissa didn't hesitate. She leaned forward and gave him a hug. He breathed deeply, letting the familiar aroma of her orange blossom scent surround him. He stayed there for a few seconds, enjoying the feeling of her pressed against him.

When she pulled back, he was more than a little sorry. 'Hey,' she said, smiling brightly, 'we came up here to clear our heads and enjoy the view.' She swept her arm out to Mont Coeur beneath them. Nestled in the valley, with mountains and snow surrounding it on all sides, Mont Coeur glistened with yellow lights and exuded warmth. From here it looked like something from one of those Christmas cards adorned with glitter that sat on people's shelves every year.

It gave him a strange pang to realise that he'd never really celebrated Christmas the way he'd always longed to—in an environment where he felt as if he was loved and belonged. Last year's Christmas had been spent in an exclusive restaurant in New York with a visiting work colleague and an annoyed girlfriend. When he'd received the letter from his parents he'd been both excited and nervous about what Christmas might hold this year, all for his hopes to be dashed. It just proved to him he was better off on his own.

He turned to face Anissa again—the brightest spark he'd met since he'd got here. She had her head tilted a little, watching him through enquiring eyes without actually saying anything. It was almost as if she was giving him time for his thoughts. She'd said she came up here to think. He could understand why.

She smiled. 'We're also supposed to enjoy the skiing.' She gave him a sympathetic glance. 'Want to go down to an easier slope? We can do that. You might be more comfortable.' She was being sincere, trying to let him down gently. It seemed he'd fooled her more than he'd planned to.

His stomach gave a little twist. They'd just opened themselves up to each other. Anissa had been going for gold. A gold medal. She'd been *that* good.

And somehow? He wasn't surprised.

He couldn't begin to imagine how much her life had somersaulted. What had happened to her coach? Her team? The sponsors he could almost understand. But the rest?

It made him angry for her. Angry that she was forced to spend her days cleaning other people's chalets and teaching the basics of the thing that had been her passion.

She deserved better.

But she was still thinking about him. She patted his arm. 'It will be fine. Honest. People come up runs all the time that they aren't really equipped to deal with. We'll get you back down and find something safer. Something easier.'

It was the way she was patting his arm. Nicely. Reassuringly. All the while thinking he was probably about to fall on his backside.

Now his wicked streak was beginning to emerge again. He straightened up and looked down the slope. 'How about a little race?'

'What? No.' She was totally surprised. 'This is a run for experienced skiers. I thought you were—but I've obviously overestimated things. It's far too dangerous.'

'You think?' He couldn't help himself, he easily adopted his true skiing position and winked at her over his shoulder as he pushed off.

'Leo!' he heard her shout as he started skimming down the surface of the run. It was fast, glistening in the dark night against the bright white and blue lights adorning the run.

He bent low, picking up speed and bending into the turns. Despite the small lie he'd told Anissa, it had only been a few months since he'd skied and he'd always seemed to have a natural rhythm for it. He loved the feel of the cold air on his face and the speed and freedom of virtually flying down a mountain. Within thirty seconds he heard the swish of skis behind him and heard her calling to him. 'Why, you dirty, rotten…'

He laughed and looked over his shoulder. Sure enough, Anissa was catching up fast, a determined look on her face.

'You lied!' she shouted.

'I was economical with the truth.' The words were lost in the air behind him, but Anissa was there, almost on his shoulder.

'I'll give you a race,' she yelled, bending lower and edging closer.

His competitive edge would normally take over at this point, but inside he was already laughing.

Laughing at the fact he'd fooled her, and laughing at

the fact she was determined to win. Anissa Lang played to win. Just another thing to like about her.

There was a flash of black to his right-hand side just as he was about to bank right. He instantly straightened a little, giving Anissa the opportunity she'd obviously planned for as she whizzed past.

He tried to get lower to match her speed. But she was too well in tune with the mountain, too experienced on this slope. She was a natural, moving easily and with ever-increasing speed.

As the bottom of the run loomed ahead his stomach clenched.

'Slow down.' He said the words automatically through gritted teeth. She was still moving at a lightning pace, completely focused, with one intent—to win.

Panic swept over him. But it was as if someone had flicked a switch. All of a sudden she straightened, bending her legs to slow and guiding herself with one pole. It was the most graceful of moves. Perfect. Professional.

He slowed himself, but much sooner than she had. By the time he reached the bottom of the slope she was standing, waiting for him, with a large grin across her face.

She waited until he swept up to join her. She raised one eyebrow. 'Thought you would be a smarty-pants, did you?'

He raised his eyebrows back. 'Now, there's an expression I haven't heard in a hundred years.'

She waved one hand. 'Thought you would fool me?' She put her fingers in the air. 'Let's pretend we can't ski, let's act like a fool, let's see how long it takes her to catch up.'

He opened his mouth in mock surprise. 'Did you catch up? I didn't notice.'

'I chewed you up and spat you out.' She was being

snarky but she had a wide smile on her face. 'You wish you could catch me—but you didn't have a chance.' She was taunting him now, obviously picking up on his competitive edge.

He folded his arms. 'I could have caught you.'

She folded hers too. 'Really?'

He nodded. 'I think so. I was being kind. I let you win.'

She pushed down the latch at the back of her boot with her pole and stepped out of one ski. 'Oh, you *let* me win?'

He kept smiling as she pushed down the latch on the other. 'Sure I did. Didn't you know? I'm a gentleman. A gentleman always lets a lady win.'

Now she was free of her skis, Anissa moved around. She crouched down in the snow.

'Who says I'm a lady?' Something flew through the air and smacked him square in the face. For a second he was stunned, choking on the tightly packed snow. Then he spluttered, shook his head and brushed the snow off his jacket. He stepped out of his skis. 'Oh, it's like that, is it?'

She smiled, 'I play to win.' Another snowball hit him in the chest and a second flew over his shoulder.

He didn't need to be baited twice. He reached down and grabbed the nearest mound of snow, packing it together and taking aim. Anissa was good. She moved at lightning speed—even in her ski boots. And her hands were even quicker at forming and throwing snowballs.

Pow. Pow. Pow.

'You New York boys,' she yelled. 'Always think you're better at everything!'

'That's fighting talk,' Leo shouted back as he threw snowballs wildly, each one missing the target.

Anissa's laughter rang throughout the night. Leo didn't hesitate. He ran at her, stumbling in his boots. For a second she looked surprised, trying to work out what he was about to do.

But she realised just a fraction of a second too late. Leo yelled as he dived on her, sending her flying onto her back.

Whoomph!

Anissa lay flat on her back, looking up at the stars. She was momentarily stunned.

Leo couldn't stop laughing. He had a leg on either side of her and his hands in the snow beside her head.

She blinked, several thick snowflakes landing on her cheeks and lashes. 'You don't play fair,' was all she said.

He kept laughing. 'Play fair? How am I supposed to race a potential gold-medal winner down a slope? Did you tell me before we got up there? Let me know what I was really up against?'

She flicked her head from side to side in the snow. 'I wasn't planning on telling you at all.'

He stopped laughing for a second. She still had a smile on her face. He lowered his face closer to hers. 'I get that. But you were just too cute up there.'

'Cute?' Her eyebrows shot up again, but he knew she wasn't offended, she was still smiling too much.

'We need to stop meeting like this.'

'In the snow?' He nodded in agreement.

She shrugged as she lay there, apparently not minding the fact that the snow was probably soaking through her ski clothes. 'Maybe it was fate? Maybe we were meant to meet?' Her words were light but they struck a strange chord with Leo.

He stopped for a second as he rested back on his legs. 'You believe in fate? After you've been dealt such a harsh blow?'

As he said the words out loud, he realised how much

they reflected on his own circumstances. Both of them had had something they'd wanted literally snatched from their fingertips. Trouble was, Anissa had always wanted her goal. Leo hadn't dared to hope, and by the time he'd realised how much he would have liked a relationship with his parents, the chance had gone.

Her answer was quiet. 'I have to believe in something, Leo. There isn't much left.'

His heart squeezed in his chest. Her blonde hair and pale blue eyes were highlighted by the white, white snow behind her head.

He couldn't resist. He bent towards her, brushing his lips against hers. She tasted sweet. She tasted good. And the wave of familiarity from the previous night swept around him.

A tiny part of his brain questioned his actions. What if she objected? But Anissa wrapped her arms around his neck and didn't hesitate when she kissed him back.

Right now, she was all he could think about. And it was a relief. A relief to be wrapped in the arms of a warm, fun, loving woman who he already knew had other issues going on.

It made him feel not quite so alone.

It was crazy. But when Anissa had invited him today for some night-time skiing, he'd known there was no place else he'd rather be. It was odd how two lost souls were being drawn together, both wrestling their demons while trying to get on with their lives.

Her hands threaded around the back of his head. She pulled her lips from his and whispered in his ear. 'Is this how you plan to win the next race, by distracting me?'

He laughed and whispered in her ear, 'Whatever it takes…'

CHAPTER FOUR

HER STOMACH WAS in knots. It had been a long time since a guy had made her feel like this. Attractive. Important. Wanted.

She tugged at her top. Black with a criss-cross back, casual but not too casual, paired with jeans. Her hair was down, and she had put on a little more make-up than usual and worn lipstick for the first time in for ever.

Lucy and Chloe sat perched on her sofa, laughing as she frowned at her reflection in the mirror.

She spun around. 'How do I look?'

'Perfect,' said Chloe with a deadpan face as she took a sip of her wine. 'Just like you did ten minutes ago.'

Anissa glanced down. 'Are you sure?' She walked back over to the sofa where a whole array of tops were scattered. 'Maybe I should have gone with the blue? Black's too night-time, isn't it?' She sighed as she turned back to the mirror. 'It's like I'm trying too hard, right?'

Lucy laughed out loud. 'Anissa, you look perfect. Gorgeous. The guy is lucky you agreed to go out with him.' She lifted her glass of wine and raised it towards her. 'And, anyway, it might only be two p.m. out here, but somewhere in the world it's after five.'

Anissa glanced at her glass of untouched wine on the

sideboard. The girls had come over to help her get ready. And, of course, they'd brought wine.

She sagged down onto the sofa between them. 'Is it totally pathetic how nervous I am?' She wrung her hands in her lap. 'I'm twenty-eight years, old for goodness' sake. And I feel like I'm thirteen again and going on my first date.'

'You went on your first date at thirteen?' Amy raised her eyebrows and nodded at Chloe. 'Early starter.'

Anissa gave her leg a playful slap and took the wine glass from Amy's hand, stealing a sip.

She put her hand on her stomach. 'What stops nerves?'

'Wine!' said both girls together, laughing.

Chloe nudged her. 'What's to be nervous about? Been there, done that. He's a handsome, rich bachelor who is clearly attracted to you. Just go and have some fun.'

Amy put her hand over Anissa's. 'It's been a crap year, honey. This is your chance to enjoy yourself. To have some fun.' She stopped smiling for a second and squeezed Anissa's hand tightly. 'You deserve this.'

Amy stretched over and lifted Anissa's wine glass, taking it as her own and raising her glass so they all could toast together.

'Here's to late lunches, having fun and some, very, very handsome men.'

'Cheers!' they all shouted as their glasses clinked together.

Leo watched the door. The restaurant was central and popular. He could have easily afforded one of the more exclusive restaurants in the resort but he wanted Anissa to feel comfortable—and this place had been her suggestion.

She strolled in a few minutes late and he breathed a

sigh of relief. Nerves were a new thing for him. They'd appeared the moment he'd received the letter from his mother and father and had danced around him ever since.

He'd dated plenty of women in New York for the last few years, even though his priority had always been his business. But none of those dates or eventual brief relationships had resulted in him feeling nervous. He had always been in control. Always polite but slightly distant. Happy to let things progress if they worked out that way, equally happy to let things slide when appropriate.

None of those dates—at any point in the last ten years—had made his stomach churn like this.

It was odd. After the knocks of childhood he'd been so determined to be a confident adult. And he had been— right up until he'd got that letter and the permanent feeling of wondering if he was good enough had made the crows of doubt constantly circle.

So watching Anissa walk through the door towards him was like a breath of fresh air.

She gave him a shy kind of smile as she joined him at the bar.

'Drink?' he asked.

She nodded at his beer bottle. 'I'll have a beer.' He ordered swiftly and they threaded their way through the crowd and found a booth near the back. A waitress appeared promptly with menus. 'Back in five.' She waved.

Leo smiled as he slid into the booth. 'And here was me thinking that everyone came to Mont Coeur to ski.'

Anissa smiled across the crowded bar. 'It's an expensive place to come to stay in a bar all day. Seems like such a waste.'

He looked at her carefully. 'You really love skiing, don't you?'

She sighed. 'It feels like it's in my blood. I can't...

not do it. I love it. I love the freedom. The speed. The exhilaration. If I miss it for even one day, I'm itching to get back out there.'

He nodded in appreciation. 'It's great that you've found your passion but—' he chose his next words carefully '—it must have been really tough when you were injured.'

She blinked, and it seemed as though her eyes were wet almost instantly. 'It was.' She swallowed uncomfortably. 'Twelve long weeks. I had to have two separate operations, with six weeks healing in between each. Then I had physio for another twelve weeks.' She gave a wry laugh. 'But I wouldn't stay off the snow. I couldn't.'

'How does your leg feel now? Do you have the strength back?' He was curious but cautious. Would someone really ever recover fully from an injury like that?

She wiggled her leg under the table, brushing it against his. 'Most nights it's still a little sore. Particularly if I've been on the mountain all day. I have to take painkillers. But I was sore every night after training too. So that's nothing really new.'

'But if you don't ski, you don't need the painkillers?' He couldn't hide the concern in his tone.

She gave a shrug. 'I wouldn't know. I never don't ski.' She said it very matter-of-factly, as if the thought had never occurred to her.

'Do you keep in touch with anyone from before?'

Something flashed across her eyes. A jolt of hurt. She shook her head. 'I'm going to wait until I know I'm back at peak performance before I talk to anyone again. The circuit is small and I'd rather be fully ready before I try to find a new coach.'

He gave a nod. He knew immediately it was about what she wasn't saying. He'd answered enough questions like that himself over the years.

The waitress appeared back at their side. 'Ready to order?'

Anissa smiled. 'I'll have the regular Swiss burger, well done, with everything.'

Leo shook his head. He hadn't even glanced at the menu yet, too caught up in the conversation with Anissa. He handed his menu back with a smile. 'I'll have what she's having.'

'So, didn't you have business to do today?' Anissa leaned her head on one of her hands as she watched him.

He waved one hand. 'Three calls to New York, about a hundred emails, and I have a conference call with Japan later.'

She wrinkled her nose. 'Oh... I meant family business. Isn't that what you're here for?'

He took a breath. Truth was, he wasn't exactly sure what to say. 'I'm kind of in limbo at the moment. I'm just waiting to hear a bit of news before I decide my next step.'

It wasn't untrue. He was still hoping his lawyer would find some magical loophole that would set him free from the terms of the will—even though he'd already been told it was highly unlikely.

He stayed silent for a few seconds as Anissa ran her hand up and down the neck of the bottle. 'What do you do in New York?' she asked. 'A businessman—what is that? It's like a multitude of sins.' She gave a little smile then leaned back in the booth, keeping her eyes fixed on his. 'Maybe you're a serial killer? Or a spy?' She raised her eyebrows. 'Or maybe you're one of those crazy guys who do real estate in New York and star in that reality TV show.'

He couldn't help himself. 'Do I look like a reality TV star to you?'

She ran her eyes up and down his body as if she were really contemplating it.

He laughed. 'Wrong question. I should have asked if I looked like a serial killer.'

Now she laughed too and clinked her bottle against this. 'Thanks for this, Leo. I needed a little fun.'

He stopped for a second and licked his lips, looking at her appreciatively. 'So did I.' And he meant it. Every word.

This was ridiculous. He couldn't wait to get out of Mont Coeur. He never should have been here in the first place. And it was the last place he'd ever expected to meet someone. But somehow meeting Anissa had made the last few days a bit more bearable. Made the waiting game not quite so difficult.

Christmas was everywhere in Mont Coeur. And for Leo right now it was whipping up a whole range of emotions he didn't quite know how to deal with.

The waitress appeared with their food and set it before them.

Even though it was just early afternoon, the place remained busy and as they chatted the noise levels were rising.

Leo found himself leaning closer and closer across the table to talk to Anissa. She didn't seem to object, mirroring his movements and shifting in her seat until their heads were almost touching. Her hair fell forward and the scent of strawberry shampoo drifted towards him.

From the first time he'd met her he'd been attracted to her. But the more time he spent around her, the more he seemed to learn. Each encounter made him think that he'd peeled back another layer.

Anissa had qualities he admired. A real edge of determination. The ability to work hard. Drive. But all of these things were partially clouded by a veil of something else—something he strongly suspected was a woman who'd been hurt at some point, and not just by her injury.

It only made him relate to her all the more, and today she seemed more relaxed and at ease around him than she had before.

He was noticing things. Little things. The kind of things that he didn't normally take the trouble to notice. When she chatted she always toyed with the earring in her left lobe. She preferred to tuck her hair behind her right ear. She was observant—and it wasn't that he thought she was bored by him—or at least he hoped she wasn't. But she seemed to love to people-watch, remarking on the things she noticed.

'The girl in the red jacket. Do you think she's on a first date?'

Leo looked to where she was watching, seeing the girl shifting uncomfortably in her chair and sitting stiffly as a guy in a black jacket tried to engage her in conversation.

Leo cringed. 'She doesn't want to be there, does she? Look at that poor guy. He obviously can't stop talking. He looks so nervous.'

Anissa nodded to the right. 'What about the four girls in the booth over there? I sense trouble…'

Leo checked them out and smiled as he sipped the last of his beer. 'I think you could be right. Things look as if they're getting fierce.'

Sure enough, a few seconds later one of them grabbed her bag and jacket and stomped out the front door.

Leo couldn't stop watching Anissa. 'You like this, don't you?'

She finished her beer. 'What? People-watching?' She gave a little shrug. 'Of course. Doesn't everyone? I just usually don't get time. I normally have a shift in the chalets in the morning then I do lessons most afternoons and sometimes into the evenings. It's nice to get a little downtime.'

She gave a wicked kind of smile. 'I sometimes like to imagine whole other lives for people.' She gestured with her head to the couple behind them. 'Those guys? They look normal, but she's actually a princess from some principality and he's her bodyguard. But...' She leaned forward and whispered behind her hand, 'They're actually in love with each other.'

Leo shook his head but couldn't help but smile as Anissa continued. 'And those two over there—at the bar?' She winked. 'They might look like they're just your average couple who just spent the morning skiing, but they're actually time travellers. He's a Roman warrior and she's an Egyptian queen.'

Leo leaned forward conspiratorially. 'You have a very vivid imagination.'

She gave him a naughty nod. 'Oh, believe me, you have *no* idea.'

He liked this. He liked this a lot.

Her phone screen lit up and she leaned forward and smiled, reading the message and tapping out a quick reply.

He couldn't help but ask. 'Who is it?'

'My mum and dad. They're still at home in Austria and they text me every day.' She rolled her eyes. 'Except when we're all watching the latest episode of our favourite sci-fi show at the same time. Then we text every five minutes.'

Her comments were easy and throwaway. She obviously had parents who loved her and supported her. A relationship he hadn't experienced in the past and couldn't develop in the future. The thing that surprised him most was now much that actually gnawed away at him. How much it unexpectedly stung.

The waitress appeared beside them again. 'More drinks?'

Leo reached over and grabbed the cocktail menu. Another drink. Exactly what he needed right now. 'Do you have a preference?' he asked Anissa.

'This early?'

He shrugged, 'It's afternoon. Anyway…' he leaned forward again '…don't we have more people-watching to do?'

She nodded her head, 'I guess we do.' Then leaned her head on her hand. 'So, surprise me.'

His eyes ran down the cocktail list. 'We'll have two of these—the Stormy Slopes.'

The waitress gave a smile, disappeared for a few minutes then returned with two tall glasses.

Anissa leaned over and breathed in. 'Hmm, interesting.' She took a sip through the straw. Almost immediately her eyes sparkled. 'Wow, that's nice. What's in it?'

Leo took a drink from his too and gave a nod of approval. 'Rum, ginger beer and lime. Tasty. Not too heavy.' He gave her a smile. 'Afternoon cocktails. We don't want to fall over. Not yet, anyway.'

She studied him for a second. 'Have you visited any of the shops yet?'

He shook his head. 'Apart from the ski shop? Not a chance. I've been too busy. I've spent most of my time on the phone to New York.'

'Not much of a holiday,' she reflected.

'It was never meant to be a holiday.' His tone had changed and she looked up sharply and licked her lips but she didn't talk. She didn't try to fill the silence, just ran her fingers up and down the side of her glass.

It was another of her habits. Another thing he'd noticed about her.

He took a deep breath. 'The shops. Are they any good? Anything you'd recommend?'

She gave a little smile, knowing that he was changing the subject. 'Maybe. There's lots of quirky shops in Mont Coeur. Do you have anyone to buy gifts for in New York? I can probably show you where to get something a little different.'

His stomach gave a little flip. This would have been the first year he could actually have bought something for his mother and father. The effect was instant. Underneath his jersey T-shirt his skin prickled. Christmas. The time of year he liked to best avoid. What about Sebastian and his family? What about Noemi? Should he buy gifts for his brother and sister, and what on earth could he buy them? He barely knew them.

The face of his PA floated into his mind. Keisa had worked for him for the last six years. He usually bought something online and had it delivered. 'I always buy something for my PA.'

'Male or female?'

'Female.'

'What age?'

He wrinkled his brow. 'I thought I wasn't allowed to ask that?' He smiled for a second. 'I think she's probably early fifties.'

Anissa nodded. 'I know a few shops we can go to. You can see if there's anything she'll like.'

They finished their cocktails and wandered out into the snow-covered streets. The light was already beginning to fade. People were bundled up in a variety of coloured parkas, hats and scarves.

Although it was bitterly cold, there was a warmth about Mont Coeur that afternoon. It might have something to do with the fact that this was the first time she'd really been on a proper date in years. Although she knew there was no chance of this going anywhere, no chance of things progressing—his life was in New York as a businessman and hers was here, focusing on her skiing plans for the future—it was nice to be around someone again. It was nice to look at someone and feel as if they were really interested in what you were saying. The electricity in the air between them didn't hurt either.

But she was still curious. He'd mentioned the other night that he was here on family business. But he hadn't mentioned any family he intended to buy Christmas presents for. She hadn't seen anyone else visiting his chalet, so wasn't he close to his family? Mont Coeur was a long way to come from New York if he wasn't particularly close to his family.

They window-shopped along the street, Anissa pointing out a women's fashion store, a traditional Swiss chocolate shop and a jewellery store.

But none of them seemed to capture Leo's attention. Eventually she stopped and folded her arms. 'Okay, what do you normally buy Keisa?' She shook her head. 'Don't tell me. You internet-shop. You buy her perfume. Or some kind of designer scarf.'

Leo's brow furrowed and he turned towards her. 'Have you been spying on me?'

She studied his face and felt a little wave of sadness for him. Why would a guy as nice as Leo only have a PA to buy for at Christmas? It seemed…lonely.

'Why don't you use your imagination? Look at these gorgeous shops. Think about Keisa. What kind of a person is she? What does she like? Has she ever told you anything that would give a hint of what kind of gift might be a little more thoughtful, a little more personal?'

He gave a slow nod. 'Okay, then. Let's see if I can...' he gave her a wink '...use my imagination.'

As they walked further along the street, his hand brushed against hers. Whilst the little bolt of energy was still shooting up her arm he took her hand in his. She didn't object. In fact, it sent a flash of something through her head.

Her ex hadn't like public displays of affection. He'd never held her hand. He'd never put his arm around her while they'd walked in the street. They'd dated for four years and had practically lived together for the year they'd been engaged. But deep down she wondered if they'd ever really been close.

Everything had been about skiing, about racing. About getting the best times. About coaching. They had never really had many of the traditional 'dates'. Any dinner together had generally been work-related with other ski professionals from different countries. Any visit abroad had always been for a competition or about the sponsors. Just the simple act of taking her hand and Leo had made something pang inside her chest—made her feel as if she'd missed out.

'Wait a minute, what about that place?'

Leo pointed across the street to an old-fashioned shop with tiny squares of window glass outlined in white wood. There was a small Christmas tree front and centre in the window.

Anissa nodded. 'Yes, I'd forgotten about this place. They have lot of wood carvings, Christmas tree decorations, and I think they do some crystal jewellery too.'

Leo pushed open the door and a waft of cinnamon, pine and oranges surrounded them. The whole shop was filled with coloured twinkling lights. They walked around slowly, admiring the carved Christmas scenes, the array of coloured glass pendants and rings, and a whole host of unusual Christmas baubles.

Anissa pointed to a mauve-coloured pendant. 'What about this one?'

Leo bent down to look at the oval-shaped stone. He wrinkled his nose. 'It's nice... I suppose, but...' Then he looked up and his eyes widened. 'Oh, wow.'

Anissa followed his gaze. The back wall of the shop was covered in rows and rows of cuckoo clocks.

Leo stepped over, moving from one to another. Each one was completely individual. Anissa had never really looked closely before at cuckoo clocks, but now she could appreciate the workmanship. She reached a hand up to touch one, hesitating, 'I wonder how many hours one of these takes?'

Leo was moving along the line, studying each one. 'The wooden Christmas scenes,' he murmured. 'Keisa has a whole collection. A whole village. She's told me about them before. A bakery. A school. A Ferris wheel. A skating rink. A church.'

He smiled. 'But she doesn't have one of these.'

She could see the sparkle in his eyes. He turned to face her. 'A cuckoo clock. I know that Austria, Germany and Switzerland all make them. But it's kind of unique.'

Anissa smiled. 'More personal than a bottle of perfume.'

He turned back and kept studying the clocks on the wall, before taking a sharp breath. 'It's this one. It's definitely this one.'

Anissa moved closer to him and looked up. It was a beautiful wooden hand-carved cuckoo clock. Even from underneath, Anissa could see how intricate it was. It was a variety of shades of wood, with some areas carefully painted. There was the traditional cuckoo at the top behind a red door, two little balconies, one with a carved rocking chair, the other with a few birds perched on the edge. Underneath on one side were two children playing on a see-saw, a dog at their side. And on the other side was a Christmas tree with tiny red and blue baubles and a gold twinkling star on top. The whole clock was decorated with a dusting of snow. It really was a work of art.

Anissa felt a tear form in the corner of her eye. 'It's beautiful,' she breathed.

'Anissa.' Leo appeared behind her, putting one hand at her waist and leaning over one shoulder. 'What's wrong?'

She reached up and brushed the tear away, shaking her head. 'It's nothing. I'm just being silly.'

'Silly about what?'

No matter how hard she tried, she couldn't stop her voice from trembling, 'It's just…it looks so perfect. But you can tell the hard work, how painstaking it must have been to create.' She held her hands out in front of it. 'It's like someone's hopes and dreams have materialised right in front of you.' Her mouth felt dry. 'Not everyone gets that lucky.'

Leo's other hand closed around her waist and he pulled her back against him, holding her still. Anissa was very conscious of her chest rising and falling. The wide, supportive feeling at her back.

Leo's warm breath danced across her neck. His voice was low. 'I know what you mean.'

She tensed. She knew Leo was distracted by family issues but she didn't really know what they were. He was a billionaire—at least he must be if he was staying in one of those chalets—so hadn't he already been lucky?

She took a deep breath. 'You said you were here to

see your family. Is something wrong? You haven't mentioned them, just that things are…difficult.'

She watched as he swallowed and she saw the deep flash of pain in his eyes. 'I… I guess you could say we're estranged. My brother and sister—it was the first time that we've met.'

'You just met?' He'd already told her he was thirty-eight. Why on earth had it taken that long to meet his siblings?

He gave a slow nod. She could tell he was struggling already with what to say. This wasn't her business. She knew that. And she didn't want to push him to say more than he was ready to.

'Up until a few months ago, Sebastian and Noemi didn't know I existed—or I them. The first meeting was hard. I'm not sure how things will work out. I'm not sure I'm the kind of person to be part of that family.'

There was so much unsaid there. So much visible hurt. Pushing him at this point would be wrong. She turned to face him and reached out and ran her fingers through his hair.

She tried to keep her voice steady as she gave him a sad kind of smile. 'So I guess you don't feel so lucky, then?'

He shook his head. 'Do you?'

She gulped and turned back to look at the beautiful clock. 'Not right now,' she admitted. 'This year has been tough.' She held up her hands. 'Even Mont Coeur, it's the place I need to be, somewhere I can get the chance to practise, but, honestly, for the last year it's felt like a permanent reminder of what I've missed out on, what I *should* have been. What I still want to be.'

His hands slipped around her waist. He didn't say a word, just continued to hold her in his arms. She felt comfortable there. And that was stupid. Because they'd only just met.

She leaned her head back against his chest. She wasn't sure why but it felt safe to talk around Leo. It was even easier to talk when she didn't have to look him in the eye. 'Nothing like getting bad news and turning to your fiancé for support, only to see him move away so quickly he almost wins gold medals himself.'

'That's what happened?' She could feel Leo stiffen behind her.

She nodded her head. 'Yeah. No coach. No fiancé. No wedding. Way to help a girl when she's feeling down.' She was trying to sound ironic but instead she sounded tired and she knew that. But the truth was she *was* tired. Tired of trying so hard all the time on her own.

Leo's lips brushed against her ear as he bent to speak low into her ear. 'Well, one thing is quite clear, the guy didn't deserve you—not for a second.'

His phone buzzed and he moved back. She hated how much she didn't like that.

He spoke quietly. 'Yeah, yeah. Hmm.' He looked at her as she turned around. 'Can you give me a minute?' he said into the phone.

He turned back to her. 'Okay?'

She nodded and tried to pull her thoughts together. 'Should I ask the owner to parcel up the clock while you take your call?'

He nodded. 'That would be great,' he said as he strolled towards the door.

Anissa turned back to the clock. It was beautiful. It was a work of art. A masterpiece. Just like she eventually hoped she could be.

Leo didn't like anything he was hearing. A business deal he'd been working on for the last year had developed a last-minute hitch. 'Why hasn't this been dealt with? He said what?'

Leo groaned. The business associate he was dealing with was an older man. It had taken a good few years to even begin the negotiations. Joe trusted him. He couldn't leave this to anyone else. He had to deal with these problems himself. He gave a huge sigh, 'Okay, I'll come back. I'll get the first flight.'

He finished the call. New York. He'd wanted to go back there for days. But somehow he knew when he got there, the chances of getting a flight back to Mont Coeur to spend Christmas with his new family would get slimmer and slimmer.

Here, he'd had the benefit of a little time. Everything in New York was generally about work, even down to the Christmas charity ball he was obligated to attend. As soon as he returned to the States...

He looked back through the window of the shop. Anissa was talking to the store owner as they wrapped the cuckoo clock in tissue paper and bubble wrap. His stomach clenched. The Christmas ball. The place he always took a date.

For the first time, the prospect of consulting his little black book suddenly didn't seem so appealing. He felt for his wallet and strolled back into the store to pay for the clock.

'Nearly done.' Anissa smiled as he approached.

'I have to go back to New York.'

Her face fell. 'What?'

His skin prickled. She was upset. He hated that. He hated that fleeting look of hurt in her eyes. Within seconds she plastered a smile on her face. 'Oh, of course.'

'It's business. A particularly tricky deal.'

Anissa pressed her lips tight together and nodded automatically.

The seed of an idea that had partially formed outside burst into full bloom in his head. He hated that flicker of pain he'd seen in her eyes when she'd talked about being in Mont Coeur and being permanently reminded of what she'd lost. It had seemed so raw.

Maybe, just maybe he could change things for her. Put a little sparkle and hope back into her eyes. Something that he ached to feel in his life too.

'Come with me.' The words flew out of his mouth.

Her eyes widened. 'What?'

He nodded, as it all started to make sense in his head. 'You said you've never really had a proper holiday. Come with me. Come and see New York. You'll love it in winter. I can take you sightseeing.'

Sightseeing. The thing he'd never really got around to in New York.

Anissa's mouth was open. 'But…my job. I have lessons booked. I have chalets to clean.'

He moved closer to her. 'Leave them. See if someone can cover. If you can only come for a few days—that's fine. But come with me. I have a Christmas ball to attend and I'd love it if you could come with me.' His hands ached to reach for her, but he held himself back. 'I called you Ice Princess before, how do you feel about being Cinderella? Going to the most spectacular Christmas ball in New York? It will take your breath away, I promise.'

Her mouth was still open as her eyes widened. He could almost see her brain processing the invitation. She was considering it. She was actually considering it. And that built a whole host of hopes in his chest that still took him by surprise.

He moved closer. Close enough to drown out the

Christmas scents from the shop and to let him just smell her. Anissa.

'Come on, Anissa. Live a little,' he whispered.

He could see her hesitation. See her worries.

But her pale blue eyes met his. There was still a little sparkle there. Still a little hope for him.

Her lips turned upwards. 'Okay,' she whispered back as he bent to kiss her.

CHAPTER FIVE

'YOU'RE GOING. YOU'RE definitely going.'

Anissa stared around her chalet, trying to still the rising panic in her chest.

She'd said yes on a whim. How could she look into those bright blue eyes and say anything else? Particularly when she'd been overwhelmed by emotions.

It was odd how looking at the care and attention to detail in one intricate clock could align itself in her head with someone completing their dream—and leaving her feel so far away from her own.

Chloe and Amy were staring at her expectantly from the sofa.

Anissa shook her head again. 'I can't. I must have been mad to agree. I've got lessons, shifts in the chalets.'

Amy stood up and shook her head. 'We can cover them. Between us. We can cover those shifts. Ore and Anouska will help too.'

Anissa breathed in. 'But the lessons...'

Chloe smiled as she turned her phone around. 'Regan just texted. His dad's better. He's coming back. He can cover your lessons.'

Anissa gasped. Regan was one of the other ski instructors, who'd had to take time off at short notice to go home and visit his sick father.

Chloe nudged her. 'You covered his lessons for more than a week at short notice. I'm sure he'll cover yours. It's time to go on the first proper holiday of your adult life. We're sorted. Now, let's see what we can pack.'

She bent over and scribbled something on a bit of paper. 'Here's my cousin's contact details. She stays in New York. She's at fashion college there. You need anything, or you change your mind about being there—give her a call.'

Amy had already made her way to the cupboard and dragged out a suitcase. 'New York. New York. Here she comes.' She danced about in front of Anissa in excitement, then struck a pose, with one finger on her chin. 'Hmm, what do we think our fair maiden should wear when she's with her handsome billionaire in New York?'

'I have ideas,' piped up Chloe. Anissa laughed. She couldn't believe it. Things were actually coming together. She was going on holiday. She was going to New York.

With Leo.

Her heart gave a little flip-flop.

What on earth did this really mean?

His mind was full. Full of business dealings, full of family dealings, and full of a sense of relief that he was going to get out of Mont Coeur, at least for a few days.

The car he'd sent for Anissa pulled up in front of the private airport terminal. Anissa jumped out, frowning and flicking her head from side to side. 'Where are we?'

He smiled. Today she had on a long bright blue wool coat, a black hat and leather gloves. Her blonde hair framed her face and the colour of the coat was reflected in her pale blue eyes, making them look more intense than ever. She was wearing make-up. Her lips were a little redder than before and her eyelashes longer and thicker.

For a few seconds Leo's feet were frozen to the ground. He'd always thought Anissa was naturally pretty, but today...she was stunning.

She touched his arm. 'Leo? I thought we were going to the regular airport?'

He snapped back to attention and signalled to the driver to get her case. 'No. I have my own plane. Makes things simpler.'

She blinked, then blinked again, as if she was processing what he'd just told her. 'You have your own plane,' she repeated as he led her up the small detachable stairs and into the comfortable aircraft, nodding a greeting to the steward and stewardess.

There was no waiting. The flight plans had been lodged and cleared, and despite the surrounding snow and temperatures the plane and runway were ready for take-off.

The main part of the plane had large cream leather chairs and glossy wooden tables, complete with entertainment systems. Anissa looked around as if she was waiting to see where she should sit.

Leo waved his hand. 'It's just you and me, you can sit anywhere you please. There's Wi-Fi if you need it. Or, if you want to sleep, there's a bedroom in the back.'

'A bedroom?' Her eyes were wide. She looked at the eight large chairs then turned back to him. 'Leo, just exactly how rich are you?'

He smiled and waited until she'd slipped off her coat and picked a chair then he settled down in the one next to her.

Anissa turned and looked out of the window. 'Anything to eat or drink?' She shook her head. 'No, I'm fine, thank you.'

She seemed a little nervous. 'Once we take off you can use these buttons to move the seat back and these ones to access the entertainment system.'

She gave a nod of acknowledgment and turned to stare back out the window as the plane started to taxi down the runway.

Leo settled back into his seat and pulled out his two computers. He had multiple things to work on during the flight.

It took Anissa a little time to relax, but eventually she fell asleep for a few hours, waking up when the steward came to ask what they wanted for dinner.

'How long to New York?' she asked when she came back from freshening up.

'Just another few hours. It will be evening there when we arrive.'

She gave a little nod and sat down beside him. He glanced at her entertainment system. She had a popular movie frozen on screen in front of her. The setting? New York at Christmas.

He'd been so engrossed in his work for the last few hours he'd been a poor host.

The truth was he'd asked Anissa to join him on the spur of the moment. Maybe it was wrong but it had made perfect sense in his head at the time. The look on her face had been so sad. Plagued by unhappy memories and feelings of not being good enough. She'd said it out loud. Someone else fulfilling their dream. And it had made his heart twist in unexpected ways.

Because he completely and utterly got it.

He'd always had that feeling of not being good enough. His adoptive parents had never really been interested in him. It seemed as though the 'idea' of adopting a child hadn't really aligned with the reality of it.

The fact was they'd never really been interested in parenting. They hadn't wanted to go to parents' evenings, school shows or sports events. And it seemed the harder he'd worked the more they'd ignored him.

As he'd got older he'd realised that their resentment ran deep. They'd often mention the business deals they could have done or the opportunities that had slipped through their fingers because they were tied with a child. And they'd never forgotten to add that his own parents hadn't wanted him—now something that he knew wasn't true. It was as if he was supposed to be eternally grateful to them for their sacrifice in taking him.

It hadn't taken him long to realise what a destructive relationship that really was. College life had opened a whole new world for him. He'd worked three jobs so he could enrol at New York College, support himself and study business. He'd never missed an assignment and had been top of his class the whole way through. One of his professors had even spoken to him about one of the business proposals he'd pulled together, giving him the confidence to know that his plans were solid with a real possibility of success.

Most importantly, at college he'd met friends with families who loved them dearly, and had included him in the mix with open, welcoming arms. He'd watched the relationships between fathers and mothers and their sons, none of them similar to his experience at all. It had made him realise how much he'd missed out on. But it hadn't allowed him to shake off the internal sense of not being good enough. The one that had been ingrained in him all his life.

So when he'd recognised that same feeling in Anissa, he'd wanted to do anything he could to help her. He'd watched her on the mountain, knew she was talented.

But was she being realistic? Was her dream still truly achievable?

He had doubts. But he couldn't say that to her. Did any potential gold-medal athlete get back to their best after such a severe accident?

She'd been constantly surrounded by the ski life. Had she even sampled the rest of the world? Did she know what other opportunities lay out there?

He'd invited her to New York for partly selfish reasons. He hadn't really wanted to leave her, and he knew she would be a perfect partner for the ball.

But what could he do for her in return?

He turned towards her as they ate their freshly cooked pasta, prepared on the plane. 'You told me you'd never really had a proper holiday before. Is there anything you'd like to do in New York? Anything you'd like to see, to do or anywhere you'd like to go?'

She pulled back in her seat a little. 'Apart from you, there's only one person in New York I'd like to meet. One of the chalet maids, Chloe, wants me to look up her cousin, Jules. Won't you be busy? You said you had to go back for work and emergency meetings.' She gave a smile. 'Jules is my back-up plan in case you disappear the second we get there.'

He gave a nod of his head. 'I do have work to do. Business is business. But you are my guest. New York comes alive at this time of year. Christmas is huge. There are a million things we can do.'

She looked intrigued. 'Like what?'

He racked his brain. He'd been in New York for years but had never really done any sightseeing. He was probably the world's worst person to show someone around New York. But there was so much to see and do that he could come up with a standard supply of answers.

'We could walk around Central Park. Visit the museums. Go ice skating. Shop. Then there's the Empire State Building and the Rockefeller Center. Times Square. the Statue of Liberty. I'm sure we can find plenty of things to do to keep you busy.'

'All in a few days?' She looked a little disbelieving. He hadn't really specified how long they'd be here— because he wasn't really sure how long this business would take to conclude.

'Don't forget the charity ball,' he added. 'You'll love it.'

She gave a nervous swallow. 'Yeah, a ball. I'll need to find a ballgown. Might have forgotten to pack one.'

Leo sensed her hesitation. 'Don't worry about that. We can sort that out when we land. Keisa, my PA, will know exactly where to send you.'

She held his gaze for the longest moment, immediately making him think that he'd said the wrong thing.

But eventually she peeled her gaze away and continued with the pasta. 'Sounds good,' she said quietly.

Leo licked his lips. This might be a little tougher than he'd first thought.

As the flight prepared to land, Anissa stared out of the window, watching the bright lights of New York appear beneath them. He'd always loved this part.

The feeling of coming home.

But this time? It was a little different.

This time he felt unsettled. Where, exactly, was home?

First it had been the plane. Then the mention of the ball. Then the throwaway remark about brushing her off onto his PA.

This had been a bad idea. This was a very bad idea.

But as New York had emerged beneath the smoky

clouds she'd felt a tiny spurt of exhilaration. If everything else was a disaster, at least she had a few days in a whole new place. A few days to do things that a normal tourist might do. It could even be fun.

A car had been waiting for them at the airport and after their suitcases had been put in the trunk they'd set off into the city. Leo had squirmed for a few seconds.

'What's wrong?' she asked.

He pulled a face. 'This is going to come out all wrong.'

She shifted uncomfortably. 'Well, whatever it is, just say it.' Had he changed her mind about her being here?

'I forgot to book a hotel for you.' He pulled his phone out of his pocket. 'I'm sorry, I'm so used to being on my own and I was so busy thinking about my business deal that I didn't plan ahead.' He gave his head a little shake. 'In my head it makes sense to stay in my penthouse, but now that we're here... I realise how presumptuous that sounds.'

She understood. She understood completely. They'd already seen each other naked and now he was feeling awkward about where she should sleep.

'We've done everything back to front,' she said quietly as New York flashed past outside.

'I can book you into a hotel,' he said quickly. 'I don't want you to feel uncomfortable.'

'I don't want *you* to feel uncomfortable,' she replied quickly, because the truth was, right up until this second she hadn't thought about any of this. It had just flown off her radar, just like it had his. And now he was mentioning it...well, it was making them both feel uncomfortable.

He sighed, as if he realised just how stilted this all sounded, then turned to face her and put his hand on his chest. 'Anissa, I asked you to join me in New York because I wanted you to join me. But I don't want you to feel any obligation to me whatsoever. This is supposed to be fun. My penthouse is big. I have three separate bedrooms and you're welcome to sleep in any one them—alone. Please don't think that by asking you to come I have any other kind of expectation.' He gestured to the streets flashing past outside. 'Or I can book you into any hotel you choose.' He nodded slowly. 'I'm sorry. I should have thought about this sooner—I guess I'm just so used to being on my own. You decide. Do whatever makes you feel most comfortable.'

She took a few seconds to think then met his gaze. 'Thank you for being so honest. The truth is, as a stranger to a new town, and someone who is not used to travelling alone, I'd probably feel safer staying at your penthouse—as long as you don't mind someone who is most comfortable padding around in thick socks and huge pyjamas.' She gave him a smile. 'Glamour is my middle name.'

'You're sure?'

She nodded, as a feeling of relief spread through her. 'I'm sure.'

He sighed and sagged back against the leather seat. 'Thank goodness. My first guest at the penthouse and I thought I'd just made a big faux pas.'

'I'm your first guest?' Now she really was surprised.

He nodded. 'Sure. I've had other friends visit over the years, but they've stayed at hotels. Probably because I've been so wrapped up in the business.'

Half an hour later the car slid into an underground parking area and Leo took her to a private elevator.

Seconds later they emerged into a glistening penthouse. It was like something out of a film. The tinted glass windows stretched from floor to ceiling, laying the city out before them. The floor was a dark slate colour and the furnishings cream and glass. It was immaculate—like a place where people didn't actually stay.

And, while it was beautiful, it struck Anissa that there was nothing about this place that said 'Leo' to her.

The kitchen was open-plan, looking into the sitting area with large leather sofas and an extremely expensive-looking dining table and chairs.

She walked over and ran her fingers along the table. 'You get to sit here every morning and eat breakfast looking out over New York City? It's quite a view.'

'It is, isn't it?' He gave a slow nod. 'I should take more time to appreciate it.'

He strolled through to the kitchen and opened one of the glossy white cabinets. 'This is the most important thing.' He waved a package at her. 'Coffee pods. There's a whole variety in there so just pick your favourite.' He stood in front of a fancy machine that probably cost more than she earned in a month, flicking a few switches and pressing a few buttons as he slid one of the pods into place and slotted a latte glass underneath. 'This is all you need to do. Simple. Right?'

She blinked as the liquid frothed into the cup and hid her smile. 'It seems simple,' she agreed. 'But I feel as if I should come with an equipment warning.'

'What do you mean?'

She sighed and waved her hand in front of her stomach. 'It's like I've got an internal magnet. Dishwashers, coffee machines, computers, microwaves all seem to die in my presence.'

He laughed. 'Really?'

She nodded. 'And that's *before* I touch them.' She wagged her finger. 'So, don't say I didn't warn you.'

He glanced at his watch. 'Then let's leave coffee. How about wine? Even your internal magnet can't mess with a bottle opener.' He lifted two wine glasses down from the cupboard. 'What would you prefer, white or red?'

She paused for a second. 'Actually, my favourite is blush. Do you have any?'

He looked amused. 'Hmm, blush. Interesting choice. Yes, give me a minute.'

He pressed a button and a whole wall of the kitchen slid back to reveal a hidden wine rack. Anissa felt her eyes boggle. Really?

He selected a bottle from the rack and turned back, opening it with the corkscrew and pouring a little into one of the glasses. 'Care to check?'

Anissa laughed. 'Honestly? It looks like the right colour, so I'm sure it will be fine.' She rolled her eyes. 'How the other half live, eh?'

She watched as Leo filled both glasses and they walked over and sat down at the table. She looked out at the array of glistening lights.

'So, teach me about New York,' she said.

He gave a nod and pointed, 'That's the Empire State Building, over there is the Rockefeller Center, there's a giant Christmas tree down there and a skating rink we can visit.' He gave her a nod. 'There's also a really cool bakery on the other side of the street.'

'I like how your brain works.' She smiled as she took a sip of her wine.

'Over there, and down a bit, is Times Square. It's more fun at night. I'll take you there and you can climb the stairs and see where the ball drops at New Year.'

'Oh, yes. I'd forgotten about that.'

'There's another Christmas tree at Bryant Park, one at the Met and another at the Natural History Museum.' He looked at her carefully. 'And if you like shopping, there's always Fifth Avenue.'

She gulped. 'I'm not sure I'll be shopping on Fifth Avenue, *window*-shopping maybe. But not actual shopping.'

Leo opened his mouth as if he were about to say something else then quickly closed it again. Thank goodness. The last thing she wanted was for him to offer to meet her shopping bill. Not everyone had his income, and although Anissa had savings, she always worked hard to stay within her own budget.

And shopping on Fifth Avenue was way above her budget.

'What about Central Park?' she asked. 'I imagine it's going to be beautiful at this time of year, all covered in snow.'

He nodded. 'We can do Central Park but beware, it's a lot bigger than some people think. And it will be cold. Very cold.'

'As cold as Mont Coeur?'

Leo nodded. 'On a par. The trouble with New York is that every time we have snow, half the city grinds to a halt. Flights get grounded at the airport and some of the public transport stops working.'

Anissa looked out over the snow-dusted city. 'But surely the snow is no big surprise?'

He shrugged. 'You'd think. But every time there's a heavy snowfall there are problems.'

Anissa stood up and looked out the window. 'I like New York in wintertime. It's pretty.'

He moved next to her, his wine glass still in hand. 'So do I. I guess it's just been a long time since I stopped to notice.'

Nerves were starting to work on her. Either that or it was the combination of jet lag and wine. All of a sudden she was conscious of him standing next to her in his fine knit black jumper and black trousers. Conscious of the rise and fall of his chest. The heat emanating from him. They were side by side but she could see his reflection in the window. In Mont Coeur, Leo Baxter had been handsome. Here? In his own environment, there was something else. An assurance, a confidence that hadn't quite seemed so natural in Mont Coeur. Now he was back on his own turf it seemed to ooze from his pores, drawing her in like some kind of magnet. She almost laughed out loud. Maybe she did have a magnet inside her, and instead of being repelled by another, it was just heightening the attraction.

But her curiosity was sparked. What had hampered Leo's confidence in Mont Coeur? Was it the family business he'd referred to? He'd told her a little, but she was sure there was more to the story. She hadn't really noticed it to begin with, but now they were here, she could see the difference in his personality.

This apartment was beautiful—a showpiece even. But she was still struck by how little of him there was here. It didn't exactly feel like a home. When she closed her eyes and thought of home her mind went immediately to her mum and dad's house in Austria. Set on a hillside, with old trophies of hers scattered across the shelves, a sofa with two mismatched chairs and a whole array of family photographs, it really was a different place.

She gave herself a mental shake. Each to their own. Who was she judge a billionaire on his apparently impersonal home—particularly when he was letting her stay?

He turned towards her and raised his wine glass. 'How about a toast?'

She smiled and nodded. 'What did you have in mind?'

'To New York. To new beginnings.'

She tilted her head. New beginnings for her or new beginnings for him?

She held up her glass and clinked it against his.

'New beginnings,' she agreed as she turned and looked back out over the city. Her heart beat a little quicker.

New York. A world of new possibilities.

He strolled through to the kitchen and opened one of the glossy white cabinets.

When she got up the next morning, it was the first time in for ever her leg hadn't ached. She was so used to the feeling, it was strange, but she almost missed it. Her hand reached automatically for the painkillers she normally took first thing in the morning and then she stopped herself. She didn't need them.

Ever since her accident there hadn't been a single day that her leg hadn't ached unbearably.

Maybe it was the extremely comfortable bed? But she wasn't stupid. On average she spent six hours a day on the slopes. Yesterday had been the first time she hadn't.

She showered and pulled on some clothes, fully expecting Leo to have left some kind of note about working today. But, instead, he was sitting at the dining table, finishing a phone call.

He looked up as she walked through. 'I thought you promised me pyjamas and thick socks?'

She shook her head as she looked down at her jeans and simple blue jumper. 'I'm saving them for later. After a hard day's sightseeing—what could be more perfect than collapsing into my pyjamas?' She couldn't take her eyes away from the view again. Daytime New York and night-time New York were equally beautiful.

'It's like a window to the world up here,' she said breathlessly. She pressed her nose against the glass and looked down. People looked like ants darting purposely beneath her in a myriad of colours.

She spun back around and leaned against the glass. 'I thought you had urgent business to attend to. Isn't that why we came back?'

His face was serious for a second. 'Yeah, I've just spoken to Joe. He's quite the traditionalist. He wants to meet for dinner.'

'What does that mean?'

'That means that we have the day free to sightsee.'

Anissa's stomach fluttered. She liked how that sounded. She liked it a lot. 'So, where to, then?'

He held out his arms. 'Your wish is my command.'

The first place he took her was an all-American diner near Central Park that was his favourite breakfast hangout. It didn't look much on the outside, but one large stack of pancakes later Anissa was convinced.

He'd been too embarrassed to tell her he had virtually no food in the house—his lone bachelor status meant he rarely prepared meals—and that included breakfast. So he'd dashed off a quick email to his housekeeping services to stock his fridge before they'd left the apartment.

She was wearing that long blue coat again, the one that brought out the colour of her eyes, and he found himself fixating on them.

Next, it made sense to go to Central Park. They tramped through the snow together across the Bow Bridge and down towards the Angels of the Water fountain. Then they wove their way through the park towards Belvedere Castle.

'I never knew there was a castle in Central Park,' said Anissa as they turned towards it.

'It was renovated in the eighties. I think up until then it had been almost neglected. Now it's one of the visitor centres.'

A huge smile broke out on Anissa's face. 'It's perfect, isn't it? Small, but there's something so personal about it.'

'It's been used in some movies.'

'Really?' She spun around and held out her arms. 'Just think, I wonder if a real-live princess ever stayed here.'

Leo was looking at her with an amused expression on his face. 'I'm not sure that anyone—royal or otherwise—has ever stayed here.'

'But isn't it nice to imagine?' she said quickly.

New York was sparking something inside her. Or maybe it was Leo. Or maybe it was just being away from the thing that had surrounded her for most of her life—skiing.

'Look at the gorgeous view across the park.' She turned around and held up her hands. 'Not that the view from your penthouse isn't magnificent. But this, this is just different.'

His shoulder touched hers as he stood next to her on the ramparts. 'Don't you get tired of seeing snow all the time? Have you never longed for a sunny beach and the lapping ocean?'

It wasn't the strangest question in the world but it kind of took her unawares. 'I've never had a beach holiday,' she murmured, wondering what it would be like to run about in a bikini all day.

Her hand went automatically to her stomach. 'Imagine having to think about holding your belly in all day. Or whether you had enough sunscreen on the places you couldn't reach.'

He gave a small laugh. 'I can assure you, you don't need to worry about your stomach. As for the places you can't reach? That's what other people are for.' His face grew serious. 'Anissa, how old are you?'

She wrinkled her nose a little. 'Twenty-eight. But I'm sure you're not supposed to ask me that.'

'You really haven't had a proper holiday before, have you?'

Her brain flooded with a whole host of memories. Alain, her ex-fiancé and coach, had always been about the skiing. Always about the lucrative sponsorship deals he could score for her—or, now that she thought about it, for them. Any time they had gone away she'd always been training for the sport and had never had a chance to see the sights. His idea of love had been to push her to be the best skier that she could be.

At the time that had seemed right. But now, standing in Central Park, she wasn't so sure.

She sucked in a deep breath, letting the air come back out slowly, forming steam in the air in front of her.

'Anissa? What's wrong?'

Leo's arm slipped around her body, his arms overlapping hers. 'You're shaking. What is it?'

She couldn't stop the tremble in her voice. 'I'm just remembering things. I'm just realising the number of places I've visited but never actually seen.' She turned around in his arms so that she was facing him. It felt safer this way. Safer than staring out into the expanse of the park.

'I'm just wondering how much I've missed out on.'

She couldn't look into those blue eyes. She didn't want pity. Now she was feeling foolish. Foolish that it had taken her until this moment to see what had been happening in her life. She gave her leg an unconscious rub.

It wasn't sore. It wasn't aching. She'd thought about that this morning. The last time she'd talked about skiing to Leo she'd told him she couldn't bear the thought of not skiing every day. But now she was here—now she had

a chance to think about something *other* than skiing—
she was wondering how she'd let her life feel so closeted.

Tears formed in her eyes as she tried to swallow the
huge lump in her throat. Leo pulled her towards his chest.
'I'm supposed to be making you happy,' he whispered,
'not sad.'

She did something automatic. She hugged back. And
it felt good. It felt warm. Even though the temperature
around them was zero.

'It's not you, Leo. It's definitely not you.'

He pulled back with his hands on her arms. 'What,
then?'

She shook her head. 'I can't explain. But I feel like
I'm just waking up.' She gave a wry laugh. 'I'm twenty-
eight and I'm just waking up.'

She was embarrassed by how she was feeling. Embarrassed by the whole host of emotions sweeping around
her.

Leo tilted her chin up towards him. 'Well, in the spirit
of waking up, how about we do something else? What
do you say?'

She sucked in another breath to steady herself. 'I say
that sounds great.' She pulled her phone from her pocket.
'And I know exactly the place I want to go.'

Five minutes later they had coffee in their hands from
one of park vendors and, after a long walk and consulting the map on her phone, she led Leo to an exit halfway up the park.

He laughed when he saw what was ahead. 'You're
taking me here?'

She held out her arm. A little buzz of excitement
spread through her. 'Where else does any kid want to
go but the American Museum of Natural History? Dinosaurs. A giant blue whale. Meteorites. Hours and hours

of fun.' She gave another little sigh. 'Childlike distractions. Maybe we both could do with some.'

Leo gave a slow nod of his head. 'I've stayed in New York all these years and I've never managed to get here.' It was almost as if he was talking himself into it. 'One of the guys in the office raves about this place.' He reached out and took her hand. 'Okay. Let's do it.'

He'd felt a wave of panic earlier when he'd seen how upset she was. But something had told him not to pry—not to press too much. Just to step back and be her friend.

But thinking of Anissa in only friendly terms was a feat in itself. More than once he'd padded through to the kitchen last night and stared at the closed bedroom door, wondering about the woman lying on the other side.

He would never have knocked—no matter how much he'd wanted to.

But even sharing his space with someone else was new to him. No one had slept overnight in the apartment before but him, and it felt different knowing someone else was there. Leo had sometimes prided himself on his own space, his own privacy, and just having her there was an adjustment. It gave him a weird vibe—one that he wasn't quite sure about yet.

Then today, when she'd been standing in front of him in her blue coat, with the snow in Central Park framed behind her, the sight of her had made him catch his breath.

It was odd. Their meeting had been a fluke—entirely coincidental, with a whole set of circumstances they could never have predicted. Who knew he would have been in Mont Coeur at all? His parents dying had been a horrible event. The will reading in Switzerland? He would never have expected that. And for Anissa to be training and have an accident at the exact moment he'd come by…

Then there was the spark. The one that neither of them could deny. And on top of all of that was the fact she'd been sent to clean his chalet.

In another life they would never have met. But they'd met in this one. And it felt strangely right.

Part of this was probably how he was feeling right now. The flood of feelings from childhood and his insecurities had come back with a vengeance. He'd spent most of his adult life determined to shake them off, and for a while he'd thought he had.

Even having that face-to-face conversation with his mother and father would have helped. At least he thought it would have. And that constant sense of being cheated wouldn't leave him.

'Hey, Leo, I've got the tickets.' His head jerked up. Anissa was at the desk, waving the tickets at him.

His hand went automatically to his wallet. 'Oh, sorry, here, let me.'

She shook her head. 'Absolutely not. My treat.' She was smiling with the tickets held up against her cheek. There was a twinkle in her eye—one that had been missing in the park.

He crooked his elbow towards her. 'Okay, Ms Lang, let's have some fun.'

She'd never laughed so much. They'd spent hours in amongst the dinosaur skeletons, wondering at their size and immense power. For a few moments Leo had seemed a bit quiet. 'Always wanted to visit a place like this,' he'd murmured.

'You must have gone to museums with your mum and dad,' she'd said.

'Not often,' was the reply.

But the melancholy moment had left him as soon as

it had arrived. If he hadn't been to many museums in his childhood, it seemed he was using this one to make up for it.

Anissa took pictures of them comparing themselves to the huge footprint of the Titanosaurus. Then they wandered through the hall of mammals and the wonders of the ocean exhibit. She couldn't help but gasp at the site of the giant blue whale suspended between two floors.

He nudged her as they looked down onto the floor below. 'Do you know you can stay here? Spend the night?'

'What? No way!' She couldn't hide her excitement at even the thought of it.

'Yep. Guess what's it called?'

Was it a trick question? 'Don't know.'

'"Night at the Museum".'

She let out a burst of laughter. 'After the movie? Oh, I love it!'

He nodded. 'One of the other guys at my work has two kids. When they did it, they got to go around the dinosaur exhibits in the middle of the night with flashlights. He said it was one of the best nights of his life.'

She clasped her hands to her chest. 'Oh, I want to do it. I want to do it.'

He shook his head, smiling. 'Think you have to be between six and thirteen.' He leaned forward and whispered, his lips brushing against her ear, 'I think we might have left it a bit too late.'

She scowled and stood back, looking him up and down. 'Well, you've definitely left it too late. But me?' She held up her hair in pretend bunches and gave him a cheeky smile. 'I could maybe pass for thirteen if I tried really hard.'

He gave her a playful shove. 'No way. If I don't get to

hunt dinosaurs at night, neither do you. We could always steal some kids if we have to.'

She nodded her head until a mother walked past with a kid screaming in a stroller. 'Okay,' she whispered, 'just promise me it's not that one.'

She slid her hand into his. 'You know, I did do this kind of thing with my mum and dad—just not enough.'

'Why not?' He seemed curious.

She gave a little shrug. 'I was so passionate about ski-ing. At times it was the only thing I wanted to do, and in a way I was lucky because my mum and dad supported me, but now...' She stared back up at the giant whale. 'For the first time I wonder how much I missed out on. I wonder if at some point they should have said no to me.'

He turned to stare at her. 'How would you have felt if they had?'

His bright blue eyes were intense. It was almost as if he already knew the answer. She gave a laugh and shook her head. 'Oh, I'm sure I would have been quite the lit-tle diva. I didn't like it when I didn't get my own way.'

He arched one eyebrow. 'You? A diva? No way.'

She laughed and slid her arm into his.

Next, they spent time in the human and culture halls before heading to the planetarium.

'I love this,' breathed Anissa, as she lay back in one of the tilting chairs and looked at dark universe above scattered with stars. Music was playing around them as the show continued.

'It is pretty amazing,' agreed Leo as he lay in the chair next to her. She turned her head. He was staring straight up, his dark, slightly messy hair crinkling at the collar of his button-down shirt. Most men had their hair cropped quite short, but she liked the longer look. It suited Leo.

And every time she looked at that hair she had to fight the urge to run her fingers through it.

There was hardly anyone around them and for a few moments it felt as if they were only ones appreciating the marvels above them.

She reached over and threaded her fingers through his. If he was surprised he didn't show it. He didn't pull away. 'Thank you for bringing me here, Leo,' she whispered.

He turned his head in the darkness and smiled at her, just as the planets appeared behind him. 'I think you brought me,' he joked as she let out a gasp.

It was odd. She'd seen lots of wonderful things today, and snapped a hundred photos. But this was image that would stay in her mind. Leo, lying back in the chair, smiling at her with the planets behind him.

He glanced behind him and nodded at the scene. Settling back in his chair, his thumb traced little circles in the palm of her hand as the show continued. 'I wish I'd done this as a kid,' he murmured. She could see him glancing at the few other people—many families—in the theatre.

'You must have done some stuff like this as a kid?'

He shook his head. 'No. Never. No parks. No museums. No arcades.' He gave a sad kind of smile. 'Obviously, I did school trips—and we went to some fun places then.'

Her stomach rolled. It was almost like he was trying to make excuses for his parents. What kind of people had they been? It made her heart pang. 'Not all families get time,' she said, trying to be conciliatory.

He gave a sad sigh as he continued to trace little circles in her palm. 'Even if they'd had the time, they still wouldn't have brought me here.' He turned to face her.

'But it doesn't matter now. Because I'm here with the right person.'

Tingles shot up her arm and straight to her heart.

It was crazy. She knew it was crazy. They'd done everything back to front. Her actions that first night had been so out of character for her she hadn't even recognised herself. She'd thought she'd have been filled with a lifetime of regrets.

But…something, something had just clicked.

If someone had told her this time a few weeks ago she'd be in New York, staying in a billionaire's penthouse, she would never have believed it.

She wanted to ask him what he meant about the fact his parents still wouldn't have brought him here. And she still hadn't really worked out why he'd only just met his brother and sister. His whole family dynamics seemed complicated and it was obvious he played his cards close to his chest. But now didn't seem the time to ask. Not when he'd just told her he was glad he was with her.

She turned back to him and smiled again, hoping to distract him from any sad thoughts he might be having.

'I wonder if there's anything out there?' she said.

'Who knows?' asked Leo. 'And what do you think they'd make of us?'

Her head fell back, 'Well, that's the million-dollar question, isn't it? We have all this beauty and we've ruined some of it.'

He nodded in agreement, his finger still moving soothingly in her palm. 'You're right. But for now let's just lie back, appreciate the stars and try to imagine a place where everything is perfect.'

There was something about his words. It was like a warm blanket being snuggled all around her. There were a hundred things she could stress about right now. Training. Her job. Her finances. And whether she would ever have a chance of competing professionally again. Sometimes it made her brain ache.

Today had been her first day of a proper holiday. And she'd loved every minute. Or almost every minute. Right up until she'd realised what her life before had been like.

It was almost as if a fog was being lifted from her eyes and she was finally getting clear vision. And the person clearly in her vision right now was Leo.

She smiled again and settled back in her chair. Above her the planets were aligning with stars, sending beautiful streaks across the sky.

It was almost like a message. A message that she was going to take some time to consider. And she knew just who to do that with.

CHAPTER SIX

LEO HAD ALWAYS been familiar with the tourist spots in New York but he'd never really visited them.

The time at the Natural History Museum had tugged at something inside. In one way, he'd felt a wave of anxiety when he'd seen the tears in Anissa's eyes at Belvedere Castle. It had pulled at all his primal instincts to protect her, and try and take away the hurt she was experiencing. The museum had been the nearest place to go that might distract her.

But it had done a whole lot more than that. She'd come alive in there. He'd almost felt her confidence build as they'd moved around the museum. He'd loved watching the excitement in her eyes at some of the exhibits. She could find joy in the smallest things, and had a million ideas, opinions and questions—all things he'd never really thought about before.

Being around Anissa was fun. The truth was at Mont Coeur there had been an air of sadness around her—even if she hadn't known it. He knew it was likely due to her uncertainty and her change of circumstances, but the more hours she spent in New York, the more he could see her gradually shaking off those worries and feelings. And he liked that. He liked that a lot.

Because she was having an effect on him. Today he'd

sent a text to Noemi. It was ridiculous. It had taken him nearly an hour to decide what to send.

Hi there, had to return to New York for urgent business but will be in touch soon. Won't do anything to jeopardise Cattaneo Jewels.

He'd wanted to be reassuring. Noemi had replied straight away, saying that she hoped everything was okay.

He'd felt a little bad that he hadn't spoken to them before he'd left. But he wasn't used to this family stuff. He wasn't used to keeping in touch with people.

Watching Anissa send frequent texts to her mum and dad had made him feel guilty.

He really needed a chance to try and get his head around all this.

But now wasn't the time. Because right now he was steering Anissa along Fifth Avenue.

She stopped outside one store then another. He watched closely. He could see when something caught her eye. 'Want to go in?'

She shook her head. 'Not a chance. I'm a window shopper. That's it.'

He tried to be tactful. 'Well, one of things I wanted to take you to was the Christmas ball. It's fancy. You'll need something formal. And obviously it's my treat. So if you see something you like and want to try, go ahead.'

She hesitated for a second, apparently struggling to find the words. 'Leo... I'm really honoured you want to take me somewhere like that...and I'd never want to embarrass you, but I'm not quite sure how comfortable I feel about you buying me something that...' She held out her hand and gestured to the store behind her. 'That will probably cost more than I earn in a few months.'

He'd somehow known Anissa might feel like this. 'But it's my treat. I want you to buy something. Something you like and feel comfortable in.'

She pressed her lips together. 'Let me think about it. I'm just not sure.'

He nodded his head. He had to respect her wishes. 'Of course. But don't leave it too late. We only have another three days until the ball.'

She glanced along the street. 'Enough of Fifth Avenue. Let's have some fun.'

'What kind of fun?'

She pulled something from her pocket. 'I have a list. I made it last night.'

He sidled up to her and tried to look over her shoulder. 'You made a list?'

She whipped it away so he couldn't see it as she laughed. 'Yep, I wrote down all the things I could possibly do in New York.'

She pulled out her phone and stared at it as it buzzed. The weirdest expression flashed over her face.

'Who is it?'

She gave a little shake of her head. 'It's someone I used to deal with.'

'Your coach—your ex?' He couldn't help it. It was first person that sprang to mind. It didn't matter he'd never set eyes on the guy, there was a definite flicker of jealousy.

She shook her head harder as she still stared at the buzzing phone. 'No, no. It's someone who worked on the championship skiing committee.' She genuinely looked puzzled. 'I have no idea why they want to speak to me.' She pressed her lips together and hit the reject button, sending the caller to her voicemail.

'You don't want to speak to them?'

'No. Not now. Not here.' She still had the list in her

other hand. She waited for a second then put a smile back on her face. 'This is about us. This is about New York.'

He wanted to ask more questions. But it was clear she was trying her best to put Mount Coeur behind her. 'Okay, then, what's next on the list?'

She concentrated hard for a few seconds, laughing as he kept trying to duck behind her to see the list.

'Okay,' she said, tucking the list back into her pocket. 'I'd really like it if we could see the view, either from the Empire State Building or the Rockefeller Center—whichever you think is best.'

'I think this is my time to cringe,' he admitted.

'Why?'

He pulled a face. 'I've never managed to get up either, but...'

'How long have you actually lived here?'

He gave a rueful shake of his head. 'No. I think I'm going to take the first amendment here. I don't want to implicate myself at all.'

She held out her hands. 'Well, just think. We get to do a first thing together.'

He couldn't help but be surprised. And a little impressed. 'Yeah, that's a cool way to look at it. In fact—' Another thought sprang into his head. 'There's actually something else that would be a first—that we can do together.' He gave a slow nod. 'Actually, it makes it easier for me to decide which place we go to for the view.'

He held out his hand towards her. 'Want to see a little more of New York?'

She shot him a huge smile. 'Absolutely.'

The tree was stunning. She'd never quite seen anything like it before. It was around seventy feet tall and stood right in front of the Rockefeller Center, overlooking the most perfect ice rink.

He leaned over the barrier alongside her. 'If we stay here for another week we could see the Christmas tree-lighting. They do it live on television now. It's a big deal.'

She sighed. 'Oh, that would be great. But we'll be back in Mont Coeur by then, won't we?'

There was an almost wistful tone to her voice. Didn't she want to go back to the place she was currently calling home?

Mont Coeur. It was odd. But the name made it feel as though a dark cloak had settled around his shoulders. So much uncertainty. So much still to sort out. He wasn't quite sure if was ready for all this.

'Probably,' he said finally.

She was watching the people skating underneath them. Some were clinging onto the barrier at the side, others were stumbling around the rink and a few were spinning around and skating backwards with ease.

'Want to go skating too?' he asked.

She pointed at one girl who was twirling around in the middle of the rink. 'Just so you know, that's not going to be me, not even close.'

He pointed to a guy who was trying to gain his feet at the side of the rink—and failing miserably. 'Is that going to be you?'

She laughed. 'Let's just wait and see.'

She looked upwards. It was afternoon and the sky was beginning to darken above them. 'Are we going to up?'

He nodded. 'Let's go. This is the perfect time. You'll get to see the city at the end of the daylight, then you'll get to see it in the dark too.'

They made their way inside and he bought the tickets and they boarded the elevator. By the time they exited above the viewing platform sixty-eight floors above, the sun was just starting to descend in the sky.

Anissa couldn't believe the view. There was a glass wall straight in front of them. 'You can walk right around?'

Leo nodded. 'There's a three-hundred-and-sixty-degree view up here.'

She walked over to a set of binoculars and fumbled in her pocket for some change. Leo was quicker and slid some coins in while she still trying to make sense of the American currency.

'The Empire State Building is amazing,' she breathed as she peered through the binoculars. 'The rest of midtown is just amazing.'

'Is that your favourite word today?'

She looked up from the binoculars. 'It could be, but let's wait until we've done the skating.'

They moved around all sides of the viewing platform, spending time looking over Central Park and then east towards Brooklyn.

She gave an appreciative nod. 'The view from your apartment is good, but this, this is just...'

'Amazing?' he finished with a laugh.

'Yeah,' she agreed. It was over an hour before Anissa finally decided she was done. By then, she'd worked her way back around to the south view in time to see the Empire State Building light up.

'It changes colour all the time,' said Leo. 'Traditional is white, but if there's a big sporting event, a special day or support for a charity, or a past historical event then the colours change.' He gave a smile. 'Then, of course, there's Christmas. It usually lights up in red and green just a few days before.'

She gave a rueful kind of smile as she stared over at

the Empire State Building currently illuminated in white, her head rested on his shoulder. 'We'll miss that. We'll be back in Mont Coeur.'

His hand slid around her waist and it seemed only natural to turn around to face him. 'Thank you for bringing me to New York, Leo,' she whispered, her warm breath steaming in the cold air around them. With his Italian good looks and sincere eyes he almost took her breath away. For a few moments, even though there were people around them, it felt like it was just the two of them—no one else.

For a second she wondered what he might do, then his head lowered towards hers, his eyelashes brushing against the skin on her cheeks as his lips met hers.

She slid her arms up around his neck. She couldn't think about anything else. Just his lips on hers. She could feel all the tension she hadn't even realised was there melt from her body as Leo deepened their kiss and pulled her even closer. His hand slid down to her backside and the spark she'd felt that first night flooded through her again, coupled with the connection she'd felt today when they'd lain in the planetarium, watching the night sky above them, with their fingers entwined. Leo Baxter was getting well and truly under her skin.

They broke apart naturally, both trying to catch their breath. She let out a little laugh and stepped back as she saw a few other people staring at them.

He stepped back too, with a nod of his head.

He gave her a nudge. 'How about a visit to a bakery in the next street, then we can try the skating?'

Her stomach gave an automatic rumble and they both laughed. 'Well, okay, then,' she said.

The elevator ride down was swift and the white-trimmed popular bakery was right around the corner with a queue out the door. One of the servers gave Leo a wave.

'You know them in here?' Anissa asked, her eyebrows raised.

'Perhaps.' He shrugged. 'Have a look in the counter. They have cupcakes, scones, desserts, pies, cheesecakes, speciality cakes.' He pointed to one end of the counter. 'They even do a speciality cupcake every day.' He squinted around the guy in front of him. 'Today's is banana, pineapple and pecan with cream-cheese icing.'

She groaned. The smell in the bakery was wonderful and was making her hungrier by the second. The queue shuffled slowly forward. 'Okay,' she asked. 'What would you recommend? Somehow I think you might have tried a few of these.'

'Guilty.' He gave a grin. 'Honestly? It would have to be the banana pudding.'

She was kind of intrigued. 'What's in that?'

'Vanilla wafers, fresh bananas and creamy vanilla pudding all topped with chocolate shavings. Once tried, never forgotten. I promise you.'

Her stomach rumbled again. 'Okay. I'll go with that.'

Two minutes later they had piping-hot coffee and small tubs with spoons. It was growing even darker outside with the cold air starting to bite. 'Oh, this is perfect,' Anissa said after the first mouthful.

Leo was watching her anxiously. 'Glad you didn't fold and get a cupcake or a brownie?'

She took another spoonful and shook her head. 'Not a chance.' She glanced over her shoulder. 'But when does it close? We should have bought some cupcakes for the penthouse.'

'Don't worry. They deliver,' he said as they walked back towards the skating rink.

The lights were on around the rink now and it was busier than before. They stood for a minute, finishing their coffee and pudding, before Leo headed over to the skate hire. A few minutes later he came back with two sets of blue skates. Anissa quickly laced hers and stood up, wobbling, while Leo handed over their boots. 'Who is the gold statue?' she asked.

The giant statue overlooked the rink in front of the Rockefeller Center. 'It's Prometheus, and it's made of bronze. I think it's supposed to depict him bringing fire to mankind.' It glistened against the dark night sky, surrounded by the colourful flags of many nations and twinkling lights in the trees around the sunken plaza. 'This whole place is just magical,' breathed Anissa as she tucked her hands back into her gloves.

Leo was waiting for her at the entrance to the rink. He held his hand out towards her. 'Ready?'

She took a few precarious steps towards him. 'Oh, I'm ready. Let's go for it.'

His bravado lasted around five seconds. Long enough to realise he should have held onto the edge.

Anissa stared open-mouthed as he landed flat on his back. Then she couldn't help pull him back up for laughing. People moved past them, a few shuffling, others moving gracefully.

'Hey!' shouted Anissa as he grabbed onto her legs to finally balance himself. A few seconds later he was facing her, breathing hard. 'Right. Let's try this again.'

She burst out laughing once more. 'Whose idea was this?' she asked as she spun away and did a wobbly kind of twirl.

'Hey, cheater. You said you didn't know how to skate!'

She shook her head as she glided back towards him.

'No. I didn't.' She gave a wicked grin. 'I might have hinted that I wasn't very good.' She gave his chest a prod. 'Just like someone else did on the slopes. Are you trying to play me again?'

He put his hands down to her waist, anchoring her next to him. 'Oh, I promise you. I'm definitely not trying to play you. This seemed like a good idea at the time—but I might live to regret it.'

'What's a few bumps and bruises between friends?' Her eyes were twinkling underneath her blue hat and her cheeks had a glow about them, lighting up her normally pale skin.

A warm feeling spread through him. She was blossoming. She was blossoming in New York, being here with him. What must it have been like, spending most of her life concentrating on training? Had she ever really had time for herself or for friends?

Maybe she'd just needed the break—the freedom to get away and try and find out who she was, what she really wanted to do. Back in Mont Coeur she'd seemed so determined, so focused.

He took a deep breath. 'Have you thought about what you might do if it the skiing thing doesn't work out?'

He could see her whole body tense. Her jaw clenched. 'Why would my…' she lifted her fingers '…"skiing thing" not work out?'

Wow. She was instantly mad. Interesting. He thought carefully. He could skirt around the edges but he got the distinct impression that might be what everyone else did. 'You've had a horrible injury.' He gestured down towards her leg. 'And you've been lucky.' He could see her jaw tense even more and sensed she wanted to butt in, but he was determined to keep talking. 'You've had surgery. Rehab. And you've got your mobility back. You're up, about and walking, with very few problems.' He licked his lips. 'There might be a chance you won't quite reach where you were before. What will you do then?'

For a few seconds it looked as if he'd swept the feet out from under her. She blinked a few times and her eyes looked glassy. He was determined not to fill the silence. After a few minutes she licked her lips and spoke carefully. 'Maybe I am lucky—I guess it's just not really a word that I thought applied to me. You're right. There are other sportspeople who've had horrible career-ending injuries and never got...' this time when she put her fingers in the air she didn't seem mad '"back to normal" like I have.' She sucked in a long breath. 'But my normal was a woman who had the chance of winning championship gold. I'd feel like a quitter if I didn't try to get back to where I was before.'

His hand moved and rubbed her back in reassurance. 'I know, I think it's great. But you've got to have a back-up plan. Even when I throw everything into a business deal, I always have a back-up plan. It's sensible.'

He was trying his best to ask the question without being quite so blunt.

She attempted a smile. 'A back-up plan. I guess it is the sensible option. The grown-up option. I guess I need to look at other things too.' She rolled her eyes and pointed at the ice rink. 'So, Leo, what's your back-up plan for this?'

Now he rolled his eyes too. 'I might need to fake an injury.'

She shook her head and laughed. 'Oh, no. Come on,' she said, obviously taking pity on him and sliding her hand into his. 'You just keep your feet still and I'll pull you round.'

He could tell she wanted to change the subject and

move onto something else and that was fine. He'd asked the question and it was clear it was something she'd need to consider. Right now, he had more immediate problems. He couldn't help but look down at the glistening ice, trying to focus on keeping his balance as she tugged him along. The first time he looked up, he started to wobble and Anissa skated around behind him and put her hands at his waist. 'Here, this might be easier. I'll help you keep your balance, and you try and move your feet.'

He tried a few steps, still wobbling furiously. But her hands were steady, and after a few minutes he started to get a little more confident.

Leo almost laughed out loud as a kid stumbled past with his mother holding onto his waist the same way Anissa was. It made him straighten up a little. He could see other people around him struggling too. He bent his knees a bit more and tried to push himself along a little better, trying to glide. His arms were held out on either side as he fought to keep his balance. Anissa leaned around from behind him, her blonde hair coming loose from her hat. 'That's better. You're getting it. Keep going.'

And he was. Little by little he made his way through the rest of the jostling skaters. After a few circuits of the busy ice rink, Anissa released her grip on his waist and appeared back at his side, slipping her hand into his. They looked like any other couple at the rink, laughing and joking on their way around.

He'd never done this before. Never. In fact, there were a number of firsts he'd had in the last few days—all with Anissa. The truth was he'd come back to sort out work issues and he should have been concentrating on convincing Joe to go through with the deal. But Joe was being stubborn, just as Leo had known he would be. He'd agreed to dinner, but not until tomorrow night. Under any other set of circumstances Leo would have been anxious. He'd have been planning ways to either charm Joe or convince him with facts and figures. Whichever strategy worked best. But he hadn't done any of that. He'd been too busy entertaining Anissa.

By the time she tugged him towards the exit of the rink, both of them were breathing a little faster. 'That was fun,' she said.

He let out a wry laugh. 'Yeah, fun.' Then he stopped for a second. 'Actually, it was…better than I thought it would be.'

She leaned on the barrier. There was a distinct gleam in her eye. 'You thought you'd be better, didn't you? You thought you'd just go on out there and ace it.'

She was spot on. He ducked down to unfasten his skates so she wouldn't notice the flush of colour in his face.

But Anissa was just as quick. She knelt down next to him. 'Yes, Leo Baxter. Mr Wonderful at Everything.'

She was joking—of course she was—but the words made his stomach twist.

For a split second their gazes connected and the words just spilled from his lips. 'If only that were true.' He couldn't hide his bitterness.

Her eyes widened and her hand reached over and gripped his jacket. 'Leo?'

He pulled away, embarrassed that he'd let her see his old resentment bubbling over. She fumbled to pull off her skates and quickly changed into her boots. He could see her hesitation as she reached towards him again. It was busy at the changing station. Lots of people were queuing to hire skates. But when her warm hand came into contact with his face he couldn't deny the buzz.

It didn't matter that it was busy. It didn't matter that the level of noise around them was distracting. All he was conscious of was her touch on his face.

She stepped right up to him, her body in full contact with his. It was almost as if a bubble formed around them. A quiet descended, letting the world outside dissipate. Now he couldn't hear the people chattering, now he wasn't conscious of the flashes of colour as people pushed past. All he could see was the pale blue eyes looking up at him.

Her hand was still on his cheek. 'Tell me, Leo. Tell me what's wrong.'

His first reaction would always be to brush things off. To walk away. To change the conversation to something else entirely.

But, somehow, with Anissa, he didn't feel as if he could do that.

His chest grew tight. The weight of his mother and father's deaths. The strained relationship with his new siblings. The pressure of the will.

How could he explain any of that in a few words? He didn't even know where to start. Leo had never had a confidante. Never really disclosed any of his past to friends or colleagues.

He was the original child who kept things close to his chest, and he'd carried that trait into adulthood. No one could protect him or look after him as well as he could look after himself. He'd just believed that for so long.

It had affected everything. Every relationship he'd formed. Whether that had been work or personal. He'd never dated for more than six months. After that, women had expectations about what they thought should happen next. That didn't work for Leo. He hadn't wanted to play the doting husband or father.

He'd never seen that relationship. He'd never had that example.

And now? He never would.

The pain struck him like a crushing blow to the chest. He bent over, trying to suck some air into his chest.

'Leo? Leo? What's wrong? Are you sick?'

Anissa's arm was around him instantly, her head down next to his.

In his mind right now all he could see was the funeral. Of course, he had gone. It hadn't mattered that he'd never met his brother or sister.

Because Salvo and Nicole had been so well known for their business the chapel had been packed. No one had noticed one more Italian-looking man slipping in wearing a black suit. When the family had entered Noemi had been openly weeping, Sebastian's face like a mask.

The two caskets had been side by side at the front of the chapel, a simple white wreath on top of each one.

The congregation had sung a song that his mother had apparently loved—something Leo had never learned. The priest had spoken at length about their lives and love for each other. And their family. Sebastian and Noemi. It had been like a knife twisting in his gut. Leo, the unknown and forgotten child.

He wasn't quite sure what he'd expected to get from the funeral. Essentially he'd been saying goodbye to the parents he'd never got to meet. There had only been a few telephone calls. And for the shortest time he'd felt hope... hope that the one thing he'd always longed for might finally be within his reach—only to have it snatched away from his grasp so cruelly.

It played on his mind, along with the permanent feeling of never being good enough—the one his adoptive parents had continually perpetuated. Even now, Sebastian had resurrected those feelings by his reaction to the will's decree. His face and demeanour at the idea of Leo being involved in the family business had said it all.

It still made him angry. Sebastian had no idea how hard Leo had worked, or just how successful he was. Penthouses in New York and private jets didn't come cheap. Or maybe he did know—and just didn't care.

It turned around in Leo's head. How would he feel if someone came right now and told him he had to share the controlling interests in his business with other people? He'd be angry. He'd be furious. Just like Sebastian clearly was.

Leo's brain was in overdrive. He'd been trying so hard not to overthink everything. He'd been trying so hard just to let himself be distracted for a few days.

Anissa.

It was as if that quiet bubble around him vanished. Anissa's orange scent drifted around him, and the noise from the ice rink and bright lights seemed exaggerated.

Wonderful—that's what she'd said. Leo Baxter wasn't wonderful. Even though he'd tried to be at various points in his life. He wasn't wonderful at being a son, a brother, or at any kind of relationship. Wonderful was the last thing he felt. Especially while all this was going on.

Her hand was at his side. He could see the worried expression on her face and the concern in her eyes. But all of a sudden he didn't want to know.

He needed some space.

He stepped out of her reach. 'I need to go. Is there somewhere else you wanted to see? You mentioned you had a friend to catch up with.'

'Leo?' She blinked then added quickly, 'Of course. Jules. I can give her a call and see if she's available.'

He knew he sounded detached. 'Good. I have business to deal with.' He grabbed his wallet from his jacket pocket and pulled out a couple of cards. 'Here. Use this for the cab—or for coffee, or drinks—whatever you need.' It was almost as if something flicked on in his head. 'Or if you have time go shopping with Jules, get a dress for the ball.'

He turned and walked away before she had a chance to say anything.

Before she had a chance stop him.

And he walked. Pushed his way through the Christmas crowds and as far away from the merriment that he possibly could.

Anissa was stung. What had just happened? What had she said? She stared down at the cards in her hand. One was a credit card, the other the entrance key to the penthouse.

Someone jostled her from behind and she almost dropped them. 'Get a dress,' he'd said. Did he really think she would just go and spend his money?

She wanted to run after him. She wanted to find out what on earth was wrong—what on earth she'd said.

But something told her not to. Something told her he needed time on his own. She still hadn't really got to the bottom of what was happening in Leo Baxter's life.

She moved away from the ice rink. The joy and excitement she'd experienced earlier deflated—just as if someone had pricked her with a pin.

Her feet carried her back to the bakery. She stared at the card in her hand. There was a tiny flare of anger. He had no idea what kind of person she was. She glanced at the designer store across the road. She'd never been a fan, but she could go in there and come out with a bag, shoes, jeans and coat that would easily total around ten thousand dollars.

For a few seconds she actually contemplated it, staring down at her worn black boots. There was a mannequin in the window dressed in cream coat, black shiny boots and a gold bag. But what use would a cream coat be anyway? She'd get it dirty within the first five minutes.

She sighed and joined the queue in the bakery again, ordering twenty-four cupcakes to be delivered to the penthouse. Her hand wavered as she gave the server Leo's card, wondering if she should just pay for them herself.

But the server moved at lightning speed, handing the card back and packaging up the variety of cupcakes in a cardboard box.

Anissa started walking slowly back down the streets. Maybe she should take a chance and call Jules, even though she didn't really know her. Her hand fumbled in her pocket, rustling a scrap of paper as she tucked the cards inside. She stopped and pulled it out.

The contact details Chloe had given her for her cousin. She swallowed and looked around. She didn't want to go back to the penthouse yet—not if Leo was there. And she didn't really want to wander around alone. Maybe Chloe's cousin could tell her somewhere fun to go for a few hours—somewhere safe, and hopefully warm. She pulled out her phone and started dialling.

One hour and one subway ride later, Anissa was on her second bottle of beer with Chloe's cousin, Jules.

Jules had been happy to hear from Anissa and invited her to join her and her friends in a local bar. Jules was dressed in a variety of black clothing with her thick dark hair swept over to one side. Her fingers picked at the foil around the neck of the bottle of beer. 'So you're telling me that some billionaire gave you his credit card, told you to spend, and you didn't do it?'

Jules was looking at Anissa as if she were entirely crazy.

'I bought cupcakes.' She shrugged.

Jules shook her head. 'Cupcakes.' She reached across the table and grabbed Anissa's hand. 'Girl, you're in New York. You could have bought just about anything! A pair of Louboutins. A Louis Vuitton bag. And you bought cupcakes?'

Anissa sighed and leaned her head on one hand.

'Your guy sounds like a bit of a tool,' remarked Jules.

'He's not my guy.'

'Then what is he?'

Anissa shifted uncomfortably on her bar stool. She wasn't quite sure what to call Leo. 'He's just…just…a friend.'

Jules eyebrows shot up. 'A friend? But not your guy.' She counted off on one hand. 'So, he flies you to New York in his private jet, installs you in his penthouse with no strings. Takes you sightseeing and ice skating. Invites you to some party. Kisses you at the top of the Rockefeller Center, then abandons you at the ice rink and stomps off in a huff somewhere.'

Anissa rolled her eyes. 'When you put it like that…' She sighed. 'And it's not a party. It's a ball. He told me to buy a dress.'

Jules sat a little straighter on her stool. 'Ball? What ball?'

Anissa waved her hand. 'I don't know. Some Christmas charity ball. It's in that famous hotel on Fifth Avenue, next to Central Park.'

Jules's chin almost bounced off the bar. 'Wh-what?'

Anissa felt a wave of discomfort. 'What?' she repeated.

Jules's eyes were sparkling. 'You're going to *the* Christmas charity ball. The one that the whole of New York talks about. It's on Saturday.' She looked back at Anissa and squeaked. 'It's on Saturday—and you don't have a dress!' A strange kind of smile came over her face and she put her hands on her hips. 'Well, aren't you just the original Cinderella.'

Anissa stood up from her bar stool. 'Okay, stop. You're making me nervous. Is this a big deal? I didn't know it was a big deal. Leo didn't make it sound like that. He just told me I needed a formal dress.'

Jules slapped her hand on her forehead. 'Mercy! The girl has a ticket to the hottest gig in town and doesn't even know it.' Her eyes ran up and down Anissa's length. 'Hmm...' It was almost as if something flashed through her brain. She clapped her hands together. 'You don't have a dress!'

Anissa frowned. 'You've said that—several times.'

Jules grabbed her jacket and bag, 'Come with me. Come with me now. I have the perfect thing. Perfect.'

Anissa couldn't think straight. Jules waved goodbye to her friends, jerked her hand and Anissa had to stop to grab her own jacket before she was dragged out onto the cold street.

Jules kept muttering all the way along the street. 'This will be great. This will be perfect. It will suit you. Your name's written all over it.'

She pushed Anissa towards a building and led her up a flight of stairs to an apartment. As soon as Jules pushed open the front door Anissa sucked in a breath. It was like walking into another world.

There were mannequins everywhere, each wearing

a unique dress design, each one a little more spectacular than the one next to it. And although Jules seemed to dress exclusively in black, there wasn't a single black item to be seen. Green. Blue. Red. Silver. Purple.

Anissa's foot hovered on the threshold. It was like the story from her childhood where the kids stepped through the back of a wardrobe into another world.

Jules seemed not to have noticed her hesitation. She marched straight over to a pale blue gown, glittering with jewels.

She turned to look at Anissa, her face filled with pent-up anxiety. 'What do you think?'

Anissa stepped inside, closed the door behind her and followed to where Jules was standing.

Jules paced around the mannequin.

'I made this for my fashion show. As soon as you said you needed a dress, it just flashed into my head. I can see you in it. I can see you in this dress. It's perfect. It suits your complexion and your eyes.' Jules pressed her hands together in front of her. 'What do you think? Would you consider it? Would you consider wearing one of my designs?'

Anissa couldn't talk. She couldn't think straight. She walked around the dress. It was pale blue with a sequined and beaded bodice with a slash neck, and a skirt made of layers and layers of pale blue tulle hanging completely straight. It was quite simply the most beautiful dress Anissa had ever seen.

She put her hand up to her chest. 'You want me to wear one of your designs?'

Jules immediately started babbling. 'Well, only if you want to. Only if you think it's good enough. But it would mean so much to me—having a dress I've designed worn by someone attending *the* Christmas ball of New York. It's my dream come true.'

Anissa couldn't believe her ears. The dress was stunning.

'You w-want me to wear…this?'

'Don't you like it?' Jules's voice was instantly defensive.

'I love it,' breathed Anissa. 'Will it fit?' she hardly dared to ask.

Jules nodded enthusiastically. 'Let's try it. As soon as I looked at you I thought it might work. We can make adjustments, if needed.'

Jules released the zipper at the back of the dress and slid it off the mannequin. She pushed Anissa towards her bedroom. 'Go in there. Try it on.'

Anissa stepped through to the bedroom. After a few hesitant moments she slipped off her clothes and tried the dress on. The satin lining slid over her skin easily. It felt almost like a second skin.

She couldn't fasten the zip so stepped back outside so Jules could do it for her.

Jules stood her in front of a full-length mirror and fastened the zip.

Anissa let out a little gasp. The dress was magnificent. The beaded and sequined bodice enhanced her neat curves, the slash neckline demure and flattering. The straight layers of tulle fluttered as she moved, swishing then falling back into place.

Jules put her hand up to her mouth. 'You look like an ice princess. It's just stunning.' She moved behind Anissa and nipped the dress in a little at the waist and grabbed a few pins. 'This needs only minor alterations.'

She finished pinning then stared into the mirror at Anissa's reflection, giving her a scrutinising glance.

Next she shook out Anissa's blonde hair and pulled up the sides, leaving some tendrils around her ear. 'Have you thought about how you might get styled?'

Anissa was still staring at her reflection in an almost mesmerised way. 'Why would I need it styled?' she asked.

Jules pulled her hair a little tighter. 'What?'

Anissa let out a yelp as Jules bent around her. 'Tell me you are joking?'

Anissa tried to shake her head, but it was difficult when Jules had such a grip of her hair.

Jules let out a laugh. 'You really are a newcomer to all this, aren't you?' She sucked in a breath. 'Okay, do you trust me?'

Anissa looked at Jules and back to her reflection in the mirror. This dress was the most perfect thing she'd ever seen—and definitely the most gorgeous thing she'd ever worn. 'After you showing me this dress? Of course I trust you.' She turned from side to side as something flooded into her mind. 'He called me Ice Princess when we first met. And that's exactly how I feel in this dress. Like an ice princess.'

Jules was still eyeing her critically. 'Okay, it's just a few minor adjustments. I can do them in the next few days. Get yourself a pair of shoes.' She scribbled on a piece of paper. 'Heels no higher than this? Got it.'

Anissa nodded. This was all happening so fast.

Jules smiled. 'I have a friend who can do your hair and make-up. You'll be perfect.'

Anissa pressed her lips together. 'But after what happened today—what if this is all for nothing? What if he's changed his mind? What if doesn't want me to go any more?'

Jules shook her head. 'I've said it before and I'll say

it again. This guy brought you to New York. He wants you to be his date for this ball. No matter what happened today, he'll still want you by his side.'

Anissa glanced back in the mirror. She liked how much she loved this dress, and how it made her look like someone else entirely. She gave a slow nod. 'Okay. I love this. Truly love it. How much do I owe you? This dress is spectacular. I can tell the hours and hours of work you've put into it.'

Jules shook her head. 'No. No way. All I want you to do is tell everyone who asks at the ball that the dress was designed by me. Give them my cards. I'll give you a whole pile.' She gave a broad smile. 'That's my dream come true.'

Anissa couldn't believe it. 'Really? You don't want me to pay you?'

Jules kept shaking her head. 'Honestly? You wearing my dress could give me so much publicity. It could really make me as a new designer.'

Anissa reached over and grabbed Jules's hands. 'Thank you so much for this. I don't know what I would have done without you.'

Jules put her hands on her hips and gave a slow nod of her head. 'It's my pleasure, but one thing. Have a think about Mr Billionaire. He might have whisked you off to New York, but don't let him take you for granted.' She raised her eyebrows. 'Maybe you should let him sweat a little about the dress. Let him think you haven't bought one.'

Anissa smiled. 'Jules, you have a wicked streak.'

Jules nodded. 'And I bet you do too…'

CHAPTER SEVEN

LEO WAS FEELING like complete and utter crap. Just exactly as he should.

He'd left her. He'd left her alone in New York, a strange city where she knew practically no one. All because of one lousy freak-out in his head.

What was wrong with him? What if she couldn't get hold of her friend?

Up until that point they'd virtually had the perfect day. Anissa was interesting, fun and gorgeous. Everything he could ever ask for. And yet...

He'd let her down. He'd let them both down.

He stared at the phone for a few seconds. He'd almost picked it up at least dozen times now. He couldn't quite decide which one to phone—Noemi or Sebastian. Maybe he should phone both? Maybe he should phone neither?

But the constant texting between Anissa and her parents had set something off in his brain. She was part of a family. It didn't matter where she was in the world, or what she was doing, she was still part of a family and it was clear she loved it.

He had a different set of circumstances, but this constant feeling of not being good enough wasn't Noemi's or Sebastian's fault. It was down to his own upbringing, added to by his own misgivings. Every part of him was telling him to make an effort. And that wasn't just his business brain talking. Part of it was his heart.

Anissa was having an effect on him he hadn't expected.

He picked up the phone and dialled the numbers quickly. Noemi answered on the second ring. 'Leo? How are you? It's so nice to hear from you.'

She sounded genuinely happy to hear from him. Something spread through him. A warmth he hadn't really experienced before.

'Hi, Noemi,' he said as he settled back in the chair, 'I just wanted to check in…'

Anissa pulled out her phone as she headed from the subway. Although she wasn't used to New York, she felt safe. The streets were busy and well lit. Her phone buzzed again. It was Hans from the Championship Skiing Competition. They hadn't spoken properly in eighteen months. She couldn't imagine why he'd phone her twice in one day.

Last time she'd ignored the call. This time she pressed it to her ear.

'Hans?'

'Anissa! At last. Where are you?'

She looked around. It felt like a trick question. 'New York?'

'New York? What on earth are you doing in New York?'

She pulled a face, 'A holiday?' she answered, as if it was a question. What kind of answer did he expect?

'Darn it! I'm in Mont Coeur. I thought you were here.'

Her stomach crunched. Hans had gone to Mount Coeur to speak to her?

'Well, sorry. I've left for a few days.' She pressed her

lips together for a second. 'Hans, did you want something?'

He cleared his throat. 'I was actually hoping to speak to you in person.'

Now she really was nervous. This seemed strange. 'What about?'

There was a long pause. 'It's just…that there's potentially an opening on the Skiing Championship Committee. I wanted to have a chat to see if you might be interested.'

She stopped walking. She was stunned.

'Wh-what?'

'I know we haven't spoken in a while,' Hans said smoothly, 'which is why I wanted to speak to you in person.'

She still couldn't really answer.

Hans kept talking. 'One of our members plans to resign in a few months—ongoing health issues—and we were talking about who would be perfect to take their place, and your name came up. We want someone young. We want someone who knows the sport inside out. They asked me to sound you out.'

Her head was spinning. Her name had come up? With the Skiing Championship Committee? She still couldn't quite believe it. She needed to clarify things.

'But what is it exactly that they wanted you to sound me out about?'

'It's probably better if we do this in person.'

Anissa looked around. She didn't know what to think. Her legs were actually shaking.

'When will you be back in Mont Coeur?'

'I don't know.' There was slight panic in her chest. 'I'll be in New York for at least the next four days.'

'Oh, okay.' Hans paused. 'How about if I email you

some information and then we can chat when you're back in Mont Coeur. It will give you a few days to think about things and decide how you feel.'

Her brain was still in overdrive. She still wasn't exactly sure what he was saying to her. She stuttered out her email address.

Her heart gave a little leap as she hung up. She had no idea what this meant. But that horrible churning feeling in her stomach that had been there for the last year—the one that wondered if she would ever make it back to championship skiing again—suddenly lessened a bit. She'd never really considered other career opportunities. She actually didn't think there were any—apart from teaching skiing or being a chalet maid. This was different. Could this be the back-up plan that Leo had suggested to her?

This felt like the possibility of a light at the end of a very long tunnel.

Leo was pacing by the time he heard the elevator ping at the entrance to the penthouse. 'I'm sorry,' he said as soon as she stepped through the doors.

He'd spent the last few hours regretting his actions. He couldn't really explain them to himself so how on earth could he explain them to Anissa?

It all felt like too much. The stuff with his parents. The will. Meeting his brother and sister under difficult circumstances. And on top of all that—Anissa. He liked her. She was slowly but surely finding away under the shell he'd built around himself. He liked her laugh. He liked her questions. He liked her work ethic and her striving to do well.

But he also liked the way she clearly adored her parents and was in contact with them every day. He liked the way she always tucked a bit of hair behind her right ear. And he worried about how disappointed she would be if she didn't get back to championship skiing. He'd only known her a few weeks but he cared about her. He'd wanted her to enjoy herself in New York—and he'd almost ruined it today. All because of the torrent of emotion that had flooded over him.

He'd spent the last few hours feeling guilty, wondering where she was and hoping she would return. He'd had his phone in his hand so many times to try and call her—but that seemed ridiculous after he'd left her on her own.

It hadn't helped that an hour ago a delivery had arrived from the bakery store—twenty-four rich and gorgeous cupcakes. He hadn't ordered them, which meant that Anissa obviously had.

But now the constant ache in his stomach was gone. She was here.

Anissa's cheeks had a glow about them and her eyes were sparkling. Her gaze narrowed and she got straight to the point. It seemed as if some time alone had focused her mind. 'Are you going to tell me what was wrong earlier?'

The words stuck somewhere in his throat. He'd been ready to churn out a whole load of excuses. But now that she was standing in front of him, her blonde hair peeking out from under hat, her blue coat fastened to her neck and dusted with snow, and her pale blue eyes focused entirely on him, his prepared excuses just seemed to disappear into the air around them. 'It's just...'

She unfastened her coat and hung it up. 'Just what?'

When he couldn't find the words, she gave a sigh. After a few seconds she walked into the kitchen, lifted the lid of the cupcakes box and gave a little nod. Then she grabbed a bottle of wine and took a glass from the cupboard. 'It's late, Leo. I'm tired. I... I had fun today. Or I thought we did. Until we didn't.'

She sighed as she poured the wine into a glass. 'Leo, you brought me here on the spur of the moment. You had business to do. You took me sightseeing. You brought me to stay in your penthouse. You invite me to a ball. Then you thrust your credit card at me and tell me to use it for the cab, drinks or…whatever I might like. You told me to use your credit card to shop. Have you any idea how insulting that is? As if…you're trying to buy me or something?'

Leo walked over to one of the windows. He stood with his hands in his pockets. In the darkness outside he could see all the glimmers of lights across the city. He wasn't used to sharing. He'd never really had anyone to confide in before. Today's conversation with Noemi had been… interesting. It finally felt as if he was starting to move in the right direction with his family. And now Anissa was asking him outright what was wrong.

Something caught his eye. A flicker to the side. A helicopter. New York was full of them.

It felt like an elephant had just put a foot on his chest.

Anissa appeared at his side, holding her glass of wine.

As he watched the light from the helicopter flicker across the sky the pain in his chest intensified. It was almost as if everything had finally come to a head and he just had to let it out.

'The family stuff.' His voice was croaky.

'Yes?' asked Anissa.

'I was in Mont Coeur for the reading of my mum and dad's will.' His words were stilted.

'Your parents died?' She was clearly surprised, 'I'm so sorry.'

He took a few moments to find the rest of his words. 'I didn't even get a chance to know them.' His eyes fixed on the helicopter again. 'When they came to meet me in

New York for the first time, they…they were killed in an accident.'

Anissa stepped in front of him, blocking out the blackness and twinkling lights of the city beyond. Concern was laced across her face. 'What kind of accident?'

The words choked in his throat. 'A helicopter crash. They died coming to meet me.'

He swayed just as Anissa's hands reached out to him. 'Leo.' Her wine sloshed on the floor as she guided him back to a chair.

He crumpled into the chair as the emotions that had been building inside him for the last few months bubbled over.

'If they hadn't discovered me, if they hadn't got in contact they would never have died. It was my fault. Mine. I should never have answered that letter. I should never have agreed to meet them.' Tears started to stream down his face.

Anissa knelt in front of him and took his hands in hers. 'Oh, Leo, I'm sorry. I'm so sorry. But it's not your fault. You could never have predicted something like that.' Her brow furrowed. 'But I don't understand. Why didn't you know your parents? You mentioned them before—but said they didn't bother much with you.'

He ran his fingers through his thick hair. 'I… I… I didn't know them because they had me adopted as a baby. They weren't married, they had no support and they told me they'd had no choice but to give me up.'

She reached up and cradled his cheek with one hand. 'Oh, Leo,' she said softly.

It was the touch. The pure worry in her voice that gave him the strength to continue. 'I didn't know them. I didn't know them at all. My adoptive parents had always told me that I wasn't wanted—that I'd been abandoned.

They were the ones who didn't bother much with me. I spent my whole life feeling not good enough—for them, or for my real parents.'

'But you were a kid. Why on earth would your adoptive parents tell you that? That's cruel.'

It was like a little light switching on in his head. He nodded. 'Yes, it is. It's how they were.' He straightened a little and put his hand over hers. 'They weren't really interested in me. I think the thought of having a kid was better than the actual experience. They always made me feel as if I was constantly a bother.'

'That's terrible. How dare they? Where are they now? Do you still talk?'

He shook his head. 'I left when I was twenty and never looked back. When I got the letter out of the blue from my real parents I was stunned. I didn't believe it at first. It took me a few weeks to get in touch.'

She nodded as if she could understand. 'And when you did?'

He took a deep breath and lifted his head. 'Salvo and Nicole were anxious to meet me. They said they'd been looking for me almost since they'd given me up. But they wanted a chance to tell Sebastian and Noemi about me. Apparently, they'd been so racked with guilt they hadn't told my brother and sister about me.'

She was almost afraid to ask. 'And did they get a chance?'

He gave a shudder. 'Not the way they wanted to. Noemi opened my reply. She confronted her mother about it. She was upset they'd kept me a secret—and, to be honest, so was I.'

'But you arranged to see them—to meet?'

A single tear snaked down his face. 'I did.' His voice broke again. 'I wanted to meet them, Anissa. I did. I'd never had a real family, not one where I felt as if I belonged, where I felt as if I was wanted. And then, all of a sudden, it seemed like it might happen.'

'Oh, Leo.' Her words were so soft, so full of empathy.

'And...then...' he shook his head '...they were gone. They'd arrived in New York a few hours early and decided to take a tour of the city in a helicopter.'

His hands were shaking. He couldn't help it.

'And then there was the funeral...'

Anissa's hand was warm on his cheek, the other clasping his hand. 'So you didn't meet Sebastian and Noemi then?'

He flung up his hands in exasperation. 'How could I? I wasn't sure what they knew about me. I didn't even know if Sebastian knew I existed. I could hardly reveal myself at the family funeral as the missing son.' He hated how this made his heart ache. 'I went. I just stayed at the back. There were hundreds of people there. I was just another Italian-looking guy in a suit. One of many.'

He hated how bitter and twisted that sounded, but he hated even more how bitter and twisted it made him feel.

'They must hate me. They must really hate me— Sebastian and Noemi. If my parents had never found me, they would never have been in New York. They would never have had the accident. Life would still be good. The business would still be in safe hands.' He sucked in a shaky breath. 'It's my fault. All my fault.'

This feeling had been sitting heavily over him like a dark cloak from the second the accident had happened. It haunted his dreams at night, had sat on his chest like a heavy weight during the funeral, and hindered every step he'd taken in the snow to go and meet his brother and sister.

Guilt was horrid. Guilt was like having something

drain the life out of you slowly but surely. At least that's what it had been like the last few months.

'Of course it's not your fault, Leo. How could you have known? How could you ever have predicted that? It was just a horrible, horrible accident. And stop saying that. That's the second time you've said it. It's not your fault. Stop believing that.' She shook her head. 'You said they'd spent most of their lives searching for you. It sounds as if they would never have stopped.'

He tried to take in what she was saying. In his head he knew it probably made sense. But he just couldn't accept it. Not yet.

'From what you said about the funeral, it sounds like your parents were very popular.'

Leo nodded his head. 'Oh, they are—they were. You might have heard of them—the Cattaneos.'

A frown creased Anissa's brow and a second later he saw the flash of recognition in her eyes. Most people in Europe had heard of the Cattaneos.

'The jewellery people—your family are the jewellery people?'

He sighed and leaned back in the chair. 'Yeah. That's why things are so hard right now. They named me in their will.'

Anissa shook her head. 'But so they should, you are their son.'

Leo closed his eyes for a second. She made it sound so simple.

He let out a long, slow breath. 'Apparently, they did this a long time ago. They put a clause in their will to say that I have to assume the controlling stake in the family business for six months. If I don't accept it, or try and walk away during that time, the business gets dissolved.'

Anissa's eyes widened. 'What? No. That's terrible. It's an awful position for you to be in.'

He nodded. 'I know. Imagine how Sebastian and Noemi feel. Mystery brother appears out of nowhere and gets given the ability to ruin the family business completely. Is it any wonder Sebastian is angry? I can't help but imagine how I'd feel if the company I'd spend my life building got handed over to someone else.'

He leaned his head back against the leather recliner. 'I have no idea what happens next. I've been on my own for so long. But the question I have to ask myself is do I really want a family? My mother and father aren't there now, and they're the people I'd really wanted to form a relationship with. So, with Sebastian and Noemi, this hasn't been the best of starts. I've been left in a charge of their family business—how they can trust me, or me them? Let's face it, they have to be nice to me for the next six months—whether they want to or not.'

Anissa moved and sat on the edge of the chair next to him. After a few seconds she threaded her fingers through his hair. It was an intimate move. The move of someone who cared. 'Could it be that you're just feeling overwhelmed by everything? It sounds as though it's all happened so quickly. You didn't even get a chance to say goodbye to your parents properly.'

He was drawn by her touch. His hand automatically wound its way around her waist and he pulled her towards him, sliding her from the armrest and onto his lap.

She put her hands on either side of his head and pressed her forehead against his. 'Leo, who have you talked to about all this?'

He breathed slowly. 'Just my lawyers. I've been trying to find a way out without destroying the jewellery business.'

Her eyes fixed on his and she was so close her eyelashes were brushing against his skin. 'I meant who have you talked to about this for *you*, Leo. Not for business. Not for legal reasons. Who have you spoken to for you?'

He gave his head the slightest shake. 'No one.'

It sounded so lonely. It made it sound as if he had such a solitary existence.

Words choked in his throat. 'I've seen how close you are with your parents. I've never had anything like that. I don't even know how I should be with my brother and sister. I phoned Noemi earlier today. But it felt so stilted—not her, me. I just don't know how to have that kind of conversation. Not yet. Not while all this business stuff is hanging over our heads.'

'Leo, I can't imagine how hard this has been for you. And this time of year—Christmas—always seems to magnify things.' Her hands wove back through his hair and she gave him a smile. 'But I want to tell you one thing. You *are* good enough, Leo. You've always been good enough.'

Her lips brushed against his cheek and his head instinctively turned to capture her lips with his.

Heat flooded through him. There was so much electricity between them—it had been there from the very first time they'd met. But now it was more. It was deeper. The connection stronger. And he liked that. It meant so much. That feeling of finally connecting with someone. To want to feel her skin under his. He wanted to feel the heartbeat in her chest against his.

Whatever he'd done today, however mixed up and guilty he'd felt about everything, it seemed that Anissa had a more forgiving heart than he could have hoped for.

She tugged at his jumper, pulling it over his head as she stayed on his lap, matching his every kiss. Every cell in his body was roaring. It wasn't just the attraction. It was the empathy and understanding. Her words. Her reassurance. The complete and utter belief in her eyes when she'd looked at him and told him that he was good enough. It had made his heart soar in a way he'd never felt before.

This was new. This was all new to him.

And no matter what happened, whatever decision he made about the family business, something in his heart was telling him that for the first time in his life he'd found something that could be worth holding onto.

And as he picked Anissa up and carried her to his bedroom, he'd never felt surer of anything in his life.

CHAPTER EIGHT

Wow. For the first time in for ever her muscles ached in good ways instead of bad.

Last night she'd come home prepared to be angry at Leo. But one look at the expression on his face as he'd crumpled in front of her had almost been the end of her.

She'd had no idea what he'd been going through. She couldn't imagine the devastation of losing her parents— or the set of circumstances he'd described to her. Every part of the story had made her heart twist in her chest a little more at what Leo had missed out on. Every word had made her relish the good relationship she had with her parents. How must it feel to have never had that? And when it finally seemed like a possibility—to have it ripped away?

No wonder he was devastated. No wonder he was all over the place.

Now she understood the bravado and business face that Leo tried his best to keep in place. It was his mask. The thing that held him together.

Because he didn't have anyone else.

He didn't have anyone to share things with. His new-found relationship with his brother and sister had never had the chance to develop—and, thanks to the contents of the will, possibly never would.

But it was that overall feeling of not being good enough that she could relate to most.

It lit a little fire inside her. He was good enough. Surely his family would see that? Surely everyone could see it?

'Hey.'

The voice beside her made her start. She rolled over in the bed to face a sleepy-eyed Leo. Darn, he was sexy in the morning.

'Hey,' she replied as her lips automatically turned upwards.

'What do you want to do today?' he said huskily.

'Do I still get to play tourist?' She was almost holding her breath, wondering what he would say.

'Absolutely. Tell me where you want to go today and I'll take you. Tonight I'd really like it if you'd come with me when I have dinner with a business associate.'

'You would? Do you think he'll be okay with me being there?'

'He'll have to be. Joe is the reason I came back. He's playing hard ball on a business proposal that I thought we'd wrapped up.' Leo lifted one of her hands and kissed it. 'Who wouldn't want a smart, intelligent lady at their table? He'll have to understand that I'm entertaining my guest. Anyway, I think he'll like you. Who wouldn't?'

She couldn't help but be flattered. Chalet girl by day... girlfriend by night? She still wasn't quite sure.

She nodded. 'Where's dinner? What do I need to wear?'

He pulled a face and groaned. 'Did I make a huge mess of things yesterday, giving you a credit card and telling you to buy something?'

She nodded. 'You might have done. But don't worry. The ballgown is sorted.' She'd been offended before when he'd said his PA would find her something, but now she'd much rather sightsee than spend the day shopping. It was time for a compromise. 'How about you give me the number of your PA and I can tell her what size I am, what colour I prefer and what style of dress I like. I'm pretty easygoing and, as long as it fits and covers me, I'll wear it. That way neither of us has to go near a clothes store today.' She leaned a little closer. 'Anyway, I'm all about the water today. I have something much more fun in mind.'

One of his eyebrows rose. 'The water?' He was obviously curious.

She nodded but didn't give anything away.

Leo leaned over to kiss her. 'Your wish is my command. Now, let's go and have some fun.'

It only took her ten minutes to get ready and have the conversation with Leo's PA. She switched on the coffee machine while Leo was showering and fired up his computer to check her messages.

Her heart gave a little leap as she noticed the email from Hans straight away.

The email was detailed. It gave her a full outline of what her role and responsibilities would be. They had a clear job description for her with a wide remit, complete with salary and expenses—more than she could ever have imagined. She'd be right at the heart of the championship skiing committee.

But not as a competitor.

Part of it made her feel happy. She'd never have thought they would have considered her in a million years. But the other part of her brain was irrationally insulted. They assumed she'd never get back to professional skiing. Surely they knew she was training again?

Almost automatically her hand started rubbing her leg and her other hand reached for her handbag and froze. She was looking for painkillers. The ones she took every day.

The ones she currently didn't need.

She stopped and pushed herself up from the chair, filling a glass with water while she waited for the coffee. Taking the painkillers had become automatic.

Except for…now.

She did a few gentle stretches. The truth was since she'd got on her feet again she'd never stopped training. She'd thought she just had to learn to live with pain and medicate it.

She'd never actually imagined that if she'd stopped skiing the pain wouldn't be there any more. How stupid was that?

The machine clicked next to her and she exchanged Leo's full cup of coffee with her empty one. She inserted a new pod and pressed the button as she tried to process her thoughts. Was she reaching for something she could never achieve? Was she damaging her body for a dream that would never come true?

Tears pricked in her eyes as she looked out over the snow-dusted city. Out there was a world of possibilities. Maybe she needed to consider her options a little more rationally—take the emotion, history and heart out of things—but could she do that?

Leo appeared at the door smiling, rubbing his hair with one towel, another wrapped around his waist.

He fixed on her with those bright blue eyes. 'Brilliant, I smell coffee.' His fresh, clean scent drifted around her as he moved beside her and shot her a sexy grin. 'So, Anissa. Surprise me. What are we doing today?'

* * *

She was definitely infectious. And he liked it. He liked it a lot.

They started by taking the Staten Island Ferry past the Statue of Liberty. But one sighting wasn't enough and Anissa wanted to do the whole tourist thing. So they took the boat to Liberty Island and climbed the stairs to the pedestal, statue and finally the crown.

'Isn't it great?' she whispered as they looked out over New York Harbor and Manhattan.

'It is, isn't it?' he agreed, wondering why he'd never done this before.

She nudged him. 'It's freezing today. Do you think the Hudson will be frozen?'

He thought for a second. 'Parts of it could be—why?'

She smiled. 'Because it might make where I want to go next even more special.'

'And where's that?'

She kept grinning. 'Not saying. I want it to be a surprise,' she said teasingly. 'I've checked the directions and I'll tell you when we get there.'

An hour and a half later he frowned as he looked at a sign in front of him. 'You want to go here? Really?'

'Are you joking?' She held up her hands. 'Of course I want to go here.' She pointed to the river. 'Look, a submarine surrounded by frozen ice, how cool is that?' She gestured to the hangar high above them. 'In there is a space shuttle. Have you ever seen a space shuttle before? Touched one? I haven't. And I can't wait.' She spun around and pointed directly above. 'And up there, are the old war planes. Don't you remember that movie? The one where the guy is the last man left in New York with the zombies and he plays golf from the top of one of the war planes?'

Leo frowned, taking a few seconds to place the film, before it finally clicked in his brain. 'Of course!' He grabbed her hand and pulled her towards him. 'You're just a big kid really, aren't you?'

Her cold nose brushed against his chin. 'Maybe I am,' she said quickly. 'Or maybe I'm just reassessing things. Deciding what's important.'

The look in her eyes as she said the words tugged at his heart. There it was again. The sign that they were on the same wavelength. She lifted her hands and rested them on his shoulders. She licked her lips. 'Maybe we both need to have a think about things. Tell me more about your chat with Noemi yesterday.'

He rolled his eyes. He couldn't help it. 'It was fine. She was chatty. Asked lots of questions. Mainly around when I'd be back.'

Anissa nodded her head. 'She wants to get to know you better, Leo. It's a natural response. And I'm glad.'

He nodded. 'I guess. It was apparently a dream of Mother and Father's that they would have all their children together around the table at Christmas.'

Anissa took a few seconds. 'Does Noemi want to fulfil that dream?'

He nodded. 'But isn't it too late? They're gone.'

She gripped his shoulders firmly. 'But you're not gone. Noemi and Sebastian are not gone. This is your family, Leo. The people you should get to know. The people you should get to love.'

She was right. He knew she was right. But it just seemed like such a big leap into the unknown.

She kept talking. 'Christmas is a really special for

families. I always love spending this time of year with
my mum and dad.'

'Are you going home for Christmas?' Something
panged inside him. He wasn't quite sure how he wanted
her to answer this question.

She shook her head. 'I promised I'd work. I'm going
home a few days before Christmas then coming back
on the twenty-third. It will be fine. My mum will make
Christmas dinner early and we'll celebrate then.' She
gave a shrug. 'I always keep my commitments and someone has to work.'

She'd be there. Inside his heart gave a little leap. If he
decided to go back for Christmas, Anissa would be there.
Somehow that made things not seem quite so daunting.

She tilted her head to one side. 'Noemi was the easy
one to call, wasn't she? The person you really need to
call is Sebastian.'

He let out a wry laugh. 'How come you never beat
around the bush? How come you just go straight for the
jugular?'

She laughed too. 'Because life is too short. And, anyway, you know your brother was angry about the will. I
bet he was hurt. He must have spent his whole life working for that position and now he feels as if it's been ripped
away from him and all his hard work counts for nothing.'
She wrinkled her nose. 'What's Noemi's stake in this?'

'She's a silent partner. But I'm not sure how happy
she is about that.'

Anissa put her hand on his chest. 'You don't know
what else is going on in their lives—apart from the fact
they've just lost their parents and found out about a secret brother, there could be other stuff.' She stood up on
her tiptoes and whispered in his ear as she hugged him

tight. 'Take a breath, Leo. Take a chance. Once they get to know you, they'll think that you're great.'

His stomach gave a flutter. He'd never, ever had anyone support him as much as Anissa was doing now. And he wanted to reciprocate. He wanted to do the same for her as she was doing for him.

But that could mean asking her questions she didn't want to be asked. Asking if her she really could make it back to championship skiing. And right now the last thing he wanted to do was hurt her. Or damage the most valuable relationship he'd started to form.

He kissed her swiftly on the lips and lowered his voice. 'Okay, tourist, how would you like to see the inside of my submarine?'

She laughed. 'Now, how could any girl resist an offer like that?'

Five hours later they'd just had enough time to dash back to the apartment and dress for dinner. Anissa hadn't checked to see what Leo's PA Keisa had sent over. She'd just grabbed the hangar and rushed into her room to shower and change. She blasted her hair with the dryer and applied some make-up quickly. Her heart gave a little flip at the box of shoes on the bed. Black patent leather stilettos with red soles. Probably cost more than she earned in a month. She unzipped the clothes bag and shook out the dress.

It was gorgeous—red, a colour she rarely wore. It had a straight neckline, falling from her hips with a small red flounce around the bottom stopping at her knees.

She stepped into the dress and the shoes and took one quick glance in the mirror before hurrying out to Leo.

'Wow.' He was standing waiting for her in a dark suit and tie, a glass of red wine in his hand. The lights in the penthouse were dimmed and she loved the way his eyes sparkled as she sashayed towards him.

She gestured down, 'Well, I haven't met Keisa but she sure has impeccable taste.'

Leo nodded appreciatively. 'She does.' Then he gave a little smile. 'I might have sent her a photo.'

'Of me?' She was surprised. 'When?'

'Today.' He shrugged. 'We took masses of pictures at the statue and the Natural History Museum the other day.'

She moved forward and tapped his chest. 'And I have a spectacular photo of you pretending to hold a giant blue whale from the other day.'

He laughed. 'I forgot about that one. You could use it as blackmail material.' Then he nodded and wagged his finger. 'Actually, I have a really good picture of someone with their head inside a T-Rex's mouth. Now, *that* would be a good blackmail picture.'

She slid her arms up around his neck. 'You'd really blackmail me?'

His hands rested on her hips and his gaze was loaded. 'I could be persuaded not to.'

She moved closer, so she could feel the full length of his body against hers. 'Tell me about tonight. Tell me about Joe.'

He met her gaze. 'Are you worried about dinner?'

She pulled a face. 'Not worried, really. But… I know this is a big deal for you. I don't want to say anything wrong. Is there anything I should avoid?'

He shook his head. 'Just be yourself. You're perfect. Joe will love you.'

It was like warm honey spreading through her. Since he'd opened up to her last night it was as if all the walls had come down. He seemed easier, more relaxed. She didn't doubt he was still considering what to do next about his family, but the dark, hooded look had left his face. It was almost as if he was relieved to have finally shared how he was feeling about things.

She stepped back and slipped her hand into his. 'Come on, then, Mr Baxter, take me to dinner.'

It was his favourite restaurant—and it was Joe's too. The restaurant slowly rotated as they ate, meaning that in the space of an hour they got to see all the views of New York.

Service was smooth and quick. And just like he'd predicted, Joe was charmed by Anissa. It was the first time Leo had ever taken a date with him to a business meeting but somehow this had just felt right.

Anissa had enchanted Joe with stories about her childhood in Austria, and then intrigued him with tales about her international skiing experiences.

As she spoke Leo couldn't help but notice the far-off look in her eye or the slightly wistful tone in her voice. He wasn't quite sure what to say or how to react. As their main courses arrived, she turned towards both of them.

'I've had an interesting job offer.'

'You have?'

She nodded hesitantly. 'From someone I used to have a lot of dealings with—there's a vacancy on the International Skiing Championship Committee.' She seemed a little nervous. 'They've considered me.'

Joe leaned over and squeezed Anissa's hand. 'Of course they have. They know talent when they see it.' He seemed to pick up the fact she didn't reply right away. 'They've considered you—are you considering them?'

It was the careful way Joe turned the question around. He was a wily character with years of experience in dealing with people. Leo held his breath. He wanted to know the answer to that question too. Anissa hadn't mentioned the job offer earlier—why not?

She toyed with the food on her plate. 'I'm not sure,' she said finally.

Leo couldn't help himself. 'Why not? It sounds wonderful.'

She gave a little sigh. 'Because if I say yes, that's it. It's almost like I'm saying I'll never compete any more—I'll never get the gold medal. I don't quite know if I'm ready to do that.'

Joe nodded. 'You said earlier you had an accident. Do you honestly think you'll get back to championship level?'

Leo shifted in his seat. He'd asked Anissa to consider a back-up plan, but he hadn't been quite as blunt. It seemed that Joe's age allowed him to be me much more direct.

Anissa's face was blank. She didn't reply.

Joe gave her hand a squeeze again and waved his other hand. 'Well, whatever you decide I'm sure it will be right for you. After all, you need to do what makes you happy.' He picked up his wine glass and raised it in a toast towards Anissa. 'To Anissa, a beautiful woman with a beautiful future, whatever it may be.'

Anissa picked up her glass and raised it back to Joe, tentatively taking a sip. She looked sad. She looked unsure. And Leo hated that for her.

His heart gave a squeeze as his head finally caught up.

He loved her. For the first time in his life he actually loved someone.

He wanted her to be happy. He wanted her to know she was good enough, and to choose the career path that was right for her. But more than anything he wanted her to be with him.

It was almost like someone had just lit up the sky behind him with fireworks.

He lifted his glass and clinked it against hers. 'To Anissa,' he agreed. 'You can be whatever you want to be.'

She met his gaze. Her eyes still looked unsure.

But he'd never more sure of anything in his life.

Joe was an old charmer. He could be brash, he could be flattering, and he could definitely charm the birds from the trees. Business between him and Leo had been wrapped up within five minutes. There had been a few disagreements backwards and forwards but no bad blood. It was clear that both men respected each other and she liked that. She liked it that Joe respected Leo's business acumen. Joe thought Leo was good enough. And that made her happy.

Dinner finished relatively early and since it wasn't far to Leo's apartment they waved the car away.

She extended one leg and pointed to her shiny new shoes. 'You do know that walking on these red soles essentially ruins them.'

Leo frowned. He obviously didn't get it. 'But shoes are for walking in. What else are you supposed to do with them?'

She shook her head. 'Never mind. Let's walk.'

His hand slid around her waist, pulling her closer.

She decided to ask the question she'd wanted to ask all night. 'Have you had any more thoughts about what to do about your family?'

He pressed his lips together for a second. 'Well, you're right. I probably should talk to Sebastian at some point—try and reassure him that I'm not interested in taking his place at the company.' He sighed. 'I've already told him, but I don't know if he's ready to listen yet.'

'Are you sure you don't want to be part of the family business?'

'What do you mean?'

She stopped walking for a second and looked at him. The Italian blood in him was strong, his sallow skin, his dark ruffled hair. His bright blue eyes were startling. His lithe body and build. He was Italian through and through. Even if he hadn't found out his ancestry, she could have guessed it.

'This is your family business too, Leo. Your mother and father left you the controlling shares for a reason. They loved you. You were their son. They wanted you to be part of the business—to work with them and your brother and sister. Do you really want to walk away from this, without thinking about it properly?'

He had a confused look in his eyes and he shook his head slowly. 'How can I? How can I take away what is theirs?'

She gripped his arm. 'Because it's yours too.' She stopped for a second and took a deep breath. 'Don't just walk away without thinking about it. Sebastian's reaction is making you feel as if you're not entitled to this. But you are, Leo. I don't want you to walk away and then regret it years down the line.'

She couldn't help the passion in her voice. Last night they'd connected. She'd seen how broken he'd been—how confused. But what she could also see was the yearning to belong. To be part of a family.

Her heart ached for this gorgeous man who tried to hide his emotions. Maybe waiting the six months then walking away from the family business was exactly what he should do. But she didn't know that. And, more importantly, Leo didn't know that.

She didn't pretend to have a head for business. But

Leo clearly did. He might have ideas and skills that could enhance the business. If only he would take the time to speak to Sebastian. If they could put the family business aside and get the chance to get to know one another.

She sucked in a slow breath. She was an only child and, like most only children, had longed for a brother or sister. How would she feel if she found out now that she did have one?

She knew in her heart she'd want to know everything about them. But Leo still hadn't answered her question. His brow was furrowed as if he was mulling over what she'd said. Something clicked in her brain.

'Your brother, Sebastian. You said you didn't meet his family because they hadn't arrived yet.'

He nodded. 'Yes.'

'Do you have a niece or a nephew?'

'I have…a nephew, I guess.' He honestly looked as though he really hadn't processed that. 'I'd never really considered the fact I was an uncle.'

'What's his name? What age is he?'

'His name is Frankie. He's…two, I think.'

Anissa clapped her hands together. 'A two-year-old nephew? That's brilliant.' She tugged at Leo's arm. 'You do know that New York has some of the best toy stores in the world.'

Now he looked really confused. 'Wh-what?'

She put a hand on each of his arms. 'Leo, in a few weeks' time it's Christmas. Whether you decide to go back to Mont Coeur or not, what you can't do…' she shook her head fiercely '…what you absolutely can't do is ignore the fact that this is the first Christmas you've known about your nephew. You have to get him something—just like you got something for Keisa.'

She gave him a little shake. 'This time, Leo, it's not

a present for your loyal PA. This time it's for family. A nephew is a gift.'

It was as if a light came on in his eyes. His lips turned up slightly. 'So,' he said slowly. 'I have to go gift shopping?'

She nodded. 'Finally, you're getting it.'

He held out his hands. 'What on earth do I buy a two-year-old boy?'

She winked at him. 'You should know. You used to be one.'

He groaned but she wouldn't let him away with it. She pointed one finger and pressed it into his chest with every word. 'You. Are. Going. To. Be. A. Great. Uncle.'

He put his hand to his chest. 'I am going to be a bruised uncle.'

She glanced at her watch. 'Darn it, the toy stores will be closed by now.'

Leo raised his eyebrows and pulled out his phone. 'Most places can be persuaded to open. Particularly if you'll make a charitable donation to a place of their choosing.'

Her heart gave a little leap and after a five-minute conversation Leo hailed a cab and named one of the most well-known toy stores. 'We're in luck,' he said as they climbed in. 'Apparently, it's a major stocktake night on the run-up to Christmas. Staff are already there.' There was a gleam in his eyes. 'We can go in.'

'Brilliant.' She rubbed her hands together as the cab wound its way through the snowy New York streets.

The lights were still on in the toy store but the shutters were pulled across the storefront. A member of staff was watching and waved them round to side entrance. He held out his hand. 'Leo Baxter?'

Leo nodded and shook his hand. 'Thanks for doing this.'

The man laughed. 'Anyone who'll make that big a donation to the children's cancer foundation gets my attention. Do you want one of the staff to help you shop—or do you just want to look around on your own?'

Leo glanced back at Anissa. She was already dying to find her way around the toy store. 'I think we're good.' She nodded.

The manager smiled and waved his arm. 'In that case, enjoy yourselves.'

She couldn't help herself and clapped her hands together excitedly. 'Come on, Leo. Let's go.'

Leo seemed a bit bewildered by the packed aisles and colourful signs everywhere. They moved from computers, to board games, to action figures, cars, laser guns and then on to game consoles, bikes, skateboards, roller skates and outdoor play furniture. Leo shook his head. 'I've just no idea where to start. I've never even met the kid.'

He sighed. 'And if he's anything like his dad, he'll probably hate me.' She hated the defeated look in his eyes. She walked over and wrapped one hand around his neck and ran the other through his hair. 'Leo Baxter, stop thinking like that. Stop thinking the glass is half-full. Start thinking about the whole new adventures you could be having.'

Being around him tonight had given her a spurt of new energy. She wanted to help Leo believe in who he was. She wanted him to know his value as part of the family.

He put his hands around her waist and spoke quietly. 'The truth is I could buy the entire contents of this store. But what good would that do?'

She nodded. 'You're right. What you need to do is

think of something you loved as a kid. Something you would want to buy for your own son.' She gave a playful shrug. 'If you ever have one.'

His eyes locked onto hers, his gaze intense. For a second it took her breath away. It was almost like he was staring right into her very soul. Seeing every part of her. No one had looked at her like that—ever.

His voice was husky. 'How come you didn't tell me about the job offer?'

The words took her by surprise.

Of course. She hadn't told him. Because she hadn't really had time to think about it properly yet. It had just come out in the course of the conversation with Joe this evening.

When she didn't answer straight away, Leo started talking again. 'It sounds like a great opportunity. They must think a lot of you if they got in touch. Wouldn't you love to do something like that?'

She could see genuine enthusiasm in his eyes and her stomach coiled as she knew it wasn't mirrored in her own. 'I... I...don't know,' she stumbled.

Leo was still enthused. 'They obviously think you have the knowledge, the skill set and the respect of the skiing community to offer you a position like that. Just think how much you could influence things, shape the future of professional skiing.'

But I won't have a gold medal.

The thought seemed to be implanted in her brain. It had felt as if it had been on a loop from the moment that Hans had called her.

Maybe she was being ridiculous, but she just couldn't shake that thought.

Leo was still talking all about how wonderful she

would be. What a brilliant opportunity it was. Encouraging her to be the best she could be.

All of a sudden she felt overwhelmed. New York had been fabulous. But her whole life was upside down. She couldn't concentrate long enough to make any decisions. And in amongst all this she'd met a wonderful man who'd shared some really personal moments with her and maybe even stolen a little part of her heart.

Had she really just thought that? After only a few weeks?

She gulped. Leo was still talking. She gave herself a little shake and patted her hand against his chest. 'Hey. We can't stay here all night. The staff will need to get home. What was your number one toy as a kid?'

Right now she would do anything to distract him from the subject of her, and her job offer.

For the briefest second he looked a little surprised at her interruption, but then there was a flash in his eyes. 'Dinosaurs!' he exclaimed. 'Dinosaurs were the thing I absolutely loved.'

'Of course,' she agreed quickly. 'What kid doesn't love dinosaurs?' She grabbed his hand. 'Come on, I'm sure they're just around the corner.'

Ten minutes later they had a mat with volcanoes, jungles and rivers, along with every dinosaur that the store stocked. Leo's arms were full.

Anissa bent down and picked up a few human figures and a toy jeep. She laughed. 'Collateral damage. We need some people that the dinosaurs can eat.'

'Good idea,' he agreed as they headed to the cash desk. His footsteps faltered and he turned to face her. 'Anissa?'

'Yes?'

He took a moment. 'Thank you.'

'What for?'

'For this. For thinking about Frankie. For being there for me. For everything.' His voice cracked a little.

It was like a vice gripping her heart. She didn't want him to say anything else. Wasn't ready for anything else. She was still getting used to the fact her leg and back didn't ache constantly. She was still trying not to think about what her life could look like. Most of all, she was still trying to work out how she felt about the gorgeous billionaire who'd whisked her halfway around the world.

She painted a smile on her face. 'That's what friends are for.'

CHAPTER NINE

THE LAST FEW days had been good, but even though physically they were closer than ever, emotionally Anissa felt distant. At times Leo watched her staring off into space, clearly mulling things over—things that she wasn't sharing with him.

It felt as if it was time to take some action. To try and let her see herself as he saw her. Not as a sportswoman who'd had an accident and had had her dreams snatched from her fingers but as a beautiful, intelligent woman who could re-evaluate her life and what she wanted to achieve.

When he'd seen the hurt in her eyes as she'd talked about her accident, he'd imagined that taking her away from Mont Coeur would give her a chance to rethink things. A chance to see what her life could be like outside skiing. But it seemed that Anissa was still fixated on that gold medal. He hated the fact that he wondered if it would actually be in her reach or not.

'Anissa?' he asked. 'How are you doing?'

She'd disappeared for a few hours to get her hair and make-up done for the Christmas charity ball, then as soon as she'd returned she'd ducked into one of the other rooms to change. He still wasn't sure what she would be wearing.

All he knew was that his credit card only had a charge for a pair of shoes, and that made him *really* nervous.

'I'm fine,' came the muffled voice from inside the room.

'Need any help?'

There was a long minute's silence and then the door opened. 'Nope,' she said simply as she stepped towards him.

His breath caught somewhere in his throat. Anissa's blonde hair was piled on top of her head with a few loose tendrils around her face. She was wearing a pale blue floor-length dress, with beads and sequins on the bodice and skirts that seemed to shimmer as she walked.

It was like she'd cast a magic spell all around him. 'You look like an ice princess,' he breathed.

She smiled as she stepped up to him. 'That's what you called me in Mont Coeur. I kept it in mind.'

There was a tiny shimmer of glitter on her cheeks. Her lips were a rich rose colour, and her eyelashes longer than he'd ever seen them.

'Where on earth did you get this dress? It's perfect, the exact colour of your eyes.'

She looked down and held out the skirts. 'I can't quite believe it. Do you remember me telling you about Chloe's cousin being in New York? Turns out she's a fashion student. When she found out where I was going, she asked if I'd consider one of her dresses.' She spun around, letting the light catch the few scattered sequins on the skirts.

Leo's heart tightened in his chest. She looked stunning. She was stunning. Inside and out. And tonight, at some point, he was going to tell her how he felt about her.

He gave her a bow. 'Okay, Ms Lang. Let me take you to New York's finest ball.'

* * *

It was everything she could ever have dreamed of. The black limousine pulled up to a red carpet outside the famous hotel. Cameras flashed instantly. It seemed the ball was even more prestigious than she'd thought. As soon as they entered the foyer Leo started nodding to people. It only took a few seconds for a woman to grab hold of her arm. 'Your dress. It's exquisite. Who is the designer?'

Anissa smiled. 'Oh, it's someone new. Her name is Jules Chen.' She looked down at the pale blue gown. 'I think she'll be the next big thing.'

The woman nodded in agreement. 'Well, if your dress is anything to go by, I'd say she will be.'

Anissa felt a little swell of pride as she pressed Jules's card into the woman's hand. She'd need to tell Jules.

Leo led her further through the foyer. The ballroom had a beautiful curved staircase on either side, leading down to the black-and-white floor.

As if they'd planned it especially for her, the lighting was blue and gold, and the huge chandeliers above sent a myriad of rainbow lights across all the walls. The whole room was decorated for Christmas, with strings of elegant twinkling lights. Slim and unusual white Christmas trees were decorated with glittering blue baubles, and blue and gold garlands were wound around the pillars in the middle of the room.

From the second they arrived waiters with silver trays appeared with glasses of champagne and trays of tiny food she couldn't even identify.

A large orchestra had been set up in one of the adjoining rooms and the music flowed through the ballroom.

Leo introduced her to couple after couple, each one more glamorous than the one before. Dozens of people asked about her dress and each time she told them

Jules's name and pressed a card into their hand she felt a little buzz of excitement. Hopefully the more people who heard her name, the more people would talk about her and seek out her designs. Finally, after they'd talked to everyone and circled the edges of the ballroom more than once, he turned to her and extended his hand. 'May I have this dance?'

She smiled and placed her glass of champagne on one of the tables. 'I thought you'd never ask.'

As the music started around them he led her into the middle of the dance floor. Dancing was formal, with most couples in traditional waltz holds. 'You know how to do this?' she asked as her stomach gave a few flips.

'Don't you?' He grinned down at her.

'Let's just say I didn't have much time in the past for balls,' she said wryly.

He bent to her ear, his lips brushing against her. 'It's easy,' he whispered. 'Just follow my lead.'

And so she did. He steered her elegantly around the dance floor to the popular slow Christmas pop song. It seemed that even famous balls couldn't escape the clichéd cheesy pop ballads. But she liked this one, and naturally picked up the rhythm and tempo of the steps.

'Told you I could teach you,' he joked.

'If you can ski, you can do anything,' she answered with false bravado.

His eyebrows rose. 'Is that so?' Before she could think any further he spun her around, turn after turn, until the whole ballroom was flashing before her eyes. She leaned her head forward onto his chest. 'Stop,' she groaned. 'I feel dizzy.'

'I haven't even started yet,' he joked as he slowed their steps. 'Hey,' he continued. 'You can always just stand on my shoes.'

'With these heels? I'd spear you to the floor.'

He spun her once again, still laughing, her skirts swirling out around them and the sequins on her dress glimmering in the pale blue lights. She felt like a princess. And definitely not an ice princess. Her heart was beating so fast she thought it could power the whole of Manhattan.

No one had made her feel like this before. Alain had never made her heart beat like this—and he'd never her treated like this. It didn't take money to treat a girl like a princess—or to make her feel that way.

Leo, no matter what else he was going through, seemed to do this seamlessly.

Every look, every smile made each cell in her body stand to attention. She couldn't deny the attraction between them—or the buzz of electricity that seemed to sizzle around them.

But what were Leo's expectations of her?

She could see people looking at them as they danced past. With his tall and broad frame, Italian looks and bright blue eyes he was easily the best-looking man in the room. The guy was a billionaire. And he was with her.

Anissa Lang. Chalet girl and ski instructor.

Why? Why had he chosen her?

If she hadn't slipped that night when practising it was likely that they would never have met. Never have made that connection. If she hadn't been assigned to clean his chalet they might never have seen each other again.

That made her stomach squirm. A series of coincidences had brought them together. What did that really mean?

She could sense herself rapidly losing her heart to this guy. A guy who stayed in New York. A guy who had success at his fingertips.

Why would he consider a girl who didn't even know what she wanted out of life?

The thoughts started to overwhelm her. Maybe she was reading too much into all this. Maybe once Leo had time to think and resolve the issues he had with his family he would forget all about her.

Her chest tightened. That scared her. The thought of never seeing Leo again? The thought of never being around him made her stomach twist in a way she hadn't expected.

He was still smiling at her with those bright blue eyes. He held out his arm and spun her underneath it, sliding his arm around her waist and leading her off the dance floor.

'Let's take a break,' he said smoothly. 'We need to talk.'

It was weird. She thought she could hear the beating of her heart in her ears. How was that even possible?

They moved out of the now-crowded ballroom, past the orchestra, and through to another room that looked out over part of Central Park.

He took her hand in his. 'I called Sebastian today.'

'You did?'

He nodded. 'When you went to get your hair and make-up done, I decided it was time.'

Her heart swelled a little. She knew how wary he'd been about making that call. 'How was it?'

He pressed his lips together. 'Still a bit awkward. I'm just not sure where, or if, I fit in this family.'

She nodded slowly. 'But you're taking steps. That's the point.'

He sucked in a deep breath. 'That's what I want to talk about.'

Her skin prickled as if a cool breeze had swept over

her skin. She wasn't quite sure where this was heading. 'What do you mean?'

'Steps. I'm not sure what comes next with…my family.' He stumbled over the last words. 'But all that stuff—finding my real parents, then losing them—has given me a chance to re-evaluate my life. To look at what I want. To decide what I want to do with it.'

His words were coming out quicker. He was getting more excited.

Anissa's mouth was dry. 'What do you want to do with it?'

He took her other hand. 'It's more about who I want to do it with.'

She could almost swear her heart stopped beating.

Her voice was barely audible. 'Wh-what?'

Leo's eyes were sparkling and his smile wide. He closed both hands over hers. 'I want to do it with you, Anissa. Stay with me. Stay with me in New York. Have a clean break from your past life and take your time to decide what you want to do. You've been different these last few days. It's like the shadows have lifted from your eyes and you've come out from under a cloud.'

Her heart twisted at those words—partly because they might be true—but Leo kept talking, his enthusiasm brimming over.

'Stay with me. Take some time. Decide what you want to do and where you want to be. We both know that you might not make it back to gold-medal level again. But you're brilliant, Anissa. There's a world of opportunities out there for you. You just need to decide which one you want. So take your time. Stay with me. Get away from the slopes. New York could give you the time and space you need to make some plans for the future.'

She bristled at those words. He'd said her fear out

loud. He'd said that she likely wouldn't get back to the standard she needed to get the gold medal. It had played on her mind constantly for the last year—everyone had spoken with their silent disappearance from her life— but Leo was the first person to actually say the words to her face. And she didn't like them.

Leo reached up and touched her cheek. 'Please tell me you'll stay, Anissa. Now I've found you, I don't want to lose you. I love you.'

Her heart burned in her chest. Part of her wanted to shout out in joy and part of her wanted to burst into tears.

She'd met someone she'd connected with. Someone who, with one glance, could set her pulse racing. She'd seen into his pain, into his feelings of inadequacy, and completely understood. What's more, she'd wanted to help. She hated that this wonderful, caring man felt like that.

Maybe she should be laughing. Maybe she should be throwing her arms around his neck and telling him that she loved him too.

Because she did.

But she just couldn't. Not now. Not here. Not when he'd just said those other words.

It didn't matter that it was the most romantic setting. It didn't matter that most of other women in room would think she was crazy.

She wasn't ready to give up on her dreams. It just seemed too much. Those slow feelings of being over-whelmed that had developed in the last few days were now gathering speed like snow tumbling down a mountain in an avalanche.

She could almost hear a ringing in her ears. The tightness across her chest had spread. Although she could breathe in, she was struggling to get it back out. Her head started to swim.

She stepped back. Out of his reach, out of the smell of his deep woody aftershave and away from the heat emanating from his body.

She needed space. She needed time.

His eyes widened as if he'd finally realised something was wrong.

'Anissa?'

She pulled her hands back against her chest and shook her head.

There was noise behind them. An ornamental clock striking midnight.

It was like the spur she needed.

She shook her head and gathered her skirts in her hands. 'No, Leo.' The words choked halfway in her throat. 'I'm sorry.'

As she headed to the stairs she stumbled and tripped, leaving one of her silver jewelled sandals behind. For a second she hesitated, wondering if she should pick it up. But Leo was still staring at her, his face a picture of confusion.

She couldn't take the chance he would come after her—would try to persuade her to stay.

Tears clouded her vision. She had to get away before the pressure in her chest became too much. She turned and fled down the stairs as the last strike of midnight sounded.

Leo was stunned. What had just happened?

One second he was inviting the woman that he loved to stay with him. The next second she was crying and running away.

For a few seconds he was frozen to the spot, wondering how he could have got things so wrong. Wondering if he'd completely misread where he and Anissa could go.

The pain in his chest was sharp. A woman next to him coughed loudly, giving him a disapproving stare as if he'd just done something terrible.

He took a deep breath and started pushing his way through the crowd towards the stairs. What had he said? What had he done?

He stopped and picked up the silver sandal lying on one side. His insides coiled. She'd been so anxious to get out of there she'd actually left a sandal behind.

He'd thought offering her the chance to move somewhere new and make a fresh start would be just what she needed—and just what she would want.

But he'd obviously got it wrong. Badly wrong.

Or maybe the thing he'd got wrong was that fact that he'd told her he loved her. He couldn't deny how he felt. But it was clear Anissa didn't feel the same way.

He reached the top of the stairs and stopped for a second as the hairs on the back of his neck prickled. Maybe she'd felt pressured by what he'd said. If Anissa didn't feel the same way, how must his declaration of love have felt?

Had he imagined the sparks and electricity between them—was he really that out of touch? He grabbed the banister to steady himself.

He'd been happy. He'd been caught up in the atmosphere of the night, the beauty of the woman in front of him and his own raw emotions.

He loved her. He loved her. He wanted her to be happy. He'd thought his offer of staying here and not worrying about training any more would have been a relief to her.

How wrong he'd been.

When she'd mentioned the other job he'd assumed

she'd been considering it. She'd just been so much brighter and happier since they'd reached New York.

But it seemed she hadn't quite realised that yet.

He hurried out into the foyer and glanced from side to side, the elegant silver sandal in his hand. Surely she couldn't have gone anywhere without it?

The irony gripped him. He'd called her Ice Princess, but the truth was she was his Cinderella.

And she'd slipped right through his grasp.

CHAPTER TEN

SHE'D PANICKED. SHE'D run straight out of the main entrance of the hotel into the snow-covered streets and flagged down the first taxi that she'd seen.

The cab driver had looked a little bewildered at the girl with one shoe, a silver purse hanging from her wrist, and a pile of skirts in her hands, but—being New York—he'd probably seen a whole lot more.

But when he'd asked her for an address her brain had frozen.

He gave a nod and started the cab, driving a few blocks and pulling over again. 'Okay, girl?' His question was quiet. There was concern on his face.

Her brain snapped back into focus. She knew what she must look like. He must be wondering if something had happened.

She nodded her head quickly. 'I'm sorry. I'm okay.' He raised his eyebrows a little and she nodded again. 'I promise.'

The kindness of strangers. It brought a tear to her eye. She wondered what else this taxi driver had seen over the years. She rattled off the first address that sprang to mind. Jules. The only other person she knew in New York. She thought about pulling out her phone and checking to see if Jules was in. But the truth was, whether Jules was in or not, she'd no place else she felt she could go.

If Jules wasn't in she could always just wait outside.

The taxi driver gave a nod and pulled back out into the traffic.

The city that never slept. There was never a truer word. Even though it was after midnight, the streets of New York were still busy. Lots of people were laughing and joking in the streets—it was almost just as busy as it had been during the day.

She started to say a silent prayer that Jules hadn't gone out for the evening. What bar had they met in before? Maybe Anissa should try there. She glanced down at the ballgown and pulled a face. She might just be a little overdressed for a bar.

The taxi pulled up outside Jules's apartment and Anissa thanked the driver and jumped out, her bare foot instantly coming into contact with the freezing ground as she limped to the doorway.

She winced and pressed Jules's buzzer. 'Please be in, please be in,' she repeated, hoping against hope it might have some magical effect.

Thankfully, as soon as she'd sounded the buzzer Jules answered the door. Her eyes swept up and down Anissa's length before she stepped outside and slid her arm around Anissa, ushering her in.

Anissa was embarrassed. She'd allowed the hem of Jules's beautiful gown to be caught in the dirty snow on the streets of New York.

'I didn't know where to go,' she gasped. 'I'm sorry for turning up so late.'

Jules's face was set firmly. She hurried Anissa across her living room and settled her on the sofa before sitting on the low table in front of her.

'What happened?'

Anissa couldn't help herself. She started babbling. 'Oh, the dress. I'm sorry. I didn't mean to get it dirty. But I lost a shoe on my way out and couldn't go back for it. I'll pay for any repairs.'

She was suddenly conscious of the fact she was back in Jules's living room. All around her was the gorgeous array of glittering dresses on headless mannequins. She gave a little shiver as she pulled the firm bodice of her dress away from her skin.

She'd practically ruined one of these beautiful dresses. Jules would be mad. She would be right to be mad. Something else Anissa had messed up.

Tears started to fall down her face. 'I'm sorry, lots of people asked about the dress. I told them who designed it. I told everyone who spoke to me.'

Jules shook her head and frowned, leaning over and putting her warm hand over Anissa's cold one. 'Stop it. Stop talking about the dress.' She picked up the tablet sitting on the table and spun it around. 'I know you told everyone I'm the designer. You've already hit the news websites.'

Anissa let out a gasp and pulled the tablet towards her. There she was, standing on the red carpet with Leo's arm around her waist. They were looking at each other and smiling as though there wasn't anyone else around them. As if they were actually in a private bubble all of their own.

They looked like a golden couple. And in Jules's stunning dress she looked like a princess.

Jules pointed to the headline: *'Billionaire's Date is Belle of the Ball'*.

She spoke carefully. 'You've done me a million fa-

vours by wearing my dress. But push that aside. What's
wrong, Anissa? What happened tonight? Are you hurt?'

Anissa's throat was tight. Hot tears spilled down her
cheeks and her whole body tensed. 'No. No. No one hurt
me.'

Jules watched her for a few seconds, eyeing her carefully before giving a little nod of acceptance. 'Okay, so
you're not hurt. So why have you turned up here…' she
looked down at the floor '…in the middle of the night
and missing a shoe?' Jules gave her head a little shake.
'What did Mr Wonderful do?'

Anissa had finally started to breathe again. Her head
was beginning to clear. She was here. She was in Jules's
house. She could stop. She could think.

'He told me he loved me and asked me to stay.' The
words just burst from her mouth and she dissolved into
tears again. This time it wasn't just a few tears streaming down her cheeks. This time it was all out sobbing.

After a few quiet seconds Jules moved from the table
and sat on the sofa next to Anissa, putting her arm around
her and letting her rest her head on Jules's shoulder while
she sobbed.

It was almost as if everything that had been bubbling
under the surface for so long had finally erupted. All the
pent-up frustrations about who she was, what she was
doing, and whether she'd be good enough again flowed
from her. Her feelings for Leo had just brought everything to the surface. After years of being driven by an
ambitious ex, she'd finally met someone who loved her
for who she was—not who she could be.

After a while Jules patted her back. When she spoke
her voice had an amused tone. 'Anissa, I'm trying to work
out why it's such a disaster that a gorgeous billionaire

has told you that he loves you, and asked you to stay in New York?'

'Don't say it like that,' Anissa pleaded, knowing exactly how ironic it sounded.

'How would you like me to say it?' asked Jules.

Anissa's phone buzzed again. It had buzzed almost continuously on the journey over here. She didn't even have to turn it over to know who it was.

She shook her head fiercely. 'I can't. I just can't. He told me that the gold medal was probably out of my reach. He told me to consider other plans. He wanted me to have a back-up plan. I'm not ready.'

Jules pulled back a little and gave her a look that was way beyond her young years.

'That's it,' she said succinctly.

Anissa wiped some tears away. 'What's it?'

Jules gave a nod of her head. 'That's what the issue is, Anissa. And now you have to ask yourself why.'

Anissa was thoroughly confused. 'What do you mean?'

Jules pushed herself up and walked through to the kitchen and switched on the coffee pot. She turned to face Anissa. 'You said you're not ready. That's the crux of the matter. Now, you have to ask yourself why. *Why* are you not ready? He hasn't said anything to you that you haven't already considered yourself.'

Anissa shivered, even though the room was warm. She wasn't sure she liked this line of questioning.

'Do you love him?' The question seemed to come out of the blue.

'I... I... I...' Anissa stumbled over the words.

Jules raised her eyebrows and walked back from the kitchen with a mug in either hand.

'Do you love him?' This time she was much firmer.

This time she didn't think, the answer just bubbled over. 'Of course I love him.'

There it was. How she felt. How she'd been feeling these last few days. She'd finally admitted it—she'd finally said it out loud.

Now it was real.

Jules eyebrows were still raised. 'And that,' she said as she waved the cups in the air, 'is why we need coffee.'

Four cups of coffee later the early morning light was streaming into the room. Jules was lying on the sofa, her eyelids heavy. But Anissa hadn't slept at all. She'd switched to hot water with lemon but every part of her body was still jangling.

The pale blue dress was now back on one of the mannequins. The bottom edges looked as if they had been dragged through a muddy puddle, and even from across the room Anissa could see that some of the sequins were hanging off.

She'd changed into a T-shirt and jeans belonging to Jules, along with a pair of thick socks and baseball boots.

Jules gave a groan and snuggled into one of the cushions on the sofa. She was obviously all talked out.

Even though Anissa had been drinking for hours, her throat still felt dry. Leo had told her that he loved her and she'd run away. He'd asked her to live with him and she'd practically bolted.

Instead of focusing on the fact she'd met a good, kind-hearted man who made her heart swell, she'd focused on her past. She'd focused on failure.

Her breathing stuttered and, as if in sympathy for Leo, the muscles in her legs and back ached.

The chronic, persistent and sometimes unbearable

ache she felt after skiing. The thing she'd ignored before her accident, and even more so after.

Her body telling her that she'd never reach the gold medal. Not now, not after she'd done so much damage. The truth was, even if she spent the next five years practising every day, she still wouldn't be able to match her previous skill and speed.

Her body had been telling her for a while—her brain just hadn't been listening.

'I'm never going to get a gold medal,' she breathed as she stared at the ice-cold New York street outside.

'What?' Jules rubbed her eyes. 'What did you say?'

'I'm never going to get a gold medal.' This time her words were more assured. 'I'm never going to be good enough to compete. I'm never going to reach the speed I need.'

It was the oddest sensation. Like self-discovery. Her brain had finally put the pieces together. But saying them out loud was like an affirmation. A confirmation to herself that this was real. She swayed, her legs instantly feeling like jelly. She bent down and put her head in her hands.

Within a few seconds she realised Jules had rolled herself off the sofa and come over next to her. Jules's warm hand closed over her own as they clutched her head. Her hair was still on top of her head. She couldn't even imagine what it looked like at this stage.

'I've been a fool,' she whispered as she lifted her head to meet Jules's weary gaze. 'I've been such a fool.'

Jules sighed and collapsed on the floor next to her. 'Okay, I'm too tired. And my phone has been buzzing all night. You're going to have to spell it out for me.'

Anissa nodded. Then stopped and shook her head instead. 'My head has been full of skiing and winning the championship for so long, it's like I just couldn't imagine anything else.' She brushed away one of the tears in her eyes. 'Leo brought me here to show me another world. He knew. He knew I'd probably never get back to professional skiing, but he was trying to tell me that there's so much more out there. He wanted me to see a whole other world.' She sat back on her heels. 'But I just wasn't listening,' she said sadly.

Jules screwed up her face. 'But your heart was listening. You told me that you loved him. Surely that's all you need to know.'

Anissa sat up straighter, her hands going automatically to her heart. The panic that had gripped her last night was starting again in a weird, different kind of way.

'I have to find Leo,' she said, pushing herself to her feet.

Jules squinted up at her. 'What?'

Anissa reached for her purse. 'I have to get back. I have to get back to Leo. I didn't tell him. I didn't even tell him that I love him too. What if he thinks I don't?'

Jules gave a smile. 'Does this mean I can finally get some sleep?'

Anissa reached over and gave her a huge hug. 'Jules, you're wonderful. You can definitely get some sleep. And you are the most fabulous, talented dress designer on the entire planet. Thank you for helping me out.'

Jules shook her head and stood up, dragging herself over to the sofa and flopping back down. 'Go.' She waved her arm.

'Go and tell your billionaire that you've finally worked things out and that you love him.' She laughed as she closed her eyes and pulled the cushion over her head. 'Please, do it now.'

Anissa nodded and headed straight to the door. She

could phone. He'd texted her for the first few hours after she'd left. But the phone didn't seem right. Not for now. Not for this.

She stepped out into the cold morning air. She had no jacket. She'd forgotten to ask Jules for a coat and the biting wind chilled her to the bone.

She waved her hand wildly, trying to flag down a cab. After a few minutes one appeared with its light on and slowed down. She climbed in and quickly recited Leo's address, settling back in the seat and praying her heart would stop thudding by the time she reached there.

New York had never looked so grey. Leo had finally stopped texting Anissa and just prayed she was safe. He hadn't slept a wink. He was still wearing last night's tux. Maybe she'd booked into some random hotel rather than come back here. Or maybe she'd jumped on a plane back to Mont Coeur—anything rather than see him again.

There was a click behind him and he spun around. Anissa stepped out of the penthouse elevator, her cheeks flushed pink. Her hair was still piled on her head in a lopsided kind of way. He could see remnants of last night's glitter on her cheeks, but she'd completely changed her clothes. She was wearing a rumpled T-shirt, jeans and baseball shoes and she was rubbing her arms frantically.

He couldn't stop himself. 'Where have you been?'

She stepped forward. 'I'm sorry. I'm sorry. I just didn't know… You took me unawares… I wasn't expecting… I mean… I just…' She couldn't seem to get the words out.

All he could feel was relief that she was actually here. Actually back in his apartment. After last night, he'd wondered if he'd ever see her again. And the thought of that, of never actually seeing Anissa again, had made him feel physically sick.

'Take a minute, Anissa.'

He wanted to reach over and put his arms around her. But he wasn't sure what she wanted. She might just be here to pick up her things and leave again, and that just tore his heart apart.

She stepped up right in front of him. She was trembling. Was it because she was cold or was it because of something else? All he could see was her wide pale blue eyes. Her skin was almost translucent.

Her cold hands reached out towards him. Her touch sent a pulse of electricity up his arm. But he still didn't want to move. He'd already got things so wrong. He didn't want to presume anything.

'You brought me here,' she started. She gestured to the world through the windows behind him. 'You brought me here to show me another world. One I'd never experienced before. I'd been so focused on skiing. It was everything.' She clutched her hands to her chest. 'My life. My passion. My heart. I couldn't think outside the skiing box. Not even when I was injured. Not even when I should have taken a step back to reassess.'

He was holding his breath. He wanted to hear what came next.

'You've shown me a whole other world, Leo. One with possibilities. The chance to work on the skiing committee is a big one. And if I'd still been in Mont Coeur, training every day, I would never have considered it—not for a second.'

She gave her head a shake and smiled a sad smile. 'I was so focused on winning a gold medal. I thought it was the only dream to have, the only goal to dream about. I couldn't see past that. And because I couldn't see past that, I've missed a whole life. I've missed a whole world.'

She pressed her lips together and met his gaze. 'You showed me something else, Leo. You showed me that someone can love me for being me. Not for being a potential gold-medal winner.' She pulled one of her hands back and put it on her heart. 'I've never had that before. I've never experienced it, and I didn't know it was possible.' She took a deep breath. 'I've never thought I was good enough.'

He opened his mouth to speak but hesitated when she shook her head. She gave a soft smile. 'I'm so sorry, Leo. I've been having doubts about myself for the last year. Something I didn't want to admit to, and was trying to totally ignore. I was taking painkillers constantly to try and deal with the agony I'd be in after training hard. I'd begun to accept it as normal, rather than take a deep breath and ask myself if it was right for me. Getting away from Mont Coeur and actually having a holiday was completely new for me.' She reached out to him again.

'And I know you've had so much going on. I understand how hard everything has been for you. Every day I've spent with you, I've realised just how much you mean to me. It doesn't matter that it's only been a few weeks. I've managed to get to twenty-eight years old without feeling like this. It scared me, Leo. It scared me. I'm sorry. I'm sorry I ran out last night.'

Now he wanted to breathe. Now he actually wanted to hope.

She touched his cheek as tears filled her eyes and her voice shook. 'I love you, Leo Baxter. I've never met anyone like you. You have the biggest heart in the world, and I want you to share it with me. I want you to share it with your family. I want you to know how lucky they are to have you. I want you to know that your parents would be proud of the man you've become. They couldn't have possibly hoped for any better.'

If he held his breath any longer he might fall over. This time he wasn't scared to reach out and touch her.

'When you ran away last night I thought I'd got everything wrong. I thought I'd imagined the connection we had. I thought I'd scared you off.'

She stepped closer and ran her fingers through his hair. 'You didn't imagine the connection, Leo. It's been there from the first second. I just couldn't let myself acknowledge it. I thought I only had room in my life for skiing, for reaching for that gold medal. I was wrong, Leo. I've never loved anyone before like this—that's why it's so scary.'

He chose his words carefully. 'Anissa, you can be anything you want to be. If you still want to pursue your dream of skiing, I'll support you completely.' And it was true. He'd be there for her whatever she decided to do.

She shook her head as she pressed her lips together for a second. 'I needed to get here, Leo. I needed to get to this place myself. I needed to realise what I was doing to my body and that I wasn't being realistic with my dreams.'

She couldn't hide more tears as she blinked. 'I can't pretend it hasn't been hard.'

He understood that. He knew that. But she gave another smile. 'You've helped me, more than you could ever know. Thanks to you I know there's something else out there.' She shook her head. 'I don't want to pursue my dream of skiing. But I would like to take up the offer from the Championship Skiing Committee. I'd like a chance to encourage others to realise their dreams.'

The excitement was in her eyes. He could see she'd actually found something to be passionate about.

'That sounds perfect.' He spoke cautiously, wondering what that meant for them.

She nodded slowly. 'But I only want to do it if we can be together. I don't want to be at the other side of the world from you. I love you, Leo. I want to be with you. If I take that job it will mean lots of travel, all over the US and overseas. But the truth is I don't really want us to be apart.'

His heart swelled in his chest. It was just what he wanted to hear. He pulled her towards him and put his lips on hers. She returned his kisses passionately, wrapping her arms around his neck. 'It's just as well, then, that I own a private jet and can take you, and follow you, to the ends of the earth. When you need to go overseas, I can come with you—if you want me to—and work from there. When you're in the US, we can base ourselves here, in New York. We can make this work, Anissa. I know we can.'

'I thought I'd been a fool,' she whispered. 'I thought I'd lost you.'

'Ditto,' he whispered, then he pulled back a little and laughed. Having Anissa back in his arms felt so right.

It was almost as if his head had finally started to clear. Realising he loved Anissa was just the starting point. 'I might have done something that would surprise you last night.'

She tilted her head to one side. 'What?'

'I phoned Sebastian again.' He stopped for a second and tried the words again. 'I phoned my brother.'

She pulled back, her eyes wide. 'You did?'

He nodded. 'I did.'

'What on earth did you say to him?'

'I told him I'd brought the woman I loved to New York

and I'd messed up. I told him that I'd asked her stay with me and she'd run away.'

'What did he say?' Anissa asked cautiously.

Leo gave an amused nod. 'I think it took him a few moments to get over the shock that I'd called—and that I'd told him all that.'

'And then?'

'And then he told me to take a deep breath. He said if I loved you, I had to give you space. I had to respect your decision. He said I should wait and let you come back to me—if you wanted to.'

Anissa looked a little surprised. 'He didn't tell you try a big gesture, or to hunt the city for me?'

Leo shook his head. 'No. Because that's exactly what I wanted to do. He told me I'd made the big gesture and I had to let love decide what happened next.'

She slid her arms around his waist. 'Wow. From a guy who hated you to a brother who gives advice.'

Leo nodded slowly as he looked out over New York. He sighed. 'I love this place. But I need to get to know Sebastian and Noemi. I don't want to be part of the jewellery business, but I need to find my place in my family. It scares me, Anissa. It scares me more than you can know.'

She gave his waist a squeeze. 'But I do get it, Leo. More than you can understand. I had to make a decision. I had to be brave. Twice. I had to decide to walk away from the only career I had known. And I had to decide to give my heart to someone.' She stood on tiptoe and whispered in his ear, 'And once you do it…it's not that hard. The thought is actually a lot scarier than the process.' She winked at him. 'And you've already done one.'

A slow smile came over him as a warm sensation swept over his body. She was right. He knew she was right. Exposing his heart to Anissa had been his first step. The first step to forming real relationships in his life. Maybe, with her help, he could take the next step.

He pulled her backwards with him and sat in one of the big chairs, pulling her onto his lap. 'The beauty of a private jet means that you can more or less go anywhere you want, anytime. So, if I asked the woman I love to come with me—to come back with me to Mont Coeur to meet my family—what would she say?'

Anissa wound her hands back around his neck as she settled in his lap. Her eyes were shining brightly. 'I would say try and stop me.'

And then she kissed him and made him forget about everything else.

* * * * *

UNMASKING
THE MAVERICK

TERESA SOUTHWICK

To the brave men and women of the United States military. Thank you for your service and sacrifice.

Chapter One

The poor kid from Prosperity, Texas, who hated fixing other people's trash for a living had come full circle.

On the upside, his father would be proud. But Brendan Tanner had a lot of mileage on him since those resentful teenage days. The Corps had a way of turning an ungrateful kid into a buttoned-up, battle-hardened marine. And it was the best thing that ever happened to him.

Now he was in Rust Creek Falls, Montana, fixing a broken toaster. He was living at a place called Sunshine Farm. After seeing something online about it being a welcome place to get a fresh start, he'd reached out to Luke Stockton, one of the owners, and the cowboy had invited him to stay as long as he wanted. The name made him smile, although the upward curving of his mouth felt a little rusty. In the last eighteen months there hadn't been much to smile about.

It disappeared when he heard a sudden high-pitched squeal. Those battle-hardened marine instincts kicked in and he automatically took a defensive stance, then realized the sound was a child's laughter. Slowly he released his breath. The reflexes were still sharp, but apparently so were the bad memories.

The kid in question burst through the open door of his temporary barn workshop and came to a stop in front of Brendan. The blond, blue-eyed little guy stared up at him and chewed on his index finger.

"Hey, buddy. Where's your mama? Did you go rogue?"

The kid babbled something that could have been a foreign language for all Brendan knew, then pointed to his tall rolling toolbox. It had belonged to his father, one of the few things he'd brought with him from Texas. When word got out that he was handy, he'd found a use for the tools. Something told him this kid could put them to use, too, but there would be hell to pay.

His next thought was all about heaven when the prettiest redhead he'd ever seen appeared in the workshop doorway.

"Jared! There you are, you little stinker." The reprimand was spoken with such affection that it wasn't a scolding at all. Then she smiled at Brendan. "Hi."

"Ma'am." He nodded and touched the brim of his Stetson. She was a little breathless, probably from running, but it was just about the sexiest thing he'd ever seen. "I wondered where his mom was."

"Oh, I'm not his mother. Aunt by marriage. My sister Fallon married Jamie Stockton, who was a widower, and she became a mom to his triplets—Jared, Henry and Kate."

Brendan watched her grab the kid when he made a move toward the toolbox. Instantly the boy started squirming to escape. If Brendan was in her arms, escape would be the last thing on his mind.

Then it sank in. Triplets. "There are two more like him?" he asked.

"Triple joy." She laughed and held on to the little wiggle worm. "Or triple trouble. It changes from moment to moment."

"Dat." Jared pointed a stubby little finger at a screwdriver sitting on the workbench. "Want dat."

The kid's determination increased his twisting to get free, but to her credit the redhead hung on. Brendan had trained in hand-to-hand combat in the Marines and wasn't sure he could have managed to wrangle the boy. He'd never been around kids, but even he knew giving this small human a sharp tool was a bad idea—no matter how determined he was to have it. He could offer to supervise, but there were too many ways for the situation to go sideways. Then he had an idea.

Underneath the workbench was a basket of broken toys. Eva Stockton, the wife of Luke, who owned Sunshine Farm, had given it to him. She'd said she kept them around for her niece and nephews and asked him to repair any he could. The kids were hard on them, she'd said, and after meeting Jared he understood what she meant.

He pulled the stash out into the open. "Maybe he'd like to look through these?"

"You're a lifesaver." The woman looked at him as if he'd hung the moon.

The lifesaver part was truer than she knew, Brendan thought. He'd saved lives, and buddies had saved his, too. They shared a bond unlike anything he'd ever known, the tight-knit family he'd never had. A brotherhood forged in battle. But a different sort of skirmish ensued when the redhead set little Jared on his feet. The toolbox was forgotten as he started in on the toys.

"Car!" Jared held one up that was missing a wheel. He squatted down and set it on the hard-packed clay floor and made the universal sound effect used by boys to simulate an engine revving.

"Here's to the short attention span of a two-and-a-half-year-old." The woman's eyes were big and blue and beautiful. The laughter shining there was really something special. "He hasn't seen those broken toys for so long they're like brand-new to him."

"I haven't had a chance to check them out and see if they're salvageable."

"Eva and Luke are keeping you busy?"

"Understatement. Fix a broken clothes dryer and suddenly you're a Jedi knight who can use the force to put Humpty Dumpty back together." He shrugged. "And they tell all their friends."

"So, do I call you Sir Jedi? Or do you have a name?"

He nearly winced. Obviously his social skills were as rusty as his smile. "Brendan Tanner."

She held out her hand. "Fiona O'Reilly."

He took her hand and something crackled up his arm, shocking the words right out of his head. He barely managed to mumble, "Nice to meet you."

While his brain was frozen, the rest of him was hot as a Texas sun on the hard-packed plains.

Before it turned awkward, Jared struck again. He'd emptied every last toy from the basket. Apparently the process of taking them out *was* playing with them and he was on to bigger and better things. Like the toolbox he'd temporarily forgotten. He opened a metal drawer, the one with various saw blades.

Without thinking it through, Brendan grabbed him up before he could touch anything and hurt himself. There was an instant screech of protest.

"I think they heard that in the next county." He looked at Fiona. "Sorry. Didn't mean to startle him, but those things are sharp."

"You have pretty good reflexes." Instead of being

upset, she looked impressed. The kid, however, was ticked off and held his arms out to her. She took him and ignored the loud grunts and the struggle to get back down. "No way, Jared. How come you don't know by now that I'm not a soft touch?"

Brendan begged to differ with her on that. She looked plenty soft to him, in all the right places. But he knew that was not what she meant. "I can't imagine herding two more like this one."

"That's why I'm here. Luke and Eva invited the family to dinner and I'm part of the reinforcements. Fallon has Henry. The last time I saw them he was chasing a chicken and she was hot on his heels. Jamie was keeping Kate from going headfirst into the horse's water trough. And I drew the short straw. We call him jackrabbit because he's so fast." She kissed his cheek and made smacking noises, getting a giggle out of the squirmy boy.

The sight of this woman with a child in her arms struck a chord deep inside Brendan. Her brightness flashed a light on the dark emptiness he carried around, the dusty place where he stored any hope of having a family.

"There you are." Luke Stockton walked into the workshop.

It was getting like Grand Central Station in here, Brendan thought. For some reason he didn't completely mind the invasion. He had liked Luke Stockton the first time they met and hadn't changed his mind since he'd been here at Sunshine Farm. His blue eyes projected honesty, integrity, and the deep tan was a result of hard outdoor work.

He shook hands with Brendan, then looked at Fiona and his nephew. "Your sister was getting worried. About you. And keeping up with Jared."

"Oh, please." Fiona rolled her eyes. "I'm onto this little man."

"I see you two have met," Luke said, glancing between her and Brendan.

"We introduced ourselves," she confirmed.

Luke took the squirming little boy, who was holding out his arms. Probably hoping this time he'd get put down. But Luke held him tight. "What are you up to, jackrabbit?"

"He's not happy," Fiona said. "Brendan wouldn't let him juggle the saw blades in his toolbox."

"You've got a mean streak," Luke teased.

"That's me. Making kids cry. It's a gift," Brendan said.

"Yeah. Speaking of gifts…" Luke looked at Fiona. "This guy can fix anything from a can opener to a car engine."

"So I heard." Fiona's eyes sparkled with amusement. "You're working him so hard the poor man hardly has time for anything else."

"Me?" Luke shook his head. "I just mentioned to a couple of people that he's got some skills repairing broken things. It's not my fault folks in Rust Creek Falls ran with it."

"So he should be flattered while working his fingers to the bone?" She folded her arms over her chest.

Luke lifted the wriggling kid above his head and got a snort of laughter out of him. "It's clear to any enterprising person that there's a need around here for this kind of service. I'm trying to talk him into opening a repair shop."

"And?"

Brendan noticed a questioning look in her eyes, along with something that might have been female interest. If he was right about that, the attraction was mutual. "And

I keep telling Luke that I will likely be gone in a few months."

"That's not a definite," the other man said. "I'm telling you there's money to be made and we need to spread the word."

"If there's one thing folks in Rust Creek Falls are good at, it's talking. It's almost a competitive sport around here," she joked.

"A business venture isn't the *only* reason to stick around." Luke glanced at Fiona, then back. "This is a close community with good people."

Brendan couldn't swear to it but he'd bet money that Fiona blushed.

All she said was, "This town has a charm, for sure."

And then another redhead appeared in the workshop doorway, holding an identical version of Jared. That must be Henry. And if the feather he was tightly clutching in his little fist was any indication, he'd caught up with that unfortunate chicken.

"See?" He held it up proudly.

"So the party is in here." This was Fallon Stockton.

Even if Brendan hadn't already met her, he would have guessed a sibling connection to Fiona just because of the coloring. She was pretty enough, but...she wasn't Fiona. And he was going to forget that thought had ever entered his mind.

"It is getting crowded in here," Luke agreed. "Also it's not a safe place to turn these little guys loose." Again he held up Jared, who squealed with delight.

"Eva sent me to find everyone. Dinner will be ready soon. We have to get the kids washed up," Fallon said.

"On it." Fiona took Jared. "Nice to meet you, Brendan."

"Likewise." Politely he touched the brim of his Stetson.

"You should join us for dinner," Luke said to him.

That caught him off guard. "I don't know…"

"Eva cooks enough to feed half of Rust Creek Falls. On top of that, Fiona brought her famous four-cheese macaroni dish and it is not to be missed."

"It's kind of last minute," he hedged.

"There's plenty of food," Fallon confirmed.

"Tell him, Fiona," Luke urged. "He hasn't lived until he's tried your homemade mac and cheese."

"I don't like to toot my own horn."

No one could accuse Brendan of picking up on social cues, but even he didn't miss the obvious matchmaking. Apparently neither did Fiona. The look on her face said she could cheerfully strangle Luke Stockton.

"I appreciate the offer," he said, "but I'm pretty busy here. I promised to have these things back in working order by tomorrow."

"Okay." Luke nodded. "If you change your mind, there will be a place set at the table for you."

"Thanks anyway."

A place at the table, he thought, watching them all walk away. A family thing. He hadn't experienced much of that in his life and it was probably better for everyone if he stayed away. And by "everyone" he meant Fiona. He'd seen the wary look on her face when he'd been invited. It was so different from her smile when he'd used a basket of broken toys to fix a toddler's tantrum. Damn it. He wanted to hang the moon for her again.

In battle it was an unwritten rule that you never left a man behind. But watching her leave made him feel as if someone was and he had a bad feeling that man was him.

At the house, Fiona made a dash for the bathroom to see just how bad she had looked for her meet and greet with the hunky new guy. Her worst suspicions were confirmed. The overall effect was almost as bad as if she'd been mud wrestling. Come to think of it, chasing after little Jared Stockton wasn't much different, but still...

Red hair had escaped her ponytail and hung around her face. The freckles on her nose, which she hated more than anything except the five extra pounds on her hips, were like dots begging to be connected. It's what happened when a girl didn't put on makeup because, hey, it was just family.

If the universe had given her a clue that she would meet the best-looking man in Montana, she would have made more of an effort to minimize her flaws. No wonder he'd turned down the dinner invitation. That and Luke throwing her at the poor man.

Now that she had a little distance from the power of his sex appeal, she could finally think straight. It was probably for the best that he hadn't come to dinner. The last time someone pushed her at a man, things ended badly. And that time it was public.

Fiona opened the bathroom door and nearly tripped over Jared, who was waiting for her. She picked him up. "Hey, bud, at least you love me."

"Wuv you." He put his hands on her cheeks and kissed her.

"You're a heartbreaker in training, that's what you are. Let's go help Aunt Eva and Uncle Luke get dinner on the table."

With the child in her arms, Fiona walked down the hall and found her way to the dining room. It was crawling with Stocktons. Altogether there were seven Stockton siblings, but only four were here. The oldest, Luke, sat at the head of the table next to his new wife, Eva Armstrong. Bella was a Jones now, married to her husband, Hudson. Daniel Stockton and his wife, Annie, had a preteen daughter, Janie. Last was Jamie, who was married to Fiona's sister Fallon.

The family had been split up after their folks died. In recent years they'd been coming back together, and these Sunday night dinners were important to all of them.

The dining room table was set for what looked like an army. Eva was directing everyone like a general executing a battle plan. The triplets were settled into booster chairs with Jamie and Fallon in between to oversee them. The other couples took their places, and Fiona was directed to one of the two empty seats at the end of the table. The Stocktons had one single male brother left and she had a bad feeling.

She sat next to the empty chair. "Is Bailey coming?"

Luke laughed at her question. "He was invited, of course, but politely declined."

"Politely?" His wife, Eva, sat at a right angle to him in the place closest to the kitchen. "I think he said something about preferring horses to people."

Bella sighed. "That's just it. We're not people. We're family."

"He's got some issues to work through." Jamie spooned peas onto Jared's and Kate's little plastic plates and passed the bowl to Fallon to serve Henry. "Give him time. He'll come around. When he meets the right woman."

Here we go, Fiona thought. She was a woman. She was nice. She was single and getting very close to the ripe old age of thirty. They'd better not ask why she wasn't married unless they wanted to unleash a redhead's legendary temper.

"So, who is the extra plate for, then?" Fallon asked.

"We have a guest staying in one of the cabins. Brendan Tanner," Eva explained. "He fixed our dryer and some other things here at Sunshine Farm. Luke invited him to dinner."

Just hearing his name made Fiona's stomach feel funny. Nervous and excited. In a "crushing on him" kind of way. It was time to shut down this topic. "He said he couldn't make it."

"I'm hoping he'll change his mind," Luke said. "The man saved us the cost of a new clothes dryer. The least we can do is feed him dinner." As if on cue, a knock on the front door interrupted him. "Come in."

A moment later Brendan Tanner walked inside and stopped cold when he saw everyone looking at him. "You didn't say the fifth infantry, third battalion would be here."

Funny, Fiona thought. She'd been thinking an army was coming, too, when she'd seen how many places were set at the table.

"Always room for one more." Luke waved him closer. "Sit there next to Fiona. Glad you changed your mind. We're ready for you."

Good for them, Fiona thought. She wasn't ready for this at all. And if the look on Tanner's face was anything to go by, he wasn't, either. But there was something in his green eyes when he looked at her, an intensity that made them glow. Heat pooled low in her belly and her hands started to shake when he walked over and sat down. She'd give him this—the man had courage.

And he showered, she thought. His damp, freshly combed hair was a clue, as was the fresh scent of soap that clung to his skin. He'd changed his clothes, too. The plaid snap-front shirt tucked into jeans highlighted his narrow hips and broad shoulders. Eye candy for sure.

And she'd been staring. *Oh, boy, say something bril-*

liant. She cleared her throat. "So, Brendan, what made you change your mind?"

"Macaroni and cheese."

"The one I made?" She was feeling a little tingly and flattered.

"Is there another one?"

"I don't think so."

He shrugged one of those broad shoulders. "It's one of my favorites. Box or scratch, count me in."

"I see." Her tingly feeling went up in smoke. "So any bozo could throw ingredients together and you'd be first in line."

"I— That's not exactly what I meant—"

She grinned. "Just kidding. But seriously. If the dish I made for this dinner doesn't bring tears to your eyes then something is very wrong with your taste buds."

He smiled, and the power of the look enveloped her in a sort of golden haze. It was a little like floating close to the sun all by herself. Bright and quiet—

She suddenly realized how quiet this room was in spite of the large group around the table. They were all staring at her and Tanner. She'd once been the center of attention at a social gathering, and the horrible memory had humiliation pouring through her now as it had then. That time it was about a man, too.

She felt as if she was living out a comedy sketch. In a noisy room when you said something embarrassing at the same moment everyone went silent and heard you. This was like that. Even the triplets, who could usually be counted on for sounds in a pitch only dogs could hear, were mirroring the adults around them and staring.

You could cut the awkwardness with a butter knife. Poor Mr. Tanner looked as if he wanted the earth to swallow him whole. She had to do something.

"I'm starving. Let's get the food going." Fiona started to grab her macaroni casserole, but it was as big as the state of Rhode Island. Instantly Brendan reached out and lifted it for her. She put some on her plate and his.

"Thanks."

"You're welcome."

As if a switch had been flipped, everyone was taking food and passing platters around. Attention had been successfully diverted away from them.

Her relief was a little premature because when everyone had filled their plates it got quiet again. She said the first thing that popped into her mind. "So, Brendan, where did you learn to fix things?"

He finished chewing and swallowed before answering. "My dad taught me."

"He must be very proud of you," Fiona said.

"He was. He passed away not too long ago."

"I'm sorry." The words were automatic and felt so inadequate when a sort of sad, haunted look slipped into his eyes.

"Thanks."

"I haven't seen anything that Brendan can't repair," Luke said. "Your dad must have been a good teacher, and the skill he gave you is invaluable."

Brendan looked thoughtful. "Funny you should say that. We didn't have much, but dad's knack for patching up what people threw out or paid him to fix put food on the table."

"An honest living," one of the men said.

"I suppose." He looked down at the full plate of food in front of him. "Necessity was the mother I didn't have."

It was like a curiosity bomb went off in Fiona's head. Follow-up questions exploded in her mind. But one of the triplets—Jared—made a bomb of his own and Fallon excused herself to change him.

The moment for interrogation passed when Hudson started talking to Brendan about horses. In Rust Creek Falls, that was like guys discussing cars anywhere else. It turned out that Brendan had worked on ranches in Texas for extra money. Was there anything he couldn't do?

That wasn't something she was going to ask. The less she knew about Brendan Tanner the better. She would bet he had a sad story, one that would engage her emotions. But he was a stranger and by his own admission was only in town temporarily. Matchmakers could throw them together until hell wouldn't have it but they couldn't make her play along.

Not again.

Chapter Two

Last night's dinner ranked up there as one of the best meals Brendan ever had. He'd eaten enough to feed a whole platoon. The Stocktons were friendly and caring folks who opened their farm to a stranger looking for a fresh start and they kept on giving. He was grateful for that. If not for Fiona O'Reilly, he could check off every box of a perfect evening.

It was bad enough that she made the best macaroni and cheese he'd ever tasted, but she was also the sexiest mac-and-cheese maker he'd ever met. Her eyes were beautiful. That curvy body had him itching to touch her. And her smile promised heaven at the same time it sent him to hell. All night.

When he hadn't tossed and turned from thinking about her, he'd been dreaming about having her in his bed. She was whip smart and wickedly funny, which was an irresistible combination. It meant danger up ahead, but only if he chose to go down that road. All he had to do was take a detour and avoid her.

That took care of his conscious mind. With luck the warning would filter down to his subconscious and keep her out of his dreams. He was a tumbleweed and she had deep roots here in Montana. Smart money was on sticking to his plan: get back in shape and reenlist in the Marine Corps where he belonged.

After an early morning run and workout, he went to the barn. Sunshine Farm made no demands on its guests but Brendan hated feeling useless and had gotten in the habit of helping feed the stock every morning. Today was no exception. He walked into the stable and grabbed a pitchfork to help spread hay for the horses.

Luke walked over and jammed his own long-handled tool into the bale. "Morning."

"Back at you."

"Glad you decided to join us for dinner last night. Any regrets?"

A few. None of which he'd talk about. "Best meal I've had in a long time."

"Did I lie about the macaroni and cheese?"

"No." Last night he'd been full and had still taken another helping. Eating for pleasure, which included the pleasure of rubbing elbows with the lady who'd made it.

"So, what do you think of Fiona?"

What did he think? Brendan was pretty sure that he was thinking about her more than he should be, and in ways that he didn't want to. "I think she makes a mean macaroni."

"Seriously? That's it?"

"What else?" He sighed. "She seems nice."

"I think she's interested in you," Luke commented. "Looked to me like there was a sparkle in her eyes when she stole glances at you."

She was stealing glances at him? That didn't suck. Then he shook his head. "You're imagining things."

"Nope. Eva saw it, too."

"You talked to your wife about this?"

"We talk about everything. She's my best friend, and then some," Luke said. "Besides, in Rust Creek Falls, talking and spreading news is how we roll."

He remembered Fiona saying something like that. "I think you're both imagining things."

"I disagree."

"For the sake of argument, let's say you're right. The question is, why me? I'm boring."

"You're new in town and single. And—don't take this the wrong way—but you're not a bad-looking guy."

"Stop. I'm blushing." The corners of his mouth curved up.

Luke laughed. "And Fiona is single, too."

"A woman who looks like her must have men lined up around the block."

"Not so much."

Brendan stuck his pitchfork in the bale of hay and leaned on it as he looked at the other man. "Why?"

"You'll have to ask her that."

No, he wouldn't be asking her anything, because it was unlikely there would be an opportunity to do that. "None of my business."

"That could change."

He grabbed the tool again, then forked up some hay and spread it in a nearby stall. "I don't think so."

"Time will tell."

After that the two of them worked in silence until all the horses were taken care of. Brendan knew from being on ranches in Texas that these animals had small stomachs relative to their size and needed to be fed two to three times a day to maintain their weight. He made it a point to be around when that happened.

"Any other chores I can help with?" he asked.

Luke didn't miss a beat before saying, "You can give

serious consideration to opening a repair business here at Sunshine Farm."

"You're persistent. I'll give you that."

His friend smiled. "There is something. In a couple of days my brother Jamie is rounding up cattle from their summer grazing spot in the hills and bringing them back for the winter. I'm giving him a hand but he could use another man. You game? He'd be appreciative."

"Glad to."

"Good. Thanks."

"Least I can do." Brendan sincerely meant that. He was grateful to be here and wanted to give back. There was something about this sunshine-yellow barn that brightened the dark places inside him.

Luke left shortly after that and Brendan went to his temporary shop in the barn. On the worktable was a food processor he'd started to take apart yesterday, before impulsively giving in to Luke's dinner invitation. The lady who dropped it off was annoyed that it crapped out right after the warranty was up. She didn't give the thing much of a chance at a second life and told him not to waste too much time trying. The thing was, after his morning workout he had nothing but time.

He removed a couple of small screws to separate the outer casing from the motor in order to assess the problem. Just as he was pulling it apart, his cell phone rang. He tapped the answer icon.

"Hello."

"Hey, it's Fiona O'Reilly."

"Oh. Hi." His voice sounded rusty but he resisted the urge to clear his throat.

"Hi." She hesitated a moment. "How are you?"

"Fine," he lied. Hearing her voice brought back visions

of her red hair and the teasing smile that had tension curling in his gut. "You?"

"Great." Her voice sounded rusty, too, but she cleared her throat. "So, dinner last night was good."

"Yeah. I'm not used to a spread like that."

"If you stick around long enough, the calories will catch up to you." She laughed ruefully. "I carry the proof of that on my hips."

In his opinion her hips were perfect, along with the rest of her. But saying so seemed out of line. "I added an extra couple of miles to my morning run."

"Speaking of running," she said, "last night you disappeared after clearing the table and just before dessert. A less secure woman might think you were trying to get away from her."

He had been, but not for the reason she probably thought. She was equal parts temptation and complication. Marines believed retreat wasn't an option but he'd made an exception for her. Because he'd also been trained in survival.

"If I'd stayed any longer, I'd have had another helping of everything and that would've just been embarrassing."

"Yeah. Eva outdid herself. She does the baking at Daisy's Donuts, but she's an all-around outstanding cook, too."

"I found that out." He waited for her to say something and when there was silence, he thought he'd lost her. "Fiona?"

"I'm here." She cleared her throat again. "I have something to ask you."

He frowned. Was it something he'd said at dinner? His remark about necessity being the mother he never had was one he wanted back in a big way. Bracing himself, he said, "Okay."

"I was wondering if you could bring your fix-anything

reputation out for a spin to my place and look at the tractor here on the ranch."

Part of him wanted to say "no way," but another part was ready to get there as fast as he could. Still, he was a civilian, a guest here, and that meant he needed to be especially polite to everyone because he owed the Stocktons.

"Look, Fiona, I don't know if I'm the right guy—"

"Just a quick look. My dad usually can repair the ranch machinery but he's stumped. I've called a repair shop in Kalispell but they can't send someone for close to a week. It's already October and winter is coming. There are time and weather-sensitive projects pending. You'd really be doing me a favor if you could swing by."

That is a really bad idea, he thought. "I don't know if that's possible…" He let the words hang there, hoping she'd bail him out.

After several moments, she sighed. "That's okay. It was just a thought. Apparently Luke mentioned to my father that you were handy with mechanical stuff and Dad asked me to call. But don't worry about it. We'll make do. Thanks anyway. I know you're really busy."

The disappointment in her voice grabbed him and wouldn't let go. It felt like he'd just turned his back on a helpless kitten. Damn, hell and crap. "I'm not that busy. I'll give it a look."

"Really? I appreciate it so much. Thanks."

He got directions, said he'd be right over, then disconnected the call and saved her number to his phone, shaking his head and muttering to himself. Suddenly Fiona O'Reilly had become his business and it ticked him off that Luke had been so right, so soon.

Fiona waited for Mr. Fix-it on the front porch. The interior of the O'Reilly family's rambling ranch house wasn't big enough for her and the nerves jumping around inside her. She hadn't expected to see him at all and definitely not this soon. It made her wonder if fate was taking a page from Luke Stockton's matchmaking book or just having a laugh at her expense.

She saw a black F-150 truck turn off the main road and head toward the house. That was a cue for the nerves to stop the jumping jacks, pull together and form a knot in her stomach. Why was she being such a twit? He was just another guy and didn't even want to be here. She'd practically twisted his arm and he was simply doing it as a favor because she'd played the "Dad asked me to call you" card. Paddy O'Reilly would survive if Brendan had said no. But Brendan didn't know that and now she had to see him.

The truck stopped in front of her and she noticed his Texas license plate in a United States Marine Corps frame. Pulling her denim jacket tighter against the chilly north wind, she left the porch to meet him as he exited the truck. Then he grabbed a red toolbox from the rear bed.

"Hey, thanks for coming."

"No problem." Politely he touched the brim of his Stetson. "If you'll point me in the right direction, I'll take a look at the tractor."

"Can I get you a cup of coffee or anything? I've got an extra to-go mug. My father and brothers, Ronan and Keegan, use them all the time." She was babbling and he was letting her. It wasn't easy but she stopped talking.

"No coffee. Thanks anyway."

"Okay. The tractor is parked in the shed down there next to the stable."

"This is a nice spread," he said as they walked. "I saw the sign as I drove in. Rusty Bucket Ranch. Interesting name."

"Kind of whimsical but down to earth." She smiled up at him. "My ancestors emigrated from Ireland. They made their living from the land and wanted to do that in America. So they came West and found this property. After buying it, as the tale goes, they had nothing left but a rusty bucket. The name stuck."

"And they prospered."

"Yeah. We have all this." She gazed from the white, split rail corral fence and stable to the other ranch buildings and the barn her brothers had converted into their living space. "And a tractor that won't start."

"Let's see what we can do to change that." He followed her into the shed.

"You can set your toolbox on the worktable there." She went to the other end and opened the doors to give him more light, then came back. Her breath caught when she saw that he'd removed his long-sleeved flannel shirt. The olive green T-shirt he wore under it was snug and fit him like a second skin that highlighted every luscious muscle.

She swallowed, then said, "So, here she is. Sorry about the tool explosion there. My dad left all his stuff out. He was going to take another look at it. Just between you, me and the goats, that would involve less looking and a lot more colorful language. When he's working on this tractor, the words run more to the four-letter variety."

While she nattered on, he'd opened the side panel to inspect the inside. Without looking up, he said, "What about you?"

"Oh, I've been known to swear, but only when necessary. And always in a ladylike way." She heard him chuckle and that brought a smile to her face. Resting her back against the workbench, she settled in to keep him company. Hand him tools. Admire the way his back muscles moved and bunched under that snug shirt. Check out his world-class butt in the worn jeans. "And I guess I also have a way with words that are more than four letters."

"How's that?" He didn't look up but kept poking around in the tractor engine.

"I write freelance articles about ranch life for farm and outdoor magazines."

"What kind of articles?"

"A recent one was about recycling bent nails, rusty hinges and old bottles. A rancher's motto is 'Use it up, wear it out, make it do or do without.'"

"I know all about that," he said wryly.

She remembered him saying he'd grown up making do. "I'm working on an article now about preparing for the winter. Cold weather in Montana isn't for sissies."

"I bet."

"So, between my writing job and chores on the ranch, I keep pretty busy."

"Sounds like it. A good life."

"It is. I love what I do."

"You're lucky."

She couldn't see his expression but there was a wistful tone in his voice. Since he had his head buried in the engine, this might be a good time to ask some of the questions that had been rolling around in her mind when she couldn't sleep last night.

She'd hoped he would open up a little while ago when she called, but he didn't. Maybe he would now. What was the worst that could happen? He'd take his tools and go home? She was willing to risk it.

"So, dinner last night was awkward. Did you notice how we got paired off?"

"Yup." He still didn't look at her. "This morning when I was helping with chores, Luke asked what I thought about you."

"No. Really? What did you say?" That was unexpected.

"I told him you make a mean macaroni."

And? Her heart skipped a beat waiting for…what? Didn't matter because he didn't come through with more. "At least you didn't say *I* was mean."

"Actually, I said you seem nice."

"I think I am. But Luke was probably just making polite conversation. Not necessarily matchmaking."

"There's more. He underlined the fact that you're single and I'm single."

"And?" she prompted.

"And I asked him why you're still single."

"What did he say?"

"That I should ask you. So, why are you still single?"

"Because I'm not married," she said.

"Smart-ass. So why aren't you married?"

If that question had come up at dinner last night she would have been angry and defensive. With so many people watching her reaction, it would have felt too much like the public way she'd found out the man she'd expected a proposal from had cheated on her and gotten a girl pregnant. But now they were alone, and Brendan wasn't even looking at her, so it felt like the solitude of the confessional.

"So many reasons for being single," she started. "I'm too old—pushing thirty, a spinster by Old West standards. Not thin enough. Men seem to like stick women who have to run around in the shower to get wet. On top of that there are no men here in Rust Creek Falls—"

"Don't look now but—" Without turning he lifted a greasy hand. "Man. Says so right on my driver's license."

"Okay. That last one deserves some context. I grew up in Rust Creek Falls. Spent my whole life here and most of the guys have, too. They're friends of Ronan and

Keegan and, by extension, like my brothers. So…ew. It's too weird. That makes meeting men a challenge."

"Okay. I respect your honesty." He glanced over his shoulder. "Luke was just doing his part, then."

"Exactly." She beamed at him. "Look at you paying attention and participating in the conversation."

"I've been told I'm too quiet. So I've been making an effort since I got out."

By "out" she assumed he meant leaving the military. Since he was doing his best to take part, she'd give him an opportunity to share. Maybe the fact that he was elbow-deep in a tractor engine would help.

"I noticed your license plate holder. So you were a marine?"

"Yup. From Prosperity, Texas." He picked up a tool from the workbench beside him. "I loved the Corps. It was a good career."

She could hear respect, reverence and regret in his tone. And, frankly, he sounded a little lost. "Why did you leave, then?"

"My dad got sick. Cancer. I came home to be with him."

"That must have been a difficult time. I bet you miss him."

His movements stilled for a moment. "Yeah."

Fiona knew about Luke and Eva's plan to offer a stay at Sunshine Farm to someone going through a hard time in order to pay their happiness and good luck forward. They were always looking for someone in need of a fresh start. With these bits of information Brendan had revealed, she could see why they'd opened their arms to him. "So you're trying to figure out what to be when you grow up?"

He didn't answer but straightened from his trouble-shooting position over the engine and climbed up on the tractor. The key was in the ignition and he turned it. Instantly the engine rumbled to life. He nodded. Anyone else would have pumped their arm or woo-hooed in triumph. A victory boot scoot wouldn't be out of the question, either. But not this man. His reaction was quiet satisfaction.

He turned off the machine and climbed down. "Mission accomplished."

"What did you do?"

"There were some wires way down in the belly, hard to see, right next to the housing for—"

She held up a hand to stop him. "My head will explode if you say one more word."

"Okay." He grinned as he grabbed a rag and wiped the worst of the grease off his hands.

The look was so darn cute it liquefied her brain cells. That's when she realized talking to him without eye contact was much easier. *Pull it together, Fiona*, she told herself. "If my dad wants to know what you did I'll just have him call you."

"Okay."

"Seriously, though, thank you so much. Come on up to the house and I'll give you a check for your work. What do I owe you?"

Without missing a beat he said, "Dinner."

That surprised her. This was business and usually that involved taking payment for one's work. So maybe she'd misunderstood. "I'd be happy to buy you dinner, but—"

He shook his head. "A gentleman would never let a lady pay. I want to buy you dinner."

She almost blurted out, "Shut the front door," but managed to hold back. "Let me get this straight. You fixed my dad's tractor and want to take me to dinner as payment?"

"Yes. Tomorrow night. On one condition."

"What?" she asked, a little suspicious now.

He grabbed his flannel shirt, slung it over his broad shoulder by one finger and met her gaze. "Just you and me. No family."

He wanted to be alone with her? *Pinch me*, she thought. This had to be a dream. A handsome man, single and sexy, was asking her out to dinner? This was shocking. She'd been so sure he was running away from her last night.

"Fiona?"

"Oh. Right." She smiled. "I'd like that very much."

"Then I'll pick you up at six thirty. Is that okay?"

Heck, yes. But all she said was, "That would be fine." What in the world was she going to wear?

Chapter Three

What had he been thinking?

"Tanner, you're an idiot. Asking the woman to dinner. In payment for services rendered, no less." And now he was talking to himself. The downward spiral into hell was picking up speed and momentum.

His father must be turning over in his grave about this. He could just hear it. *That's no way to make a living. Since when do we not take money for our work?*

Since the woman he did the work for looked like Fiona. That smile... When the tractor engine sputtered to life, she'd looked at him again as if he'd hung the moon. A man could get used to that.

"Knock, knock."

Brendan turned away from his workbench and saw an older woman standing in the doorway. She was probably in her sixties, not very tall and had shoulder-length silver hair. There was spitfire in her eyes and a blender in her arms.

She moved closer and looked up at him. "Are you Brendan Tanner?"

"Yes, ma'am."

She held out her hand. "Edna Halstead."

"Nice to meet you."

"Same here. Luke Stockton says you can fix anything."

"I wouldn't say that, but I'm pretty good at repairs." He nodded at the small appliance she was holding. "Having trouble with that?"

"Blasted thing just quit. They don't make things like they used to. It's practically new."

"That's always the way. I'll see what I can do."

She handed it over. "Just when I got my husband to drink protein shakes, too."

"I'm guessing he'd be just as happy if I couldn't fix this." He put the base and pitcher on the workbench then looked back at her still staring at him. "Was there something else?"

"Mind looking at it now? I'd rather not make another trip out here. Unless you're too busy…"

"No, ma'am."

"Good. I wouldn't expect it would take long. It isn't the space station. If it's a goner, I expect you'll know that right away."

"Yeah." He picked up a small screwdriver to take apart the base.

"I don't expect a lifetime warranty," she said. "Still, you should get a little more time out of something."

"Yes, ma'am."

"It's not expensive to get another one, but just on general principle I don't want to do that."

"No, ma'am." He checked out all the connections and the cord, then cleaned and tightened anything that looked to be loose while the woman chattered away.

"The thing is, my husband, J.T., and I are retired and on a fixed income, so we have a budget."

"Understood."

"Are you military, Mr. Tanner?"

"Was." And he missed it, even more after losing his dad. He missed his brothers. Missed doing work that was important. Now he had no mission, no focus except to be in the best possible physical shape for reenlisting.

"What branch of the service?" Her eyes glittered with interest.

"Marine Corps."

"*Semper fi.* Your service is much appreciated and welcome home."

"Thank you." He stopped working and met her gaze. "Were you in the military?"

She shook her head. "Only by marriage. J.T. was a marine."

"Vietnam?"

"Did my age give it away?" she teased.

"No, ma'am. What is it they say? Fifty is the new forty?"

She laughed. "I'm a little north of that. Almost seventy. And you know it."

"Doesn't show. And what I know is a lot of service members who served their country during that conflict were never properly welcomed home. That wasn't right."

"No." Her mouth pulled tight for a moment. "Since then folks have learned to separate service to country from politics. Hopefully that will never happen again. Some make the ultimate sacrifice. Others live with physical disabilities."

Something in her expression said she knew about that. "Your husband?"

"He lost a leg—above the knee."

"Sorry to hear that, ma'am."

"Stop calling me that. 'Ma'am' makes me feel like I lived through the Revolutionary War. Edna, Ed or Eddie will do."

"Yes, ma—" He saw her glare and stopped. "Eddie."

"Good choice." She grinned. "And don't be feeling sorry for J.T. He's taken it in stride, if you'll pardon the pun. He's one tough marine. The few—"

"The proud. The Marines," he finished.

"Oorah."

He closed up the blender base. "There's no real obvious sign of trouble. I tightened a few loose wires and made sure the rest was shipshape. Let's plug it in and see."

"Sure do hope you're as good as Luke claims."

"Here goes." He saw her cross her fingers.

He plugged in the blender and with one last look at her he pushed a button. The thing came to life and the woman smiled her appreciation.

"Looks like you're back in the protein shake business," he told her. "Hope your husband is happy, too."

"He'd rather have his bacon, eggs and fried potatoes. But we have a deal. A healthy breakfast earns a scoop of ice cream after dinner."

"Seems fair."

"He doesn't think so but we both know who the commanding officer is."

"Skipper." Brendan saluted. "Only an idiot would mix it up in a skirmish like that."

"Speaking of idiots…" There was a gleam in her eyes. "What woman did you ask to dinner?"

He froze. "What?"

"You were mumbling to yourself about it when I came in."

"You heard that?" he asked.

"It's a popular misconception that all old people are hard of hearing. For the record, there's nothing wrong with my ears. You apparently are having second thoughts about asking a woman to dinner. So I'd like to know what woman we're talking about and I can tell you whether or not you're right about being an idiot."

He already knew he was. He momentarily toyed with the idea of saying *we* weren't talking about anything, but something told him Eddie Halstead would have a big problem with that response.

"I fixed a tractor at the Rusty Bucket Ranch earlier today and—"

"Fiona O'Reilly." It took her all of a second and a half to put it together.

"How did you know?"

"You don't seem the type to hit on a married woman. Her sisters, Fallon and Brenna, are. To Jamie Stockton and Travis Dalton respectively." She nodded firmly. "Since Fiona is the last single O'Reilly daughter and lives on the Rusty Bucket Ranch, she must be the woman in question."

"You're not wrong."

"And you're not an idiot," she said. "Why would you think so? She's beautiful, smart and dependable."

"It's complicated."

"Bravo Sierra," she snapped, using marine slang for BS. "That just means you don't want to talk about it."

She was dead-on about that. "Look, if it's all the same to you—"

"Eddie Halstead." Luke walked in and gave the older woman a big hug. "I saw your car outside and had to come and say hello."

"Good to see you, Luke." She glanced at Brendan. "You were right about him. He fixed my blender."

"So, J.T. will be back in the business of drinking his breakfast," the rancher guessed.

"A shake is healthier than bacon and eggs," she said stubbornly. "Especially if he's going to keep up with his chores."

"Eva would agree with that."

"And my stubborn man isn't getting any younger. He's got arthritis in his hands and one good leg. These days, climbing on a ladder is like a combat mission." She looked from Brendan to Luke. "He's pretty handy but I don't like him on a ladder. Ladder fall figures increase with age and physical condition. The man is sixty-eight years old, although you wouldn't know it to look at him. Don't tell him I said that. The point is, he's too old to be on a ladder even if he had two good legs. Gonna make putting up Halloween decorations a challenge this year."

"I'd be happy to help out." Brendan looked at her. "Say the word and I'll swing by."

"Come to think of it," she said as she tapped her lip. "The refrigerator is making a funny noise."

"Make a list," he said.

"I would sure appreciate it. The thing is, J.T.'s proud, if you get my drift."

"Sure do," Brendan said. "But if he gives you any trouble, just tell him it's one marine helping out a brother."

"I don't want to take up your time," she said.

"He's got plenty to spare," Luke interjected.

"Seems so," Eddie said. "He just fixed the O'Reilly's tractor and instead of taking money he's taking Fiona out to dinner."

"Well, well." Luke grinned. "All because of a house call."

"Marines work fast," the older woman said.

Luke snapped his fingers. "I just had an idea. You could expand the repair shop and go mobile with it. For the things people can't drop off."

"Now why would I want to do that?" Brendan asked.

"Because making money is a good thing," Eddie said.

"Unless you ask all of your customers to dinner. Then you're flirting with a negative cash flow."

"Understood," Brendan told her. "But that's not what I meant. I don't want to make long-term plans."

"How's that?" she asked.

"Because I'm only here temporarily."

"Why?" she asked. "You have somewhere better to be?"

That's what he was here to figure out.

No matter how many times she reminded herself that Brendan wasn't staying permanently, Fiona couldn't tamp down her excitement to see him. Telling herself this wasn't a date didn't help, either. For some reason it was how he was taking payment for fixing the tractor.

And that was where her thought process went off the rails. He wouldn't accept money but wanted to take her to dinner. Maybe he wanted more than that, but she didn't think so. If that didn't go to a girl's head, she was the Queen of England. The logical conclusion was that he wanted to see her. Alone. Without family.

And she was stoked.

She'd even bought a new dress—a hunter green, long-sleeved knit that minimized her curves even as it hugged them. A contradiction that paralleled the coming social occasion she refused to call a date. The dress's hem teased the top of her new low-heeled, knee-high black leather boots. They were a splurge, but when she got paid for her latest article, her budget would be just fine. Tonight it was important to look like a woman, not a ranch hand.

She checked out her appearance in the full-length, free-standing mirror in her bedroom, the one she used to share with Fallon and Brenna. There were times, like now, when she missed her sisters being around to tell her whether or not the neckline of this dress was too plain and begged for jewelry. If her hair was too curly, too straight or just right. Did her newly perfected smoky eye make her look like a hooker?

Brenna would always flop on the bed and give her two cents. *You look too prudish. Lower the neckline, shorten the skirt. Show more skin. A little cleavage couldn't hurt.*

Fiona turned from side to side, studying the way the soft material clung to her breasts. "Make him wonder about what he can't see," she told her reflection.

The first time they met she'd looked like a pig wrestler. Yesterday she'd had time to brush her hair and put on some tinted sunscreen along with sheer lip gloss. Tonight she was going for something between demure and dynamite. Just to show him she could. If only her sisters were here to confirm that she'd pulled it off.

Fiona glanced at the clock beside her bed and her heart skipped a beat. He would be here soon. There was still time to tone it down if her mother thought she'd gone too far.

Grabbing her heavy wool shawl and black clutch purse, she headed downstairs, where Maureen O'Reilly was fixing dinner. The kitchen was a big, open room with lots of counter space, a farm sink and a big round oak table with eight chairs. Years ago, when all of them had been under one roof, they'd totaled seven.

Now, Fallon and Brenna were happily married and sharing living space with their respective husbands. Her older brothers, Ronan and Keegan, had bachelor quarters here on the ranch where they worked. The two showed no sign of settling down and it worked for them. Her mother was thrilled to have them close by.

Maureen was checking something in the oven, then straightened and turned when she heard Fiona's footsteps on the wood floor. "Hey, sweetie. You look beautiful. That emergency shopping trip yesterday afternoon really paid off."

Fiona looked down at the slightly flared skirt and smoothed her palms over her hips. Unlike Fallon and Brenna, their mother might sugarcoat her opinion.

"You don't think it's too—"

"It's not *too* anything." She set pot holders on the counter beside the pot simmering on the stove. "Not too dressy, just casual enough."

That had been the challenge since Fiona didn't know where they were going to dinner. "Really?"

"Yes."

The back door opened and in walked her tall, handsome, brown-haired, blue-eyed brothers. Women were drawn to them like dieters to donuts. And both stopped dead in their tracks when they saw her.

Ronan, the oldest, whistled. "Look at you. Got a hot date?"

Brendan was hot, but this wasn't technically a date. "I'm going out."

"With who?" Keegan asked.

"No one you know," she hedged.

"How do you know who we know?" her oldest brother challenged her.

Instead of answering, Fiona blew out a breath and met her mother's gaze. "Why are they here?"

"It's pot roast night," Keegan said, as if that explained why these two, who often fended for themselves, had shown up for dinner.

"So what?" She knew she sounded like a ten-year-old, but it couldn't be helped. The knuckleheads would not help get her to a Zen place before Brendan showed up. In fact, they'd do just the opposite. "Mom could fix pheasant under glass and the two of you couldn't be counted on to put in an appearance."

"Are we unreliable?" Ronan asked his mother.

"Yes."

He walked over and affectionately slid his arm across her shoulders. "Am I still your favorite?"

"I do not have favorites where my children are concerned. I can, however, confirm that you are still the oldest of five."

"And Fiona is the oldest girl." There was a teasing gleam in Keegan's eyes that women seemed to find adorable, if Rust Creek Falls gossip was anything to go by. "She's the only one of my sisters still here for dinner. Oh, wait, she's wearing a dress. The world has gone crazy."

"I've changed my mind—" she started to say before Keegan interrupted her.

"Along with your tomboy look."

"It's official," she said. "Brenna isn't the dramatic one. You are."

"I'm Irish." Keegan grinned. He was awfully cute when he did that. "Drama is a badge of honor."

"And so is being good with words," Ronan pointed out. "Which you are, sis. You've verbally danced around the question of who you are going out with. Now, fess up. Who did you put on a pretty new dress for tonight?"

"What are you? The fashion police? You don't know that it's new." Since when did he get hit with the observant stick?

"You're deflecting again," he countered. "This could be serious."

"Or, to say it a different way," Keegan chimed in, "what poor, unsuspecting guy are you trying to snag?"

"That's ridiculous," she countered.

"Is it?" He arched an eyebrow and held up three fingers while he ticked off his reasons. "Oldest girl. Still not married. Pushing the big three-oh."

"I'd like to push you off a cliff," she mumbled. "And for your information, not that you deserve any consideration, but I am not looking for a husband. I don't need one to enjoy a full and happy life."

"That's very enlightened of you." Keegan nodded approvingly. "I could have told you that. All you had to do was ask."

"Can we talk about the fact that you're alone?" Fiona made a scoffing sound. "Because, judging by your track record, you are the very last person I would take advice from."

"Why me?" There was mock innocence on her brother's face. "Ronan is the one who set you up with Tate Gibbs."

A new guy in town that he'd met at Ace in the Hole, the local cowboy bar. The jerk had turned out to be a liar and cheat.

She noticed a guilty expression on her oldest brother's face. In spite of her annoyance with these two, she didn't want him to feel bad about what happened. Ultimately she'd made the choice to fall for her ex. It was her own bad judgment that got her heart broken. Lesson learned.

"I'm not looking to get married," she said firmly. "I've stopped looking for a man. Period."

"Keep an open mind, honey." Up until now their mother had stayed out of the verbal volley and simply listened. Now, though, she stepped in. "When you least expect it, that's when love will happen. When you've stopped looking, it will find you."

Another tired saying that should be stitched on a sampler and hung on the wall. Fiona envied her parents' thirty-plus years of marriage. They were still happy and deeply in love, stealing kisses like teenagers when they thought no one was watching. More than once someone would teasingly tell them to get a room. But that kind of love was exactly what she wanted. It just didn't seem as if it was in the cards for her. And there was no way she'd settle for less.

Brendan Tanner was intriguing, she would give him that. And there was something inherently heroic about him. The way he'd handled little Jared with patience and kindness spoke to how he would be with kids of his own. And the fact that he was taking her to dinner instead of letting her pay him to fix the tractor made him seem like a really good man. But she'd been wrong before.

He was basically another stranger in town and she was definitely against getting burned again. He was certainly a pretty package and she was curious about him. But her only goal was one nice evening out.

Before she could tell the boys to go jump in the lake, the back door opened again and her father walked in, followed by his dog, Duchess. Paddy O'Reilly was a big, handsome man and his sons took after him. That was even more painfully clear when he stopped and stared at her the way they had.

"No one told me we were dressing up for dinner tonight," he said, absently rubbing the dog's golden head.

"Fiona's not eating here," Maureen told him.

"She has a date but won't tell us who she's going out with," Keegan informed his father.

"Whoever he is, he's a very lucky man." Paddy's eyes were filled with paternal pride. "You're the image of your mother and she had the men falling all over themselves for a chance with her."

"Thanks, Dad." Fiona felt a lump in her throat.

"So who is this fortunate fella?" His eyes twinkled, proof he knew he wasn't fooling her. Information was what he wanted. "Are we going to have an opportunity to meet him?"

"Not if I can help it."

Oh, dear God. He would be here any minute and she wanted to spare him the awkward family once-over. Now the guardians of the Galaxy were standing shoulder to shoulder, ready to grill the guy. The poor man had done them a favor and this was how they repaid him!

With her shawl and purse in hand, she turned on her heel and hurried to the living room, planning to slip out the door. But the plan was doomed to failure and if she wasn't so darn nervous that would have been clear to her.

All of them followed in her wake, including her mother. They were assembled behind her like the Atlantic Wall on D-day. And before she could even tell them to back off, there was a firm knock on the front door.

This was going to be a disaster. The worst part was that she actually cared her night was going up in flames. And not in a good way.

Chapter Four

The door opened onto Fiona standing there in a dark green dress, and Brendan could only stare. The material hugged her curvy body and made him ache in places he never knew he had. And the earthy color of it released the fire in her red hair. Not for the first time he thought she was the most beautiful woman he'd ever seen. So beautiful, in fact, that it took him several heartbeats to take his eyes off her long enough to notice the four other people lined up behind her. An older man and woman, probably her parents, and two big strapping men. No doubt the brothers she'd mentioned—Ronan and Keegan.

Right then he felt really stupid in general, but even more so with the single rose in his fingers. Her family was staring at it—and him—as if he was from another planet.

Brendan held the flower out to her and said, "This is for you."

"I figured." She glanced over her shoulder at the lurkers, then met his gaze and rolled her eyes. "Brendan Tanner, these are my parents, Maureen and Paddy O'Reilly. And my older brothers, Ronan and Keegan. Everyone, this is Brendan."

"Tanner," Paddy said as he shook his hand. "So you're the fella who fixed my tractor when I couldn't."

"I've seen the problem before, Mr. O'Reilly. I've worked on a lot of ranches that had tractors, a lot of different models. Including that one. I knew what to look for so it wasn't a big deal."

"I suppose that makes me feel a bit better," the older man said a little grudgingly.

"It was very nice of you to come by and look at it." Maureen O'Reilly was still a beautiful woman and her daughter was her spitting image. "And very neighborly of you not to charge us for your time."

He glanced at Fiona, who wouldn't quite look him in the eyes. So she hadn't told them that his fee had been taking her to dinner. She'd apparently told them he did it as a favor, out of the goodness of his heart. That almost made him laugh, since the jury was out on whether or not he had a heart.

Actually he was glad she hadn't told them the whole truth. He would feel ten times as stupid as he already did. Neighborly wasn't exactly how he felt looking at her in that dress. And the three men staring him down knew it. Could this get any more uncomfortable?

"So, how do you like Rust Creek Falls?" Ronan's tone was friendly enough, but the look in his eyes said, *Hurt my sister and I'm coming for you.*

"It's a nice town." Brendan met his gaze, refusing to look away.

"People around here have each other's backs," Keegan said. "We protect our own. It's how we roll."

"Understood." Brendan met the other man's steely gaze and took some satisfaction when Keegan blinked first.

"Where are your manners, Fiona? We've been talking out here and you should have invited the man in." Maureen looked at her daughter, then back at him. "Would you like to come inside, Mr. Tanner?"

"Mom," Fiona said, "we have a dinner reservation."

Brendan was pretty sure the look she gave him was saying she knew that probably wasn't true but just go with her on it. That worked for him. "We should get on the road. Thanks anyway, Mrs. O'Reilly."

"It's Maureen."

"Yes, ma'am." He looked at Fiona. "You ready?"

"So ready." She slid a black shawl around her shoulders and stepped outside, onto the porch. "'Bye, everyone."

"Nice to meet you all," Brendan said, then settled his hand at the small of her back. The gesture was polite, but also selfish, an excuse to touch her. And it backfired. The contact made him want to pull her close. Suddenly, being polite was the last thing on his mind.

After opening the passenger door, he glanced over his shoulder and saw light still spilling out from the front door, telling him the family continued to watch. Maybe the reminder to mind his manners wasn't such a bad thing, after all. He helped her inside the truck and closed the door. When he walked around the front of the vehicle, he gave the O'Reillys a farewell wave, then got in and headed for the road that would take them out of Rust Creek Falls.

"About that having a reservation remark—" Fiona started. "I was afraid you were going to take my mom up on the invitation to go inside."

"No." He couldn't imagine the seventh level of hell being more uncomfortable than that. "Hope that's okay."

"Very much okay."

"Good." That meant he'd interpreted her look correctly. His instincts in a combat situation had saved lives more than once, but understanding a woman's expression was a thousand times more complex. He often read women's signals wrong but tonight wasn't one of those times.

"Ironically," he said, "I did make a reservation."

"That's good."

"No big deal. I did it online."

"I meant the part where I wasn't actually lying to my mother. That's never good."

"I guess not."

Probably he'd told his mother whoppers but he couldn't remember because he'd been five when she left. And growing up watching his dad be sad without her was pretty bad. No one had ever come right out and said it was Brendan's fault, but he figured a case could be made.

"I'm sorry about that." Fiona's voice broke into his dark thoughts.

For a couple of beats he was afraid he'd spoken out loud, then realized he hadn't. So he was forced to ask, "About what?"

"You specifically said no family. Most of the time mine is scattered. Everyone doing their own thing. Sadly, this wasn't one of those nights. If they made you uncomfortable, I apologize."

"That's not necessary. I'm tough. And they obviously love you."

"I know." She sighed. "But I'm not a teenager and this isn't my first rodeo."

"You're lucky to have them." Said the man who had no one.

"Agreed." She blew out a small breath and looked out the passenger window, but it was too dark to see anything. "So, where are we going?"

"That's a surprise."

"Am I overdressed?"

Yes, he thought, glancing at her in the passenger seat,

then returning his eyes to the road. He would give almost anything to see her without that sexy green dress. But that's not what she meant. And from the online intel he'd gathered, what she had on was perfect for the restaurant. He'd added a navy sport coat to his long-sleeved light blue dress shirt that was tucked into his newest jeans.

"You're fine," he said. "You look really nice, by the way. I should have said so earlier but the welcoming party kind of threw me off my game."

"And I should have thanked you earlier for the rose. But my family circled the wagons and sucked all the oxygen from the air." She let out a sigh. "And you look very handsome."

"Shucks, ma'am—"

She laughed and the sound was like sunshine. It was warm and bright and made him grin. Smiling wasn't natural but there was no holding it back even if he wanted to.

The light moment dissolved his tension and he felt relaxed for the first time in longer than he could remember. Between military deployments and watching his father waste away from cancer, there hadn't been much to smile about. But he'd had a clear understanding of his mission in each case. Sunshine Farm had caught his attention because it was a place where someone could find a fresh start. So far he didn't feel the objective was coming together. So he continued his plan to get back in shape and reenlist.

"It's awfully quiet over there," Fiona said. "Except for the part where I can hear you thinking."

"Oh? How?"

"There's a strange sort of whirring, clunking sound."

"That's just me concentrating on the road." He chuckled again, feeling his connection to her strengthen.

"Hmm," she said thoughtfully. "I could help you watch

the road if I knew where we were going. Although it has to be Kalispell. There aren't many places in Rust Creek Falls that require a reservation."

She was right about their general destination, but he wasn't going to confirm. "Good try, but I'm not going to reveal anything."

About thirty minutes later the lights of the city glowed and twinkled in the distance. From browsing the internet he knew Kalispell was a city of about twenty-two thousand. It was definitely bigger than Rust Creek Falls, which had a nice restaurant at Maverick Manor. He just figured the two of them would draw attention there, which he didn't want. This would be better. Just dinner; no expectations. Always best not to have any.

Enough with the dark thoughts. As best he could, for the rest of the night he was turning them off. It was just a couple of hours. Surely he could manage that.

A short time later he pulled into the restaurant parking lot and turned off the truck engine. "Surprise."

"North Bay Grill. This looks nice. How did you find it?"

"How does anyone find anything these days?"

"Internet," they both said together.

Brendan did a quick scan of the outside and surrounding area. An old habit from deployment days. The wood siding was light blue with white painted shutters bracketing the windows. There were neatly trimmed shrubs and flowers around the perimeter.

"It looks like a New England fishing village." Fiona glanced over at him and smiled.

There it was again. That look as if he'd done just the right thing.

He stared at her for several moments, soaking it in.

Then he forced himself to mobilize and open the door. It was either get moving or kiss her, and he couldn't do that.

"Let's go in," he said.

He went around to the passenger side to open her door but she was already sliding to the ground. Shame. He would have liked an excuse to put his hands at her waist and lift her down. Side by side—he was careful not to touch her—they walked to the entrance and he opened the door for her. It was a weeknight and the place wasn't busy. Apparently a reservation wasn't necessary. The hostess showed them to a table for two by the dual-sided rock fireplace in the center of the room.

Fiona sat down, then looked around at the pictures of ships on the walls and the antique fishing paraphernalia decorating a shelf near the ceiling. "Very cozy on a cold October night."

"Yeah."

A waiter in uniform black pants and a crisp white shirt walked over. "Good evening. My name is Jeremy. I'll be your server tonight. Can I get you something to drink?"

They ordered—chardonnay for Fiona, beer for Brendan—then perused the menu. By the time their drinks arrived, they'd both decided on salmon. Jeremy put a basket of freshly baked cheddar biscuits on the table, then discreetly withdrew. Fiona took one and buttered it before biting.

"Mmm." She closed her eyes and savored the taste.

The look of ecstasy on her face was the sexiest thing he'd ever seen. She looked like a woman who'd been well and thoroughly made love to and he badly wanted to be the man who was responsible for it. The knot in his gut tightened another notch.

Fiona pushed the basket closer to him. "You have to try these."

Anything to take his mind off sex. He snagged one, buttered and bit into it. "Good."

"That's the best you've got? It rocked my world."

Before he could answer, the salads arrived and they both dug in.

Fiona wasn't one of those women who ate two leaves and called it a night. She enjoyed her entire meal and he liked that about her.

"Wow," she said, setting her fork on the empty dinner plate a while later. "I was hungry."

"Me, too." He took a swallow of beer and sat back. "So tell me, have you finished your article?"

She nodded. "I'm working on another one now."

"Already?"

"The extra money is nice." She shrugged.

"What is this one about?"

"Holidays in a small town. 'Tis the season coming up and the best rule is to write what you know." She toyed with the stem of her wineglass. "Halloween isn't far off and next thing you know Thanksgiving will be here. Big cities have their professionally decorated store windows but the people of Rust Creek Falls are every bit as enthusiastic about our traditional ways of celebrating."

"So you're going to write about it."

"Yes. I'll give you a copy and you can let me know what you think."

"I look forward to it."

She glanced at the flames crackling nearby, then back at him. "What do you think about Rust Creek Falls so far?"

"Nice town."

"That's what you told my brother. I was hoping for a couple of details. I guess you're meeting a lot of folks, what with fixing their stuff?" She picked up her glass and took a sip of wine.

"Yes. And being busy is good."

"The fact that you are should tell you something."

"Like?" He watched her settle her hands in her lap.

"There's a real call for what you do. You're providing a necessary service or you'd be twiddling your thumbs."

"Did Luke put you up to that?" he asked.

"What?"

"He said the same thing. I just wondered if he recruited you to talk me into his repair shop whim."

"Maybe it's not just a whim. Maybe he's onto something." She held up her hands to stop him from interrupting. "And no, he didn't enlist my help."

"Okay. Just crossed my mind. He's not shy about sharing his ideas."

"What else is he talking up?"

"We already talked about him doing a little matchmaking."

"Are you saying he's responsible for you asking me to dinner?" Was there an edge to her voice?

Brendan hated to admit it but the man had gotten into his head some. Luke had said he thought Fiona was interested. That thought had been rattling around when he'd fixed O'Reilly's tractor then asked Fiona out to dinner. But no one had held a gun to his head; the words had come out of his own mouth.

"Luke is absolutely not why I asked you to dinner. What he would call this is public relations. Your father will pass on to someone else the positive experience he had with me." He shrugged.

"Publicity through word of mouth," she mused aloud. "A good marketing technique. Especially in Rust Creek Falls."

Brendan ignored the part of his rational mind that suggested Luke's words had fallen on fertile ground and taken root. He wanted to ignore the connection he felt with Fiona. It was happening too fast. It was scary that he felt anything at all. He wanted her bad but that wasn't going to happen. His certainty about it had nothing to do with her not being that kind of girl and everything to do with the fact that he had never felt this way about a woman. He wouldn't let himself go there. He wouldn't end up a sad man, brooding for the rest of his life about the woman who left him.

For Pete's sake, why hadn't he just let Fiona pay him for fixing the damn tractor?

After dinner they left the restaurant and returned to the truck. Fiona climbed into the passenger seat while Brendan held the door for her. The gentlemanly gesture seemed as normal to him as breathing and she found it so darn appealing.

"Thanks," she said.

"You're welcome." His tone was polite but cool all of a sudden.

Why? What had changed now that there wasn't a cloth-covered table between them?

He got in and started the engine. After backing out of the parking space, he headed for the exit and the street beyond that that would take them back to Rust Creek Falls.

In spite of the fact that Luke Stockton seemed to be playing Cupid, she had to admit she'd had a good time. There was no harm in one fun evening out and she wasn't ready for it to end. Fiona wanted to keep it going as long as possible.

She glanced over at Brendan, and in the lights from

the dashboard she could see that his features had settled into what she thought of as brood mode.

Unacceptable.

Since he didn't seem inclined to break the silence, she would. The question was, how? She needed a conversation starter and the idea gods were with her when she came up with something that just might engage him.

"So, that was a nice place," she started.

"Yeah."

"I would definitely recommend it."

"Affirmative."

She wasn't discouraged by the one-word responses. This was leading him right where she wanted to go. "Kalispell is a nice town."

"Yup."

"Okay, look. It's a bit of a drive back and it will be more entertaining if we chat. Don't you think?"

"Sure. About?"

She was ready. "Tell me something about yourself that would surprise me."

Frowning, he glanced over at her, then returned his gaze to the road. "Is that a trick question?"

"Not when it got five words out of you as opposed to one." She was pleased to have his attention. "It's a conversation starter."

"I'm just not sure what you mean by surprise you."

"Well…" She thought for a moment. "I know you were in the Marines and that you're good at fixing things. And tools are your friends. You're a man's man." *Be still my heart*, she thought. "So I'd like to know something about your softer side. Maybe you knit body armor. Use lavender vanilla motor oil. Prefer salad to rare steak. Maybe quiche."

There was a half-smile on his face for a moment before it disappeared. "I left the Marine Corps to help my father when he got sick. The military taught me to fight, but cancer is a battle he and I couldn't win. That's a tough reality for a warrior."

"I can imagine. But I already knew that."

"It was more than that, though. I realized soon enough that the mission changed. I appreciated spending time with him and I nursed him."

"You mean taking him to doctor appointments?"

"That, too. But I handled his meds. Made him as comfortable as possible." There was sadness in his voice. "At the end I fed him when he was too weak to pick up a fork. I made sure his final wishes were attended to."

"He was lucky to have you."

"There wasn't anyone else," he said.

Why? she wanted to ask. What happened that he had to grow up without a mother? It seemed too forward to ask, so she didn't.

"I'm so sorry for your loss. I know that doesn't help, but it's all I've got. I have no frame of reference to understand how you feel except that it must suck to lose a parent. If there's any comfort to be had, it's that he *was* lucky to have you."

"Leon, my dad, said as much, but I'm not sure I believe him. Fathers have to say that."

"Not mine. Paddy O'Reilly doesn't hesitate to say if any of his children are not living up to his high standards." She toyed with the rose he'd given her earlier, which she'd taken with her. "He also would tell you that he loves you unconditionally in front of the whole town at the top of his lungs. The good stuff carries a lot of weight when you know that he won't hold back on the bad."

"I can see how that would be the case." Brendan had

one hand on the steering wheel, easily controlling the truck on the straightaway road.

"So, you never knew your mother?" The words popped out of her mouth and hung in the air between them. She glanced at his profile and noted that he wasn't frowning any more than usual. Neither had he responded to the question.

When he did say something, it was clear he didn't intend to answer. "Your turn. Tell me something about you that would surprise me."

She figured it would take a lot to surprise him and just went with the biggest shock she'd ever gotten. "My boyfriend got a girl pregnant and married her. In that order. I found out at a baby shower. Not for the trollop in Thunder Canyon that he dumped me for. A friend of mine in Rust Creek Falls was having a baby."

Brendan was quiet for a moment then he said, "So, he's not your boyfriend anymore, right?"

That surprised a laugh out of her. The cheating and the public way she'd found out about it had left deep, painful scars. Never in a bazillion years would she have expected to laugh about it.

"No, we are no longer together. He was a stranger in town that I thought I knew. We got close pretty fast and everyone in Rust Creek Falls expected me to flash an engagement ring any second." Surprisingly the painful memory didn't cut as deeply as it once had. "Instead he left. I suppose I should have suspected something when phone calls became infrequent texts that suddenly stopped. But obviously he worked fast and I didn't want to see it, I guess. Then I went to Paige's baby shower and friends from Thunder Canyon who didn't know about my relationship with him shared the 'good' news."

"That falls into the 'really sucks' column."

"You'll get no argument from me." She sighed. "I have more than one regret about the whole awful mess, but the biggest one is that I never got to tell him off."

"Now, that surprises me. You don't strike me as the kind of woman who holds back."

"I'm not. And I thought a lot about what I'd say. Maybe I was waiting for him to do me the courtesy of a phone call to end it." She glanced over at Brendan. "For the record, there are worse things than a breakup text. Radio silence means you were too insignificant to even waste a couple of seconds composing a message."

"And you didn't call him."

It wasn't a question. "I didn't want him to think he was important enough to spend that much emotional energy on."

"I'm pretty sure guys don't contemplate the meaning of emotional energy. If nothing else it would have made you feel better."

"Yeah. But that was a couple years ago and the moment is gone. He's nothing to me now." Except the man her brother Ronan had set her up with. The whole experience was now just a cautionary tale.

He turned onto the road that led to her house. "Almost there. You were right about talking making the time go faster."

"It flies when you're having fun." And reliving painful memories. Her house was just ahead and the front porch light was on.

Brendan parked the truck and turned off the engine, throwing them into darkness. So, here they were, and she'd just bared her soul about the man who'd done her wrong. Now she was facing the "how do you say goodnight?" moment. Hug? Handshake? Kiss on the cheek?

Lip to lip was her preference, but there was no reason to expect that.

She grabbed her purse and the rose in one hand, then opened her door and slid out. Meeting his gaze across the truck's interior, she said, "Thank you for dinner, Brendan. That was very nice of you. I'm sure we'll see each other around. Good night."

She closed the door and headed for the walkway to the porch. Behind her, she heard him get out of the truck, and moments later he fell into step beside her.

"The least I can do is see you safely to your door."

"Don't take this the wrong way, but this isn't a Halloween slasher movie. It's highly unlikely that someone will jump out of the shadows to attack me."

He shrugged. "Call me old-fashioned."

Naturally. And call her a sucker for courtly manners, she thought. A glow started inside her, and she felt sure it was visible from space.

They walked up the steps onto the porch and stopped a few feet from the door. She turned to him and looked up—way up.

"Well, thanks again," she said. "I had a really nice time."

"Me, too."

Was it her imagination that he leaned toward her? She held her breath, and her heart beat so hard it sounded in her ears. Anticipation poured through her.

And then he took a step back. "Good night, Fiona."

In stunned silence she watched him walk away and get in the truck. So, this was a horror movie, after all. But it was her expectations that were slashed. She'd been so sure he was going to kiss her. Until he didn't. And she'd bought a new outfit for this? Some impression she'd made. Apparently he just wasn't that into her.

Never one to miss a chance to see the silver lining,

Fiona rationalized the heck out of this. It was déjà vu. Brendan Tanner was a stranger, a nice hunky one, but they'd been pushed together by a well-meaning man. It was for the best that he didn't kiss her because around him her wisdom and willpower seemed to evaporate. If history was anything to go by, giving in to the attraction would not end well.

But none of that rationalization took away the sting of her bruised ego or the smarting of rejection.

But she'd handled it once. A little chocolate along with reading a couple of sarcastic blogs to shore up her attitude and she would be just fine.

Chapter Five

"We're almost there." Luke glanced over from the driver's side of his truck.

"I was wondering if you were lost," Brendan said.

Luke had asked him to help with roundup this year and they were headed to the cabin to make good on his promise. In October ranchers went into the hills and gathered up cattle that had been grazing there during the summer. Luke had explained that this operation took about three days, and the staging area with cabins, pens for the cows and a stable to put up the horses was a three-hour drive from Rust Creek Falls.

Of course Brendan had been happy to do it. But that was before he found out he'd have too much time to think about Fiona. Too many miles to remember every detail of their dinner the other night, including the fact that he hadn't kissed her good night. He'd wanted to—bad. He was pretty sure letting that opportunity get away from him would be at the top of a long list of regrets.

But on the drive home from Kalispell, because he'd been talking about his father after Fiona had asked him to surprise her, the warning his old man had pounded into him was right there in his head. Brendan still remembered the exact words: *Don't fall in love, son. Don't you dare do it. Then no woman can hurt you like your mother did me.*

Brendan had figured it was pretty important to his dad since the warning was one of the last things Leon said to him before he died. But it wasn't necessary. Brendan had lived the message. His father's wife walked out and later a long-term girlfriend did the same. The experiences hollowed out Leon's heart and made him a two-time loser. Brendan's own growing-up years were all the warning he'd needed, and he swore a long time ago not to let any woman in.

Then he met Fiona O'Reilly.

"You're not very good company," Luke said. "I have better conversations with my horse."

"He's back there." Brendan angled his thumb toward the horse trailer that was hitched to the truck. "I'm happy to switch places with him."

"Now that's what I'm talking about." Luke grinned as he guided the vehicle off the paved road onto a solidly packed dirt one. "I could have used much more of that guy for the last three hours."

"That guy is up for the challenge."

"Too late. We're here." His friend came to a stop beside two trucks already parked in the small compound.

There were two log cabins, side by side, with a couple of wooden picnic tables out front. A short distance away were several empty enclosures that, presumably, would hold the cattle they rounded up. Next to that was a barn—open on both ends—with a roof and stalls to stable the horses. The land was hilly and covered with grass and scrub.

Overhead the sky was a cloudless blue, letting the sunshine take some bite out of the chill in the air. The word *idyllic* came to mind, and it would have been if he hadn't spent the last three hours thinking about a woman he wanted but needed to avoid like the flu.

"Jamie's not here yet. The slacker," Luke teased.

"The man has triplets," Brendan reminded him. "Maybe you should cut him a break."

"I'll give it some thought."

"You might want to decide before those three kids are teenagers."

"Three teens at the same time." Luke shuddered. "I don't know what you were like at sixteen, but I wouldn't wish three of me at that age on my worst enemy. And one of them a girl. You're right. That's when he'll need the slack."

That said, the two of them got out of the truck and looked around. Brendan didn't recognize the other vehicles. "If Jamie's not here, who do those belong to?"

His question was answered when Fiona walked out of the cabin nearest them. A feeling rolled through him that felt like Friday afternoon of a long holiday weekend. Happy to see her didn't do justice to what he felt and he wasn't especially thrilled about that.

When Luke stopped beside him, Brendan said low enough so only his friend could hear, "You didn't mention the O'Reillys would be here."

"No?" Luke shrugged and met his gaze. The expression on his face was just a little too innocent. "The O'Reillys are here. The cattle carry the brands of our respective ranches. Every year we combine our resources to round up the animals and separate them into pens. I hope that's not a problem."

Brendan saw Paddy, Ronan and Keegan come out of the barn and head in his direction. He blew out a long breath. "Not a problem for me."

Then Brendan's gaze zeroed in on Fiona's mouth. *That* was a problem.

"Hello, Luke." Paddy led his brood in handshakes.

"You've all met Brendan, I assume?" Luke's question was met with nods all around. "He's helping us out this year. He has some ranching skills being that he's from Texas. I told him Montana would show him the right way."

Paddy laughed, but his boys didn't react. Apparently glaring at him took all their concentration.

"Good to see you, Tanner."

"How are you, Mr. O'Reilly?"

"Can't complain," the older man said.

Brendan suspected his sons could and would answer differently. He would admit to not always treating women with the respect he should have—promising to call when he had no intention of following through, classic crap that guys pulled—but he hadn't put a disrespectful finger on Fiona. If they were aware of that, it didn't seem to matter.

"How was the drive?" Luke asked the older man.

"Good." Paddy looked up at the perfect sky. "But the weather is due to take a turn. You know how unpredictable October can be in Montana."

"Yeah. I think we're getting this done just in time." Luke nodded. "Jamie's on his way. I planned to give my brother a hard time about always being late but Brendan reminded me he has three kids who will all turn into teenagers at the same time. Figured he needs to save up energy for that."

"Amen." Paddy glanced at his adult children. "It's a load off a father's shoulders when his kids grow up to be fine human beings."

"Thanks, Dad." Fiona smiled at him. "That might be the nicest thing you've ever said to me."

"Don't let it go to your head," he teased her.

"I'm going to take care of my horses," Luke said. "Fiona, would you do me a favor and show Brendan around? Give him the first-timer tour?"

"Sure." The brim of her brown Stetson shadowed her eyes so there was no way to read her reaction to the request. "Grab your gear and I'll show you where to put it."

"Okay." He opened the rear of the four-door truck and took out his duffel, then turned to see she was waiting for him.

His intention was to make eye contact, but damned if his gaze didn't go rogue and land on her lips again. If he'd gone with his instincts that night, he would already know how she tasted instead of letting his thoughts run wild with the unknown. But he hadn't kissed her and was now forced to use his imagination.

"This way." Fiona pointed to the cabin closest to the holding pens.

He fell into step beside her. For some reason he felt the need to break the tense silence. "How've you been?"

"Fine."

He waited for her to take over the conversation and run with it, but that didn't happen. "How's the latest article going?"

"Good."

Zero for two, he thought when she didn't elaborate. Miss Get the Conversation Started didn't seem inclined to want to follow her own advice.

She had surprised him with the story of her bad experience. Brendan was no saint but he would never cheat on a woman and he wanted five minutes alone with the guy who'd done that to her. Even though he had no right to it, anger burned through him, bright and hot.

They stepped on the porch and their boots thudded on the wood. She pushed open the door and led him inside.

"It's basic," she said, "but there's running water and indoor plumbing." She pointed out the open room. "Kitchen, eating area, a couple of bedrooms and bath downstairs. Upstairs are two more bedrooms and a loft. Pick a spot and stash your stuff."

"Okay. I assume your family is in the other cabin?"

"Yes."

This was not the carefree, happy woman he'd had dinner with. He wanted that woman back.

"Are you okay, Fiona?"

"Fine."

Liar, he wanted to say. *Tell me what I did.* But he didn't get a chance to say anything because she turned abruptly and started toward the door.

"We trade off cooking meals for everyone," she said over her shoulder. "Jamie handled it last year so meals will be in our cabin this time."

"Okay. If you need help I can—"

"No." She glanced around, everywhere but at him. "That's it, then. Dinner is at six." And without another word she walked out the door.

Brendan dropped his duffel and followed her. She was headed for the other cabin and he started after her. Before he could catch up, someone behind him called out his name.

It was Ronan. "I need a word, Tanner."

The snarl in the other man's voice said this wasn't going to be a "welcome to the neighborhood" conversation. He turned and faced Fiona's older brother. "What can I do for you, O'Reilly?"

"Why are you here?"

"Like Luke said. To lend a hand."

The other man folded his arms over his chest. "That's it? Just helping out?"

Brendan knew where this was going, but he didn't plan to make it easy. "What other reason would there be?"

"Maybe your motivation has something to do with my sister?"

"I didn't know she would be here. Luke didn't mention that any of you were coming."

All of it was true but Ronan didn't look like he was in the mood to believe that. Brendan wouldn't have agreed to come if he'd known, but it was unlikely this pissed-off older brother would believe that, either.

"So you're here out of the goodness of your heart?"

Luke had asked on Jamie's behalf and Brendan couldn't say no to the man who had given him a place to get a fresh perspective. He considered him a friend who asked for a favor. That was good enough. Did that fall into the "goodness of his heart" category? Close enough. "Yeah. I'm a prince of a guy."

"Then why is Fiona upset?"

"She's your sister. How am I supposed to know?"

Ronan's gaze narrowed on him. "She was fine until you took her out to dinner. She was cheerful, happy, taking care of everyone like always. She was just…Fiona."

"And what? She turned into someone else?" Brendan couldn't resist needling this guy, but he braced himself. No telling how hotheaded he was.

Ronan's glare intensified. "Don't be an ass."

"Too late."

"On the drive up here she was good. When you showed up she wasn't. I don't know. Her mood changed."

"I have no idea what's going on with her. Maybe you should try asking her about this."

"I will." The conviction in his tone said he would do just that. "And one more thing."

"There always is." Brendan barely held back his annoyance.

"I saw the way you looked at her."

"And how was that?" Again with the knee-jerk comment. Brendan knew *exactly* how he'd looked at her.

"I think you can figure that one out for yourself." If possible, Ronan's expression turned even hotter. "Fair warning. If you hurt my sister—"

"Before you finish that thought, you should know I'm an ex-marine. I have advanced hand-to-hand combat training."

"All the same…you've been warned. No one hurts her again."

He walked away before Brendan could respond. He was aware that big brothers could be protective, but this man had a level of hostility that took it up a notch. And the best explanation was that Ronan felt he was somehow to blame for her being hurt. Why?

Brendan meant what he'd said. He wouldn't do anything to make Fiona unhappy and the best way to avoid that was to keep his distance. But damn it. Being warned off made him want her even more.

Of all the roundups in all the world, Brendan Tanner had walked into hers. *How is that even fair?* Fiona thought. At dinner she'd managed to avoid him, and everyone turned in early to rest up for a long day in the saddle. She'd tossed and turned all night and was now in said saddle and feeling tired and pretty doggone crabby about the whole situation.

She and Ronan had paired off and were riding in the hills. From previous years they knew the cows wandered off a fair distance and it was best to start there, then head back to the staging area with as many animals as they could find. The strategy avoided having to double back while keeping the strays together.

It was a Montana Visitors Bureau kind of day. Blue sky dotted with puffy white clouds. The air smelled of earth and shrubs and early morning dew. She loved riding and taking in the beauty of the great outdoors. All these sensations were going into a journal for an article she was planning to write about the experience.

Normally she loved roundup, but this time she wasn't feeling it. Normally she made an effort to chat up whoever she was riding with, but she wasn't feeling that, either. After all, this was Ronan, and her brother didn't care whether or not she kept him entertained with witty conversation. Although he kept giving her funny looks.

"What?" she finally said.

"Excuse me?"

"You keep staring at me. Why?" she snapped.

"I know you're going to bite my head off for saying this, but—" he blew out a breath "—is it that time of the month?"

"Are you seriously asking me that?"

"It's a legitimate question," he defended.

Fiona noted that he looked a little skittish and took some satisfaction from that. Her big, badass, chick-magnet brother might just be a little afraid of her. For however long it lasted she had the power and would abuse it to the best of her ability. And, yes, she realized her pique was directed at someone else and Ronan was in the wrong place at the wrong time. Tough noogies.

"Define a legitimate question," she said.

He squirmed in the saddle as the horses walked side by side. "It's just that you're usually so perky. Asking about everyone else and—"

"Are you saying I'm not pulling my weight this year?

Because that's just baloney. I've fetched, carried, cooked and done my fair share of the chores."

"That's not what I meant."

"It sounded like that's what you meant. So explain it to me." She gave him a look that would have lasered paint off the side of a barn. "For once try talking about your feelings."

"Okay." There was irritation in that one word. "I'm *feeling* that you're not yourself. That you're ticked off about something and not especially cheerful or fun to be around."

"Excuse me. I didn't realize that amusing you was part of getting the job done."

"Not fair, Fiona. There's a burr under your saddle and you're taking it out on me."

Guilty, she thought. He was more emotionally aware than she'd given him credit for. "There are other reasons for a woman's bad attitude besides it being that time of the month."

"So I'll take that as a no on the monthly thing." He met her gaze and she confirmed with a nod. "At the risk of pissing you off more, it's a little early to be wearing the Halloween witch costume."

She really couldn't argue with that characterization. "I'm just having a bad day."

"That's not like you," he commented. "Usually you're so cheerful and optimistic it makes my teeth hurt."

"Then your teeth should be thanking me," she snapped.

"See, that's what I'm talking about. That was a sarcastic comment. Usually those same words would have been teasing."

"Are you saying you don't like my tone?"

"Yeah, pretty much."

"I say again—tough."

"Come on, Fee, I'm your big brother. You can talk to me about anything. We established it's not that time of the month so—" He suddenly stopped talking and his gaze snapped to hers. "Are you late? Does that mean you're pregnant? I'm there for you. You have to know that. It will be okay—"

"Take a breath, for Pete's sake. I'm not pregnant."

One had to have sex for that to happen and she hadn't for a long time. That thought brought back the humiliation of Brendan not kissing her. She would have been putty in his hands but he didn't want her at all. Unexpected tears gathered in her eyes and she looked away. The last thing she wanted was for Ronan to see her cry.

"You have a vivid imagination. Maybe you should be the writer," she said.

"I'm not an idiot. And don't tell me that's open to debate," he warned. "Something's up. Why won't you tell me what's going on?"

It was a valid question. She was close to her sisters and discussed everything with them. But since Brenna and Fallon had fallen in love and set up housekeeping with their respective men, Fiona had grown closer to Ronan. He was there on the ranch. Living in the converted barn, but just a short walk from the house. And he took his responsibilities as big brother very seriously.

She didn't really want to talk about it. There was nothing anyone could do. Rejection was her issue to work through and put behind her. But still. Although he hid it pretty well, her brother was a good guy with a soft heart. He didn't deserve this from her.

"You know," he said, "your mood was just fine until Tanner showed up yesterday. Does he have anything to do with your foul temper?" His voice was barely audible over the *clip clop* of their horses' hooves, but intensity wrapped around every single syllable of those words.

"It's not what you think," she said.

"What do you think I think?"

"That he got out of line when he took me to dinner the other night."

"Did he?" Ronan looked at her, his eyes narrowed dangerously.

She laughed, but that was about irony, not amusement. "Actually, it was just the opposite. He couldn't get away from me fast enough."

"So there was no chemistry between you." He sounded both relieved and pleased.

That's just it, Fiona thought. She was pretty sure there were buckets of chemistry and not just from her. When he touched her it was electric. The looks he gave her sizzled. He'd asked her to dinner, and why would he if not for some feeling on his part? If her man radar was that far off, she would give up her matching black lace bra and panties.

"If you must know, he didn't kiss me good night."

"All right, then." There was a high five all over that statement. Then he looked at her face. "Oh. You wanted him to."

If she wasn't on a horse, Fiona believed there was a very real possibility that she'd have cheerfully choked him just then. "Give the man a prize."

"So, he hurt you. Damn it." His horse danced sideways, probably sensing his anger. "Well, you can be sure he won't do it again."

It took several beats before the words sank in, but when they did Fiona's stomach knotted with dread. "How can you be so sure about that? Now that I think about it, you were talking to him yesterday and neither of you looked like it was a friendly chat about the weather. What did you say to him?"

Ronan shrugged. "Doesn't really matter. You're obviously not going to give him another chance."

"Seriously? You can read my mind?" What if Brendan wanted a second chance? That was unlikely, but what if? Did Ronan scare him off? It would be good to know the context of that tense conversation. "What did you say to him, Ronan?"

"I warned him not to hurt you."

Too late. "Why on earth would you do that?"

"Because he's a drifter. Just like the one who broke your heart."

"Oh, Ronan—"

"What? Do not tell me I should have stayed out of it. What kind of big brother would I be if I didn't look out for my little sister?"

He meant well, but that didn't stop her irritation from bubbling to the surface. "While I appreciate your honorable intentions, I'm a big girl. I can take care of myself, thank you very much."

"Because you did such a good job of that?" Ronan said. As soon as the words were out of his mouth it looked as if he'd give almost anything to have them back.

"You fixed me up with that jerk," she shot back.

"I introduced you," he defended. "I met him at Ace in the Hole and thought he was a good guy. Obviously I was mistaken. You will never know how sorry I am about that. I feel terrible about what happened."

And suddenly she got it. The acute overprotectiveness. "You got in Brendan's face because you're trying to make it up to me."

"Maybe."

"Look, it's very sweet of you to be concerned and I

love you for it. But that bad choice and any I might make in the future are mine alone."

"Are you telling me to stay out of your love life?"

"I—" There wasn't anything to stay out of, but this was a stand for her independence. She'd made it an issue and he deserved an answer to the question. "Yes."

"I can't promise you that." He held up a hand to stop her words. "I can tell you that I'll give anyone who comes calling the benefit of the doubt, but if there's anything I don't like, I'm sticking my nose in. If you don't like it— tough."

"Fair enough. Just give me room to make my choice."

There wouldn't be any reason to interfere in her love life because she was never going to be stupid again. Her head was on straight now. Brendan Tanner *was* a drifter and falling for him would be a check mark in the "stupid" column. She was many things, but stupid wasn't one of them.

Chapter Six

"Good chili." Brendan had no idea who made it but he put the words out there anyway because that was the truth. At six he had joined Jamie and Luke Stockton in the O'Reilly cabin around a wooden picnic-style table where meals were being served.

"Glad you like it," Ronan said. "It's my world famous recipe."

His brother snorted. "You never make it the same way twice. *Recipe* is a stretch."

"Keegan, you wouldn't know a recipe if it came up and kissed you on the mouth." Ronan elbowed his younger brother.

"You're not foolin' anyone," his father said. "Throwing beans, meat and seasoning into a pot is the best you can do to get a meal together since our Fiona's ultimatum."

"Which was?" Luke asked.

"She refused to do all the cooking for roundup just because she was the only woman," Paddy explained. "So the boys and I agreed to each be responsible for one evening meal."

"Heaven help us when it's Keegan's turn," Ronan teased.

"I barbecue a mean steak," his brother shot back.

"The corn bread is good, too," Brendan continued. "Practically melts in your mouth."

"Now, that was Fiona's doing," Paddy said proudly. "She's a good cook. Her mother taught her everything."

"I'll never be as good as Mom," she said.

"I don't know about that," Jamie offered. "That macaroni and cheese you make is enough to make a grown man cry. And it's stopped my triplets from shedding tears a time or two."

"Isn't that the truth," Paddy agreed.

She smiled at her father, who was next to her. The "boys" were sitting across from them. Jamie was on her left with Luke on the other side of the table from him. Brendan was on the end, odd man out. There to lend a hand with rounding up the cows but not really a part of this tight-knit group.

That was just a fact. But what he found truly aggravating was that since giving him the two-cent tour, Fiona had gone out of her way to ignore him. And after a long day in the saddle he was tired and hungry—but not for food. He'd been looking forward to seeing *her*. Now she wouldn't even look at him.

The good-natured banter continued between the O'Reilly brothers, who pulled siblings Luke and Jamie into the joking. Without a word, Fiona stood and stepped over the bench before grabbing her plate and eating utensils. She took them to the sink and washed everything by hand, then put them in a dish drainer on the counter. Brendan decided to do the same and joined her there.

"So, I'll just clean up after myself."

"Knock yourself out." She moved away, then grabbed her jacket from a peg on the wall.

Quietly she let herself out the door. The men were still talking and laughing. They didn't seem to notice she'd left, and Brendan figured he sure wouldn't be missed. He set his washed dishes with hers, grabbed a jacket and slipped outside, too.

It was a chilly night but there was a full moon that bathed the landscape in silvery light. He could see Fiona in the distance and followed her. A couple times he lost her along the winding trail, or trees and bushes blocked his line of sight. But he kept on and heard the sound of gurgling water, which was a clue to her final destination.

Moments later he emerged from the trees and saw a clearing by a stream. Fiona was sitting on a fallen tree trunk facing it. Moonlight turned her red hair into a bright beacon, leading him straight to her. If this was a combat situation, his warrior sense would be warning him to stand fast. Danger ahead. Now that he was a civilian, he called it his better judgment and that was telling him to walk away. Turn around and don't look back. But he ignored it.

"Hi." His boots made noise on the rocky river bank and she'd no doubt heard his approach, but he wanted to make sure he didn't scare her. "It's just me."

She glanced over her shoulder, then turned her gaze back to the stream. "Thought you'd be hanging out with the menfolk. Telling off-color jokes."

"No." So, she still wouldn't look at him. "Is that why you came out here? To give them space?"

"I just wanted some fresh air."

"You didn't get enough of that rounding up cows today?"

Instead of smiling, her mouth pulled tight. "I was with Ronan. It was air, all right, but not what I'd call fresh. He's something."

"Yeah."

"This is a pretty spot."

So, they were changing the subject. "It is. Mind if I join you?"

That got her to look up at him and there was surprise in her eyes. Then she shrugged and said, "Suit yourself."

It was the same tone she'd used with her "knock yourself out" comment. As if his presence made no difference to her one way or the other. That rankled and he decided it suited him to sit next to her. So he did.

His shoulder brushed hers and he'd swear there were sparks spiraling in the crisp night air. That would explain why his brain shorted out for a couple of seconds. When he could manage a coherent thought, the best he could come up with was, "There are wild animals out here. Probably best not to be alone."

"Is that why you're here? To wrestle mountain lions who get any ideas?"

There it was. Her teasing humor and biting wit. He'd missed them more than he'd realized. "I have a certain skill set."

"Apparently the male protective streak is strong here in Montana," she said wryly.

"I didn't notice."

"Oh, please. I know Ronan got in your face yesterday. I saw you talking to him. And I know my brother. He was doing that thing he does. Some older brother/younger sister code he feels obligated to uphold."

"It was nothing I can't handle."

"Still, if he made you uncomfortable, I apologize."

"No need." Because he wanted so badly to take her in his arms, Brendan rested his elbows on his knees and clasped his hands together between them. "I would do the same thing if I had a sister as pretty as you."

"Hmm. I don't know whether to say thank you or you need your eyes checked."

"I'd suggest going with the first one. I don't say things I don't mean."

"That's refreshing." There was a trace of sarcasm in her tone.

"It's the truth," he said quietly.

"I wasn't implying that you are in the habit of telling falsehoods—" She sighed. "The thing is, a little context might explain my skepticism and help you understand why Ronan acted the way he did."

"I'm a guy. I get it."

"It's more than just macho swagger. Remember I told you about the guy who I thought was going to propose?"

"And got a girl pregnant?"

"That's the one," she confirmed. "Ronan introduced me to him."

"He fixed you up?"

"Yeah. They met at Ace in the Hole. My brother liked him and he set up a meet."

"Mr. Matchmaker," he commented, trying to reconcile the cupid image in his mind with the Ronan he'd met.

"If you say that to his face…duck." Her smile came and went in a heartbeat. "The thing is, the jerk told me he had to go back to Thunder Canyon for a while. Some things to take care of."

"That's one way to put it."

"I know, right?" She stared at the gurgling water, moonlight reflecting off the ripples. Her delicate jaw clenched, hinting at the anger and hurt she still felt. "He asked me to wait. Promised he would come back to me. Idiot that I am, I believed him. So I waited."

He remembered her saying that communication between them was sporadic before it stopped. "And he didn't have the guts to tell you himself that he's a cheating bastard."

"Yeah. So Ronan feels lower than pond scum and has gone into protective, "touch my sister and die" mode. I'm sorry he confronted you when there's not even anything going on between us."

"If there was," he said, "I would never string you along. I'd never break a promise like that. When I joined the Marines, I took an oath to protect the Constitution of the United States. I still feel the weight and commitment of that vow in a lot of ways, but especially my personal behavior. I don't make promises I don't intend to keep."

"You're a good man, Brendan Tanner. I appreciate knowing that. Even though we're not a thing," she added.

"You're sure about that? Us not being a thing?"

"If we were, you would have kissed me after we had dinner the other night." There was regret in her voice.

That was something he knew all too well. Remorse for things he'd done and things he hadn't. Just yesterday he'd kicked himself six ways to sundown for not kissing her when he'd had the chance. To miss another opportunity would just be wrong. Because Fiona by moonlight tempted him to his limit.

The conflict raged inside him and he didn't make a conscious decision, but he must have instinctively moved toward her. She met him halfway and the next thing he knew, they were kissing. For just a second he was afraid the pressure of her lips was only his imagination, but it was so much hotter that he knew this was real. Even better, he finally knew the texture and taste of her lips—soft as clouds, sweet as candy.

Just like that he was on fire and wanted more. He took her in his arms and pulled her into his lap, where she snuggled against his chest. Their jackets were in the way but he tightened his hold anyway. She slid her fingers into the hair at the nape of his neck and his whole body went hot and hard.

His heart was pounding and he couldn't get enough air into his lungs. He felt like a man drowning, a man sinking into the feel of Fiona, the scent of her skin, the need to touch her everywhere. Her breathless little moans drove him completely crazy and he wanted her here and now.

Then, through a haze of lust, he heard a nearby twig crack, loud as a gunshot in the quiet night. Whether it was an animal or a man, it was enough to break the spell.

He pulled his mouth from hers. "Fiona—"

"What?" She pressed her kiss-swollen lips together and blinked up at him.

"I need to get you back to the cabin before both your brothers and your father come looking."

"Oh. I guess you're right." Reluctantly she pushed herself out of his arms and stood in front of him. "Okay."

Side by side they walked the path back. Neither of them spoke and the air between them crackled with tension. Thoughts tumbled through his mind like rocks rolling down a hill. According to her reasoning, a kiss made them a thing. But he told her he would never promise her something he couldn't deliver.

As badly as he wanted to kiss her and have her in his bed, he could never do that. Fiona wasn't a fling kind of woman, but a fling was all he could give her. It was inevitable he'd let her down. He'd told the truth about not breaking vows and he wouldn't break the one he'd made to himself about never hurting her.

After three and a half awkward days, one of which included the best kiss she'd ever had, Fiona was relieved that it was finally time to pack up and go home. Luke, Ronan and Keegan were driving the cattle back to the ranches.

They were at the barn saddling horses and making sure everything was stowed away and organized for next year. Jamie and Brendan would take two trucks while she rode with her dad. She wanted to brainstorm some ideas for ranching articles with him. Anything to keep from thinking about the way Brendan had distanced himself after that excruciatingly romantic kiss in the moonlight.

At dinner in Kalispell they'd had a great time, and then he skipped the good-night kiss. When he finally did kiss her, she was ready to go wherever he would take her. Which, apparently, was nowhere, based on the fact that he'd barely said two words to her since. That night by the stream it felt to her as if he couldn't help himself, but afterward he resisted her just fine.

She was getting so many mixed signals, this "thing" was giving her whiplash.

"I'm done thinking about him."

And now she was talking to herself as she shoved the last of her clothes into a duffel, then carried it downstairs and out to the truck. She tossed it into the back seat and slammed the rear passenger door.

Her gaze was drawn to the horse trailer hitched to Luke's truck, where Brendan was sweet-talking one of the animals inside. Her heart did a little flip that made a liar out of her. She couldn't seem to stop thinking about him.

If only he wasn't so gosh-darn good-looking. Even as she thought that, she knew it wasn't just about him being handsome. If he wasn't a decent man, Luke and Eva wouldn't have him at Sunshine Farm.

"Something wrong, Fee?"

"Hmm?" She glanced around as her father walked up behind her. "I'm sorry, what?"

"Looked like you were a million miles away." Paddy

put a box of supplies in the bed of the truck, then met her gaze. "Something on your mind?"

"Always. You know me," she said vaguely.

"I do. Better than you think." There was a curious intensity in his eyes. "And I suspect what you're thinking has something to do with the new fella."

She flicked a glance in Brendan's direction. Now he was leaning against the horse trailer, patiently waiting to head out after loading the animals. Looking as if he didn't have a care in the world. What would it take to shake that casual attitude?

"Why would you say that?" she asked her dad.

"There it is." Her father nodded knowingly.

"What?"

"The tone. The one telling me I'm just a man and couldn't possibly understand women. Your mother uses it on me all the time."

"And you always tell her she's right."

"Mostly she is. And she likes hearing it." He grinned, showing a hint of the charmer who'd captured her mother's heart. "But don't you believe that I'm completely clueless about this sort of thing."

Paddy O'Reilly had pretty much let her mom deal with it. Even when Fiona had been the talk of Rust Creek Falls after being dumped, her dad had only muttered that he never liked the rat bastard scum-sucking loser. But he'd never actually talked to her about it. So she was curious about his interest now.

"Define 'this sort of thing,'" she told him.

"Let's just say it didn't escape my notice that you and Tanner disappeared the other night. Together. Just the two of you."

Fiona felt heat creep into her cheeks. She'd hoped no one had noticed that. When not a word was said about it, she'd believed she was home free. "It's not what you think, Dad."

"So you know what I'm thinking?"

She didn't want to spell that out. Not to her father. "We talked. And there is no 'this sort of thing.'"

"If you say so."

"I do."

Paddy didn't respond. He just stared at her. Fiona felt like a little girl again, the one who always cracked and confessed wrongdoing under the pressure of that look. It hadn't seemed like it at the time, but life was easier when she'd been a child. Now she wasn't her father's little girl anymore. She was a grown woman and didn't have to tell him that Brendan had kissed her. And that she liked it. That kiss had rocked her world like an earthquake, but obviously she was the only one feeling aftershocks. Hence, there was nothing between them.

Paddy finally sighed and shook his head. "You're as pretty as your mother and as stubborn as me. I'm not sure that's a good thing, Fiona."

How about that? She'd stared down the master and he got nothing out of her. It was just a small thing, but she still felt proud. "I love you, too, Dad."

"Love is both a blessing and a curse." He fished the truck keys out of his jeans pocket. "I need to start her up and make sure this old girl will get us home."

Seeing Brendan here at the roundup staging area had pushed everything else from her mind. Fiona had forgotten that when they left home, the truck had been running rough. Like all the ranch equipment, her father took care of maintaining his vehicles.

"Are you worried about it?" she asked.

"No. But if there's a problem, I want to know about it before everyone takes off from here." He nodded in Brendan's direction. "Want to make sure I don't need his help. I'll take a look at everything, then start her up."

He walked to the front of the truck and lifted the hood, then leaned in to inspect the engine guts. A couple minutes later he straightened and got in behind the wheel to start it up. Suddenly there was a loud, explosive sound as the engine backfired.

Fiona happened to be looking at Brendan, who instantly dropped to the ground as if he'd been shot. She'd seen enough movies and TV shows and read articles about the challenges of combat soldiers returning to civilian life. Not all the wounds showed on the outside. She didn't have to be a shrink to realize the unexpected boom must have triggered memories of a dangerous war zone, where an explosion meant injury and death.

Almost as quickly as he'd gone down, Brendan was back on his feet. His back was to her so he wasn't aware that she'd seen.

"Doggone it." Her father slid out from behind the wheel and poked his head back under the hood. "That's never good. It could be the spark plugs or a dirty air filter. Or something else."

"Should I get Brendan to have a look?"

"Couldn't hurt," he said. "He fixed the tractor when I couldn't see squat wrong with it. The man is a genius with this stuff."

"Should I tell him you said that?" she teased.

Paddy looked up from the wires and gizmos under the hood. "Can if you want to. Doesn't mean I'm not still watching him real close."

"Don't think I don't appreciate that."

He grinned. "The heck you do. But fathers watch out for their baby girls. Before you say it, I know you're not a baby anymore. Doesn't make a damn bit of difference."

Now that she thought about it, Paddy didn't involve himself in her love life, except to say he didn't like the loser who dumped her. And he was the only one in the family who'd felt that way. What had he seen that no one else had?

"What do you think of Tanner, Dad?"

"Don't have enough information yet to answer that. I can tell you one thing. Serving this country in the Marine Corps goes a long way with me." He straightened and met her gaze. "But you're asking if I like him for you."

"No. It's not like that." Because Brendan had made it clear he wasn't for her. There was no "them." "I was just wondering what you thought."

Her father glanced at the other truck and horse trailer, where the man in question was waiting, then back at her. "It's a long ride home and there will be plenty of time to share my thoughts on everything. But if you don't get on over and ask that fella to have a look at this truck pretty quick, we may never get started."

"Yes, sir."

She headed over to Brendan. The front of him was still a little dusty from dropping to the ground and he was absently brushing it away.

"Hi," she said.

"Hey." He didn't look up.

"Are you all right?" she asked.

"Horses and gear are all loaded up. Just waiting on the others to say the word that we're ready to move out."

Fiona didn't miss the fact that he'd deliberately made her question impersonal. She could play along and pretend she hadn't seen how the truck backfiring had affected him. The others were busy, so no one but her knew how he'd reacted. Or she could ask straight out. A case could be made for either course of action, but the reality was that she just couldn't ignore he was going through something.

"So, the truck backfire was loud," she started.

He looked at her then, and there was a mix of emotions in his clear green eyes. Suspicion. Wariness. Embarrassment that someone had seen. A little residual fear, maybe.

"Could be the catalytic converter," he said.

"Actually, I wasn't asking why. It was more about what happened when you heard it."

His mouth pulled tight for a moment before he shrugged. "I jumped."

"I jumped. You hit the deck, Brendan."

"You saw that, huh?" He looked away for a moment. "Wasn't expecting it."

"Do you want to talk about it?"

"Nothing to say." He slid his fingertips into the pockets of his worn jeans.

"I don't think that's true. You might not want to discuss it but I bet there's quite a bit to fill a conversation. And I'm happy to listen. In fact, Dad doesn't need me. I could ride along with you—"

"As you've pointed out, I'm not much of a talker. Just the way I'm wired, I guess."

"You're not alone," she said. "I've got brothers and they keep things bottled up pretty tight. Probably a guy thing. So I get it."

"Nothing really to get." He lifted a shoulder. "Not much to say."

"Okay. I won't push."

"Good."

"I just have one more thing to say," she told him.

"Why doesn't that surprise me?"

"Maybe because *I'm* wired that way." She stuffed her cold hands into the pockets of her sheepskin jacket. "The other night you told me you don't ever take for granted your oath to protect and defend the Constitution of this country. I'm pretty sure you can't forget things that happened to you in the service of it."

"Fiona, don't make a big deal out of this—"

"I'm almost finished." She heard the beginning of irritation in his voice and didn't care. There was nothing to lose by giving him a piece of her mind. "You don't have to tell me anything. But it might help you to talk to someone." She stopped and looked at him. "Now I'm done."

"Okay. I'm going to see what's keeping the guys." He half turned toward the barn.

"Wait. One more thing."

"What?"

"Dad wanted me to ask you to look at the truck. Make sure you don't see something that can't wait until we get home."

"Okay." He didn't say it, but everything about his body language said he was relieved that she'd changed the subject.

Fiona's heart broke a little bit for him. Everyone needed help sometimes, someone to listen. Even strong men like Brendan Tanner. Clearly he wasn't about to confide in her, but she would really like it if he did.

She would like that way too much.

Chapter Seven

Several days after returning to Rust Creek Falls, Brendan still couldn't forget the way Fiona looked at him. With pity. It made him so mad. Not that he blamed her. She had a soft heart and wanted to help. He was ticked off at himself for not being able to control his reaction to that truck backfiring at the cabin. The unexpected sound had put him right smack in the middle of a firefight in Afghanistan.

Fiona was the last person he would pick to see him like that. He didn't want anyone to feel sorry for him, but especially not her. It was pointless to puzzle out the why of that because A, he didn't do commitment and he wouldn't do anything less than that with her, and B, he was getting into shape to reenlist in the Marine Corps.

It was early afternoon when he pulled his truck to a stop at the curb of a cute little house on South Broomtail Way in Rust Creek Falls. An American flag was proudly displayed in front. Eddie Halstead had asked for his help with a couple of projects. On top of the fact that her husband was a former marine, Brendan wasn't much enjoying his own company right now and figured it couldn't hurt to give them a hand.

The siding on their home was painted green, a shade that reminded him of his woodland utilities uniform. Shutters framing the windows were white. A sidewalk led to three steps and a covered porch. The grass was cut and neatly edged, bushes and flowers strategically arranged. The property was buttoned down, he thought. It definitely passed inspection.

He exited the truck and retrieved his portable toolbox from the back, then headed up the walkway. Moving closer, he saw a sign above the door that said, *"Semper fi." Semper fidelis*—always faithful—the Marine Corps motto.

Brendan felt emotion and pride and something that could have been homesickness all roll into a ball and come to rest on his chest. He missed belonging somewhere, having a purpose, someone else counting on him and him counting on them. Although, now that he thought about it, Eddie was counting on him to do some things around here that she didn't want her husband to do.

He rang the bell and waited. When the door opened, an older man stood there. He was nearly six feet, with silver hair cut military-short and sharp, clear brown eyes. He stood straight, his shoulders back, as if standing inspection.

"You must be Brendan Tanner. The tools are a clue." He glanced at the metal box. "I'm J. T. Halstead."

Brendan shook the hand he held out. "Nice to meet you, sir."

"It's J.T. And just so we're clear, son, it's Eddie's idea for you to be here. I'm perfectly capable of getting on a ladder, but I agreed to please her. Plus, if I fell off and didn't kill myself in the process, she'd never let me live it down."

"Yes, sir." Brendan figured J.T. was a lucky man to

have someone care about him that much. Fiona would care that way.

J.T. shook his head. "I'm still trying to decide whether or not to thank you for fixing that blasted blender. A man drinking his breakfast is just wrong."

"Roger that, sir. Did you sabotage the blender?"

"Wish I'd thought of it," he said wryly.

"Are you going to ask the man in, J.T.?" Eddie's voice was coming from somewhere beyond the doorway. "Hurry up and close the door. I can feel a cold draft all the way back here."

"My bride." There was amusement in the man's expression. "Feel free to salute her. She likes that."

J.T. motioned him inside then shut the door. He turned and started walking toward the back of the house. His gait was uneven, the left leg stiff as the man sort of swung it forward from the hip. The prosthetic leg. This marine had come home from war physically changed yet had figured out how to move on, and Brendan was impressed.

They walked into the kitchen, where Eddie was standing at an island in the center of the room, removing cookies from a pan and setting them on a rack to cool. "Hi, Brendan. Thanks for coming over."

"No problem. Nice place." He looked around the cozy room and breathed in the delicious smell of freshly baked cookies.

On the pale yellow walls there were pictures of parsley, sage, rosemary and thyme. Womanly touches were everywhere, making the room feel like a foreign country to him. Most of his growing-up years had been just him and his dad. Testosterone central.

Then he noticed a couple other wall hangings. One said, "All men are created equal and then a few become brothers. United States Marine Corps." Another read,

"I'm not a hero, but I had the honor of walking beside a few who were." This manly touch made for a nice balance.

Eddie smiled at him and asked, "Would you like a cookie? Maybe a cup of coffee to go with it?"

"Probably I should just get started on that list of yours."

"It's an impressive one," she said, her eyes twinkling. "But when's the last time you had home-baked cookies?"

Brendan wasn't sure he ever had. "Well, if you're sure—"

"You know, Ed, someone should try one—just to make sure they're up to your usual standards." J.T. gave him a wry look. "It's the least a brother can do."

"Oorah." Brendan grinned.

Eddie set two cups of coffee and a plate of cookies on the table along with Halloween napkins. "Here you go."

He sat in one of the ladder-back chairs.

J.T. sat at a right angle to him and automatically kneaded his left thigh, as if it bothered him. But there was no evidence of discomfort in his expression when he smiled at his wife. "Thanks, honey."

"This is my day to call Kyleigh, our daughter who lives in Colorado," she explained to Brendan. "J.T., you're clear on the list?"

"Crystal," he answered.

She met Brendan's gaze. "Do *not* let him step foot on a ladder."

"Understood." He wanted to salute but resisted.

When the two men were alone J.T. said, "That look was the one she used to keep sixth graders in line when their impulse control got out in front of their common sense. She's a retired teacher."

"Could have been a Corps drill instructor," Brendan observed.

"She'd take that as a compliment."

"I meant it as one."

The other man nodded then stirred cream and sugar into his coffee. "So, how long were you in?"

Brendan knew he meant the length of his military service. "Fourteen years. I enlisted after high school."

"You always wanted to be a soldier?"

"Something like that." Mostly he'd wanted to get away from home. He'd signed up before his dad got dumped by yet another woman in his life, then felt guilty leaving Leon alone when he was going through such a rough time.

"How many tours did you do?"

"I deployed to Afghanistan three times."

"Rust Creek Falls is the polar opposite of Kabul," J.T. said.

"Unless a car backfires." Brendan hadn't meant to say that, but he saw agreement in the other man's eyes.

"How long have you been out?"

"Year and a half. My father had cancer. I came home to take care of him." Brendan stared at the coffee in his cup. "He died six months ago."

"Sorry for your loss, son."

"Thank you."

"So you're still adjusting to civilian life."

"*Still* being the operative word. In most ways it feels as if I've just started. The first year with my dad didn't seem to count. It was sort of regimented. Doctors, treatment, drugs, survival."

"And it took your mind off all the things you didn't want to think about."

"Yeah." Something clicked inside him, as if a connection was made and a current of understanding flowed freely. The memories were always there, waiting for something to trigger them. He knew that it had taken the military brass a long time to recognize post-traumatic stress as a very real syndrome for men and women who served in a theater of war.

J.T. obviously lost his leg. He'd come home and all these years later seemed to have a normal life. What had it taken to get him here?

"How did you get past it?" Brendan met the other man's gaze and knew he understood the question. "If you don't mind me asking."

"Not at all." He took a cookie from the plate and bit into it. "We got married before I was drafted and sent overseas near the end of the war. I was lucky enough to have her to come home to. Right away she got pregnant with our first child, Kyleigh. And I didn't have time to think about 'Nam. I had a family to support and I worked as an electrician for a construction company in Kalispell. Days were busy. It was at night when the war terrors came back."

"How so?"

"Nightmares. Things you push away in the day come out then and there's no way to hide it, as much as you'd like to. Eddie's no one's fool."

"What did you do?"

"I was smart enough to open up and talk about what I experienced, and then I let her love the horror of it right out of me."

"Hmm."

"She's the best thing that ever happened to me. And every day I try to let her know it." J.T. drank the last of the coffee in his cup. "Speaking of that, if you're ready, we can start here in the kitchen, replacing that ceiling light. I've got a stepladder in the garage. I'll show you where it is."

For the rest of the afternoon, Brendan chatted with the couple as he went from changing spotlights to putting up outside Halloween decorations to checking out a noise in the refrigerator. But in the back of his mind, the veteran's words rolled around. Love was the answer. If so, that was a problem. What did a marine veteran do when love was the enemy?

Fiona walked into the kitchen and smelled bacon and eggs when her taste buds had been expecting something completely different. "I thought you were going to make Grandma's pumpkin waffles."

"I was." Her mother turned off a burner on the stove. "But Grandma's waffle iron isn't cooperating."

"What's wrong?" Fiona walked over to the counter and lifted the heavy metal lid. "Looks okay to me."

"It won't heat up."

"But it's October. We always have pumpkin waffles on Sundays in October."

"I know." Maureen sighed.

She didn't miss the distress in her mother's eyes that could turn into tears any second. The woman loved her mother's waffle iron. It was one of only a few mementos she had and the thing was used frequently, keeping Grandma's memory alive. Maureen O'Reilly didn't just pull an old appliance out of the cupboard. With it came the stories, tender and quirky, about the feisty woman who had raised her.

"Isn't the batter already made? Can't you make pancakes instead?"

"I could. But the experience isn't the same without the tradition." She sniffled and blinked, stubbornly refusing to give in to tears.

"Maybe Dad can look at it. I'll go get him," Fiona offered.

"No. He already checked it out and pronounced the

thing dead. So he went to mend fences in the north pasture."

"No way. It's family day."

"I got a little emotional."

And her father couldn't stand to see his wife cry, especially if he couldn't make her feel better. "Oh, Mom—"

Maureen shrugged. "He said it was old and maybe it was time to get a new one. But they don't make things like they used to and there's no character in them. Just instructions you can't understand and buttons you don't know what to do with."

"Maybe it can be fixed, Mom."

"I already told you. Your father is ready to throw it out like a used tissue."

"No, I meant Brendan Tanner. He took care of Eddie Halstead's blender. She's singing his praises all over town."

Her mother's expression brightened. "Why didn't I think of that?"

"Because you were upset and there hasn't been anyone in Rust Creek Falls who could do it before. You should take it to him," Fiona suggested.

"That's a great idea." Maureen shook her head. "Would you mind dropping it off for me? I'm making pumpkin bread today. Halloween isn't far off and the holidays will be here before you know it. I have to start the holiday baking and freezing."

Her mother baked a bazillion loaves for gifts and get-togethers from now through Christmas. Maureen O'Reilly's pumpkin bread was a very big deal.

"Don't you need me to help you with that, Mom? The waffle iron can wait. You can drop it off on your way into Rust Creek Falls the next time you go."

Her mother arched one eyebrow. "Is there some reason you're avoiding Brendan?"

"No." Did she say that too fast? "Of course not." Was she protesting too much?

"Then why don't you want to see him?"

Maybe because she wanted too much to see him? If she said that, there would be a talk, which would be a waste of time. He'd kissed her, sampled the wares so to speak, and lost interest. Apparently she didn't light his fire.

"Who says I don't want to see him?" she protested.

"Good. Then take Grandma's waffle iron over to him today. And don't leave until you have a prognosis."

"He's probably not even there, Mom. Since he fixed our tractor, other ranchers have been after him to look at their larger equipment. His skills are in high demand."

"Good. Then just drop it off. You won't have to even see him."

As much as Fiona didn't want to take a chance on seeing Brendan, there was no getting out of this. "Okay."

Maureen O'Reilly wore stubborn like a winter coat. She put it on when necessary, then shrugged out of it when the job was done. She smiled sweetly, then hugged her daughter. "Thank you so much, sweetheart."

So that's why, a few minutes later, with a breakfast sandwich to go, she was on her way to Sunshine Farm with Grandma's on-life-support waffle iron. She couldn't shake the feeling this trip was flirting with fate, but she hadn't done much flirting at all recently. So, what the heck?

After turning off the road onto the property, she smiled. It was hard to look at the sunshine-yellow barn and be grumpy. She parked nearby, then grabbed the square appliance from the seat beside her and got out of the truck. A memory washed over her of chasing little

Jared Stockton into the barn and meeting Brendan Tanner for the first time.

In the looks department he was a standout, but she'd spent some time with him since and found he was so much more than just a pretty face. He had courage, loyalty, integrity—and baggage. Well, who didn't?

She'd really hoped to just leave the appliance and a note because he was out working on someone's tractor, but that turned out not to be necessary. He turned when she walked through the doorway of his workshop.

"Fiona." He sounded a little surprised. "Hi."

Was it her imagination or just wishful thinking that he looked pleased to see her? "Good morning. Although I guess it's almost afternoon now."

"Yeah." His gaze dropped to the appliance she was holding against her chest like armor. "What do you have there?"

She blinked at him, then remembered. Walking closer, she set the thing beside the lamp he was working on. "It's a waffle iron."

"I figured," he said wryly.

"You're probably on your way out to fix something bigger and more important. But when you get a few minutes could you take a look at this? For my mom."

"What's the problem?"

"It won't heat up." She couldn't say the same for her. Standing this close to him made her skin burn. Nonchalance would be so much easier if she didn't have vivid memories of how wonderful it felt to be held in his strong arms.

He lifted the heavy lid and glanced at the individual squares inside. "No heat makes it nothing more than a doorstop." He nodded thoughtfully. "I'll have a look right now."

"I don't want to keep you. But I have explicit orders from my mother to stay until you've fixed the thing or pronounced it dead. But it really can wait."

"I'm in no rush." He laughed. "And this sounds really serious."

Humor transformed his face, making him look younger, more carefree. It was an expression that could have a woman swooning if she wasn't careful. "I don't mean to sound so dramatic, but this means a lot to my mother because it belonged to her mother. She makes waffles and passes on the story of how Grandpa courted Grandma when they were still in high school."

"Sounds special." He was looking at the cord. "This is frayed and that means electrical current isn't getting through."

"Can you fix it?"

"Yes."

"Oh, thank God." She touched a hand to her chest. "My mom will be so relieved."

"Happy to help." He didn't look at her, but his voice took on a wistful note when he asked, "Did you know your grandmother?"

"Yes. She was so wonderful. I miss her, too. She died a couple of years ago, way too young. It's one of the reasons my mom is so sentimental about this thing."

"Hmm."

"What?" She couldn't read his expression.

"I was just wondering what it's like to have a mom," he said.

At dinner the day she'd met him, he made that cryptic remark. *Necessity is the mother I never had.* Fiona had been curious then, but said nothing. She knew him better now and if he didn't want to answer, he would change the subject.

"What happened to your mom?" she asked gently.

"She left my dad when I started kindergarten." He worked while he talked, baring the wires, stripping them with a plier-like tool.

The words and tone were conversational, but devoid of emotion, as if he was talking about someone else. But Fiona's heart hurt for the five-year-old boy he'd been. "She just walked out without a word?"

"No, there were plenty of words. She explained everything to me."

"That must have been one heck of an explanation, because I don't understand how a mother could leave her child."

"She said she'd been unhappy with my dad from the beginning. Turns out she only married Leon because she got pregnant and was scared. She didn't know what to do."

"But you were just a little boy. That's heavy stuff to lay on you."

"There's more."

"Seriously?"

"Oh, yeah." He met her gaze for a moment. "She said she picked the name Brendan because it's Celtic for *sword*. Warriors used swords and I needed to be brave."

"So she never planned to stay."

"Apparently. She waited to leave until I was in school and child care would be easier for my dad. He was handsome and a good man but she needed more excitement. The truth was she wasn't mom material and she said I would be better off with just my dad raising me."

Fiona was stunned at the amount of information the woman had unloaded on such a young child. "I have to say, I agree with her about her lack of maternal instincts."

"You think?"

"I don't know what to say. At least she didn't walk away without a word? Or she's just a selfish witch."

"My dad went with the witch one. And a few other more colorful descriptions that I can't repeat in front of a lady." Mentioning his dad put emotion in his eyes and none of it was the warm and fuzzy kind.

"How did he take it?"

"Nearly broke him," Brendan admitted. "The sadness—" He shook his head. "I was young, but even I could see it."

"I don't remember much from being five," she said. "But I guess a life-altering crisis like your mom leaving is pretty hard to forget."

He inspected the repaired waffle iron cord, then plugged it in to test it. After lifting the lid, he felt the inside and smiled at her. "Heat."

No kidding, Fiona thought. When he looked like that she could almost feel steam coming out of her ears. "My mother will be so happy. She'd give you her first-born, but Ronan might have something to say about that."

"Something tells me you're right," Brendan said wryly. "I'm glad I could help."

"Me, too." Then he looked a little sheepish and she asked, "What?"

"I didn't mean to go on about my past. Don't know why that all came out. Sorry—"

She held up a hand to stop him. "No apology necessary. What are friends for?"

"Is that what we are?"

"I hope so. And friends talk to each other about what's bothering them."

"So, let's even the score. Anything bothering you?"

"Just how much I owe you for fixing the waffle iron."

He thought for a moment. "What about a horseback ride?"

Warning bells were sounding, but she could barely hear because her heart was pounding so hard. "You fix the tractor and buy me dinner, then you repair the waffle iron and want to take me riding."

"Is that a yes or no?"

"It's a 'keep this up and I'll be your best customer.'" She felt as sunny and happy as the cheerful color of this barn. "So, yes, it's a yes."

A big fat affirmative. Because being careful was highly overrated.

Chapter Eight

Brendan wasn't sure about Fiona becoming his best customer, but she was his best *something*. At the roundup he'd looked forward to seeing her every day. When it was over, he'd missed her. When she came in with that waffle iron, he'd been so damn glad to see her. The idea of her just walking away after he'd repaired it made him impulsive. All he could think of to keep her there was a horseback ride.

He'd checked with Luke to make sure borrowing a couple of horses for a ride was all right with him. After being grilled, he had to admit that the second horse was for Fiona. That was all it took for his friend to enthusiastically give the okay. A guy would have to be exceptionally clueless not to get that Luke was all but throwing him and Fiona together. She would probably have a negative opinion after what happened the last time someone fixed her up.

But Brendan couldn't worry about that—or anything else. Not on such a beautiful day. It was cool but sunny. The sky was deep blue and seemed to go on forever. And there was a stunning, sexy woman riding beside him.

As their horses trotted away from Sunshine Farm toward wide-open land, he looked over at her. Her hair gleamed like a brand-new copper penny in the sun. She looked happy and carefree, her body moving with the animal in a graceful, fluid motion. He could stare at her all day, but she'd busted his chops about making conversation, so he racked his brain for a topic.

"I'm sorry your grandmother's waffle iron broke and upset your mother." That was a bald-faced lie. It's what brought her here. "But it's nice to see you."

"Nice to see you, too." The smile she sent in his direction was pleased and a little shy. "And I'm sorry your mom left. You can borrow mine if you want."

"I think she's got enough kids to worry about."

Brendan still wasn't sure why he'd told her about his mother. Might have something to do with his time out at the Halsteads' yesterday. Eddie baked cookies, called her daughter once a week. She was the kind of mother he'd like to have had. And then there was his chat with J.T. The veteran was the second person who'd advised him to talk about the experiences that he couldn't quite forget. Fiona had been the first.

"My mom would never shut anyone out from under her worry umbrella," Fiona said. "If someone needs to be worried about, she's more than happy to oblige."

A maternal quality his own mother had been missing. He glanced over and found Fiona looking back. A feeling crept over him that she was a lot like her mom in caring for people. The way she'd come to him after the truck backfired, quietly checking to make sure he was okay. The answer to that was yes and no. He'd had a combat flashback, but guys he'd served with had it a lot worse. He wished there was something he could do to help get them past the worst like Luke was doing for him.

"You should probably check with your mom before

offering her services to strangers." He was kidding, but her mouth pulled tight for a moment.

"I don't have to check. She's a natural born worrier. If she doesn't have something to fret about, she'll find something. Look at it this way—you'd be doing her a favor."

He laughed. Humor swelled inside him and lit up all the places that had been so dark for so long. He defied anyone to spend time around this woman and not smile. It was healing. Exactly what he'd hoped for when he'd heard about a ranch in Rust Creek Falls that offered a place to stay for someone looking to make a fresh start. Luke's invitation was making it possible for Brendan to take back the life he'd had before his father got sick.

"If I need to be worried about, I'll let her know," he promised.

"I would hope you'd let me know first," she said.

"Sure."

"Really?" She didn't look convinced.

His response had come automatically and he wondered now if it really was true. She'd given him an opening to talk about his battle baggage, but he'd brushed her off. Partly because he didn't want the hell of war to touch her in any way and partly because only someone who'd been through it could understand.

"I've been taking care of myself for a long time," he finally said. "As a soldier it's my job to take care of other people."

"But you're not a soldier now," she said quietly.

"Right." It was hard to shake the military mind-set when that was the only place he'd ever felt he belonged. "I guess fixing things for folks is still taking care of them."

"Can't argue with that. Not only is my mother over the moon that you fixed Grandma's waffle iron, the whole family will reap the rewards of a pumpkin spice waf-

fle breakfast tomorrow. Ranchers around here are ec-
static about your skills with fixing tractors and backhoes.
Rumor has it that there's a waiting list for your services.
You have so taken care of us."

"Understood." That made him feel good, and Brendan
wondered if his father had ever been able to find that perspective about the service he'd provided.

They were quiet for a while as their horses plodded
along a crude trail carved through prairie grass. In the
distance mountains stood tall and rugged. Straight ahead,
just beyond a line of trees, he spotted a stream.

He pointed to it. "That's a good place to rest and water
the horses."

"Okay."

Closer to the river bank they stopped, dismounted,
then led the animals to the water. When they'd finished
drinking, Brendan drew them to nearby grass and secured
the reins to a sturdy bush before joining Fiona, who was
leaning against the trunk of a ponderosa pine tree.

He stopped beside her and breathed in the clean air—
no desert dust, fear sweat or smell of gunpowder anywhere. Peace was taken for granted by anyone who'd
never been to war, and Brendan savored this moment,
memorizing everything about it. He studied the mountains that seemed closer and bigger from here than they
were from Sunshine Farm.

Fiona followed his gaze. "I hear Texas is flat."

"A lot of it is. But there are some mountains in the
western part of the state. Somehow this is different."

"In a good way?"

"Yeah."

"Won't be long until there's snow on them," she commented, nodding toward the towering peaks.

For some reason the words made him feel empty and

he was filled with longing. To be in the same place from season to season, year after year. Long enough to know when the leaves would change and the snow would come.

"I look forward to seeing snow. Maybe for the holidays. I've never had a white Christmas."

"Really?" When she looked at him, her eyes sparkled with happiness. "I wasn't sure you would be staying that long."

"The truth is that I haven't figured out my future yet. I can't make you any promises."

"I never asked for one." Her eyes were flashing now but not with anything good. "What makes you think I want a commitment?"

"All I said was it would be nice to see snow. I honestly have no idea what I'm doing tomorrow, so—"

"I'm not saying you have to decide. I made an innocent comment and you pushed back as if I suggested we elope next Sunday. I'm a big girl, Brendan—"

"Yeah. I noticed." Things would be less complicated if he hadn't.

She pushed away from the tree and faced him, standing just inches from him. This was not a good time to finally figure out what it meant that a woman was beautiful when she was angry. And Fiona was more beautiful than he'd ever seen her.

"I can handle the truth, Tanner. Stop sending mixed signals. You ask me to dinner then give me no good-night kiss. You kiss me in the moonlight, then ignore me. If you don't want more than friendship, I—"

"Of course I do," he interrupted.

"Well, you've got a funny way of showing it." She must have seen something in his expression because she poked her index finger into his chest and said, "Don't you dare tell me it's complicated."

"You said you could handle the truth," he reminded her.

"I can. But it's really simple. Either you feel something for me or you don't. Clearly you don't. And I'm leaving before this gets even more weird."

"Don't go." Brendan took her hand to stop her. He stared into eyes so clear and blue and innocent they could wash away all the bad he carried inside him. He took a lock of her fiery hair between his fingers and breathed in the sweet, flowery scent of her skin. He'd used up every last ounce of willpower he had resisting the urge to have her. "Do you really not know that I think you're the most beautiful woman I've ever seen?"

Her smile was slow and sweet, but she wasn't quite sure of herself. "You do?"

"Seriously? Yes." He stared at her flawless face, cute little turned-up nose, full lips. "You're killing me here, Fee."

"So, what is it you want?" She studied him, searching for the answer on his face. "I don't mean the future. I'm not talking about tomorrow or the next day. What do you want now? Right this minute."

"You." The single word came out on a whisper as his heart pounded.

She moved closer so that their bodies were touching from chest to knee. Turning her face up, she asked, "Then what are you waiting for?"

Brendan knew he had good reasons for holding back, but right this second he had no idea what they were. He touched his mouth to hers and eagerly took what she offered. Her lips were soft and every bit as sexy here with the sun shining as they'd been in the moonlight.

He traced her mouth with his tongue and she opened to him without hesitation, offering everything. He explored slowly, thoroughly, and it wasn't nearly enough. He tugged her cotton shirt from the waistband of her jeans and slipped his hand underneath, settling his palm on her bare back. Her skin was even softer than he'd imagined and his imagination had gone wild. He moved his palm to her waist and slowly slid upward, brushing his thumb to the underside of her breast.

"Oh, Brendan—" Her breathing quickened and she pulled his shirt free from his jeans, then reached underneath, skimming her hands over his abdomen and up to his chest.

She seemed frustrated, in the cutest possible way, and tugged his snap-front shirt open. Pressing her body to his, she put her arms around his neck and stood on tiptoe to kiss him until he was sure his head was going to explode.

Brendan was breathing hard when he cupped her butt in his hands, then slid them to the backs of her thighs and lifted her. She wrapped her legs around his hips and he braced her against the tree, letting his forearm shield her back from the rough bark. If they didn't have their clothes on, he'd be inside her right now. He would—

Then the truth smacked him upside the head. Reality was a bitch. It was in the top ten hardest things he'd ever done, but Brendan pulled his mouth from hers.

"Fiona—"

"What?" Her voice was a breathless whisper, but there was wariness, too.

"You know I want you more than anything, right?"

"A second ago I thought so, but now I'm not so sure." She pressed her kiss-swollen lips together and there was a bruised expression in her eyes, as if she was expecting to be disappointed.

"It's the honest to God truth that I want you so much it hurts."

"But?"

"I don't have a condom."

She blinked at him as the consequences of that sank in. "Oh…"

He could almost see the wheels turning in her head and had a feeling he knew what she was about to suggest. He put a finger to her lips to stop the words. "No. I would never risk you that way. Besides, we're right out in the open. Not that far from Sunshine Farm. There's no telling who could ride by. I won't put you in a position like that."

"You're a good man." After blowing out a long breath she kissed his cheek. Then she let her legs slide down over his thighs until her boots touched the ground. "So, we're not that far from your cabin. Do you have protection there?"

He'd resigned himself to the fact that this wasn't going to happen. What with blood flow to his brain detoured, it took a second for her question to sink in. When it did, he grinned. "Why, yes, I do."

"Like I said, good man. I'll race you." She gave him a sassy look, then slipped out of his arms and sprinted toward the horses.

"Hot damn." Brendan was right behind her.

On horseback Fiona followed Brendan until he stopped in front of one of the seven log cabins built on Sunshine Farm property. It was small, and judging by the speed at which he dismounted, Brendan was in a hurry to get inside.

"I'll take care of the horses later." He took her reins

and along with his own tied them to one of the vertical log poles supporting the porch roof.

Fiona slid out of the saddle and met his gaze. His green eyes were more intense than she'd ever seen them and all the heat there was focused on her. But there was a question, too. And she didn't have to ask what it was.

She moved to him and slid her hand into his. "I haven't changed my mind."

A slow, sexy smile curved up the corners of his mouth. "It's been a long time."

That made her heart happy. Still, she couldn't resist saying, "I'm sure everything will come back to you."

With her hand tucked securely in his much larger one, they walked inside and shut the door behind them. It was barely closed before he pulled her into his arms and kissed her as if today was their last day on earth. In a heartbeat her breathing went from slightly elevated to "can't get enough air." The ride back had not cooled off her hormones. If anything, waiting made her want him even more desperately. She pulled at the snap front of his shirt, baring his chest to her touch. Again.

"Bedroom—that way," he said hoarsely, tugging her with him.

In the small room, simple cotton curtains covered the windows but sunlight sneaked in around the edges. There was a bed, a pine dresser and matching nightstands. In a frenzy they toed off boots and yanked off clothes, not necessarily their own. Brendan pulled the bedspread and blanket to the foot of the bed, then lifted her easily into his arms and set her in the middle of it.

He slid in beside her, then drew her to him and claimed her mouth. Her bare breasts were snuggled to his wide chest and she settled her palms on his back, exploring the impressive muscles. He swept his hand down her side and over her hip, the touch setting her on fire everywhere. But that was nothing compared to what she felt when his fingers trailed over her abdomen to the most intimate place between her thighs. If she was on fire before, now her body was an out-of-control blaze.

"Oh, God, Brendan. I want you…" She dug her fingers into the thick muscles of his biceps.

"Understood."

He rolled away, just far enough to reach into the nightstand and fumble around until he found what he was looking for. He retrieved the square packet and tore it open, then put on the condom.

He took her in his arms again and gently pressed her body into the mattress with his own. After nudging her legs apart with his knee, he slowly entered her and took his weight on his forearms. He was breathing really hard.

"Fiona—" he whispered.

"Yes." She arched her hips upward, showing him what she wanted without words.

He got the message. Slowly at first, then increasing the tempo, he thrust into her. With every movement she felt the tension tighten inside her until all too soon it exploded in a blaze of exquisite pleasure. He held her until the aftershocks subsided, then started to move again. One thrust, then another and another until he buried his face in her neck as he found his own release. She held him tight while his breathing slowed.

Finally he lifted his head and looked at her, then brushed the hair back from her face. His smile was soft, tender—peaceful. "I don't ever want to move."

"Me, either." She traced a finger over his chest, really liking the masculine dusting of hair. "I hear a 'but.'"

"The horses are still outside in front of the cabin."

As the reality sank in, her eyes widened. She'd been in too much of a hurry before to worry about being seen, but that changed in a heartbeat. If no one knew about them, they wouldn't talk. Or judge. "Holy Mother of God—"

"Yeah." He rolled away from her and got up, heading for the small bathroom.

She jumped out of bed and started getting dressed. "What if someone sees them? They'll know we—you— I—"

"Had sex." He came out of the bathroom still naked and all male perfection.

The extra pounds she carried had never bothered Fiona more than they did right this minute. But that was sort of like shutting the barn door after the horse got out. "I would prefer it if only you and I knew what happened."

"My lips are sealed," he agreed.

"I'm pretty sure we can count on the horses not to rat us out, but if anyone comes by and starts asking questions—"

"I suggest we get a move on before that happens." He came close and gave her a quick kiss before putting his clothes on.

After Fiona tucked in her shirt and finger-combed her hair, she said, "This will have to do."

"You look beautiful. Like you just came from a man's bed after—"

"Oh, God."

"Or back from a ride."

"Right," she said enthusiastically. "That would explain the messy hair."

Brendan opened the door and Fiona poked her head out, making sure the coast was clear for a clean getaway. There was no one in sight and she untied the reins of her

horse. Brendan did the same and they started walking
the animals to the barn for food, water and a rubdown.

She was rocking a nice little glow now that no one was
the wiser about them having sex. The sky looked bluer.
The air was fresher. Life was better. But when they were
almost to the big yellow barn, Luke Stockton came around
the corner and there was a man with him. She recognized
Forrest Traub. The hunky former soldier walked with a
limp, the result of being wounded in Iraq. He lived in
Thunder Canyon, so the question was—why was he here?

"Hey, you two, how was the ride?" Luke asked.

Fiona felt heat creep into her cheeks. Did he know
what they'd just done? Surely not. How could he? There
was no choice but to brazen it out. "It was good. Beautiful day. Sun shining. Air crisp and clean. I brought over
my mother's waffle iron. It wouldn't heat. Brendan fixed
it." She was babbling and couldn't seem to stop. "Hey,
Forrest. How are you? How's Angie?"

"My wife is great." He looked at the man beside her.
"Who's your friend?"

More than a friend, she thought. But exactly what he
was, she really had no idea. "Sorry. Where are my manners? This is Brendan Tanner."

"He's the guy I told you about," Luke said.

"Ex-marine." Forrest nodded. "I was army."

They talked a bit, and after Brendan told him about
his father, the other man looked at him sympathetically.

"Sorry." He shifted his weight from one leg to the other
and winced from the movement. "It's tough enough to re-
adjust, but that's a really crappy thing to come home to."

"Yeah."

Fiona waited, but he didn't elaborate. Didn't explain
that his adjustment didn't really start until after his dad

died, making it feel pretty current to him. What was he thinking right now? He'd told her he hadn't figured out his future yet. Was he wishing he was still in the military? The subtext of what he'd said was that he hadn't wanted to resign but was forced to by his father's illness.

"Brendan is actually why I asked Forrest to come and check out Sunshine Farm," Luke said.

"Oh?" Fiona wasn't following.

"From experience I understand the challenges of reintegrating to civilian life," Forrest said. "Especially when there are physical changes. I had a hard time. Bitter and angry. If not for Angie I don't know where I'd be right now." He shook his head. "And I came home with just a bum leg. Some men and women have it really hard. Missing limbs. Traumatic brain injury. Then there are the emotional wounds of PTSD. Mental challenges can often be harder to measure progress."

"I'm not sure where Sunshine Farm comes in," she admitted.

"Luke contacted me because he knows I work with returning veterans and groups that help them assimilate to life stateside. He thinks a stay here might help a veteran dealing with all kinds of war-related problems."

"You'd have to ask Brendan to confirm," Luke said, "but I think R & R here has made him a little more social."

"Are you serious? Rest and relaxation?" Brendan laughed. "He's got the whole town bringing me stuff to fix. On top of that I get a call every day about fixing ranch equipment. Now he's nagging me to open a business. It's been nothing but work."

"And yet you continue to do it." Luke nodded with satisfaction. "So that got me to thinking. There are seven cabins. I helped my dad build them—one for each of his kids." Satisfaction faded and there was sadness in his eyes. "He and my mom wanted all of us to live here. If that didn't work out, they said they could always open a dude ranch."

"It didn't quite go that way," Fiona said gently.

Everyone in Rust Creek Falls knew the story. His folks died too young in a car accident, and the family got split up. Some of their kids were pretty little and ended up getting adopted by other families. The older boys—including Luke—left town on their own, and the rest were raised by their grandparents. In the last couple of years the Stocktons were finding their way back to each other.

"So what's your plan for the cabins?" she asked.

"I want to dedicate a couple of them for veterans who might need a quiet place where they can get a fresh start." He stopped for a moment. "I've given this a lot of thought and I'd like to start a charitable foundation, add more cabins. Make the existing ones more homey. But that would take some money."

"Hey, this is Rust Creek Falls. People are generous and more than happy to contribute to a good cause," Fiona pointed out. "In fact, you guys are having a Halloween party here, right?"

"Yeah," he said. "We want to make it an annual family tradition."

"Turn it into a fund-raiser," she suggested. "I'll get the word out on that. We can do a bake sale and pass the hat. All you and Eva have to do is plan the party, which I'm quite sure she has under control. Let me do the rest."

"Are you sure?" Luke said.

"Yes."

"Okay, then. I knew I could count on you. Everyone does."

Not everyone, she thought, looking up at Brendan. He

might be more social than when he got here, but he was still holding part of himself back. After what they'd just done in his cabin, she was more emotionally invested than she wanted to be. Obviously he was attracted to her, but he'd come right out and said he wouldn't make promises. There was every reason to believe she was just spinning her wheels.

Chapter Nine

For Brendan, time was now defined as before sleeping with Fiona and after. Before yesterday he'd been able to tell himself he could resist her. Today that didn't hold water. He couldn't stop thinking about her. Had sex ever been that perfect? Or was it just perfect with her?

And, damn it, how long had he been staring into space picturing her naked? If the guys in his unit could see him now, he'd be mocked mercilessly. *Back to work*, he told himself.

He looked at the broken toaster he'd taken apart and the line of small appliances on the workbench—some fixed, some waiting for his attention. He had decided to take a day off from fixing ranch equipment and try to clear off a backlog of things that folks needed in their homes. The sheer number was impressive and each one represented people who'd reached out to him.

"This town is sucking me in," he grumbled.

And not just the town. Fiona.

She was sassy and strong. Independent. And that was sexy as hell. The only part of making love to her that didn't meet a perfect standard was having to get up to care for the horses. But doing that first wasn't an option.

He'd nearly taken her by the stream. Waiting to have her was the hardest thing he'd ever done. The idea of not leaving his bed and making love to her for a week was awfully appealing, but he had a feeling even that wouldn't be long enough. And he was off again, thinking about her in his arms.

"I'm going to start calling you Sergeant Slacker." Luke walked into the workshop and set a large cardboard box on the bench in front of Brendan.

"That's Sergeant Major Slacker to you, and I'm going as fast as I can," he lied. Apparently he didn't need the guys in his old unit to mock him. Luke filled that role just fine.

"I would hope so." The other man grinned. "Because I have an idea."

"Does this inspiration have anything to do with me?"

"What was your first clue?"

"I'm pretty sure you didn't come out here to insult my work ethic." He nodded at the box in front of him. "And you brought a whole bunch of junk."

"Of all people you should see the potential here." Luke picked up a remote control car that had seen better days. "If you can fix this, it's worth something to someone. That would be found money. Maybe that's why it's called a *foundation*."

"Funny guy." Brendan glanced down at the box's contents and saw a stuffed toy with a pull on the back that presumably had made it talk at one time. There was a mirror with lights around it. If they lit up the thing wouldn't be here. And he saw a mobile with zoo animals hanging from a windup thing, for a baby's crib. "So you plan to sell these."

"If you can fix them. And I have every faith you can. Obviously you'd be donating your time," he pointed out.

"And just when am I supposed to find time to donate? What with making house calls to ranches to repair the big-ticket machinery?"

"You can teach someone how to do what you do."

The way his father had taught him, Brendan thought. "Are you planning to set up a booth in the corral to sell this stuff?"

Luke didn't look at all discouraged. "I'm going to search for retail space in town. Maybe I can talk the owner into reduced rent, or better yet, none at all, to maximize profits. Eva and I have big plans for Sunshine Farm. People coming here for a fresh start might be willing to volunteer some time, or if things go well, we can afford to pay a wage for their work."

"An awful lot of things have to fall into place," he pointed out.

"You are so glass-half-empty." Luke *tsk*ed. "Have some faith."

"I do. Faith that I may not be sticking around."

"And leave all this?" His friend glanced around the workshop that was starting to look like a trash heap with bicycles in various stages of disrepair. An electric frying pan and Crock-Pot were gathering dust. There was a leaf blower and even a chainsaw someone had persuaded him to try to work a miracle on.

"Hard to believe, I know," Brendan said wryly.

"Seriously, you should open a repair shop in town, right next to the Sunshine Farm Foundation Store. There's a real need and you'd be doing something worthwhile. It's a win-win."

"This was never a career goal," he pointed out. "Just something to keep me busy."

"Mission accomplished." Luke folded his arms over

his chest. "A man can't spend all his time on keeping in shape, you know."

That was a reference to his daily workouts. Training had been hit-and-miss when he was caring for his dad. Since coming to Rust Creek Falls, his daily routine included intense exercise in order to be physically ready to reenlist.

"I don't want folks to start depending on me."

"Hate to break it to you, my friend. They already do."

But could he depend on them? Before joining the Marines, the only person Brendan trusted was his dad.

In the military, shared experiences, hardship and danger had forged unbreakable bonds, ones that made his fellow soldiers more like brothers. But civilian life had not given him any reason to trust people.

Luke sighed. "At least think about making it permanent?"

Maybe that would keep him from thinking about Fiona. "Will do."

"So, when I walked in here just now you were deep in thought. Did that have anything to do with a certain pretty redhead who volunteered to handle the Halloween party fund-raiser for the foundation?"

It was like the man could read his mind and Brendan wasn't comfortable with that. On the day of his horseback ride with Fiona, Brendan remembered that his friend had said he was partially responsible for the idea to dedicate a certain number of cabins for soldiers. Brendan didn't want to be anyone's poster boy.

"I have a lot of things on my mind," he said.

"Are all of them named Fiona?"

The man wasn't going to let this go so it might be good to just throw him a bone. "She's a very special woman."

"You'll get no argument from me. Is it my imagination

that things have gotten serious between you two pretty quickly?"

As much as Brendan wanted to push back against that, he couldn't. That was the truth. And sleeping with her complicated everything. He hadn't changed his mind about her being the kind of woman who deserved more than a one-night stand.

"Are you asking me what my intentions are?"

"No. Yes." Luke held up a hand to stop the angry reply he was expecting. "I know I have no right. She's a grown woman, but—"

"You feel like a brother to her," Brendan finished.

"Yeah. How did you know that?"

"She told me it's hard to meet men in Rust Creek Falls because she grew up with most of them and they're all like brothers." He also knew that Fiona wasn't a fan of anyone fixing her up.

"Since I left town for years I didn't exactly grow up with her." Luke's easygoing expression disappeared for a moment, but then he seemed to shake off whatever had put it there. "Call me a cockeyed optimist—"

"You're a cockeyed optimist."

The other man laughed. "But I want everyone to be as happy as Eva and I are."

"You guys are the lucky ones."

His father hadn't been, and Leon warned Brendan not to risk his heart. So far he'd been pretty successful. Love had never been an issue because he always kept women at a distance. Somehow Fiona had breached his perimeter without firing a shot—just by being her. And suddenly the rules of engagement made no sense to him anymore.

"I am lucky," Luke agreed.

"For some of us that's just not in the cards."

"Then some of you have to make an effort to turn over

different cards." He held up a hand again. "I'm not asking why, just saying you don't have to be alone."

He'd always felt alone but that was before Fiona. And he'd never missed any woman the way he did her when they were apart. But putting up barriers was second nature now. Bringing them down wasn't easy to do and he wasn't even sure he wanted to try.

"Look, not that I don't enjoy being badgered," Brendan said, "but don't you have something else to do? Somewhere else to be? Another guy to play matchmaker for? And it has to be said. I'm not sure the Cupid thing is a good look for you."

"I'm really hurt," Luke teased. "But you're not wrong. I do have to get going. As a matter of fact, I'm on my way into town and, if you want, I can deliver some of the things you've repaired. Save you a trip."

"That's okay. I'll take care of it." His response was automatic, a default position, not depending on anyone. If he did it himself, he knew the job was done. No one could let him down. "Thanks for the offer, though."

"We're going to have to learn to work together when you eventually crack under pressure and agree to open the repair shop. When that happens, I promise not to say I told you so."

Before Brendan could tell him he was full of it, Luke walked away. Based on the man's perceptive remarks about Fiona and his own tendency to distrust others, it was hard not to believe that Luke was reading his mind.

Except if that was the case, he would also know why he felt the way he did. In the Marines, it started with boot camp. Recruits had to work together. If someone screwed up they were all punished. Others had his back; he had theirs. The training prepared them all for what was coming and the bond became stronger, literally forged in fire, during the heat of battle.

He'd never felt like he belonged anywhere the way he did in the Marine Corps. Brendan had made it through his father's illness and passing because of his resolve to reenlist when he got himself in good enough physical shape.

Then Fiona chased a kid into this workshop and his whole world tilted. The more time he spent with her, the more he felt caught in a firefight without his combat armor. It was easy for Luke to hype being married when things worked out so well for him. But Brendan had seen what happened when it all went to hell and he didn't want to set foot in that minefield.

After learning of Luke Stockton's plans for Sunshine Farm and the foundation he planned to start, Fiona got busy. The Halloween party was coming up fast and she had to get word out quickly. So, late the following afternoon, she headed to *The Rust Creek Falls Gazette* office in town. The sooner there was a notice in the paper, the better.

She needed to see the features editor, Nell Cook, who was in charge of a page called "What's Cookin'." She reported upcoming town events and a calendar of activities. If there was a bake sale, car wash for charity or a health clinic, Nell handled it. But she couldn't do that if she didn't know about it.

The office was located on North Main Street, and Fiona drove into the parking lot it shared with Bee's Beauty Parlor, Wings To Go and Daisy's Donuts. All of these businesses fronted the parallel street, North Broomtail Road. She parked and slid out of the truck, then headed around the building to the front door.

Nell was her friend. They'd gone to high school together, but the other woman was a couple of years younger. She wasn't married yet, either, but at least the big 3-0 wasn't staring *her* in the face.

Lydia Grant, receptionist and editor, sat at the front desk. She smiled. "Hi, Fiona. Go on back. Nell won't mind."

"Thanks."

She went down the short hall and found her friend's office. The door was open and Nell's back was to it. She was staring intently at the computer monitor.

Fiona knocked once. "What's cookin'?"

The other woman swiveled her chair around and grinned, then stood and walked past the cluttered desk for a hug. "Like I've never heard that before."

"Yeah. I couldn't resist. How are you?" She glanced at the desktop chaos that somehow worked for her friend. "Looks like you're keeping busy."

"That's an understatement," said the pretty brown-eyed brunette. "And you're here to give me more work, aren't you?"

"How did you know?"

"Because I know *you*. Have a seat." She indicated the unpadded chair and rested a hip on the corner of her desk, probably the only spot without something on it. "What's up?"

"Luke Stockton is turning his Halloween party into a fund-raiser."

"For what?"

"You're going to who, what, when, where and why me, so just listen without interrupting and I'll give it to you all at once." She took a deep breath and filled in her friend on all of Luke's plans. "Actually it was my idea to make a fund-raiser out of the Halloween party he and Eva are having at Sunshine Farm."

"You mean Lonelyhearts Ranch?" she said with a laugh.

"No. Officially it's called Sunshine Farm. And you can't miss the big yellow barn it gets its name from."

"That barn is visible from the moon," Nell agreed. "But the name Lonelyhearts Ranch is catching fire. As are the people who stay there, it would seem." She sighed at Fiona's look. "Don't pretend you don't know what I'm talking about. I don't write 'Rust Creek Ramblings' but I never miss a column that publicizes what goes on in this town."

"Me, either." The column contained gossip, rumors and romantic liaisons and was not to be missed. No one in town wanted to be left out of the loop. But Fiona wanted to be left out of any talk that could land her in that column. "I've noticed that fresh starters at the ranch have been featured a little."

"A little?" Nell pushed her black-framed glasses to the top of her head. "You think?"

Fiona knew her friend was driving at something but she couldn't see what. "It's all about a safe place to get your life together."

"Hmm." The other woman nodded knowingly. "Finding a relationship could also be defined as 'getting your life together.'"

"It's not about falling in love." If it were, Fiona would know.

"Maybe not about that, but it's still going on."

"What are you talking about?" That was a stall because Fiona knew exactly what she meant.

"Luke and Eva." Nell held up a hand and started counting off fingers.

"Technically they fell in love before moving to the ranch."

The other woman continued as if she hadn't said anything. "Amy Wainwright, who came for their wedding fell back in love with Derek Dalton. Or maybe they never stopped loving each other since that secret, impulsive teenage marriage."

"So the ranch didn't have anything to do with them committing to each other," Fiona argued.

"But it came together for them while Amy was staying there." She held up a third finger. "Then there's Mikayla Brown, who came to stay. Even pregnant, or maybe because she was, she ended up with millionaire Jensen Jones."

"Okay. I'll give you that. But it's coincidence that she happened to be staying there."

Wagging her ring finger, Nell said, "Josselyn Weaver came to stay and ended up with delicious widower Dr. Drew Strickland. She just came for a new beginning and found it with the doctor and his son."

"So she wasn't a lonely heart running from something." But Fiona had a feeling she was spitting into the wind.

"I'm beginning to think there's something in the water there, or a romantic vibe. So far everyone who came to visit has fallen in love."

"What's your point, Nell?"

"Brendan Tanner." There was a gleam in her eyes.

"It's certainly no secret that he's staying there." Fiona knew she was being guarded, but this conversation was headed to a place she didn't want to go.

"My point is—what's up with you and Brendan?"

"We've met."

"That's usually a prerequisite for something being up," Nell said wryly. "There's a rumor that you two are more than acquaintances."

Eva and Luke would know they'd hung out. Her parents and brothers, too. That meant her sisters, Fallon and Brenna, could know and say something to their husbands. Any one of them could have dropped a casual remark to anyone. In this town gossip spread fast, like fire in dry brush with hurricane force winds to push it along.

"Where did you hear that we're more than friends?"

"Around," the other woman said vaguely. "Is it true?"

"Is what true?"

"Oh, come on, Fiona. You know what I'm asking." She folded her arms over her chest. "Are you and Brendan Tanner an item?"

She did her best not to squirm in the uncomfortable chair under her friend's scrutiny. They knew each other so well it was possible Nell could see on Fiona's face that she'd done the wild thing with Brendan. "There is nothing but friendship between Brendan and me."

"You're lying. Something is up with you. What is it?"

"I feel like a witness on the stand. Since when is it your job to be the town's heart monitor?"

"Since you're my friend. And it's not the town's heart I'm concerned about. It's yours. I care about you." She shrugged. "Plus, I hear things."

"*Things* are thrown around in conversation every time someone in Rust Creek Falls goes into a store or business. How much of it is actually true?" Fiona argued.

"If you're talking about the Lonelyhearts Ranch, so far it's one hundred percent accurate."

The woman had a point. On top of everything else Fiona was wrestling with, she was going to have the distinction of being the first one to spoil that perfect romantic record. The quieter she kept whatever was happening with Brendan, the less likely she was to go down in Rust Creek Falls lore as a loser at love.

"Every streak comes to an end." Fiona did her best to keep her tone neutral.

"I haven't met him yet," Nell admitted. "Is he as good-looking as I've heard?"

Even better, she wanted to say. *And you should see him without his clothes on.* Sharing that, however, was not the way to avoid more personal questions. "He's very pretty, in a manly way."

"Where on the scale?"

Fiona knew she meant one to ten with ten being Hollywood-hunk gorgeous. "He's definitely above a five."

Nell removed her glasses from the top of her head and tossed them on a pile of papers littering the desk. "If I didn't know you better, I would say that you're trying to discourage me from checking him out. Is that because you've staked a claim?"

"No."

And even if she had, it would take two to be exclusive. Brendan obviously liked hanging out with her. She would have to be an idiot not to get that. But he never made a promise to her, so there'd been no vow to break. That would almost make it easier because then she could be angry. Anger was a very big shield to hide behind.

Fiona stood. "If you want to check him out, go for it. Be my guest. I have no objection."

"No, thanks." Nell grinned. "You of all people know that I don't have time for men."

What her friend meant was that she'd sworn off them, with good reason. "I better go. It's getting late. Do you want to go to Ace in the Hole for a burger?"

"If only." She sighed. "I have a lot of work here. Top on the list is writing up something about the Halloween party fund-raiser at Luke Stockton's place."

"I've never been more grateful that you're a workaholic. It's a really good thing he's going to do." Fiona stood. "Thanks, Nell."

After a goodbye hug, Fiona left the building and went to the parking lot. She glanced at the vehicles there and noticed a familiar truck with Texas plates in a Marine Corps frame. It was in a space right by Daisy's Donuts.

And suddenly she had a very strong craving for sugar.

Chapter Ten

Brendan's last delivery of the day was a repaired toaster oven. After reluctantly accepting payment, he walked away with a broken vacuum cleaner. He put it in the rear passenger section of his truck with the other things folks had given him to fix. It seemed customer satisfaction was so high he had as many broken items as before, and that didn't include the list of ranch jobs he'd promised to do. Job security if he wanted it.

The last stop had been on North Broomtail Road, and Daisy's Donuts was ahead on the right. He knew he could get a cup of coffee there and that sounded pretty good right about now. So he pulled into the lot behind the store and parked. As he walked inside, the sweet baked goods smell made his stomach rumble. He couldn't remember whether or not he'd eaten lunch.

This was where Eva Stockton worked, doing the baking, but he didn't think she'd be here now. Since it was coming up on dinnertime, most likely she would be home, cooking for her husband.

A feeling of loneliness seasoned with a dash of envy rolled through him. It was a little surprising that he so quickly recognized the emotions since they were rare for him. He'd always been a little smug about having everything he needed. Then he came to Sunshine Farm and realized he had nothing. That was another reason why he was leaning toward reenlistment.

He glanced around at the empty tables of the shop and at the glass display case. There weren't many customers this late in the day. Before he could approach the counter, the bell tinkled over the door he'd just walked through.

Automatically he turned to see who came in and recognized Fiona. He was really happy to see her, no two ways about it. Loneliness retreated and her sunny smile chased away the darkness. A man could get used to that. In fact, every time he saw her it was like the first time, when he felt as if he'd been smacked upside the head with a two-by-four. In a good way.

He was grinning like a fool and didn't care. Maybe it was low blood sugar. "Hi."

"I thought that was your truck in the parking lot." She moved close and looked up at him. "In Montana a Texas license plate sticks out like a fly in milk."

"So this isn't a coincidence."

"Only in the sense that I was at the newspaper the same time you stopped here," she said.

So it had been deliberate on her part to come inside and see him. The fact that she'd made the effort had him feeling pretty doggone good.

"What were you doing at the *Gazette*?"

"I'm following up on my promise to Luke—to organize his first annual Halloween party fund-raiser." She glanced through the big window to the newspaper building across the parking lot. "Every edition of the paper has a list of what's going on here in town. My friend works there. She'll give Luke's foundation benefit good play."

"You didn't waste any time."

"There isn't any to waste," she said. "It's right around the corner."

And the idea for it had gone down yesterday. Right after he'd made love to her. Brendan felt a hitch in his breathing and fought the urge to pull her into his arms now. But this was Daisy's Donuts, not an isolated, sun-drenched meadow overlooking a river. That one time was a slip-up. It wasn't fair to put her in that position again. Not when his future was unsettled. He wouldn't be another jerk who led her on, then walked away and hurt her.

"Hey, Tanner. You listening?"

"Hmm?" He reeled in his thoughts and saw Fiona angle her head toward the blonde teenage girl watching the shop and patiently waiting for him to order something. "Can I buy you a cup of coffee?"

"Sure."

Together they walked over to the low counter beside the glass display case. "Two coffees, please."

"Anything to go with that? Cookie? Donut? Muffin?" The blonde looked about twelve but had to be older than that to work here.

"Do you want something?" he asked Fiona.

"So very much." She sighed. "But no. Just coffee."

"Nothing else," he told the teen.

"Okay." She filled two cups and made change when Brendan paid. "Coffee stuff is over there."

Fiona took her coffee, moved to a table not in front of a window and sat down.

Brendan joined her and took the seat across from her. "No 'stuff' for you?"

"I learned to drink it black. Easier when you have to get up before God in the morning."

"Me, too."

"No sissy coffee for you?" she teased.

"That's one way to put it." Places he'd been while in the Marines didn't have frills, so black it was.

"What brings you into town?" She blew on the coffee, dispersing the steam. The movement made her lips pucker and all he could think about was how much he wanted to kiss her.

"Deliveries." His voice was hoarse so he cleared his throat. "I returned small appliances that I fixed."

"So you don't make people pick them up. Great customer service."

He shrugged. "They could if there was a rush. Otherwise I'm happy to drop them off."

"And then you needed coffee. Is it safe to assume you're so busy that the abundance of work wore you out?"

That was partly true. The other part had to do with a lousy night's sleep because he couldn't stop thinking of her in his bed and wishing she'd never left. But he only said, "Business has been good."

"So, has Luke said 'I told you so' yet?"

"No." The man only said people were starting to depend on Brendan, which might be worse. And clearly his friend hadn't given up on the fix-it shop. He told Fiona about Luke's idea of going mobile for dishwashers and refrigerators, and how he was thinking about turning trashed items into profit to benefit the foundation. "I'll admit he may be onto something. A shop like that could turn into a profitable business in Rust Creek Falls."

"Not just anyone could make it successful," she pointed out.

Only *he* could do that, was what she meant. The work made him feel good, which surprised him because he'd felt just the opposite when he was a kid. He'd been ashamed that he never had anything new. His dad cobbled things together, including a life after his mother left.

There'd been another woman for a couple of years and Brendan had gotten a taste of what a family might feel like. But it didn't last. In his experience, the only place he was guaranteed to fit in was the Marine Corps. In the military he knew he would have a place to belong, be a part of a family.

But sitting across from Fiona was temptation on steroids. She was the kind of woman his father had warned him to guard his heart against. A pretty, practical, down-to-earth woman who could make him want to give her everything, then yank the rug out from underneath him. The kind he would miss for the rest of his life.

He sipped his coffee and thought about her words. Only he could make a fix-it business successful. The question was whether or not he wanted to try. He didn't know the answer and wanted to shelve the subject. So that's what he did.

"How have you been?" he asked.

"You mean since yesterday?" The thing about a redhead's skin was not being able to hide a blush.

He really liked the way the high color made her eyes bluer and put a sparkle in them. "Yeah, since then."

Her expression turned a little shy and it was a good guess that she was thinking about what they'd done in his cabin. But she met his look directly. "I've been really good. How about you?"

"Fine." A lousy night's sleep didn't count. "Like I said. Busy."

"Me, too. In between ranch chores I sold another article."

"Which one?"

"The one I was telling you about. How to survive a Montana winter."

"And how does one do that?" he asked.

"Find a way to stay warm." Her eyes went all smoky and soft and it looked like she meant sharing body heat. In a naked sort of way.

Or maybe she hadn't meant that at all. Could be his imagination was overheated. Before he had a chance to decide which, he realized the donut shop teenager was clearing her throat, trying to get their attention. That's when he saw that the glass case had been emptied and the lights behind the counter were off.

"I'm sorry, but it's time to close up now," the teen said.

Fiona stood and carried her empty cup to the trash can. "I didn't realize. We didn't mean to keep you late."

"I normally wouldn't care, but it's a school night and I have to get home and do schoolwork." She looked apologetic.

"We are out of here." Brendan put his cup in the trash by the door. "Thanks for letting us stay awhile."

"No problem. Come back again."

"Will do."

He held the door for Fiona as they walked outside. The air was crisp and cold, a prelude to the Montana winter she had been talking about surviving. She was going to get in her truck and he'd get in his and that would be that. Saved from naked body heat.

But a feeling took hold and wouldn't let go. He just didn't want to spend another evening alone in his cabin. Not if there was a chance of spending it with her. Even fully clothed.

He put a hand on her arm to keep her from walking away. "How would you feel about going to Ace in the Hole for a beer and a bite to eat?"

"I wouldn't like to go alone."

"Smart-ass." He must be way out of practice with this

stuff. Asking a woman to eat with him shouldn't be this hard. "I was wondering if you would go with me."

"In that case, I would enjoy it very much."

That's when he turned to rationalization to justify his lapse in willpower. Lately he was very good at rationalizing. He told himself he and Fiona were just two friends having a burger together. No big deal. It was a public place. Nothing would happen.

Fiona rode to Ace in the Hole with Brendan and was pretty happy that he'd invited her along. And just a little proud of herself for taking the initiative to say hello to him in Daisy's Donuts. The evening couldn't have turned out better if she'd planned it.

After doing a mental high five, she smiled sweetly at him from the truck's passenger seat. "I didn't expect to see you so soon. It was a nice coincidence, us being in town at the same time."

"My good luck." In the light from the dashboard, his grin was clearly visible.

The words made her glow almost as brightly as she had in his bed. Then, after talking to Luke Stockton and Forrest Traub yesterday, she'd gone home without anyone the wiser. But there'd been no promise of a phone call or date. Then they both ended up in the same parking lot at the same time, so who was she to spit in fate's eye?

The drive took only a few minutes and she was almost disappointed when the neon beer sign in the window of the local cowboy bar came into view. Also on display was the big ace of hearts playing card that gave the place its name.

Brendan pulled the truck into the lot and parked. "There are quite a few people here on a weeknight."

"It's a popular place." She was reluctant to give up

the intimacy of being alone with him, but hunger won out. "Let's go."

After exiting the truck, they walked side by side to the entrance, and he opened the squeaky screen door for her. The interior was dimly lighted but she knew this place like the back of her hand. Tables and chairs were arranged on the wood plank floor to form a dance area and there were booths around the perimeter of the large room. An oak bar, scratched and scarred from years of use, took up one wall. Halloween decorations were evidence that trick-or-treat time was fast approaching. There was a plastic pumpkin sitting at one end of the bar and fake webs with plastic spiders sticking to the walls.

Brendan pointed. "Let's grab a booth."

"Okay." It was on the other side of the big room, a little more private than the tables near the dance floor.

He put his hand to the small of her back, and the pressure of his touch warmed her everywhere. They walked past a table where four women sat with drinks in front of them. A beautiful, slim blonde stared shamelessly at Brendan and there was no mistaking the flirtatious expression on her face.

Fiona glanced up at him to see if he'd noticed and his tense expression made her curious. "I bet that happens to you all the time."

"What?" He frowned at her.

"You walk into a room and have women eating out of your hand."

"First of all, it's less messy when people use plates. And second, someone that obvious isn't a person I want to get to know."

"So you did notice the ogling."

"Seriously?" His voice was teasing. "Survival training

stresses close observation of your surroundings. I was a marine. It's a hard habit to break."

"Who knew your survival skills would come in handy for civilian life?"

"Identify and evade," he said. "Sometimes it's the best way to avoid awkward, messy situations."

Interesting, Fiona thought. She guessed that he didn't like rejecting someone. To be fair, most people didn't, but if she had to speculate, the process made him acutely uncomfortable. Since Fiona was with him, her presence should keep in check any unwanted attention.

They left Ms. Ogler behind and slid into the booth across from each other. It wasn't more than a minute or two before Rosey Traven appeared. The sixtyish owner of the Ace wore a peasant blouse that revealed a hint of her ample bosom and was cinched at her waist with a wide leather belt. Her dark blue jeans were tight and she wore red cowboy boots.

"Fiona O'Reilly. I haven't seen you in forever. Almost forgot what you look like."

"Hey, Rosey." Ace in the Hole didn't have the best memories for her, what with this being where Ronan met the jerk he introduced her to, the one who broke her heart. Coming with Brendan might cancel it out. She opened her mouth to introduce him but Rosey was already talking.

"Brendan Tanner." The older woman smiled at him. Clearly they'd met. "Good to see you again."

"Same here. Where's your husband?"

"You met Sam?" Fiona asked.

Rosey laughed. "My husband knew this man was military as soon as he walked in."

"Sam was a navy SEAL," Brendan explained.

"I actually knew that," Fiona said wryly.

"Sam took a fellow veteran under his wing and they

had a lot to talk about. He's in the back, organizing inventory. I'll send him out to say hello when he's free."

"I'd like that." Brendan seemed at ease with her.

"So, what can I get you two? Need a menu?"

"Not me," Fiona said. "Burger, fries and a house cabernet."

"I'll have the same," Brendan said. "Except make it a draft beer."

"Coming right up." She glanced in the direction of the blonde who'd checked them out on the way in. "Didn't Paisley put the moves on you the last time you were here?"

"Yeah." His expression turned grim.

"Thought so." Rosey looked at him, then Fiona, as if she were sizing them up relationship-wise. But she didn't comment. "I'll send Jackie over with your drinks."

"Thanks, Rosey." When the woman walked away, Fiona met his gaze. "So you've been here before."

"Yeah. Nights get long and this is more my style than Maverick Manor."

She knew what he meant about this place being comfortable, like a broken-in saddle.

"Rosey and Sam are good people." And both of them had misjudged the jerk who romanced and rejected her. But he'd been a stranger and had fooled almost everyone. That tended to make a girl wary about someone who wasn't born and raised in Rust Creek Falls.

The young woman working the bar came over with a beer mug for him and a glass of wine for her. "Let me know if you want refills."

"Thanks." Brendan picked his glass up and took a sip. "Tastes good after a long, hard day."

Fiona sipped her own drink. "I'll second that."

They made small talk while waiting for food and, good

to her word, Rosey brought out two burger baskets in record time.

"Enjoy," she said, then moved away to chat with and check up on people at nearby tables.

Fiona ate a couple of fries to kill the hunger pains, then dug into the thick, messy hamburger. She'd eaten half of it before saying, "I'm too hungry to talk."

He pretended to be shocked. "Who are you and what have you done with Fiona O'Reilly? I thought you were all about conversation."

"I know. Priorities. Deal with it." She grinned before taking another bite.

Brendan was no slouch in putting away food, either. His disappeared even faster than hers. He pushed away the empty red plastic basket. "That was good."

After chewing the last bite of hamburger, Fiona finished up her fries and sighed. "Well, the way I wolfed that down was certainly not ladylike."

"Did you enjoy it?" he asked.

"So very much."

"Okay, then."

"Now that I'm full, I absolutely swear on Rosey's bar that I will lose the pesky extra pounds that are probably several more after what I just ate."

Brendan studied her as he toyed with the handle of his beer mug. He looked perplexed. "You don't need to lose weight."

Fiona figured he was just being nice since he'd seen her naked. "That's easy for you to say."

"The truth *is* easy," he insisted. "You are not overweight."

"I'm sure not slender like Brenna and Fallon."

"Your sisters aren't curvy and sexy like you. If I get a vote, I wouldn't change a single thing."

Fiona stared at him for several moments, not sure she'd heard him correctly. "You think I'm sexy?"

"Now you're just fishing for compliments," he teased.

"I'm really not. I sincerely want to know."

His eyes were suddenly hot and intense as he leaned forward. "I think you're damn sexy and so does every other man in here. All of them have been checking you out since we walked in. I'm not the only one getting ogled. Trust me on this, Fiona. You're the most beautiful woman in here. My humble opinion? You shouldn't mess with perfection. Stay just the way you are."

The words made Fiona go all warm and gooey inside. It could be insincere flattery. She'd been on the receiving end of that before. But then she realized that was her default skepticism kicking in. She'd bet that he wasn't a sweet talker. Heck, he wasn't much of a talker, period. Her heart melted like butter in a hot frying pan.

She'd been thrown off balance by his compliment and hadn't taken note of the jukebox playing. Some people were now using the dance floor.

"Are you in a hurry to leave?" Brendan asked.

"Are you?"

"Asked you first."

"Honestly, no. But if you're tired—"

"I'm not." He glanced over at the couples moving slowly to the ballad that was playing. "Would you like to dance?"

"Yes." More than her next breath she wanted to be in his arms again. For any reason at all.

He slid out of the booth and held out his hand to her. She took it and stood, then walked with him to the dance floor. He circled his arm around her waist and tucked her close to his body, then wrapped her hand in his and settled them on his chest. They swayed to the music, and

Fiona knew she would hold this perfect moment in her heart forever.

Too soon the song ended and they walked back to their booth. Before sitting Fiona said, "I'm going to the ladies' room. Be right back."

"I'll be here."

She smiled before heading past the end of the bar and into the hallway where the restrooms were located. The women's was blissfully quiet and she quickly took care of business and washed her hands. She'd forgotten her purse and couldn't reapply lip gloss, but Brendan had certainly seen her look worse. Roundup came to mind. And she smiled remembering what he'd said a little while ago.

You're the most beautiful woman in here... Stay just the way you are.

She was going to hold that in her heart forever, too, and pretty much every moment since she'd seen him at Daisy's Donuts She smiled happily and went back out into the hallway.

Rosey was standing by the end of the bar. "Look who moved in on your man."

She saw that Paisley woman talking to Brendan and a knot of fury coiled inside her. They were standing by the booth and he looked really uncomfortable. If the woman was an enemy combatant he would know exactly what to do. He was too much of a gentleman to tell her to get lost but Fiona wasn't too much of a lady. "He's not my man. But…"

Fiona didn't wait for Rosey's reply. She walked over and wrapped her arms around Brendan's waist, snuggling close, then smiled at the pretty blonde. "Hi. I'm Fiona. I don't think we've met."

"Paisley Ritter."

"Pretty name," she said sweetly. "I see you met my boyfriend, Brendan."

"Yes." The other woman didn't seem quite so chatty now.

"Would you like to join us for a drink?"

Paisley looked startled. "No. My friends are waiting."

Fiona rested her cheek against Brendan's chest. "If you change your mind, just come on over. Bring your friends, too."

"Okay. See you around." She didn't look at either of them before turning and scurrying away.

"Boyfriend, huh?" Brendan smiled down at her before kissing her lightly on the mouth. "You didn't even raise your voice."

"Didn't have to. Killed her with kindness. She never knew what hit her."

"They're leaving," he said, nodding toward Paisley and her friends, who were walking out the door.

"You're welcome."

"Seriously, thanks. You have no idea how grateful I am."

"I've got your back," she assured him. *Always*, she added silently.

"I owe you big-time."

"And I know just how you can pay me back. A *boyfriend* usually comes to dinner with family. And my mother wants to thank you for fixing her waffle iron. How about tomorrow night?"

He looked like he would rather take a sharp stick in the eye, but answered like the brave soldier he was. "I would love to."

Fiona wasn't sure why that's what she wanted as a thank-you except maybe so he'd be less of a stranger. It was becoming more important to her that he lose the label.

Chapter Eleven

At five minutes to six the next evening, Brendan turned onto the road that led to the Rusty Bucket Ranch. The last time he'd been here it was to pick up Fiona for dinner. It was quick and almost painless. Tonight he was staying. All he could say was, the next time he told someone "I owe you," he would find out what paying off the debt entailed. Her brothers hated him and the jury was out on her father. Her mother seemed nice. Maybe she could hold off the men if things went sideways.

What bothered him more than an evening with two hostile older brothers was that he couldn't say no to Fiona. He was pretty sure that he would have agreed to this dinner invitation whether he owed her or not. Just because she asked.

That's as far as he would go with that thought. Anything more made him feel too exposed when he was about to face the O'Reilly men on their territory.

At six o'clock on the dot he pulled the truck to a stop in front of Fiona's house, where lights were ablaze in all the downstairs windows. "Here goes nothing," he muttered.

All his senses were on high alert, not unlike the way he'd felt on patrol during his deployments. He was pretty sure there wouldn't be an IED—improvised explosive device—waiting for him, but situations could be volatile even when there was no shrapnel involved.

He stepped onto the porch and knocked. From inside came the sound of a dog barking and voices, just before the door opened. Fiona stood there looking so beautiful she took his breath away. The sight of her thick, shiny red hair, sweet smile and cute freckled nose was the best thing that happened to him all day. He made a mental note that if Ronan and Keegan made his life miserable for the next few hours, seeing Fiona was worth it. He wished that wasn't the case but he had to be honest.

"Hi. You look pretty—" Before he could say more, a fuzzy, yellow-haired dog nuzzled his hand. He rubbed her head and scratched between her ears.

"This is Duchess. She's a golden retriever, German shepherd mix."

He rubbed a hand over her back. "You look pretty, too."

"Come on in. Everyone's in the kitchen," Fiona said.

He followed her from the spacious living room through a dining room with the table already set for six. Any hope he'd had of dinner with just Fiona and her parents died right there.

The kitchen was big and cozy and loud. Maureen lifted the lid from a large silver pot on the stove. Her husband hovered and sniffed what was cooking, then slid his arms around his wife's waist and kissed her neck.

Seeing the affectionate gesture, their sons groaned loudly.

"Get a room," Ronan teased.

"My eyes," Keegan chimed in. "I can never un-see that."

"I have a room, thank you very much," Paddy retorted.

"And if you don't want to see me kissing your mother, go back to the barn where you belong."

Fiona laughed at the expression on Brendan's face. "I think I've mentioned that they actually live in the converted space. Not that these two couldn't have survived nicely with just stalls, hay and a water trough. What with them being pigs and all."

"Low blow, sis." Ronan walked over and shook Brendan's hand. "Would you like a beer?"

"Thanks." He hadn't expected that nonhostile gesture.

"Wow," Fiona said. "Since when does my big brother have company manners?"

"Always." Maureen put down the big wooden spoon she'd been using and came over to shake his hand. "Welcome, Brendan. I raised all my children to treat visitors to our home with respect. Fiona is teasing."

"No, I'm not, Mom." The sparkle in her eyes said otherwise. "Your manners training didn't bear fruit until I was born. Then Fallon and Brenna imitated my good example. The effort you put in on my two brothers was a complete waste of energy."

Paddy joined the group and shook Brendan's hand. "Hello, son. Glad you could join us."

"My pleasure, sir. Thanks for having me."

"Fiona, can I get you a glass of wine, my fair and favorite sister?" Ronan asked when he brought Brendan the beer bottle.

"I bet you say that to Fallon and Brenna when I'm not around." She shook her head. "And you're not fooling anyone with this Sir Walter Raleigh act. No one here believes you would throw your cloak over a puddle so I wouldn't get my dainty feet wet."

"Maybe Brendan does." Ronan met his gaze but there was no threat, veiled or otherwise.

"I'm staying out of this skirmish."

"Wise man." Ronan nodded. "The thing is, I wouldn't be caught dead in a cloak. It would clash with my cowboy hat. Now, little sister, do you want wine or not?"

"Yes. Thank you."

"I'd like one, too," Maureen said. "Dinner is pretty much ready. But I'm keeping it warm. It would be nice to visit a bit with our guest before we sit down to eat."

Brendan sipped his beer and braced himself. "Visit with our guest" was code for extracting information from him. What were his intentions toward Fiona? Were they friends or more than that? Was he like the jerk who hurt her? He'd tried not to be that guy. And he never let Fiona think he was staying. He'd done his best not to lead her on.

"Are you okay?" Fiona asked, studying him.

"Yes. Why?" He took another drink from his beer bottle then met her gaze.

"I don't know. If I had to describe the look on your face, I'd say it's fight or flight. Like you're waiting for something bad to happen."

"Go ahead. Be honest." Ronan handed his mother and sister stemmed glasses of white wine. "Tell us. We can take it."

As if sensing he needed moral support, Duchess strolled up beside him and nuzzled his fingers. Oddly enough, it helped.

"Okay." The comment fell into the "let's do this man-to-man" category. It was familiar territory for him. "Based on previous experiences, I was expecting hostility from Ronan and Keegan. But this friendliness has thrown me off. Maybe that's the point."

"No." Ronan grinned at his brother. "The point is that Fiona threatened to hurt us if we were mean to you."

"I did not!"

Keegan took up the narrative as if she hadn't spoken. "A man would be a fool not to take her warning to heart." He was doing his best not to laugh.

"You guys are so full of it," she accused them. "Like I could really hurt you."

"They have you on height and weight." Paddy slid an arm across her shoulders and pulled her close for an affectionate hug. "But they are putty in your hands if you shed a tear."

"True." She grinned at Brendan. "It's the nuclear option so I use it on them sparingly."

"When we were kids, she got us in trouble with dad more than once by crying her eyes out," Ronan said.

"I was the first girl after two boys," she explained.

"The little princess," Keegan grumbled.

"And don't think I didn't take full advantage," she gloated. "After Fallon was born it didn't work as well. Then Brenna came along and the boys were just plain outnumbered. I'm pretty sure there was a formal request for surrender when Mom came home from the hospital with another pink-wrapped bundle of joy."

"You call it joy," Ronan said. "I call three little sisters the seventh level of hell."

Brendan happened to be drinking from his beer and almost spit. He started laughing. "Triple the tears."

"No kidding," Keegan agreed. "If only we could send them to a drought-ravaged area where they could do some good."

"Their husbands might object," Maureen pointed out.

"Then just send Fiona." Ronan glanced at his brother who nodded. "No one would miss her."

Brendan would, but kept that to himself. This was a sibling thing and the three of them were very good at it. He wondered what it would have been like to grow up in a big, happy family like this one. It was something a lonely, only child had wanted pretty bad. The Corps was the closest he ever got. Right now he felt as if he was on the outside looking in.

"Stop it, you two," Maureen said. "You talk tough, but you would miss your sister if she wasn't here."

"Yeah," Keegan said. "Like a toothache."

"And yet again, our family happy hour deteriorates into the children fighting," their mother teased. "I think it's time to put dinner on the table."

"I'll give you a hand, sweetheart."

Paddy followed her to the stove, where they filled serving platters and bowls with meat, mashed potatoes, gravy, vegetables and salad. When they thought no one was looking, he dipped his head and kissed his wife full on the mouth.

After years together they were still close.

Brendan had never seen this before. He felt like a fish out of water and couldn't imagine why Fiona had invited him here. She could do so much better than him. The problem was, the idea of her with another man made him crazy. What the hell was he supposed to do?

Fiona stared Brendan down without blinking. She was calling his bluff. "I'll see your ten orange candies and raise you another ten."

He glanced at his cards and shook his head before tossing them on the kitchen table. "A sugar high I can't afford."

"Did you have anything, son?" Paddy asked Brendan.

"No."

"I didn't, either," Fiona said.

"Then it was a good bluff." The older man gave her an approving nod.

Her brothers had left after dinner and they were playing poker with her parents using Halloween candy corn as currency. She was on a roll.

"I like winning," Fiona gloated, raking in her winnings. "Whose deal is it now?"

Paddy stood and stretched. "Not mine. I'm out. I have to get up early in the morning."

Apparently Brendan took that as a sign and got up, too. "I should be going."

Fiona sighed inside. Obviously he had to leave at some point but she wasn't ready for that time to be now. It had been such a fun evening. Her family, even her dork brothers, had warmed to him and he'd loosened up after a while. He seemed to have a good time and the evening went way too fast.

"I'll walk you out," she said.

"Good night, Mrs.—Maureen." He caught himself. Sometime during dinner her parents had given him permission to drop the formality and use their first names. "That was a really good meal."

"You're very welcome, Brendan." Her mom hugged him goodbye. "I hope you'll come back again soon."

"I appreciate that." It wasn't a yes or no and he had a sort of wistful expression on his face. "Thanks again."

He held out his hand to her father. "Paddy. Thank you for having me."

"My pleasure, son."

Brendan headed for the front door and Fiona walked beside him. After he stepped outside on the porch, she joined him and closed the door behind her. The light was on and she could see his brooding expression again.

"I hope you didn't mind my family too much."

"They're great." He met her gaze. "And I was so sure your brothers hated my guts."

"They did." She grinned. "But that wasn't personal. It was just general principle since I'm their sister. They got over it."

"Your parents are nice."

She winced. "'Nice' could mean anything from completely awesome to worse than you could possibly have imagined."

"I meant it in a good way. You're lucky to have them." There was unmistakable envy in his voice.

"I know it." She guessed he was thinking about his own rough childhood, without a mother in the picture. "We play the hand we're dealt. I do wish I could have met your dad."

"He would have liked you."

"And I would have liked him."

"You sound pretty sure about that." He frowned. "How do you know?"

"Because he raised you. Without him you wouldn't be the man you are."

"And what kind of man am I?"

"Kind, brave, honest, hardworking, strong, generous." She smiled at him. "Want me to keep going?"

"Of course." The corners of his mouth slowly turned up.

"Humble, loyal, trustworthy—"

"Stop. Now you're making me blush."

"I mean every word," she said sincerely.

"Fiona—"

His eyes went all intense and he took a half step closer before sliding his arm around her waist, urging her nearer to his body. The heat of him warmed her deep inside and she searched his face, hardly daring to breathe. He touched his mouth to hers, soft and sweet, even as he held her tightly enough that her breasts were crushed to his chest. Their tongues dueled as he kissed her until they were both breathless.

Brendan pulled his mouth away first, but still held her body close. "If I don't go now—"

"I know." But she sighed her disappointment.

"Can I see you tomorrow?" he said against her lips.

"I'd like that." Saying goodbye wasn't nearly so hard when she knew he wanted to see her again soon.

He smiled. "I'll call you."

"Okay. Good night, Brendan."

He lifted a hand in answer, then turned away and left the porch to climb into his truck. Fiona shivered in the cold air and crossed her arms over her chest, refusing to go back inside until his taillights disappeared.

After turning off the living room lights, she passed the dining room table to make sure everything was in order. She walked into the kitchen and was surprised to see her mother still up, hand-washing the big pots she'd used to cook dinner.

Fiona hurried over to the sink. "Mom, let me do those. You go on up to bed."

"I'm almost finished." She set a large lid in the dish drainer on the countertop.

"At least I can dry them," Fiona insisted, grabbing a kitchen towel.

"Thank you, sweetie." They worked side by side in silence for a few moments before her mom said, "I like Brendan. He seems like a very nice young man."

It was always great to have parental approval for one's friends. Just because things had taken an intimate turn didn't mean they were more than that. He'd given her no reason to believe there was anything besides friendship between them.

"He liked you guys, too." She took a large skillet from her mother and started to dry it.

"I'm glad. Your father had very positive things to say and he's a pretty good judge of character."

Fiona had learned the hard way how good her dad was at pegging people. The creep who dumped her had done all the right things when he met her folks, but her dad had seen something that bothered him and could never define exactly what. Turned out he'd been right. So the fact that he was okay with Brendan meant a lot.

"Brendan's not a big talker."

"Nothing wrong with that." Her mom rinsed out the sink. "Gave him more time to look at you."

"What?" Her cheeks grew warm. Why in the world was she blushing? "No, he wasn't."

"I beg to differ. And he wasn't just *looking*, if you know what I mean."

"Actually, I don't." Fiona knew her mother would elaborate. The woman didn't hesitate to share her thoughts.

"It was the *way* he looked at you. There were a lot of feelings in his eyes."

"What kind of feelings?"

"The forever-after kind," Maureen said.

"Oh, please, Mom. You're such a romantic. It's not like that." And she was okay with it. Probably. Maybe.

"Well, I don't know what you think it's like, but that man had the same look in his eyes that your father did just before he said he loved me for the first time."

As much as Fiona wanted to believe that, she couldn't go there. That would take things to a serious place where the potential was really high for getting hurt. Been there, done that. Not again.

"I think you're imagining things."

"Do you, now?" Her mother smiled. "Then answer me

this. Why would he come here to dinner and put himself through the O'Reilly inspection process?"

"He was hungry?"

"I'll admit he showed a healthy appetite, but that's not why."

"I did him a favor." She explained what happened at Ace in the Hole last night.

"I see. You pretended to be his girlfriend so that woman would stop hitting on him." Her mother nodded sagely. "I bet playing that part came real easy to you."

Now that she mentioned it, the role was almost natural. Although she wasn't going to confirm that. "The thing is, he owed me."

"So why did you cash in that marker with a family dinner?"

Leave it to Maureen O'Reilly to get right to the heart of the matter. Fiona wasn't prepared to answer that question because she didn't know the answer for sure. So she asked one of her own.

"When Dad said he loved you, what did you say?"

"That I loved him, too." Her mother's eyes turned soft and glowy at the memory.

"Was it an automatic response? Like something you would say because if you didn't it's like a big thing hanging out there."

"Nothing hung out there," her mother said wryly. "I told him I loved him and it was the honest-to-God truth. I knew it the very first time we met."

Fiona felt a fluttering inside her, the same sensation she'd experienced the first time she saw Brendan. Was there such a thing as love at first sight? Was it hereditary? "How did you know?"

"I wish I could answer, sweetie. I'd be a rich woman because everyone would pay to know that secret. It was just something that hit me deep down inside, a certainty that Paddy O'Reilly was the only man who could make me happy."

"And he has." She had grown up watching them never miss the chance to touch each other, communicating their deep love with just a look. Kissing in the kitchen or anywhere else when they thought no one was watching. Or even when they knew everyone was. "You and Dad have the absolute perfect relationship."

"Perfect?" There was skepticism in Maureen's voice. She took the towel from Fiona and folded it, draping the material over the cupboard door underneath the sink. "Define that."

"You and Dad have set a really high bar for us kids. It occurs to me that could be why it's taking Ronan and Keegan so long to settle down."

"And you?"

"I'm resigned to the fact that I'll be a spinster."

Maureen laughed and shook her head. "Let's just clear something up right now. There's no such thing as a perfect relationship. Marriage is work. Biting your tongue when you want to be an unreasonable witch. Staying calm when he's being difficult to deal with."

"That's what I mean," she said. "You and Dad never fight."

"You never *see* us fight. There's a difference. We made a promise when Ronan was born to keep our differences private. But don't mistake that for complete agreement one hundred percent of the time. Like I said, it's work. Worth all the effort, but by no means easy."

"Well, you guys sure make it look that way. You're a very tough act to follow."

"Oh, honey. I know it bothers you that you're turning thirty and not married like your younger sisters. And I can't tell you not to let it bother you. That would be a waste of breath and you're entitled to feel any way you want to." Her mother reached out and tucked a lock of hair behind Fiona's ear as if she were still a little girl. "But I can tell you that you're better off alone than marrying the wrong man. A man you don't love. A man who makes you unhappy."

"I know."

"Of course you do. It's just sometimes you can talk yourself into feeling something just because you have a certain goal."

"You're talking about Tate Gibbs, the jackass who left and cheated."

"Yes."

"Are you saying I wasn't in love with him?"

"Only you can answer that, sweetie. I just want you to find someone who makes you as happy as your father does me."

"That's what I want, too," Fiona agreed.

"We've learned that the hallmarks of a good relationship are communication and compromise. It's the hardest work you'll ever do, but it's worth it if both people involved are all in."

"I can see that."

Her mother cupped Fiona's face in her hands. "And I think Brendan wants all in with you."

"Oh, Mom—I can assure you that we are just friends. There's nothing between us." That kiss on the porch might say otherwise, but Fiona was putting on the just-friends face. As far as anyone else knew, that's all they were. It was important everyone believe that because the details of her private life were no one else's business.

"It doesn't matter what I think, just what you do." Maureen kissed her daughter's cheek. "Now, I'm tired. Would you let Duchess out before you go to bed?"

"Sure." She hugged her mom.

"Sleep tight, sweetheart."

"You, too, Mom."

She opened the kitchen door and Duchess ran outside. While waiting for the dog to do her thing, Fiona thought about what her mother said. She wasn't so sure about the forever-after look her mother talked about. Brendan never said anything he didn't mean and he had not said a thing about what they were to each other. Obviously her mother's observation was nothing more than wishful thinking. A hope that they'd get the last O'Reilly daughter married off. Fiona had given up wishing for that.

There was a lot to be said for not wishing your life away and simply living in the moment. And right now she was going to look forward to seeing Brendan tomorrow.

Chapter Twelve

Brendan figured he'd been pretty lucky getting through his deployment unscathed, physically, at least. But surviving an O'Reilly family dinner deserved some kind of medal. The one he gave himself was spending time with Fiona. But no amount of boot camp or survival training could have prepared him for shopping.

Fiona had insisted on meeting him in town at the antiques/thrift store. After she pulled into the lot, he met her at the truck and when she opened the door he said, "Hi."

"Hey." She smiled. "You're punctual."

"Tell me again why we're going to a store that has a bunch of junk. Appliances I can understand, but—"

"I've heard that there are a lot of vintage clothes here and it's a great place to find stuff for a Halloween costume. I still don't have one."

"Are you sure your mom doesn't have some old clothes somewhere?"

She shook her head. "Never even hint in my mother's presence that something she wore is vintage. Just a warning." She shut her door. "If you don't want to do this, I can handle it on my own. I would never want to force you."

He was being a pain in the butt and she should have been annoyed with him, but there wasn't even a hint of irritation in her voice. And that's what made him want to be with her. Even if it meant shopping. He was in shape now, as good as when he'd left the Corps, and could re-enlist anytime he wanted. It was coming up on "fish or cut bait" time and the pretty redhead with the sunny disposition wasn't making the decision easy.

"Let's roll," he said.

They walked around to the front door, under a sign that said, Everything Old. On either side were half-barrel planters, baskets of stick-in-the-ground garden decorations and an old horse-drawn plow.

He pointed it out. "What would anyone want with that?"

Fiona thought for a moment. "With a little paint that could be a lawn decoration for Sunshine Farm." She looked up at him. "One man's trash is another man's treasure. You should know that better than anyone since you're a genius at fixing stuff—new and old."

"I can't tell whether I was just complimented or smacked down."

"Maybe both." She grinned. "Now man up, Tanner. We're going in."

"I've got your six."

"My what now?"

"Your back." Except his gaze dropped to her curvy and spectacular butt when she preceded him through the doorway.

The interior was a lot bigger than it looked from the outside and separated into individual booths containing everything from old furniture to glassware and small appliances. In two seconds he realized this wouldn't be a quick in-and-out.

A woman walked up to them and smiled. She was a pretty brunette, somewhere in her twenties, with big turquoise eyes and freckles on her nose.

"Hi, I'm Geneva Quinn. Welcome to Everything Old."

Fiona held out her hand. "Fiona O'Reilly. This is Brendan Tanner. I haven't seen you around. Are you new to Rust Creek Falls?"

"Yeah. And you haven't seen me because I've been working a lot of hours putting my business together."

"I love what you've done with the place." Fiona looked up at him. "There was a flood in Rust Creek Falls in 2013. Half the town was under water, homes were unlivable and people abandoned them. We went through some hard times. There was a business here but it didn't survive. It's been empty until now."

"I'm getting a break on the cost and renting out space to anyone who has merchandise to sell."

"Are there any spaces available?" Brendan wondered. "I'm asking for a friend." Luke might be interested, even though Brendan probably wouldn't be around to see whether it worked out.

"Have them come see me. Meanwhile, have fun browsing."

"We will." Fiona looked at Brendan and whatever she saw made her smile. "Brendan can't wait to get started."

"I can see that," the other woman said wryly. "But he's here and he's cute. What more could you ask from a boyfriend?"

"He's not my boyfriend," she said fairly firmly. "Just a friend."

Then Fiona took off and turned left to start shopping. He caught up with her halfway down the aisle.

"So who do you know looking to rent a space here?" she asked.

"Luke mentioned something about it. Possibly another revenue source for his foundation." If there was a God, she would not ask more questions.

"And what is he planning to sell in a booth?" She walked into a space to check out a framed picture hanging on the wall.

"He said something about donations."

"Would these donations be things that you are able to fix?" She glanced over her shoulder at him.

"The man is relentless." He knew the subtext of her question was about him sticking around and that was something he couldn't answer.

She didn't ask anything but continued perusing booths till she found a rack of old clothes—hats, shoes, an old fur coat. She meticulously looked at all the hanging items but didn't see what she wanted.

Brendan already knew what he wanted. Fiona. Every time their shoulders brushed or hands bumped, he wanted to take her in his arms and kiss her until she made those breathy little moaning noises.

"I'm going in here," she said as something in a booth caught her eye.

"Okay." He followed her. "This is your op. I'm just here to look cute."

"Mission accomplished." She gave him a flirty look, then turned her attention to a stack of clothes.

Brendan scanned the shelves holding plates, glasses, pots and pans. In a corner of the booth he saw a shelf of toys and walked over to check them out. Trucks and cars were lined up haphazardly. In the back, almost hidden by action figures, he saw a military vehicle painted in jungle camouflage. He reached past the clutter and picked it up. His stomach knotted when he realized it was an awful lot like the one his mom gave him when he was five.

"Brendan?" Fiona put her hand on his arm. "Did you hear me? Are you okay?"

Apparently she'd said something and he didn't hear because of the roaring in his ears. "I'm fine."

Her gaze narrowed. "You can talk to me."

Because that's what friends did. She'd said that before. He knew the stubborn look on her face better now and she wasn't going to let this drop. Looking at the toy in his hand was like a glimpse into the past, a place he never wanted to visit again.

"I had one of these when I was a kid." He stared at the thing. "My mother gave it to me when she broke the news she was leaving."

"Oh, Brendan—" She sighed. "Of all the memories you could have found here, why did it have to be that one?"

"Yeah. What are the odds?" He'd already told her a boatload of bad stuff, but there was more and it came bubbling up. "It took a while, but my dad moved on. He let another woman into his life."

"Good."

"I guess." Leon had been happy. She was nice and they were like a family for a while. "But she left, too."

Fiona pressed her lips together for a moment. "That just bites."

"More than you know." He almost laughed. Most people would have given the stock "I'm sorry" or something equally as useless. She told it like it was.

"What aren't you telling me?"

"I had already committed to the Marines when she dumped him. I couldn't stick around and he was alone to deal with it. In a short span he lost two people he cared about. Double whammy."

"I'm sure he understood why you had to go," she said.

"Yeah. But I know it was that much harder for him." He looked at her then, the sympathy in her eyes.

"He didn't lose you, Brendan. Children grow up and leave home—" She stopped as her words sank in. "Well, not me and my brothers. It's different with the ranch. But letting kids be independent is the natural order of things."

"I know. It's just when he got sick—"

"You felt bad that you didn't spend more time with him when you could have."

He nodded, a lump in his throat as he replaced the toy on the shelf. "If we could see the future, a decision today would be a lot easier."

She moved close and wrapped her arms around his waist, resting her cheek on his chest. "I hear it in your voice. You feel as if you left a man behind, and I know marines take pride in not doing that. But I believe if your dad was here, he would say that he was glad you found a career that fulfilled you. If leaving him was part of that, so be it. If you were happy, he was happy."

Maybe it was the hug or just the right words at the right time, but he felt as if a weight lifted from his heart. As if he'd received absolution. Somehow he knew in his soul that she was right.

"Thank you," he whispered against her hair. "That helps."

"You're welcome." She hugged him tight for a moment, then backed away and smiled. "If I was a shrink that would cost you big."

"Oh? So what do I owe you?"

"Takeout from Ace in the Hole. We'll eat it at your place."

There was a little bit of a bad girl glint in her eyes and he had a sneaking suspicion about what she had in mind at his place. "Count me in."

* * *

Fiona knew exactly what her "fee" entailed and it wasn't just dinner to go. Ace in the Hole was their first stop. Together they walked inside, up to the bar and sat side by side on a couple of stools. The place was a lot busier than she'd hoped.

She wanted to be in Brendan's arms desperately and was pretty sure he was impatient to have her there. But she knew getting to his cabin discreetly was going to be a challenge. It wasn't that she was ashamed of being with him. She just didn't want everyone in town to know about it.

He was basically another stranger. Unlike the last one, he didn't lead her on. But when he left she didn't want to be the talk of the town again. That much humiliation was enough for a lifetime. No one would pity her if they didn't know she and Brendan were a thing.

So the problem at a crowded Ace in the Hole was how to get food to go without anyone asking questions and putting two and two together. Because her, him, his bed—it was going to happen.

Rosey was helping out behind the bar and walked over to them. "Brendan. Fiona. Nice to see you again. This is getting to be a habit."

The woman was fishing for information and Fiona was going to give her as little as possible. "I wouldn't say that. We checked out that new place, Everything Old, for stuff to put together a Halloween costume and—"

"You two coordinating costumes for Luke and Eva's party?"

"We were just browsing," Brendan said evasively.

Fiona needed to lay down a distraction. "By the way, I don't know if you heard that Luke is making the party a fund-raiser for the foundation he's starting. His goal is to

fix up some of the Sunshine Farms cabins and build more
for veterans who need a place to decompress and adjust
to civilian life after deployment or leaving the military."

"I hadn't heard. And you had me at 'fund-raiser,'"
Rosey said. "But that's a real good thing he's doing. I
know Sam will be on board."

Fiona nodded, pleased that the other woman's attention
had been diverted from speculation about her and Brendan. "I knew you would get it. Luke would be grateful if
you could spread the word. And if anyone can't be there
but wants to donate, he's got a website. The information
will be in the *Gazette*."

"Happy to help." She met Brendan's gaze and nodded.
"Now, what can I get you two?"

"What else? Burgers and fries." Brendan looked at
Fiona and added, "To go."

His tone was übercasual but instantly there was an elephant in the room. Rosey's eyes gleamed with curiosity
although she didn't say anything.

Fiona felt the need to fill the silence and said the first
thing that popped into her mind. "It's crowded in here
tonight. So we're going to take the food to my house and
watch TV."

"Uh-huh." The look on the other woman's face said she
didn't buy that for a second. "Since when does Maureen
O'Reilly let anyone come into her house and eat food she
didn't cook for them?"

"I just didn't want to bother her and make a mess in
the kitchen after dinner."

"Fiona Kathleen O'Reilly, your nose is growing with
every word that comes out of your mouth."

No one used all three of her names unless she was in
trouble. "I'm sensing some skepticism—"

Rosey put her hands on her ample hips and had a look on

her face that would intimidate even the most interrogation-hardened soldier.

"Okay," she said. "Would you believe a picnic?"

"It's cold and dark outside. Do I look like I was born yesterday?" The older woman held up a hand. "Don't answer that."

Fiona gave Brendan an exasperated look. "Bail me out here. Say something."

"On it." He met the bar owner's gaze. "We're taking food back to my cabin at Sunshine Farm. After I feed her, she's going to have her way with me."

"Brendan!"

"What?" He looked unapologetic and self-satisfied. "It's the truth. This scenario doesn't leave much latitude for a believable lie."

"Still, you were a marine. I expected you to put some effort into coming up with a good cover story."

"Fiona—" Rosey reached over and patted her hand. "Honey, it's not like I didn't know the minute I saw you two."

"Why? What gave it away? Is it written on my forehead?" she demanded. "'Getting lucky tonight'?"

Rosey shrugged. "It's clear that you're determined to keep it private. I respect that. And I have a reputation to maintain. Someone tells me something while I'm behind this bar, I keep it to myself. Like attorney-client privilege." She was dead serious. "This information goes no further."

"Thanks, Rosey."

"Okay. So, burgers and fries coming right up." She turned away and headed into the back.

Brendan swiveled his stool toward her, then moved hers so that she was facing him. The only parts of their bodies touching were their knees, but she felt him all over. She sensed he wanted to take her hand, but he didn't.

"I'm sorry," he said.

"It's not your fault I suck at lying."

He smiled. It was so loud in the place that no one could hear when he said, "I really want to touch you right now."

She wanted him to. Badly.

"I'm glad you're a bad liar," he told her. "In my humble opinion, it's one of your very best qualities."

"You think I'm silly, but this town—" She rested her arm on the bar beside them. "Everyone talks and I don't want it to be about me."

Not again.

He touched her hand, just a friendly gesture to anyone who might see. "For what it's worth, I think Rosey was being honest. She won't spread anything about us."

"This place is packed." She looked around at the crowd. "Someone is bound to see that we're leaving with food."

"Even so, that could mean anything," he said. "We could be taking it to your place to watch TV."

She shook her head. "Everyone will come to the same conclusion Rosey did. My mom feeds anyone who comes over. She's got an extra refrigerator and freezer jammed with enough food to feed a small country."

"I'm sorry," he said with a sigh. "But I've been eating meals with Eva and Luke. Or they send leftovers to me. There's a small microwave and compact fridge in the place. But I haven't stocked up on supplies."

Traveling light, she thought, *because that makes it easier to take off.* He was deliberately not putting down roots. She felt a twinge of something in her chest and consciously chose to ignore it. Every moment she spent with him was a memory to pull out on a cold, lonely winter night. Maybe it was stupid, but that was all the more reason she hoped Rosey kept her promise.

"It's okay," she said.

"No." He looked down for a moment before meeting her gaze. "And if you want me to go home now, I'll take you back to your truck."

Fiona met his gaze as her inner voice firmly said "no way" to that suggestion. This was like writing a free-lance article. When an opportunity came along you took it because it might not happen again. If sex was all she wanted, prospects were abundant. But she was old-fashioned and needed to have feelings. It didn't have to be love, but she had to like and respect a man to go to bed with him. Brendan fit those criteria and then some. Her only concern was caring too much.

She shook her head. "You promised me food. And I've been told that you always keep your promises. But if I didn't know better, I'd say you're trying to get out of this."

"Oh, honey—" A slow, sexy smile turned up the corners of his mouth while his eyes caught fire. "If we weren't trying to fly under the radar I'd show you here and now just how committed I am to keeping my word."

"Okay, then." Desire flared inside her. "When our food comes, we'll—"

Rosey came out of the back just then with a large brown bag in her hand. She set it in front of them. "Order up."

"You wouldn't happen to have a bottle of wine I could buy," Brendan asked, "would you?"

"I can damn sure find one," Rosey said. "This is a bar, for Pete's sake."

"And would I be pushing my luck to talk you out of a couple of glasses?"

"Do I look like a miracle worker?" she said in mock

annoyance. Then she grinned. "You're my kind of man, Brendan Tanner. If I were younger and—"

"Not married?" Fiona said.

"That, too. I am partial to military types, as you both already know. And I'm not fooling anyone. Sam Traven is the love of my life."

"You just broke my heart," Brendan teased.

"There seems to be an epidemic of nose growing in here tonight." She laughed. "I'll get that wine and some glasses for you."

Fiona stared at him. "How are we supposed to get all of that out of here without attracting attention?"

"Leave that to a marine."

When the bar owner came back with another bag, Brendan leaned over and whispered in the older woman's ear. Rosey grinned and nodded.

In a low voice he said to Fiona, "Get ready to make a run for it."

"Really? Because us sprinting out of here with two big bags won't be noticeable at all."

"I didn't mean literally. Just wait for the signal," he instructed.

"How will I know what it is?"

"Trust me. You'll know."

A few moments later, from the other end of the bar, Rosey tapped a spoon against a wineglass to get the attention of everyone in the room. "It's awful darn close to Halloween. Let's call this trick or treat. Everyone gets a drink on the house. Come on up here and tell me what you're having."

There was a swelling of noise—voices, cheers and chairs scraping as everyone stood. En masse, people headed to the end of the bar.

Brendan grabbed the two brown bags and slid off the stool. "Now."

Fiona followed his lead and they walked out the door. She glanced back to scope out their escape. Not one person noticed them. They were all focused on getting a drink order in to Rosey.

When they reached his truck in the parking lot she said, "You, sir, have skills."

"And an impressive bar tab now." He set the bags on the floor in the back, then grinned at her. The flashing neon beer sign in the bar's window highlighted the sexy gleam in his eyes. "But you haven't seen anything yet."

She whispered to herself, "Be still my heart."

But that was an impossible order to obey. Her heart was about to jump out of her chest. Her stomach was growling, but her hormones were stirred up, signaling a hunger that went a whole lot deeper. This was something that would feed her soul.

He'd gone the extra mile of getting wine and glasses. She couldn't wait until his attention to detail was focused on her.

Chapter Thirteen

Brendan parked his truck behind the cabin and turned off the headlights. He'd never wanted a woman as badly as he wanted Fiona right now but she wanted this to be under the radar. The quicker he got them inside, the faster he could have her.

"I'll go first and take the food. You wait here and if I run into anyone, I'll get rid of them as fast as I can. Then you advance, hugging the wall. I'll leave the door partly open."

"Roger that."

"I think you're enjoying this," he said.

"Maybe a little."

He grinned, then opened his door and got out. Fiona did the same, coming around to stand beside him. The scent of her skin drifted to him and stoked the fire he'd been trying and failing to bank since she suggested takeout at his place.

"Let's do this," he said.

He grabbed the two bags from the rear seat and walked the path between cabins. There were lights on next door, but he got to the front, and the newest Sunshine Farm resident was nowhere to be seen.

Rounding the corner, he stepped on the porch, went inside and set the bags on the small table before turning on the light. Moments later Fiona slipped through the door and closed it behind her.

"I don't think anyone saw me."

Brendan had a question about why she was so intent on keeping this a secret, but he was too hungry to ask. Starving for food—and for her.

He pulled the bottle of wine from the bag along with the glasses. There was a corkscrew with a note from Rosey. It said: *This is a loaner. You're welcome.*

He owed that woman big-time.

While he opened the bottle and poured each of them a glass, Fiona removed burgers and fries from the bag and put the food in the small countertop microwave to warm.

Brendan got out plates and when everything was reheated, they sat down to eat. He'd been here at Sunshine Farm for almost two months and this was the first time he'd had a meal with anyone in this cabin. It was so damn normal and ordinary that an odd sort of loneliness bled into him. Who else could be lonely with a beautiful woman sitting across from him? Wouldn't be the first time it occurred to him that he needed to have his head examined.

After all, he was here with Fiona. He probably shouldn't be but there was a part of him that felt if he didn't have her he would implode.

It didn't take them long to wolf down the food. Then Fiona got up and cleared away the paper and bags. Brendan refilled their wineglasses. She came back to the table and stood close enough for him to feel the heat of her body, just enough to make his pulse race faster and his heart pound even harder. There was a sweet, small-town innocence about her that was irresistible. And he had to ask one more time.

"Are you okay with this, Fiona?"

"It was my idea, remember?" She smiled a little shyly. "I wanted to be with you again so much. But I was afraid you didn't want me."

"You are so wrong about that."

He took her face in his hands and kissed her. She opened her mouth and he eagerly dipped his tongue inside. She tasted of burger, wine and willingness. As he explored, a soft, pleading moan vibrated in her throat. The breathy, sexy sound fired up his blood like a lightning strike to dry brush.

One moment he was kissing her, and the next they were tugging at each other's clothes, yanking off boots, discarding shirts, jeans, underwear, leaving a trail all the way to his bed. He yanked down the spread and tumbled her onto the mattress. She laughed happily and opened her arms to him. Didn't have to ask him twice. He joined her and pulled her close, savoring the feel of her bare skin against his.

"You're so soft," he whispered against her neck.

"And you're not." Her hands went up and down his back as she nestled her breasts to his chest.

Brendan moved away, just far enough so that he could hold a breast in his palm. He looked into her passion-glazed eyes and whispered, "Tell me what you want."

"Only you."

She cupped his cheek in her hand and he was lost. He touched her everywhere and she had her way with him. Finally he couldn't stand it another second and opened the nightstand, groping for a condom. He found one and put it on. Then he rolled her onto her back and she opened to him. Taking great care, he entered her and felt her sigh.

He moved slowly, listening to her shallow breathing, waiting for a sign that she was on the edge. Then he felt her hands on his back, the almost frantic movement, and her hips arched upward, demanding more of him. He thrust deeper and faster until she cried out and clung to him, saying his name over and over.

When she nuzzled his chest and spread soft kisses on his collarbone, he started to move again. She met him, thrust for thrust, pulling him deeper as she wrapped her legs around his hips. He went higher, overdosing on the sight, sound and feel of her before light exploded behind his eyes and pleasure roared through him, leaving heat everywhere. Judging from her throaty moans, he'd brought her to another orgasm.

He held her tightly against him while their breathing slowed to something resembling normal and he could actually think again. Even then they didn't move for a while. Finally he left her just long enough to go into the bathroom and dispose of the condom. It was a weird feeling, but he couldn't shake it, as if she wouldn't be there when he got back. But she was and he slid into bed, pulling her close to his side.

She rested her cheek on his chest. "So, those skills you were bragging about…"

"Yes?"

"You didn't lie." Her voice was dreamy, satisfied.

Contentment filled him, something he wasn't sure he'd ever felt before. Something he didn't trust and shouldn't get used to. "It's not bragging if it's true. And I always do my best to tell the truth."

"It's a very good quality," she agreed. "What are some of your other character strengths?"

"Well…" He thought about that and visions of his dad popped into his mind. "Leon's life lessons."

"Care to share?"

"My dad was a drill sergeant before I knew what one was. He was always saying, 'Don't slouch. Stand up straight. Never lie, steal or cheat.' And he made sure I knew that there are a lot of ways to do all three."

"Such as?"

"Promising to love and cherish, for better or worse. Don't say it unless you mean it."

"So his life lessons were about your mom walking out," she said.

"Yeah." He held her just a little tighter.

"You know, I have no idea what it feels like to grow up without a mother. I'm trying to play devil's advocate, not be patronizing. And it will never make you feel better about what happened."

Brendan couldn't help but smile at the way she was qualifying whatever it was she planned to say. "Just spill it."

"A lot of kids don't have either parent. They're orphans or abandoned. At least you had a loving father."

"That's almost harder for me. He was a great dad— wise and supportive. And he never had anyone love him back the way he deserved."

"You loved him," she pointed out.

"It's not the same." He wrapped her hand in his and settled both on his chest. "I mean a personal adult relationship."

"That's not your fault."

"Maybe it is." He absently brushed his other thumb over her shoulder. "What if my mother left because of me?"

"What? You were five."

"And a typical boy—loud and physical. Maybe I made her nuts and she couldn't take it."

"Correct me if I'm wrong, but didn't you tell me she said your dad was good-looking but she needed more excitement?"

Brendan could still remember his mother's voice and the words. Her telling him he would be better off with just his dad. "That's what she said."

"If you never believe me about anything, believe this. She left for her own selfish reasons and it had nothing to do with you. In fact, a woman like that probably did you and your dad a favor."

Brendan recalled his dad telling him the same thing, but he didn't buy it. Somehow Fiona saying it struck just the right chord because the knot of guilt inside him seemed to unravel.

"It was her loss," Fiona added.

"Understood."

"Really?" She tipped her face up to study him. "You're not going to tell me I'm wrong?"

"Not when you're right. There's that whole 'telling the truth' thing."

"Wow." She threw her arm over his abdomen and snuggled closer. "The only thing that makes me happier than being right is you trusting me enough to share all this."

He wasn't sure why he had. Maybe it just got too heavy to carry by himself. Or his glimpse into nice and normal had him going soft. Either way, he didn't regret talking about it.

"Glad you're happy." He kissed her forehead. "Especially since the trip to Everything Old was a failure."

"I'll come up with something for a costume. My sisters will help."

Brendan envied her having people to fall back on. Now that his dad was gone he didn't have that. Unless he re-enlisted.

"Speaking of Halloween," she said, "the party/fund-raiser is coming up."

"Yeah."

"I was wondering if maybe—" she met his gaze "—you'd want to go with me."

"You mean a date?"

"Sort of, I guess. My family will be there and quite a few people from town."

That made him wonder again. "So it would be very public."

"Yeah."

"Then why did we jump through hoops at Ace in the Hole to keep anyone from knowing about us?"

"I— It's just—" She tensed and slid away. "That was different."

"How?" He missed feeling her bare skin against his. More important right now was that he was missing her point.

"It's no one else's business what I do and everyone would have jumped to the conclusion that we were going to sleep together."

Some survival instinct told him not to point out that they had slept together and were still in his bed. "But if we show up at the party together, won't they jump to that conclusion?"

"I never claimed it was rational. You don't know what it's like to be the talk of the town. And not in a good way. Everyone has an opinion and they share it with you, to your face. It's awful. The pity is hard enough, but the worst was when someone said I should have known better. And they were right." She sat up and pulled the sheet with her, covering her breasts. "It was humiliating and something I never want to experience again. So tonight I jumped through hoops because I didn't want to be town topic number one tomorrow. I didn't want it to be common knowledge that I'm sleeping with you."

And he would rather die than have her humiliated—especially because of him. He was trained to protect. It was part of who he was, the best part. "Understood."

"Okay. So I guess what I just said is that it's not you. It's me."

"Roger that."

She nodded and gave him a small smile. "I don't think it's a problem being seen together at the party. We're friends. We could meet there. What do you think?"

He thought until right this moment he'd been leaning toward staying in Rust Creek Falls. Then she asked him to the party and he realized she was starting to have expectations. He was damaged goods and couldn't give her what she needed. And it killed him that he couldn't. On top of that, he prided himself on the truth but he'd been lying to himself.

He'd drawn a line in the sand with her and crossed it anyway. Giving in just one more time tonight hadn't felt like a big deal until now, and this was where he paid the price for his mistake. She might think that keeping them a secret was protecting her, but she was wrong. Whether she knew it or not, she wanted more than he could give. So it had to stop or she would get hurt; he would do anything to keep that from happening. Putting off his decision had been selfish but it wasn't just about what was best for him any longer. And suddenly his mind was made up. He knew what he had to do.

Do it quick. Rip off the Band-Aid. Tell her the truth.

"I don't think it's a good idea for me to meet you there."

"Why?"

"I have to be honest, Fiona. I plan to reenlist in the Marine Corps. It's where I belong."

"I didn't realize you'd made up your mind. I thought you were going to stay." Her eyes grew wide—and there was a bruised look in them. "I could have sworn you belonged here. The whole town embraced you. And your business—"

"That's Luke's idea, not mine," he said. "When I came to Sunshine Farm it was to clear my head, figure out my next move. Mission accomplished. The fact is I shouldn't have brought you here tonight. I'm—"

"Don't you dare say you're sorry," she warned. The bruised look turned to betrayal, as if she couldn't stand the sight of him. "I knew what I was getting into, what I wanted. And now I want to go home."

As much as he didn't want to let her go, Brendan wouldn't try to change her mind. It was for the best. He'd already made more mistakes with her than he wanted to admit. But telling her the truth about his decision to re-enlist wasn't one of them. In fact, now that he knew the depth of the pain she'd suffered being the target of town gossip, he was absolutely sure this was the right thing. Protecting her made him feel good.

Was that selfish? He was really afraid that leaving her made him just like his mother.

Fiona dumped another bunch of dirty hay into the wheelbarrow. Shoveling crap seemed like an appropriate job the day after Brendan told her he was reenlisting. Which was just a noble way of saying "leaving." She'd known it was a possibility, but that hadn't stopped her from falling in love with him. She hadn't wanted to face her growing feelings but that didn't make it any less true. Or her pain any less real. Maybe deep down she'd believed he wouldn't go. That he would want to stay. For her. And if she'd acknowledged sooner that she loved him, would she feel any less stupid and foolish?

That brought a fresh wave of pain and more tears. It was a good thing scooping up muck wasn't a precision job because her vision was blurry.

"Hey, Fee." Ronan walked into the stall behind her. "Have you seen my wire cutters?"

"No." It was an effort to keep her voice even and normal but she was pretty sure she pulled it off. She also kept her back to him.

"Are you sure? I know you've seen them. The ones with the yellow handles you're always nagging me to put back where they belong."

"I've seen them, but it's not actually my responsibility to watch them. And if you'd taken my advice you wouldn't be bugging me now."

"Wow, someone got up on the wrong side of the bed."

There was no right side when you got out of the wrong bed. "Go away."

"Not until you tell me where to look for the wire cutters."

"Why would I have any idea where you left them? I don't know everything—"

"Fiona?" He circled around to face her. "What's wrong?"

"You can't find that stupid tool, that's what." She rubbed a flannel-covered arm over her face.

"Are you crying?"

"No." She turned away.

"So you're just in a crap mood for no reason?" Her brother sounded skeptical.

She was angry and hurt. That tended to put a dent in a girl's normally sunny disposition. "Aren't I allowed to be crabby? Everyone else in this family gets to. Why not me?"

"Because you're Fiona. The cheerful one who is always happy to lend a hand. The one who moves heaven and earth to help find the lost wire cutters. That's why we all come to you."

"Everyone comes to me for everything." Tears were rolling down her cheeks and if he saw, he wouldn't go away. And she really, really wanted him to. "The truth is I don't know where everything is. I can't fix anything. I'm an idiot—"

He moved around and in front of her. "I knew it. You are crying."

"Give the man a silver belt buckle. Now would you please go away?" She put one hand over her face. The other one held the shovel.

He took the tool from her and put it down. Then she felt his arms come around her. "Don't cry, Fee."

"What if I want to?"

"Then go for it." He rubbed her back.

"I hate crying. I'm not a crier."

"Then don't," he said patiently.

"I c-can't help it."

"Okay, then. You just do whatever the hell you want."

"I don't need your permission," she snapped.

"Got that right." He gave her a squeeze, then stepped back, hands on her upper arms as he met her gaze. "But do you want to tell me who you're really mad at?"

"No."

"Well, I'm not leaving until you do. This is me. The brother who's there to hold you when you cry." He let her go and blew out a long breath. "But I have to say this is creeping me out. It's just wrong. You falling apart. I've never seen you like this. Not even when you found out that bozo lied and cheated on you."

That's because she wasn't in love with the bozo. She'd

been upset because he'd publicly humiliated her, but there was never any soul-deep pain. Not like this.

"It's nothing, Ronan. Don't worry your pretty little head. Just let me finish mucking out the stalls. Then I have an article to work on—"

"I want a name. Tell me who's responsible for making you cry so I can beat him up."

In spite of her misery, that made her laugh. Her brother was a big guy and in really good shape because ranching was hard, physical work. But Brendan had warrior skills. He'd been trained.

"What's so funny?" Ronan held up a hand. "Don't get me wrong. I'm not sorry the blubbering stopped, but what did I say?"

"I wouldn't advise a confrontation. He probably knows three hundred ways to incapacitate a man with one arm tied behind his back."

"I knew it!" He glared, not at her, just in general. "Tanner. And I warned that bastard, too."

And he'd warned her, but she'd been so sure her feelings could be controlled. Because Brendan was another stranger who was leaving and she wouldn't be stupid again. No, it wasn't her. Love was stupid.

"It's not his fault, Ronan."

"He's the one who made you cry," her brother said angrily. "By definition that makes it his fault."

"You don't even know what's going on."

"Because you won't tell me. If I have to, I'll go get answers from him—"

"No!" Fiona didn't miss the intensity in her brother's blue eyes and could practically see testosterone churning through him. He was looking for retribution on her behalf and she loved him so much for that. But sometimes things weren't meant to be, and this thing with her and

Brendan was one of those times. It would be so much easier if someone was at fault but that wasn't the case.

"Tell me why I shouldn't give him a piece of my mind." He pointed at her, a warning expression on his face. "And don't you dare say it's because I can't spare it."

That coaxed a small smile from her, but almost instantly it faded. "He's leaving—reenlisting in the Marines."

"Oh." Ronan looked deflated, as if someone punctured his indignation balloon. "Why would he go back?"

"A lot of reasons." She thought for a moment and made the decision to reveal some of the personal things Brendan had told her. She wasn't sure why, but it was important that Ronan not hate him. "He never wanted to leave the military in the first place."

"Then why did he?"

She told him about his father.

Ronan nodded his understanding. "Tough break. Can't imagine losing Dad. Or Mom."

Fiona couldn't, either, and didn't even want to think about it. "Speaking of that... His father was a single dad and they were particularly close because of it. But Brendan really loved his career, the guys he served with. It was the place he felt he belonged."

She'd been so sure he was fitting into the Rust Creek Falls community. In her heart, hope had taken hold, along with deeper feelings. So the reenlistment news came as a shock. A deeply painful one.

Last night, when she told him she wanted to go home, he'd brought her back to town to get her truck. On the drive they'd hardly said two words to each other. Although he'd made progress being conversational, Brendan wasn't naturally talkative. From him silence wasn't a surprise. Her excuse was being numb. That wore off this morning and she really missed feeling nothing. Now she felt heartsick and it sucked.

"Well, damn it." Ronan rubbed a hand across his neck, a gesture of frustration because there was no one to focus his anger on.

"I know. It's a little hard on a girl's ego to find out she just wasn't enough for him to stay—" Emotion choked off the rest of what she'd been about to say.

"So you really care about him?"

She nodded because she still couldn't get a single word past the lump in her throat.

"If it's any consolation, I don't think he set out to hurt you. I think he probably did his best not to."

"Yeah." She pressed her lips together for a moment. "I knew he was another stranger in town who was leaving, but then I got to know him. He's nothing like the bozo. Brendan is a good man. I didn't plan on this. My eyes were wide-open." She shrugged. "It just sort of happened in spite of me."

"I'd still like to beat him up," Ronan muttered.

"Because you'd feel better if he cleaned your clock?" *Men* are *from Mars*, she thought.

"Pain is easy. But watching my sister hurting and not being able to take it away is hard." He looked almost as miserable as she felt.

"You're going to make me cry again." She sniffled. "Stop being so sweet."

"Okay." He looked down for a moment, and then the corners of his mouth turned up. "So, now will you tell me where my wire cutters are?"

"Seriously?" Playfully, she slugged him in the arm, then threw her arms around him in a hug. "Don't worry about me. I'll be fine. This too shall pass. I'll get over it."

"I know you will. O'Reillys are made of stern stuff. We might bend but we don't break."

"Now go away and let me finish my work," she said.

"Okay. Maybe Keegan has been into my tools again and I can kick his ass."

Fiona laughed as she shooed her brother away. But after he was gone she felt even more alone. What he'd said about the O'Reillys being tough must have been true, because it surprised her that she'd been able to put on a brave front. The thing was that talking it out with her brother had made her realize the awful truth.

She would go on, but now there was an emptiness inside her that could never be filled. Her heart wasn't just broken. It was shattered and would never be whole enough to love again.

Chapter Fourteen

Brendan would give anything if he could forget the look in Fiona's eyes when she got out of his truck last night. He recognized betrayal and pain. Hurting her was the last thing he wanted to do. Some hero he was. It was putting off the inevitable, but he wished she hadn't asked him to go to the party. With her family there, no less. But when she did, he knew he had to reenlist and she needed to know. So he told her his decision and now she hated him. Damn it.

Now he was in the barn workshop at the crack of dawn trying to repair an electric frying pan because he couldn't sleep. Might as well do something until he had to be at Jamie Stockton's place to take a look at his baler. The pan fix wasn't going well. He'd taken it apart and was looking for something obvious. A loose connection.

It's almost always in the wiring. His dad had told him to start there every time.

Maybe his own wiring needed a fix, Brendan thought, since he was so screwed up. He'd been completely sincere when he told Fiona she was better off without him. He would just hurt her again and he couldn't stand that.

But more unbearable was the thought of her with someone else. That was a classic example of being screwed up.

"Knock, knock."

Brendan turned at the sound of Luke's voice. His friend was standing in the shop doorway. "Hey. You don't need an invitation. This is your barn."

"Yeah." The other man walked closer and stopped beside the bench, which was covered with tools and broken-down appliances. "But you made this shop yours. Breathed life into a room full of dust and cobwebs."

"You're giving me too much credit."

"I disagree." He glanced at the small appliances, battered power tools and even bikes that were lined up to be looked at. "If this space was mine, that stuff would just be junk. From where I'm standing it looks like proof that folks around here believe you can fix them. They're counting on you."

Except for his dad, no one had depended on him since he left the Marine Corps. "Are you here to try to talk me into opening a shop again?"

"No, actually." Luke's expression was deadly serious. "I came to ask when you decided to reenlist."

"How did you—"

"It's a small town. News travels fast. That's both good and bad." The other man shrugged.

Brendan hadn't told anyone except... "You talked to Fiona."

"No. Her brother Ronan. Apparently she was upset. He dragged the information out of her."

Brendan winced even though the other man's voice was calm, not critical. When did this stopover in Rust Creek Falls get more complicated than him figuring out his next move? Stupid question, because he knew the answer. The moment he saw Fiona. She complicated the hell out of his life.

Then Luke's words sank in. She hadn't shared his plan willingly but had been too upset to hide her feelings. Her brother out-stubborned her and Brendan had to admire that, and the family. Seems she wasn't the only one who cared; she came from a long line of people who believed in compassion and commitment. That was something he'd been looking for all his life.

It was why he was returning to the Corps, the one place he was guaranteed to fit.

He didn't answer Luke's question about when he'd made up his mind, but braced himself for a hard sell. At the same time he couldn't help wondering why this guy would waste his time and energy.

"Look, Luke, I don't mean to sound ungrateful. I appreciate you giving me a place to clear my head, get in shape and figure things out." He faced the other man straight on. "I've done that. Now I'm ready—"

"Not so fast." His friend held up a hand. "Hear me out."

"You can't talk me out of it. This is the right thing." But an image of Fiona flashed into his mind, running in here with her cheeks flushed and her red hair flying. She was his passion and his pain. That realization took some of the intensity out of him.

"I'm not trying to talk you out of anything," Luke said. "I just want to tell you a story."

This was starting to grate. "I'm not a kid—"

"It's my story," the other man said. "And I think you owe me a listen."

So he was calling in a marker. Brendan folded his arms over his chest. This man had a great piece of property and was putting it to good use. His family was here, he had a wife who loved him and everyone in town respected him for his commitment to give back to the community. So what was his deal?

"Okay. I'll listen. But I'm just not sure what Mr. Perfect can say that will change my mind."

"I'm not perfect. Not by a long shot." Luke laughed but the sound was mocking. "I have so much to make up for."

"No way."

Luke gave him a look, then started talking. "I was wild and willful when I was younger. When you're the oldest of seven, you're expected to set an example. But that's not what I did. At best my behavior could be described as a horrible warning. I was young and stupid."

Brendan recognized the expression on his friend's face—haunted, guilty, desolate. He saw it when he looked in the mirror. He'd seen it on the faces of his buddies in wartime and always there was death involved.

"What happened?"

"I was in a bar. Drunk on my ass." There was self-incrimination in Luke's voice. And biting sarcasm. "Oh, I was twenty-one. Barely."

"Then what—"

"My brothers Bailey and Daniel were with me and they were underage. It was a dive where they didn't care all that much about checking IDs." He blew out a long breath. "Bailey was twenty, Dan was only eighteen. He had more sense than his two older brothers put together."

"What happened?" It was something really bad. Brendan had lived through bad and knew what it looked like.

"Bailey was drunk, too, but Danny hadn't been drinking. He was worried that neither of us could drive home and he was right. He called the folks, figuring his macho brothers wouldn't hand over the keys to him and would try to drive."

"Was he right?"

It didn't seem possible, but Luke's face turned even more darkly intense and bleak. "We'll never know for sure."

"Why?"

"Mom and Dad were coming to deal with us but they never made it." His eyes were unbelievably sad. "They were hit and killed by a drunk driver."

Brendan had seen more than his share of violence and thought he'd heard it all. He didn't think anything could shock him but he was wrong. "Man, I'm sorry—"

"I'm not finished." Luke held up a hand. "My family was destroyed. There were seven orphans and my maternal grandparents weren't prepared to take them on. Jamie and Bella stayed together and endured the resentment of our mother's folks. The two youngest, Dana and Liza, were adopted."

Brendan thought he'd had it bad, but this man was carrying around the baggage of loved ones lost and six young lives forever changed—seven if you counted his. He recalled the day he'd met Forrest Traub and Luke talked about the plans he had for the cabins that he'd helped his dad build. Now he knew what Fiona had meant when she'd said things didn't go as planned.

"The Rust Creek Falls community looks like it comes together during hard times." He said that because he didn't know what else to say.

"They do," Luke answered. "But I left town."

"What?"

"Dan, Bailey and me. We moved out and took off. We blamed ourselves and it seemed like the best thing for the younger ones. We started out working ranches together, then split up." He looked away for a moment as painful memories seemed to scroll through his mind. "It's just in the last year or so we've reunited. We found out we owned Sunshine Farm. I was lucky to find Eva and she loved me back. On top of that she was one hundred percent on board with our vision to make this ranch mean something."

"And you're changing lives for the better, Luke."

"We're trying. So far we have a pretty good track record. Getting a reputation for bringing lonely hearts together." He smiled for the first time since walking through the door.

But Brendan wasn't smiling. He wasn't looking to be part of someone's vision. Not even for Luke's redemption. "I'm not sure why you told me all that, but—"

"Here's my point. I ran away from Rust Creek Falls. I thought I could leave it all behind me, but I was wrong. For twelve years I wrestled with the past and my guilt pinned me to the mat."

"That's not the man I see," Brendan said.

"Oh, that guy's there. And he'll always be there, carrying responsibility for what happened. I'm learning to deal. But it didn't start until I came back here and faced what I did."

Brendan dragged his fingers through his hair. "I'm sorry you went through that, but I'm still not sure why you told me. What does that have to do with me?"

"Everything. Takes one to know one. I ran away and you're running, too."

"You're wrong. This isn't where I grew up."

"No. But your run started when you joined the Marines. Now you're reenlisting. It's not hard to connect the dots." Luke's look challenged him.

"I have no idea what you're talking about." That was Bravo Sierra and Brendan knew it. Luke hit a nerve and the pain was radiating through him.

He remembered why he'd enlisted in the first place.

He couldn't wait to get away from Prosperity, Texas, and what had felt like the stigma of being different, being raised by a single dad who repaired junk for a living. He hadn't seen a lot of options and his mother had said he needed to live up to the meaning of his name. Be a warrior. So enlisting had been a way to get out from under. He'd run away.

Luke met his gaze. "I'm talking about the fact that joining the Marines was the first time you ran and going back is following the same pattern. Break it, Brendan. Stay in Rust Creek Falls. You have friends here, people who care about you. And Fiona."

He looked at the frying pan in pieces on the workbench. "I have a better chance of putting this mess back together than I do of fixing things with her."

"You don't know unless you try." Luke put a hand on his shoulder, a brotherly gesture. "There's a place for you here. We need all the help we can get with our plans for Sunshine Farm. Maybe you can do more good as a civilian and find yourself in the process."

Telling that story couldn't have been easy, Brendan thought. "I appreciate what you just did, Luke. What you told me. Thank you."

"Maybe it will help. Don't sell Fiona short. Give it a try with her. What have you got to lose?"

Everything, Brendan thought.

He watched the other man walk out the door and his mind was racing. Just a little while ago he'd been looking for the loose connection and now he knew it was him. He also knew how to fix it. He just hoped that it wasn't beyond repair.

Fiona finished hand-stitching little ears to Jared's pig costume for tonight's Halloween party at Sunshine Farm.

Her sister Fallon had called in reinforcements because caring for the triplets barely left her enough time to go to the bathroom, let alone sew costumes. Their sister Brenna came, too, and the three of them were at Short Hills Ranch.

"I can't believe the kids are still napping." Brenna raised her arms in the air, stretching after sitting hunched over to sew. "They aren't sick, are they?"

"No. Jamie helped me wear them out this morning. They were running around getting all that energy out. Then they ate lunch and crashed just before you guys got here."

"Miracles do happen." *Although not in my world*, Fiona thought. She finished sewing and held up the little piggy suit. "What do you think?"

"Absolutely adorable," Fallon said. "Mine's done, too."

"So is mine." Brenna followed their lead and put her needle and thread back in the sewing box sitting on the coffee table. "It's a good thing you were able to finish the body suits. The snout and ears were time-consuming."

Fallon gave them a grateful look. "I couldn't have done it without my sisters."

"Do you remember when Dad used to call us his three redheaded piggies?" Brenna's blue eyes sparkled.

"We were little then," Fallon reminded her.

"He wouldn't dare say that to us now," Fiona told them. Especially to her, with those extra few pounds on her hips.

She used to take exception to the family resemblance. It was impossible not to know they were sisters and inevitably people compared them. But they grew up and traveled their own paths to independent womanhood. Brenna loved being a hairdresser and making her clients look and feel pretty. She fell in love with Travis Dalton and married him.

Fallon worked at Country Kids Daycare because she'd always adored children. When Jamie was a single dad raising infant triplets, she was one of the volunteers who helped out so he could work his ranch. Romance happened and she married the rancher, became the kids' mom for real.

Fiona was the single sister and that wasn't likely to change. She hated the word *spinster*, but that's what she was. Because the man she loved was leaving town and taking her heart with him.

"What's wrong, Fee?" Fallon was sitting on the sofa beside her and looked concerned.

"Nothing."

"You just got awfully quiet." From the chair on the other side of the coffee table, Brenna looked concerned now, too.

"Just remembering the ghosts of Halloween past."

"Cute." Brenna wrinkled her adorable little nose. She put the costume she'd finished on top of the other two on the table. "Not bad if I do say so myself."

"They look great," Fallon gushed. "The Three Little Pigs. Jared, Henry and Kate are going to look so awesome in these."

"They better wake up pretty soon," Fiona said. "I want to see them dressed up and get some pictures of those rascals."

"I plan to let them sleep. They get cranky if they don't wake up on their own."

"Then I'll just stick around until they do. I'll help you get them ready," Fiona offered.

"Don't you have to get yourself into costume for the party?" Brenna scooted forward to the edge of her chair.

"Yeah," Fallon agreed. "You can see the triplets then

and get pictures. If we can keep them still long enough to take some."

"What are you dressing up as?" Brenna asked. "Do you need me to do your hair?"

Well, darn it. She'd hoped to avoid telling them face-to-face that she was skipping the party. Maybe she could just say it and her sisters wouldn't quiz her about the decision. *Right*, she thought. *When pigs could fly.*

"The thing is—" She looked at Fallon beside her, then Brenna in the chair. "I'm not going to the party."

"Why not?" her sisters said together.

She couldn't tell them the truth without crying and she really didn't want to cry. "I'm not feeling great and—"

"That's a big fat lie." Brenna pointed an accusing finger at her.

"I don't want to go," she said stubbornly.

"According to Jamie," Fallon said, "you assured Luke that you would handle the fund-raising part of the party. I've never known you to break a promise."

Darn promises anyway, she thought. She and Brendan had talked a lot about that. She knew what a broken promise felt like and that would be easier to handle than the fact that he didn't love her enough to stay. That hurt so much more.

"All the fund-raising stuff was about publicity ahead of time. I got the word out," she defended herself. "No one will miss me."

"What are we? Chopped liver?" Brenna looked at Fallon and shrugged.

Then they both stared daggers at her. The two of them reminded her of their mother, when she knew something was up and was determined to get the truth. "What?"

"This has something to do with Brendan Tanner." Fallon wasn't asking.

"Why would you think that? We're just friends." At least, he thought so. She was way beyond the friend zone.

"That's not what the Rust Creek Falls rumor mill says." Brenna sounded confident about her information. "And don't try to blow me off. I do hair. Customers talk. I hear things and gossip is almost never wrong. You've been seeing a lot of that ex-military cowboy."

"Pretty soon he won't be an ex," she said sadly. "He's reenlisting."

"No." Fallon looked shocked.

"Yes," she confirmed.

"I'm going to hurt him." Brenna's redheaded temper was showing. "Travis will help me."

"So will Jamie," Fallon vowed. "I'll make sure the triplets don't see their father defending their aunt's honor."

"You guys are sweet but Ronan already offered."

"He already knows? Before us?" Her two sisters looked stricken.

"He noticed I was upset and said he would rather have a fat lip than watch me cry."

"What do you know." Brenna sighed. "That brings a little tear to my eye. Who would have guessed our big brother is so sensitive?"

"Focus, ladies." Fallon was used to keeping the triplets in line and fell into the role of maintaining the track of this conversation. "What does his going back into the Marines have to do with you skipping out on the party?"

"That should be obvious. I don't want to see him. Especially in such a public setting. Practically everyone from Rust Creek Falls will be there."

"And you don't want to be humiliated again. Who could blame you? Well, I plan to tell Brendan that he's a weasel jerk and you're too good for him." Brenna nodded emphatically.

"That's just it. He's not a jerk. He's a really good man. This would be so much easier if he wasn't."

Fallon tapped her lip. "So, let me get this straight. Has he already put something in writing about going back in the military?"

"Not that I know of. I assume he'll do that when he's back in shape."

"You know, Josselyn Weaver was at Sunshine Farm when Brendan arrived. She saw him work out every morning and told me that man's muscles have muscles." Brenna saw the way they were looking at her. "What? I cut her hair. If she's right, he's already fit, so what's he waiting for? Why isn't he already back in uniform?"

"Fiona," her sisters prodded when she didn't answer.

"You'd have to ask him that question." Fiona shrugged. "He told me he's absolutely going back into the Marine Corps."

"And you didn't try to change his mind?"

"It was already made up," she told Fallon. "What could I say?"

"Let me think. Oh, I know. How about 'Don't go.' Or, 'I care about you.' Or, 'You'll be sorry if you let me get away.'" Fallon met her gaze. "I can think of more."

"I wouldn't stand in the way of something he really wants to do."

"Oh, please. You rolled over. That's practically showing him the door and shoving him out." Brenna made an exasperated sound.

"How do you know?" she protested. "You weren't there."

"I know you. Ever since that jackass toad did you wrong you give up without a fight. Wave the white flag before a shot is fired. It's as if you're expecting to get hurt so you just turn the other cheek and take it."

"Brenna's right." Fallon moved close, put an arm

around her. "If you keep pushing men away, that bastard who hurt you continues to win."

Fiona knew her sisters were right and loathed the idea of that jerk continuing to take from her. "I don't know what to do."

"Fight for him," her sisters said.

"With what?" Brendan was the warrior, not her. "I don't know how. I'm not pretty like you, Fallon, or sassy like you, Brenna."

"You're uniquely you," Fallon said gently. "And you're beautiful. One of the most lovely things about you is that you're completely unaware of how pretty and sexy you really are."

"I'd give a whole lot to have curves like you," Brenna chimed in. "Believe me, when you walk down the street, men get whiplash turning to look."

"You're my sisters. You have to say that," she objected.

"Because we're your sisters, we really don't," Brenna told her. "And maybe he's afraid."

"Oh, please," Fiona scoffed. "He's a marine."

"And he can handle himself in a military situation," Fallon agreed. "What Brenna means is that he might have personal issues that are holding him back."

"Right. We just called you on your crap," Brenna said. "Running from commitment. Could be he's doing the same thing. If one of you doesn't bend—" She sighed. "It would just be sad to waste a good thing."

"You don't have to fight. Start with the truth," Fallon suggested. "Tell him you love him. At least you'll have tried."

"I agree," Brenna said. "Explain how you feel. It will either work out or it won't. At least then you won't have regrets." She rested her elbows on her knees. "And we know how much you love Halloween. Don't let him spoil it for you."

Fiona's eyes filled with tears but this time they weren't about Brendan. "Have I ever told you guys how much I love you?"

"Sister hug." Brenna stood and walked around the table, pulling the other two into her arms.

Fiona soaked up the sibling support and decided her sisters were right. If she said nothing she was going to hurt. If she told him how she felt and he thanked her politely, then walked away, she was still going to hurt. But she wouldn't have to wonder what might have been.

Chapter Fifteen

The hardest part of putting together his Lone Ranger costume—because he was a cowboy, too—was the black mask. After talking to Luke, Brendan felt as if the mask he'd put on for so many years had been stripped away. But for the party he managed to find a black handkerchief and cut eye holes. Now he tied it and put on his Stetson, then buckled the toy gun belt he'd been lucky enough to find at Everything Old. It hadn't taken long to modify it to fit him. Tinkering was what he did, who he was, and he knew that now. If only his father was alive to see him embracing all the things he'd learned from his old man.

At the designated time, he made his way to the area in front of the big yellow barn. Earlier he'd helped Luke string white lights, put up spiderwebs and pile pumpkins. They'd also set up chairs and tables, several of which were filled with food and baked goods donated for the fundraiser. Outdoor heaters were strategically arranged and an open area set aside for dancing later.

Already a big crowd was there and he did surveillance, looking for Fiona's bright red hair. He didn't see her and frustration knotted inside him. It was possible he'd lost the best thing that ever happened to him and had no one but himself to blame.

"Hey, Brendan."

He turned toward the male voice and smiled when he immediately recognized the man limping toward him. "It's good to see you, Forrest."

"I'm surprised you knew who I was, what with the eye patch." He was dressed up as a pirate. "What gave me away? The limp?"

Brendan laughed at the former soldier's self-deprecating humor. There wasn't a trace of bitterness in his tone or expression and he knew there had been once.

"I hate to be the one to tell you this, but the eye patch doesn't hide all that much of your face."

"Back at you, buddy. When you ride off into the sunset, no one will be asking 'Who was that masked man?'"

"Oh, please, Forrest, everyone knows the Lone Ranger." The woman with him, dressed as Princess Leia, looked up teasingly.

Forrest smiled at the pretty, brown-eyed brunette. "Brendan Tanner, I'd like you to meet my beautiful wife, Angie."

She held out her hand. "It's really nice to meet you."

"Same here."

They chatted about the fund-raiser, this community's generosity and Thunder Canyon, where the couple was from. Brendan thought about all the people he'd met since arriving here. Every one of them had acted as if they'd known him forever. Treated him like one of their own. It reminded him of the Marine Corps without the deployments. And he'd decided to walk away. Someone should stamp Idiot on his forehead. And damn, he still didn't see Fiona.

With an effort Brendan pulled his thoughts back to

what Angie Traub had said. "It's really a good thing that Luke is doing here. For people in general, but veterans, too."

"Returning service members have a lot of needs." Forrest was serious now. "And not just those recovering from wounds or PTSD. Integrating into civilian life has its own challenges. Navigating government benefits programs can be confusing. We need support groups and volunteers to run interference for them."

Brendan remembered what Luke had said about him being able to do more good in civilian life. Maybe he was right.

Speaking of Luke, he walked over to them and gave Angie a kiss on the cheek then shook hands with Forrest. "Thanks for coming."

"We wouldn't miss this," the other man said.

Luke nodded with satisfaction as he stood in front of the wide-open yellow barn doors and gazed at all the people gathered in front of them. Most in costume. Some not. "There are more folks here than I'd even hoped."

"Obviously Fiona did a great job of getting the word out," Forrest observed. "I haven't seen her yet. Have you?"

"No." Brendan had been constantly scouting the crowd. "Maybe she couldn't make it."

"I don't think so." Luke shook his head. "You can count on Fiona."

Even if some jerk broke her heart, Brendan thought. "So you're sure she'll be here?"

"Yes." Not a shred of doubt in Luke's voice. "But it's time for me to make some welcoming remarks to everyone."

He tried to get the crowd's attention without success. When the talking didn't stop, he let loose with a shrill whistle that could probably be heard all the way to Prosperity, Texas.

When there was quiet Luke said, "My wife and I would like to thank you all for coming tonight. Where are you, Eva?"

"Over here," she called. Everyone looked at Raggedy Ann behind the dessert table, collecting money for the donated baked goods.

"I won't bore you for long, but I want to say just a few words." After applause, whistles and catcalls receded, Luke continued, "When we discovered that we owned this place it felt like a fresh start for me and my family.

"Right now there are seven cabins. The idea is to give people who are looking for something, a different perspective on their life, a fresh start or whatever… This is a place to figure things out."

Brendan was watching the people listening attentively to every word. They were nodding enthusiastically and flashing thumbs-up.

"It's working out so well, I want to take things to the next level. Expand. That takes money, so tonight I'm announcing that this is the first annual fund-raiser for the Lauren and Rob Stockton Memorial Foundation—"

Applause interrupted him but emotion had already stopped his speech. Brendan could see Luke fighting for control. A brother had a brother's back. Brendan wasn't a talker, but he jumped in now. Because a friend needed backup.

"I reached out to Luke during a rough time in my life. I left a career in the Marine Corps that I loved because my father was diagnosed with cancer and I wanted to help him fight it. We lost that battle and another one started for me. I had to figure out what I wanted to do with my life, figure out where I fit. Without hesitation, Luke offered me one of the cabins. He became more than a friend and Rust Creek Falls turned out to be so much more than somewhere to stay for a while—"

Just then the crowd shifted a little and he saw Fiona. The Three Little Pigs surrounded her and he knew they had to be the triplets. They were cute, but he only had eyes for her. She was wearing black and had on a pointy witch hat. Her face was painted green and he wasn't even sure how he knew it was her. But he did.

His heart started hammering as fear and hope twisted together inside him. First he had to get through his talk. "Now Luke wants to build more cabins, help more people and set aside a couple specifically for veterans. I think some of them can lend a hand to the project while they're here dealing with their personal challenges. Honest labor for a good cause could make them feel useful, a part of something." Brendan knew that firsthand and looked at Luke, who nodded his approval. He could take over now. "So it's time for him to twist your arm for money."

Luke laughed and put a hand on his shoulder. "Thanks, Brendan. And you're right. This is the part where I ask for money. There's a bake sale going on and a donation jar." He shaded his eyes from the lights hitting him and scanned the crowd. "I see some of the Jones family out there. Just so we're clear, I expect you billionaire boys to dig deep."

Brendan heard a bit of good-natured grumbling from somewhere at the back of the crowd but all he could think about was Fiona. He needed to get to her. But when people moved back and forth again, she'd disappeared. Damn it.

"With your help, we can make this project a reality," Luke said. "Now, Eva and I want everyone to have fun."

Brendan started to walk away but Luke put a hand on

his arm. "Hey, thanks for stepping in. I didn't expect to choke up like that."

"I owe you more than I can ever repay. It was the least I could do."

"So, can I read into what you said? Are you planning to stick around Rust Creek Falls, after all?"

"That's what I'd like to know." The female voice came from behind him.

Brendan would recognize it anywhere—soft and sexy and full of sass. He turned and stared at her green face. "Fiona."

"Hey, Fee," Luke said. "I'd give you a hug but I don't want any of that green stuff on me. Good job with the publicity."

"Happy to do it." She let out a long breath, then squared her shoulders. "I need to talk to Brendan. Would you mind terribly giving us some—"

"Space?" Luke filled in as he turned to walk away. "There's nothing else I would rather do."

Fiona could hardly breathe. So, this was happening. She looked at Brendan, trying to read the expression on his face. It wasn't like the mask over his eyes actually hid anything but she had no idea what he was thinking.

"Fiona, I—"

Someone bumped into her, propelling her against him. Brendan's arms came around her and felt more wonderful than she remembered. She wanted to stay there forever but that wasn't what he wanted. So, this time when she was left behind, she was determined to have no regrets about getting stuff off her chest.

"Follow me," she said, stepping away from him. "We have to talk."

She'd been publicly humiliated once; it wouldn't happen again. She wanted privacy for what she had to say. That way when she broke down, no one else had to know.

Except suddenly her family was there—Ronan and Keegan, her parents. Fallon and Jamie. Brenna and Travis. The adults were kind of looking fiercely at him. But he ignored that and hunkered down, focusing on the triplets.

"You guys look awesome."

Jared pointed to himself. "Me piggy."

"I can see that." Brendan playfully grabbed the boy up into his arms and Jared squealed with delight. "Watch out for the big bad wolf. He'll huff and puff and—"

"Blow your house down," little Kate finished. She threw her arms around his jeans-clad leg.

"Me, too. Want up." Henry held out his arms to get in on the action.

Fiona wasn't quite sure how, but he had all three toddlers in his arms. He was growling playfully while the kids giggled and shrieked.

Finally Jared had enough. "I hungry. Want a cupcake, Mommy."

"Let's get some real food first," Fallon said. When the kids were grounded again she took two little hands in hers and let her husband get Jared. Then she gave Brendan a hard stare. "You're a complete moron."

"No name-calling, sweetheart," her mother said. "Use positive words in front of the children. Let's go find the food."

"I can't think of one that is more perfect than—" Fallon glanced at her kids, then spelled, *"M-o-r-o-n."*

"And you're not wrong," Paddy agreed. The look he gave Brendan could scorch paint and it seemed as if there would be more to say, but he followed after his wife and daughter.

Brenna gave him a long, hostile stare. "If you know what's good for you—"

"I think he gets the message, honey." Travis put his hand to her back and urged her forward. He shook his head and said, "Poor bastard."

Ronan and Keegan stood side by side, looking like twin bodyguards. Fiona loved them for it but this was her deal. "I want to talk to him. I've got this, guys."

"You sure?" Ronan looked skeptical.

"We don't mind sticking around," Keegan added.

In spite of the nerves quivering inside her and the sadness pushing them out of the way, Fiona smiled at her two brothers. For a split second, love for these big lugs squeezed out everything messy and complicated. "Thanks. But I really do have this."

With a last warning look, the two men waded through the crowd and headed toward the tables where food and drink were set up.

"Okay, then." She looked up at Brendan and said again, "Follow me."

"Are you sure that's all of them?" he asked warily.

"Yes. At least the ones I'm related to," she answered. "But I can't guarantee my town family won't have something to say to you."

"I'm not sure whether to be happy about that for your sake or very afraid." He grabbed her hand and led the way through the partygoers gathered outside and past the perimeter of light.

Fiona didn't care where he took her because his big, warm hand felt so good wrapped around hers. But she pushed the thought away. This was no time to go soft. There were things she needed to tell him and hardened herself for the conversation.

It didn't take long to see that they were heading for his

cabin. About that hardening her heart thing? No way she would end up in his bed. Not again.

He stepped onto the porch of his place and released her hand. "We can talk in here."

As long as they just talked. This would very probably be the last time she was with him and it would be so easy to let herself forget that she wasn't enough to make him stay.

"Okay." She walked through the door he opened and flipped on the light switch just inside.

As the room lit up, memories flooded her. The best times of her life had happened here. She hoped that eventually thoughts of being with him would be warm, bright and comforting. Right now it just hurt all the way to her soul. When the door closed, she blinked away tears and turned to face him.

He stared at her for a moment. "So…the green face is really something."

She touched her cheek, a little sticky from the face paint she'd used. "Yeah. I didn't want to be any old generic witch."

"So, which witch are you?"

"Elphaba." His look was blank. "From the Broadway play *Wicked*."

He shrugged. "Still nothing."

"I'm sure you can find something about it on YouTube."

"I'll check it out."

"'Defying Gravity' is my favorite song from the play. But my second fave is 'For Good'—"

As soon as the words came out of her mouth, the meaning sliced through her painfully. Because she'd known him she'd been changed for good. Fiona was aware of how awesome it was to be in love. Also because she'd known him it felt as if her heart was being ripped out. At least this time she would get closure.

"You didn't really want to talk to me about a play, did you?" His voice was so gentle she could hardly stand it.

"No." She caught the corner of her bottom lip between her teeth for a moment. "I just thought we should talk about what you told me."

"Yeah." He moved a step closer until his body nearly touched hers. "I didn't like the way we left things, either. And that's my fault. You mentioned your family and—"

"I know. They can be a lot."

"It's not that. They're great. Especially the way they support you. My dad was all the family I had. And you have so many of them."

"You're trying to say that I take them for granted," she said.

"Not exactly. I'm saying that I envy you. I didn't have any siblings. My mom wasn't around for putting together a costume or going trick-or-treating."

"Brendan—" She sighed. "I'm so sorry you had to go through that."

"Me, too. But I'm really not feeling sorry for myself. I just need you to understand why the Marine Corps is so important to me. They were the brothers I never had. The family I never had. I knew I could count on them."

"You can count on me."

He looked away. "I know—"

"It's not just lip service, Brendan. I have your back always." It was now or never. "I'm in love with you."

His eyes met hers and he blinked at her. "Fiona—"

She held up a hand to stop his words. "Let me get this out before I lose my nerve. I fell in love with you. Couldn't help it. I love you for trying to keep your distance in order to protect me. It just shows what kind of man you are." She shrugged. "And it's a perfect example of why I fell hard for you."

"Listen, Fiona—"

"I'm not asking you for anything. I just wanted you to know." She took in his handsome face, including the black mask, and smiled. "I like the Lone Ranger thing you've got going on. Very heroic."

"I'm not a hero."

"You served your country, bravely and honorably. You're everyone's hero."

"I don't care about everyone. I only want to be your hero." He shook his head. "I was afraid you weren't coming tonight."

"I almost didn't," she admitted. "My sisters talked me into it. They said I should tell you how I feel."

"I'm glad you did and now it's my turn." He untied the black mask and took off his hat, then tossed both on the couch. "I've been hiding all my life. From pain and possibility. I've been running and hiding because that's where I'm comfortable. But not anymore. Not if it means losing you."

His words seeded hope that started to grow in her heart. "What are you saying?"

"I love you. I have from the very first moment I saw you. Chasing Jared into my workshop."

"You have no idea how badly I want to throw myself into your arms right now."

"What's stopping you?"

"You are." Love was all well and good, but logistics sucked. "Or I should say the fact that you're going to re-enlist."

"No. I'm not."

She shook her head. "Don't do that. Don't you dare

give up the career you love. Not for me. I won't push you into a commitment you don't want."

"I'm not doing it for you," he protested. "I'm doing it for me. There's nothing more important to me than being with you. Because I'm in love with you. And I'm not giving up anything. I've been talking to Forrest Traub, and there are other ways for me to serve. I can do a lot. It just won't be on the front lines anymore."

"You're sure? I don't want you to resent me." Fiona searched his face, looking for any sign of doubt. She saw nothing but love in his eyes. And this was the man who never broke a promise and always told the truth.

"I want to be with *you*. I want to walk in the snow for the first time with you. Thanksgiving and Christmas were always another holiday to have hard feelings about. Now I can't wait to spend them with you." He reached for her.

Fiona took a half step back. "What about my family? You saw how they are. They're going to be around."

He laughed and the humor lines crinkled around his eyes. "I was completely serious when I said I envy you having a big family. I would very much like to be a part of the rowdy O'Reillys. I'd like nothing more."

"Nothing?" she asked sweetly.

"Nothing." He pulled her into his arms then. "Except maybe to start a family of my own. With you. If you'll have me."

She cupped his lean cheek in her hand. "You are everything I have ever wanted, Brendan Tanner."

He kissed her then, and she slid her arms around his neck. When they came up for air, she said, "You've got green face paint all over you."

There was a wicked gleam in his eyes when he glanced

in the direction of the bedroom, then back at her. "I propose we make it count, then."

"I'm in." She stood on tiptoe and kissed him softly. "Always."

Epilogue

"There should be a medal I can pin on you for meritorious service." Fiona pulled the tablecloth off the dining room table. After a holiday dinner the thing looked like it had been through a battle. She smiled at Brendan. "You just survived your first O'Reilly family Thanksgiving."

"Marine Corps boot camp came in handy. I never knew it would prepare me for taking on triplet toddlers."

"They adore you." The sight of him playing and roughhousing with the kids had tugged at her heart. Partly because what woman didn't love watching a hunky man with kids? But mostly because he'd looked so happy.

Now the two of them were clearing away Thanksgiving decorations so her mother could get out the ones for Christmas. It would be her first with Brendan. He had wandered over to the front window and was staring at something so she decided to join him.

"What are you looking at?"

"It's snowing." There was awe in his voice and something else she'd never heard before. When he looked down at her there was a gleam in his eyes, too. The excitement of seeing his first snowfall? "Will you take a walk with me?"

"Anywhere." She leaned her head against his shoulder for a moment. "Let's get our coats."

They grabbed sheepskin-lined jackets from the coat rack by the front door and tugged them on.

"Ready," she said.

"Are you sure?" There was a funny look on his face.

"Is something wrong?"

"No."

"I mean, this is your first snow and everything, but I promise I'll take care of you," she teased.

"Not a doubt in my mind that you have my six." He stuck his hand in the pocket of his jacket and seemed to relax. "I'm ready."

She grinned and opened the front door, letting in a draft of cold air. Light from the front window showed big fat, wet flakes of snow gently falling. It was slowly accumulating on the ground and turning the front yard into a white wonderland. It was magical.

"Let's go." She took his hand. "Remember it's slippery."

They walked down the steps and wandered slowly away from the house. Peace and quiet surrounded them. It felt as if they were the only two people in the world. Since Halloween her love for this man had only grown stronger, deeper. Watching him enthusiastically immerse himself in the community filled her heart with happiness until it overflowed. She couldn't imagine her life without him in it.

She tucked her left hand into the bend of his elbow and he covered it with his own, brushing his thumb over her fingers.

"Can I ask you something?" she said.

"Anything," he answered without hesitation.

"Do you regret giving up the military?"

"No." Again there was no hesitation.

"Are you sure?" she asked. "Now that you've had a few weeks to think about it. You're not sorry you didn't reenlist?"

"I haven't had time to be sorry." He looked down and there was contentment in his eyes, in his expression. "I'm partnering with Luke in the Sunshine Farm Fix-it Shop. He's taken to calling me the tractor whisperer and the backhoe badass."

"I'm not sure whether to be horrified at the nicknames or impressed that Luke is so impressed."

"I vote for impressed." Then he continued, "On top of that, I'm organizing a group of veteran volunteers with construction experience to help build cabins. And we're going to negotiate the details of renting a space at Everything Old to sell donated items I've repaired in order to raise money for Luke's foundation."

"You're going to be busy."

"That's the way I like it," he said. "And I've told you about all this. So what's wrong?"

"I just want to make sure you haven't changed your mind. About staying, I mean."

"Why in the world would I?" He stopped walking and smiled down at her. "I'm happier than I've ever been in my life. Don't look now, but we're one more positive story in the growing myth of the Lonelyhearts Ranch."

"Yeah." She grinned. "Fiona and Brendan—the legend continues."

His expression turned serious then. "You look so beautiful with snow sticking to your eyelashes and in your hair. I'm glad you're my first walk in the snow."

"I'm glad you're glad." She smiled. "There was a time when I was practically obsessed with getting married because my sisters were. I was the oldest and should have been first down the aisle."

"And now?"

"Love is the most important thing. I'm okay with being a thirty-year-old spinster. As long as I can be *your* thirty-year-old spinster."

"Don't get used to the spinster thing." Suddenly he dropped to one knee and reached a hand into his jacket pocket.

Her heart started hammering. "Brendan? What are you doing? Snow is cold, you know. And wet. You're going to get frostbite of the kneecap. This is crazy. Please stand up before you catch your death—"

"If you'll stop talking and let me get a word in, I have something to ask you."

"Okay. Stopping. Now—"

"Fiona—"

She pressed her lips together and he pulled a black velvet jeweler's box from his pocket, opened it and took out a solitaire diamond ring.

"I love you more than anything in this world and want to spend the rest of my life with you. Fiona O'Reilly—"

"Can I say yes now?"

"I haven't asked you anything yet," he said.

"So hurry up," she urged.

"Will you marry me?"

"Yes." She stuck out her left hand. "It would be my honor to marry you, Brendan Tanner."

He slipped the ring on her finger and kissed her hand. Looking up at her he said, "You're the best thing that ever happened to me."

"And you're the best thing that ever happened to me. Let's go break the news to my family."

"I think they already know." He nodded toward the house, where her parents, her siblings and their families were peeking through the window, waving and giving them thumbs-up.

She sighed. "Get used to it. For better for worse. Take me, take the O'Reillys."

"Gladly." He stood and pulled her against him.

Fiona threw her arms around his neck. Waking up that morning, she'd had no idea she would find even more to be thankful for. The list was long, but now, right at the top, was living happily-ever-after with her marine.

* * * * *

MILLS & BOON

Coming next month

THEIR CHRISTMAS MIRACLE
Barbara Wallace

'Can I get you lads something to drink?'

Thomas's breath caught. It happened every so often. He'd catch the hint of an inflection or the turn of the head, and his mind would trip up. This time, it was the waitress's sharp northern twang that sounded uncannily familiar. He looked up, expecting reality to slap him back to his senses the way it had with his cottage memories. Instead...

He dropped the phone.

What the...?

His eyes darted to Linus. His brother's pale expression mirrored how Thomas felt. Mouth agape, eyes wide. If Thomas had gone mad, then his brother had plunged down the rabbit hole with him. And, mad he had to be, he thought, looking back at the waitress.

How else to explain why he was staring at the face of his dead wife?

'Rosie?' The word came out a hoarse whisper; he could barely speak. Six months. Praying and searching. Mourning.

It couldn't be her.

Who else would have those brown eyes? Dark and rich, like liquid gemstones. Bee-stung lips. And there was the scar on the bridge of her nose. The one she always hated, and that he loved because it connected the smattering of freckles.

How….? When? A million questions swirled in his head, none of which mattered. Not when a miracle was standing in front of him.

'Rosie,' he said, wrapping her in his arms.

He moved to pull her closer, only for her to push him away.

He found himself staring into eyes full of confusion.

'Do I know you?' she asked.

Continue reading
THEIR CHRISTMAS MIRACLE
Barbara Wallace

Available next month
www.millsandboon.co.uk

COMING SOON!

We really hope you enjoyed reading this book. If you're looking for more romance, be sure to head to the shops when new books are available on

Thursday
18th October

To see which titles are coming soon, please visit
millsandboon.co.uk

MILLS & BOON

LET'S TALK
Romance

For exclusive extracts, competitions
and special offers, find us online: